P...

No...

"A nifty series." —*Booklist*

"Rusch continues her provocative interplanetary detective series with healthy doses of planet-hopping intrigue, heady legal dilemmas, and well-drawn characters. . . . Science fiction fans should expect to be hooked." —*Publishers Weekly*

Paloma

"A science fiction murder mystery by one of the genre's best . . . . A book with complex characters, an interesting and unpredictable plot, and timeless and universal things to say about the human condition." —The Panama News

Buried Deep

"An exciting, intricately plotted, fast-paced novel. You'll find it difficult to put down." —SFRevu

"A good mystery wrapped in a genuinely interesting SF theme." —*Chronicle*

"Like the other volumes in the series, this one combines elements of taut thriller, PI murder mystery, and SF."—*Locus*

Consequences

"Ms. Rusch has a knack for creating interesting characters and a future that moves and breathes. I look forward to her next puzzle." —*The Weekly Press* (Philadelphia)

continued . . .

"An engrossing, thought-provoking murder mystery."

—*Locus*

"Part science fiction, part mystery, and pure enjoyment."

—*Midwest Book Review*

"Both Miles Flint and Noelle DeRicci are interesting and likable characters. Rusch ably weaves the various plot threads together. . . . Readers who enjoyed the previous books in the series will definitely want to read this one as well. . . . It works equally well as a stand-alone novel."   —SFRevu

"Rusch mounts hard-boiled noir on an expansive SF background with great panache."   —*Booklist*

"Rusch has outdone herself. . . . There are so many stories layered together in this novel that the reader is hooked from page one and reeled in through every page afterwards."

—Wigglefish.com

"Set in a totally believable future [and] full of totally believable characters (both human and alien)."

—The Eternal Night

"A satisfying SF mystery. Flint's internal conflicts are deftly portrayed, and the gritty realism of the murder investigation meshes well with the alien setting."   —*Romantic Times*

Extremes

"A very readable and thought-provoking novel that satisfies the reader in just about every possible way."   —*Analog*

"A deft blend of science fiction and mystery devices . . . this very fine novel incorporates a nice puzzle and a well-realized lunar setting, and the interplay between the protagonist and another detective is convincing and entertaining."   —*Chronicle*

"Definitely recommended."   —*KLIATT*

"Sophisticated storytelling that works all the way . . . a futuristic detective/PI novel with the blend of contemporary and timeless relevance only the best writers can achieve."—*Locus*

"Rusch achieves a thrilling momentum, and her attention to procedure and process contributes greatly. This is a sci-fi mystery that thinks, and thinks hard, about questions of justice and survival in a universe full of conflicting imperatives."   —Wigglefish.com

"Good all around . . . an exemplary futuristic detective thriller."   —*Booklist*

The Disappeared

"Rusch creates an interesting and fairly original solar civilization. . . . It's a balanced blend of police procedural and action adventure."   —Don D'Ammassa, *Chronicle*

"Rusch's handling of human-alien interactions puts a new and very sobering face on extraterrestrial contacts that few authors have thoroughly explored. . . . I am hopelessly hooked. . . . Rusch's characters . . . keep you reading long after everyone in the house has fallen asleep. . . . *The Disappeared*, like all the best science fiction, achieves a higher purpose: to make us look at the world around us with a new understanding and question the status quo."   —Lisa Dumond, SF Site

"As well-known for her fantasy and horror as she is for her science fiction, [Rusch] especially excels in tales of the collision between human and alien cultures. *The Disappeared* is a fine example of her skill."   —Science Fiction Weekly

"An entertaining blend of mystery and SF, a solid police drama that asks hard questions about what justice between cultures, and even species, really is."   —*Booklist*

"Feels like a popular TV series crossed with a Spielberg film—engaging."   —*Locus*

"A great story: compelling, heart-wrenching, extremely satisfying and, above all, successful at making the reader absolutely want for more . . . a great read." —The Eternal Night

**Other Retrieval Artist Novels
by Kristine Kathryn Rusch**

*The Disappeared
Extremes
Consequences
Buried Deep
Paloma
Recovery Man*

DUPLICATE EFFORT

A RETRIEVAL ARTIST NOVEL

Kristine Kathryn Rusch

A ROC BOOK

ROC
Published by New American Library, a division of
Penguin Group (USA) Inc., 375 Hudson Street,
New York, New York 10014, USA
Penguin Group (Canada), 90 Eglinton Avenue East, Suite 700, Toronto,
Ontario M4P 2Y3, Canada (a division of Pearson Penguin Canada Inc.)
Penguin Books Ltd., 80 Strand, London WC2R 0RL, England
Penguin Ireland, 25 St. Stephen's Green, Dublin 2,
Ireland (a division of Penguin Books Ltd.)
Penguin Group (Australia), 250 Camberwell Road, Camberwell, Victoria 3124,
Australia (a division of Pearson Australia Group Pty. Ltd.)
Penguin Books India Pvt. Ltd., 11 Community Centre, Panchsheel Park,
New Delhi - 110 017, India
Penguin Group (NZ), 67 Apollo Drive, Rosedale, North Shore 0632,
New Zealand (a division of Pearson New Zealand Ltd.)
Penguin Books (South Africa) (Pty.) Ltd., 24 Sturdee Avenue,
Rosebank, Johannesburg 2196, South Africa

Penguin Books Ltd., Registered Offices:
80 Strand, London WC2R 0RL, England

First published by Roc, an imprint of New American Library,
a division of Penguin Group (USA) Inc.

First Printing, February 2009
10 9 8 7 6 5 4 3 2 1

For Dean

1

Ki Bowles skipped down the steps outside InterDome Media, trying not to smile. She had been offered her old job back. Twice the salary, three times the visibility.

She had turned InterDome down.

This close to Armstrong's downtown, the sidewalks were crowded in the middle of the day. Dome Daylight was on full, simulating an Earth summer day, and everything seemed etched in a kind of well-lit clarity, the kind that a domed community on the Moon didn't often achieve.

She thought it appropriate to her mood. She was seeing not only all the businesspeople around her, but the edges of the buildings and the entries into the alleys—things that were usually shrouded in a kind of permanent twilight.

No one could hide on a day like today. No one could pretend to be something other than what they were.

She stuffed the scarf she'd been carrying into the bag she had slung over her shoulder. Her long hair, which she'd dyed black, silver, and deep red just before she recorded the first in-depth independent piece, flowed around her—her old trademark look, one that used to attract attention and still did, even now.

For once, she didn't care. That was why she no longer

covered up her hair with the scarf. For the first time in almost a year, she didn't mind being recognized. She wasn't back on top, not yet, but she was clawing her way up the ladder, one treacherous rung at a time.

By the time her series on the law firm Wagner, Stuart, and Xendor ended, she would be the most famous investigative reporter in Armstrong, maybe even in the Earth Alliance. She would receive a lot more offers than the one from Inter-Dome Media, and she might not take any of them.

She might continue to freelance and keep control of her life.

Miles Flint had been right when he'd given her this story six months ago.

You're ruthless, Ki, he had said. *You want the story more than you want to protect people's lives and reputations. You have no real ethics. If you think you can bring someone down, you will, without regard to the effect on their lives.*

Much as she hated the characterization, she had finally accepted it. The difference between the woman he had accused of being ruthless and the woman she was now was that now she demanded real documentation. When she worked as an investigative journalist for InterDome, they had wanted two pieces of proof for every claim, but the pieces could be as flimsy as two different people saying the same thing without backup.

On the WSX stories, she demanded hard, cold evidence, things that would stand up in court. In case she got sued, she had stored all the documentation with Flint's lawyer, Maxine Van Alen.

And Bowles would get sued; she knew that much. There had always been rumors that Wagner, Stuart, and Xendor, the Moon's largest law firm and one of the largest law firms in the Earth Alliance, had participated in illegal deal making, but now she had proof. That proof showed that WSX had profited while harming its own clients.

She expected WSX to come after her first, followed by several of its high-profile clients. Van Alen wouldn't represent Bowles—there was a large conflict of interest that Bowles didn't entirely understand—but Van Alen had gotten Bowles the best libel, copyright, and defamation attorneys in the Earth Alliance.

But Bowles didn't trust the new attorneys enough to keep her research with them. She trusted Van Alen, who had been there when Flint hired her. Van Alen had some involvement in all of this, and Bowles didn't know what it was.

At the moment, she didn't care. She had the story of the century, and she was going to use it to revive not just her career, but her entire life.

The success of her introductory piece, which had run for the first time on the news nets only the night before, made her giddy. By morning, everyone had watched the story, and it had already made the regular news bulletins all over the galaxy.

Her face was plastered everywhere—and a lot of the coverage began with this kind of lead:

Award-winning investigative reporter Ki Bowles has returned with the first in a series of hard-hitting stories about controversial law firm Wagner, Stuart, and Xendor. Bowles, who was fired from InterDome Media earlier this year for an accurate but widely misinterpreted story about the Moon's security chief, Noelle DeRicci, claims she has documentation from confidential sources that proves WSX has sold out its clients in return for great profits throughout the Alliance.

Just a few days ago no one would have acknowledged that Bowles was an award-winning reporter, let alone the fact that the story that had cost her the job at InterDome had been accurate.

All of this was just what she had hoped for. She was going to buy herself lunch at the Hunting Club, one of Armstrong's most exclusive restaurants, just to celebrate. She wished she could invite Flint to join her, but she knew better.

He hated her and made no secret of it. Noelle DeRicci had been his old partner when he had been a police detective, before he quit it all (under mysterious circumstances) and became a Retrieval Artist. He never forgave Bowles for that piece she ran on DeRicci, and sometimes Bowles wondered whether she got this job because Flint didn't mind making Bowles a target.

He had certainly been clear about what she was getting into.

You'll be headlining these stories, he said. *WSX will come after you. If Justinian Wagner is feeling particularly threatened, he won't finesse it. He might even try to have you killed.*

Because of those statements, Bowles had added a condition into the deal she was making with Flint. She would take full ownership of the investigative reports she was doing, and he would pay for a security detail for her.

He had agreed to both conditions and had set a few of his own. He doled out files, which she had come to realize were confidential WSX files. He seemed to have a lot of them.

She still hadn't seen everything, but she didn't mind. Too much information would probably get in the way. It would be too tempting. With the slow flow of information, she was able to verify each piece, and put it in a coherent form.

Then she did her own research, interviews with former employees of WSX and digging into the public records, comparing what she knew with what had been reported long ago.

When she released each story, she released some of her notes—not the ones that could trace her back to Flint, but the ones that confirmed the information already in the files.

That last had been her salvation. Initially, no one wanted to buy the series of investigative pieces from her, so she had to sell them one by one. The only taker had been a small media player out of Earth—Upstart Productions.

Upstart hadn't paid much, but they hadn't bought much, either. So when the story caused the uproar that it did as quickly as it did, it filled Bowles's bank account, not Upstart's.

Upstart had gotten free publicity and a larger market share than they had ever imagined they would, though.

She turned down the exclusive side street that led to the Hunting Club. The club had bought the entire block, planting it with real trees that cost a small fortune to maintain, and put in grass of a kind found "in the forests of Earth," whatever that meant.

As she stepped into the club's forest, she glanced over her shoulder. The security detail hung back, like it was directed to do. She had already told the company of her plans—a visit to InterDome, followed by lunch at the Hunting Club, and then work at the studio. They had divided their team among all three locations.

She figured she would be the most vulnerable during the week after the first piece ran, which was why the team had spread out to all three locations. Usually, two bodyguards followed her everywhere, but for the next seven days members of the team would clear anyplace she was going before she arrived, as well as having two bodyguards accompany her.

A breeze blew through the trees, carrying with it the scent of green leaves and warmth. She stopped, tilted her head back, and inhaled deeply. She knew the breeze was fake, but it was a fake she could appreciate.

Especially today.

Especially when she was on the top of her world.

Then something tugged at her bag.

Bowles let the bag go like she'd been trained to do, but she was already off balance.

Someone grabbed her, wrapped an arm around her throat, and another around her waist, pulling her back into one of the trees.

"Help!" she screamed. She sent the message along her

links at the same time. She used her emergency links as well as the links to her bodyguards. "Help!"

She wasn't panicked—which surprised her—because she had been expecting an attack.

But she hadn't expected one here.

She should have.

The security company should have expected it here, too. Dammit, where were they?

The man—she was convinced it was a man, just by the hairy arm wrapped around her neck—tugged her into the trees. He smelled of garlic and sweat and something a bit more pungent—fear? What did he have to be afraid of? She was the one with an arm around her throat.

He hadn't cut off any air, although the grip on her stomach pinched. She let him drag her into the trees as she fished for her bag. It hadn't fallen off. In it, she had a small defensive laser knife, just for a moment like this.

The bag was halfway open—the stupid bastard should have tossed it—and she reached in, her fingers closing around the coolness of the laser. She found the depression that turned the weapon on full, then brought it out—

Only to have another man emerge from the trees, grabbing the laser from her hand. He turned it on her, slashing just below the man's grip on her stomach.

Hot pain seared through her skin and she would have doubled over if the bastard had let go of her. But he hadn't. She flailed at him—panicked now—striking at everything.

The other man came toward her, the red blade still active, and pointed it at her face. She turned away at the last moment, and heard the man behind her scream.

Maybe the men weren't working in tandem. Maybe the man with her laser knife was trying to rescue her. Maybe he had hit her by accident as he went for the other man's arm.

Then something red flashed near her right eye and the pain seared down her face, cutting into her cheek and her mouth. She couldn't scream if she wanted to.

She was thrashing now, kicking and flailing, her entire body as much of a weapon as she could make it.

C'mon, c'mon, she sent to the security people through her links. *Help me.*

The redness slashed across her throat and she made a gurgling sound that panicked her even more. If she survived this, she would need surgery; she wouldn't be able to talk or to breathe on her own—

Like she couldn't breathe now. Black dots ran across her vision.

She couldn't pass out.

She didn't dare.

She would die if she passed out.

She willed herself to stay awake—

And fought the darkness, even as it took her away.

2

Miles Flint hurried into the Administration Center in the Port of Armstrong. His heart was pounding, and he wasn't sure whether it was from anger or confusion or both. He headed down the familiar corridors to the offices of Space Traffic Control, where he had started his work as a police officer more than a decade ago.

After his daughter Emmeline died.

He stopped a few meters from the large windows overlooking the corridor, and made himself take some deep breaths. His old friend Murray in Space Traffic had called him less than thirty minutes before to tell Flint that his daughter was in holding.

His daughter Talia.

Talia was Emmeline's clone, and two and a half years younger than Emmeline would have been. Flint had gotten Talia when her mother, Rhonda Shindo, had died. Before that, Flint didn't even know that Emmeline had been cloned, not once, but six times.

He had no idea whether the previous five clones had lived. He wouldn't let himself investigate. If they had lived, his investigation might endanger them.

He took a step forward and peered through the window.

Space Traffic's headquarters was one large room that hadn't been updated in decades. A desk sat near the front, with some chairs for the handful of visitors Space Traffic got each year.

Talia was sitting in one of those chairs, her knees pressed against her chest. She'd wrapped her arms around her ankles. Her cheek rested against one kneecap. She had her eyes closed, but Flint knew she wasn't asleep.

He sighed. In the past, he used to imagine himself with his daughter Emmeline as she grew up. He'd envision himself holding toddler Emmeline's hand as she crossed the street, laughing with six-year-old Emmeline as they played ball in what once passed for his backyard, scaring the boyfriends of teenager Emmeline when they came to call for that very important first date.

He'd never ever imagined his daughter as a difficult thirteen-year-old who had tried to run away five times in the past six months.

He rubbed a hand over his face, then straightened his shoulders and walked past the windows. He pulled the door open, expecting Talia to open her eyes. But she kept her eyes closed, playing at being asleep.

He could play that game, too. He gently closed the door behind himself as if he were trying not to wake her up.

Murray, who had been desk sergeant since Flint was a rookie, turned toward the door. When he saw Flint, he shook his head.

"That's trouble over there, that's what that is." Murray hadn't had the enhancements most people his age got. So he looked elderly and had from the day Flint first saw him. Flint used to think Murray was long past retirement age, but now he knew better. Murray could be anywhere from seventy to one hundred and twenty. There was just no way to know.

Flint stood near the desk, angled so that he could see Talia, Murray, and the murals painted across the walls. The murals covered the entire history of the spaceships that had

traveled to the Moon, starting with the first Apollo modules
so long ago. He used to love those murals. Now they were
looking a bit faded, rather like he felt.

"What happened this time?" he asked Murray.

"Caught her boarding a freighter for Earth. Thank whatever god you believe in that the freighter captain was ethical
enough to run her through the networks. Most wouldn't
have."

Talia still hadn't moved, but she looked rigid.

She was listening.

"You didn't see her board?" Flint asked. That was how
Murray had caught her on two previous occasions—the very
first time, when she tried to sneak aboard a cargo ship, and
the last time, when she'd boarded a pleasure cruise heading
for Mars.

"That little one has figured out how to stay off my
screens." Murray gave Flint a significant look. Apparently
Murray knew Talia was awake as well. "Never said she
wasn't bright."

"Believe me, I know," Flint said.

Murray gave him a compassionate glance. Murray had
raised four children of his own. He used to regale Flint with
stories from his children's past.

"You got to hire some help. Maybe a specialist. The kid
would be a handful for anyone. For a new parent . . ." Murray let the word trail off, then shrugged his shoulders.

Meaning Murray didn't know how to handle her, either.

Flint studied his daughter. No one knew she was cloned.
He'd told everyone in Armstrong that she was the child of a
last-minute encounter with his ex-wife—and his ex hadn't
told him about the baby before she left for her new job on
one of Jupiter's moons.

Flint didn't care that Talia was a clone or that the law had
made him jump through a dozen hoops to claim her as his
own. She was biologically identical to the child he had lost,
if only a few years younger. She had been raised by her biological mother.

Talia was his, and he would have claimed her as such even if she didn't have his curly blond hair—so unusual in this part of the universe—or his deep blue eyes. Her dusky skin had come from her mother, but in all other ways, she was Flint's child, through and through.

Right down to the brilliance.

He'd been that smart at that age, just not that rebellious. For the first time in years, he wished his parents were still alive so that he could ask them how they had managed to keep his brain occupied while his hormones jumped out of control.

Which wasn't entirely fair to Talia. The bulk of her problems didn't come from her changing hormones. Her problems came from the way that her life had imploded.

In the space of twenty-four hours, she had learned she was a clone, that her mother had lied to her about almost everything, and that her mother was dead. By the end of that week, Talia had left everything she'd ever known to move in with a man she'd never met before, one who claimed to be her father even though, by Alliance law, he didn't have to.

She was angry, she was sad, and she was lonely, and he didn't know what to do about any of those things.

He pushed himself away from the desk and walked over to the chairs. He sat in the one next to hers and put his hand on her back. The knobs of her spine felt sharp beneath his palm.

"Talia," he said gently.

She didn't move. She was breathing quietly.

"I know you're awake," he said.

She let out a large gust of air and sat up so fast he had to move his hand so that she wouldn't slam it against the back of the chair.

"Now you got half the Moon spying on me," she said.

"I didn't catch you," Murray said defensively. "It was the captain."

But Talia ignored him. "You got them to change the rules.

I paid for passage. My info checked out. They should have let me board."

Flint took all that in without a blink. She shouldn't have been able to book passage without her parents' permission. Nor should her information have checked out. He wondered what she had done to make sure she seemed like a legitimate traveler.

"I didn't get anyone to change any rules," Flint said. "You just happened to get a captain who was cautious."

A captain who probably wanted to make sure the teenager in front of him had the actual right to travel on his ship. Flint wondered what age Talia had tried to pass herself off as this time. Eighteen—the age of human majority throughout the Earth Alliance? Or younger with a pass?

"You know, if you gave me access to your ship, this wouldn't be a problem," Talia said.

"You couldn't fly my ship if you tried," Flint said. His ship, which he'd named the *Emmeline* long before he knew about Talia, was a state-of-the-art space yacht with more equipment than most ships ever carried.

"It's probably got an autopilot," Talia said.

"I disabled that feature years ago." Flint hadn't disabled it because he'd been afraid someone else would try to use it. He had disabled it because he liked to pilot the ship on his own. He wanted the autopilot to be something he had to program, not the default that the ship always used.

"Of course you did." Talia put her head on her knees and closed her eyes.

Flint looked over at Murray, who was watching them closely, listening to every word. Flint suddenly realized he wanted the conversation to be a lot more private.

"Thanks, Murray," Flint said. "I appreciate the fact that you contacted me."

"No problem," Murray said. Then he leaned over the desk. "Hey, kid."

Talia sighed.

"Kid." Murray clearly wasn't going to shut up until Talia acknowledged him.

She raised her head and gave him such a sullen glare that Flint felt color rise in his own cheeks.

"Your dad's one of the most stand-up men in Armstrong," Murray said. "You should give him a chance. Stop running. See where you really are."

"I'm not running," Talia said. "I'm investigating."

Flint felt the color leave his face. She hadn't said that before. What was she investigating?

"Investigating?" Murray said. "Trying to be like your dad? It takes training to be good at investigation. Maybe you should ask him to make you an apprentice or something."

"I've been asking him," Talia said. "He won't."

She had asked him to train her to be a Retrieval Artist, before she even knew what that was. Retrieval Artists specialized in finding the Disappeared, people who went missing on purpose, usually to avoid prosecution or death by any one of fifty different alien cultures. The Disappeared were usually guilty of the crimes they'd been accused of, but by human standards, most of those crimes were harmless.

The work itself was dangerous, not just for the Disappeared, but also for the Retrieval Artist, his family, and his friends.

But Flint hadn't told Talia much of that, only that she wasn't ready to become a Retrieval Artist.

So she asked him to teach her the techniques he'd learned as a detective on Armstrong's police force.

He had said no. He didn't want her searching for the Recovery Man who had kidnapped Talia's mother, setting all of these events into motion. Nor did he want Talia to look into her mother's past.

Flint hadn't even looked too deeply into Rhonda's past. He was angry enough at her for lying about Talia, and for putting their family in danger with her work. He didn't want to know what else she had done.

"Then your father's probably got some good reasons for saying no," Murray said.

Talia made a rude noise and was about to say something when Flint said, "Talia, that's enough."

He put a hand under Talia's elbow and helped her to her feet. She was as tall as he was. When he'd first met her, she hadn't been quite that tall. She'd been lanky, though, and she still was, growing into the body that she'd eventually have.

Talia wrenched her arm from his grip and rubbed her elbow as if he'd hurt her. She grabbed a small pack with her things and slung it over her shoulder.

She didn't look eighteen, but she looked older than thirteen. She was so tall and sure of herself. She glared at him, then stomped out of Traffic Headquarters.

The stomp, at least, was pure thirteen.

"Better you than me," Murray said.

"I have a hunch you've been through this before," Flint said.

"And I'm glad it's done."

Flint grinned at Murray, then followed his daughter into the corridor.

"You should let me go," she said.

"On your investigation?" Flint couldn't quite keep the sarcasm from his voice.

"I'm not running away. I'll be back. But one of us has got to do this, and saying you won't doesn't help."

"What do we have to do?" Flint asked.

"We have to find them," she said.

He didn't know what she was talking about. "Who do we have to find?"

"My sisters," Talia said.

He froze beside her. He hadn't heard this before. Had Rhonda had other children, children he didn't know about? "Sisters?"

"The other clones." Talia said that as if he were the stupidest man on the Moon.

Maybe he was.

But he understood the temptation she was feeling. He wanted to find those children, too. Only he wouldn't let himself.

"For all we know, Talia," he said softly, "they weren't viable from the beginning."

"Oh, they were," she said. "I know they were. I got the cloning documentation."

Flint felt a deep shock run through him. "You what?"

"I got the authorities to send me my documentation. I'm the sixth of a viable line. You know what that means, right?"

"Wait," Flint said, feeling confused. "There's documentation? I was told it was destroyed."

"Most of it was," Talia said. "But they have to keep the records of a clone's creation. I couldn't get who I was cloned from or how many clones were made or what happened to the others. I just got the records of the day I was cloned and the fact that I came from a viable line. That's the important thing, you know. The word *viable*."

She was going too fast for him. He frowned. He had tried to get this information right after he'd met Talia. When he couldn't do it on his own, he had had his attorney, Maxine Van Alen, subpoena the records. Neither of them could obtain a single document.

Speidel, the corporation that had cloned Talia, had told Flint that the documentation had been destroyed.

"Who sent you this information?" Flint asked.

"The City of Armstrong sent it," Talia said. "I was reading that clones are entitled to their day-of-creation document, so I requested mine."

Flint let out a small sigh. Of course. He hadn't thought of the day-of-creation document. It was like a birth certificate—proof that a clone actually existed.

Sometimes getting information was a lot simpler than he—and lawyers like Van Alen—made it out to be.

"A lot of information had been redacted," Talia was saying, "but the day I was created was there, and the fact that I come from a viable line."

A viable line. Flint ran a hand across his chin. He knew what that meant. It meant that all the clones created from the original's DNA survived.

"There are five others, then?" he said.

"At least," she said.

At least. Talia was number six. And Talia was thirteen. Emmeline, had she lived, would have been sixteen.

Had Rhonda kept the youngest? Flint felt as confused as he had when he learned that Rhonda had created a clone of their daughter in the first place.

Why create six viable clones?

"There could be more," Talia said. "But there are at least five. They're just like me. Only older."

"Older?" he asked.

"They're twenty-nine months older. All of them."

Twenty-nine months. Flint did the math. Emmeline would have been seven months when the first clone was made.

Flint had assumed that the clones made before Emmeline died were nonviable. He had assumed they had never breathed, never even managed to develop much past early cell division.

He assumed that Rhonda had tried a final time years after Emmeline's death, and this time, the cloning had worked, creating Talia.

But what if Rhonda had created those five clones—those five *children*—as a diversion from the real Emmeline?

And what had happened to them?

"See?" Talia said. "You want to find them, too."

He did and he didn't. But Talia had opened a door, one that probably should have remained closed. If the other five clones were alive, then Talia might have just endangered them.

"We have to talk about what you did," Flint said. "And we can't do it here."

Talia glared at him. "You make it sound like I did something bad."

"No, I didn't say bad." He sighed. "But you might have been incautious."

"Incautious?" Her eyebrows went up. "What does that mean?"

"I don't know yet," he said. "But there's a reason your mother didn't tell us about the other clones. And I've come to realize this year that when your mother kept a secret, she needed to."

Talia's eyes grew wide. She clearly recognized the truth of what Flint had just said.

"What are we going to do?" she asked.

"We're going to go to my office," Flint said, "and figure out exactly what's going on."

3

Bartholomew Nyquist stood in the middle of the fake forest, annoyed at the fake breeze that blew through his hair. He wanted someone to shut the breeze off—it was disturbing his crime scene—but so far, the owners of the Hunting Club weren't cooperating.

The forest itself was intriguing—nothing like the ones he had visited on Earth during his various vacations. Although this one had real trees (oaks, he would guess, and maybe a few firs) and real grass, it still felt fake.

Maybe it was because all the trees were the same height and the same distance apart. Or maybe it was because the ground was level—something that was unusual in parts of Armstrong, let alone most places he'd visited on Earth. The dirt path threw him off as well. Something went through and raked the dirt every few minutes, smoothing it, so that it looked like nothing had ever touched it.

There were no footprints of any kind. Not even his own.

He had sent the two street cops who had initially responded to some screaming from the Hunting Club's forest to see the Hunting Club's owners. Nyquist's links didn't work in the forest, which irritated him.

Police and emergency links were supposed to work

everywhere in Armstrong. He would make sure to file a complaint against the Hunting Club, one that would stick. The fact that the victims here couldn't send for help probably contributed to their deaths—especially considering the street cops were only a few meters away when the attack happened.

That bothered him. In fact, the entire attack bothered him. He recognized the female victim. It was the reporter, Ki Bowles. He'd met her six months ago, and hadn't really liked her.

But he'd followed the news stories about her firing, which wasn't the kind of thing that usually held his attention. But shortly after he met Bowles, he'd nearly died on a case and it had taken most of those six months to heal. During that time, he'd watched a lot of vids, followed too many unimportant news stories, and gotten addicted to the crap the Gossip reporters put on the various nets.

He was trying to wean himself from all of that, but he was having a tough time. He'd hoped, when he finally came back to work, that the job would distract him.

So far, it hadn't.

It might now.

He knelt beside Bowles's body. She'd been slashed pretty good, probably with the laser knife that lay a few meters away. Her stunning face, which she had decorated with distinctive tattoos, was in tatters, her throat nearly gone. She'd bled out, which was something that almost never happened anymore.

Blood had spattered down her dress, onto her legs, and her shoes. He wouldn't be able to tell what other wounds she had until the coroner's office had cleaned her up.

Behind her lay the body of a man Nyquist had never seen before. The man was big and muscular—real muscles, not those enhanced things or the kind men built up in a gym. His arm had been slashed, and the side of his face had come off.

Nyquist wasn't sure what the guy had died of—neither

wound would have been deadly in and of itself—but maybe he had bled out as well.

If that was the case, then both bodies had been here for some time.

Nyquist couldn't find much else. The dirt beneath the grass smoothed itself out, just like the dirt on the path. The grass didn't remain flat like Earth grass, either, which led him to believe that something or some program fluffed it up. He'd lost footprints, he'd probably lost trace evidence, and he'd lost all signs of the struggle.

He had no idea whether Bowles and the man were attacked together or separately. He had no idea how many attackers there had been.

And he had no idea what the attackers had been after.

The techs hadn't arrived yet. Nyquist had been the second one to the scene. He didn't have a full load of cases— hell, he didn't really have cases at all—and the moment that two unidentified bodies had been found at the Hunting Club had come across the links, he'd sent a message to Andrea Gumiela, the chief of detectives, requesting the case.

Location probably means we have a celeb case, Gumiela had sent back to him through his links. *You up for this?*

Meaning could he handle a case that had not only the usual pressures, but also the press itself, the questions, the possible fame, and the potential damage to his own reputation?

Maybe when he'd been a younger detective, he would have fled the case the moment Gumiela had posed the question. The last thing he wanted was to be famous. But Nyquist had grown jaded with the job. Now he knew that fame was as fleeting as everything else. He might become the point man on the case, the one every reporter interviewed, but three years from now, no one would remember or care.

Nyquist crouched next to Bowles's body. She had never been a conventionally beautiful woman, but she'd had an attractiveness, a charm, that made her almost irresistible. That charm was gone now. Even without the damage to her face, she no longer seemed pretty.

She had been one of those people who was greater than the sum of her parts. He wouldn't have thought it. If he'd had to describe her before this, he would have said that it was her beauty that had given her an edge, not the fact that she had personality to spare.

He sighed. Gumiela had been right. It was a celebrity murder case. The question was simple: Was Bowles the target or had she gotten between the killer and his intended victim? Or were there more victims in the fake woods here, just waiting to be discovered?

His links were still off. The street cops were obviously having no luck with the Hunting Club's owners. He would have to deal with them himself.

He stood and ran a hand through his thinning hair. He hated leaving the scene before the techs arrived, but he was going to have to. He needed link access, he needed the damn breeze shut off, and he needed the stupid forest to stop recreating itself.

He was lucky it hadn't swallowed the bodies whole.

He stepped past Bowles's body to the path when four techs arrived. He recognized two of them, and let out a small sigh of relief.

Techs carried their equipment as they had done since the dawn of the profession. They needed their kits, and they were so cautious with evidence handling that they made sure everything remained with them.

The two techs he recognized were nearly as old as he was, and had been with the department just as long. The first, a slender woman named Hadassa Leidmann, had already put on her clean suit. Only her head showed above it, her hair shaved tight against her well-formed skull.

Next to her, Adyson Owens carried his suit over his arm. His black hair was pulled back into a ponytail, but his face was clean-shaven—the result of a lawsuit that the department filed against him and won.

Nyquist didn't recognize the other two techs, who were suited up just like Leidmann was. He waited for the group to reach him along the path.

"It's a mess," he said, "and not in the way you'd expect. This forest is self-cleaning. I sent some street cops inside to shut the place down, but nothing's happening. I'm going to have to do it."

Owens glanced at the building, several meters away. "I can go."

Nyquist couldn't imagine Owens negotiating with the owners or managers of an upscale club. The man had enough trouble with interdepartmental regulations—not the ones that required meticulousness on the job, because Owens was one of the most meticulous and thorough techs in the entire department, but the kind that regulated appearance and personal habits. Nyquist could just imagine the owners of the Hunting Club looking down their enhanced noses at Owens and treating him like the employee he was.

"It's better if I try," Nyquist said. "See if you can secure the scene somehow. We have two bodies that we know of, and one is a celeb."

"That's why we were called out." Leidmann's voice was raspy, as if she had a cold. But she always spoke like that, something Nyquist had found intriguing. Most people would have smoothed the voice, but Leidmann didn't seem to care, just like she didn't seem to care that her shaved head somehow made her seem more stylish than she really was.

"We're already on another job," Owens said, with some resentment.

Too much work. Nyquist remembered when he had had that problem.

"I'm sure they want the best on this. We're going to be scrutinized more than usual." Nyquist shook his head. "It's going to be a big case."

"It's a big case just by location," Leidmann said. "Stuff like this isn't supposed to happen near the hallowed halls of the Hunting Club."

She was absolutely right. The Hunting Club would do everything it could to minimize the publicity.

And that would be a problem, too.

Nyquist glanced toward the main building, just out of sight beyond the trees. He had eaten here once, with Noelle DeRicci. DeRicci had brought him here after he had gotten out of the hospital. She had seen it as a celebration, so she wanted to take him to the best place in town.

He had been tired and overwhelmed. He didn't like places like this under the best of circumstances, and that day had been anything but the best. He could walk again, but he was still in a lot of pain, and the doctors hadn't finished all the enhancing surgeries—not that he wanted to look perfect or even better than he had. He had just insisted on getting rid of the scars. He'd had to fight to keep the wrinkles around his mouth and eyes. He'd lost the battle on all the others.

"Anything you want us to watch for?" Leidmann asked.

"Weapons besides the one that was left so obviously," Nyquist said. "Spatter. Footprints. Any evidence of surveillance. Hell, any evidence of anyone else being nearby. And we will need to search every centimeter of this place just to see what else we can find."

"You know how big these woods are, right?" Owens asked.

"Actually, no," Nyquist said. "They can't be that big. This is the center of Armstrong."

"Ten square kilometers," Owens said. "And they've got enhanced areas, so it looks even bigger. It's going to take a while to separate the real from the not-real."

"How the heck did they get so much land?" Nyquist asked.

Leidmann smiled.

"I know, I know," he said. "Money buys everything."

"Included added dome space," Leidmann said.

"It wasn't the dome space that was the problem," Owens said. "It was the historic homes that used to be here. Don't you remember all the fighting when the Hunting Club was built?"

Nyquist shook his head. He never used to pay attention to that sort of thing. Now, if it had happened in the past six months, he would know about it. Down to which celebrity was having whose baby and what celebrity hangout had the most security breaches in the last few weeks.

"They fight everything with lawsuits," Owens was saying. "So go carefully in there."

Nyquist sighed. If he had known that, he wouldn't have sent street cops in first.

"I'll be back soon," he said. "See what you can do."

Leidmann nodded. Owens was already directing the other two members of the team, gesturing toward the open forest on either side of the path, his long hair swaying in the breeze.

Nyquist shook his head a final time at the futility of it all, then started down the path toward the club itself.

Bowles hadn't been more than two dozen meters from the club. If she had stayed on the path, she would have arrived in just a few minutes.

Nyquist wondered what she'd been thinking as she came here—excited to see someone she knew? Worried that she couldn't afford it? Embarrassed at the state of her career?

Although he wasn't certain what her career was now. After the firing story faded, he hadn't seen her on-screen for months. Now that he was back to work, he wasn't watching holos or vids as much, and he certainly wasn't downloading stories. So he felt out of touch, even though by his old standards, he wasn't out of touch at all.

Certainly the woman he'd met six months ago couldn't have afforded this place. Her apartment was upscale but un-lived in—the perfect apartment for one of Armstrong's up-

and-coming celebrities—but she'd just lost her job and didn't seem to know where or if she'd work again.

Nyquist adjusted his suit coat, knowing it was rumpled and cheap. DeRicci had tried to get him to upgrade his clothing—she had even offered to pay (which embarrassed the hell out of him), reminding him that he'd lost nearly a quarter of his original weight because of his injuries. He was thinner now, and would probably stay that way. Even though the doctors had put his stomach back together and it worked just fine, he no longer liked the feeling of being overly full. It was almost painful.

The doctors said it was all in his head, but he wasn't sure. He had been rebuilt. Whether things worked properly or not, the fact that the parts were new had to change a man.

The path widened as the trees thinned. As he approached the front of the building, the path split into two, arching around a flat plane of grass that was covered with flowers and shrubs and statues of dogs, foxes, horses, and people in hunting clothes, like those old-fashioned prints he'd seen in history texts when he was a kid.

He thought the statues the creepiest part of this place— they were often rearranged into different tableaus depending on the time of day and the season. In the fall—or what passed for Armstrong's fall (even though the Moon really didn't have seasons, not as Earth knew them), the human statues were posed on top of the horses, chasing a pack of dogs that was after a single fox.

He hated that tableau the most. Even though he knew such things used to happen on parts of Earth, he saw no reason to glorify them. He wasn't the only one: Protestors had complained about the tableaus over the years, often citing the cruelty they represented as barbaric and belonging to a bygone era.

This afternoon, however, the statues were in a calmer pose. The horses were standing outside the building, as if they were waiting patiently for someone to emerge. The human figures were separated, each with its own dog. The dogs were sniffing the foliage near them. Some kind of bird burst out of a nearby shrub. If the bird hadn't been motionless, Nyquist would have thought it was real.

The breeze had died down, leaving him feeling unusually hot. He wiped his forehead, still shocked to find it smooth. Just a month ago, he still had scars. He pulled his coat around him, straightened his shoulders, and walked up the real marble stairs to the oversized wooden doors.

They didn't swing open for him as they had done for De-Ricci that day during lunch. Instead, a cultured voice with an accent he almost recognized told him to state his name and his business.

Instead of doing that, he pressed his fist against the door-jamb, informing the club's system of his name, his identification, and his official purpose without saying a word.

The doors swung open, revealing darkness beyond. He stepped inside, blinking quickly so that his eyes would adjust. As he did, a woman approached. She wore a knee-length skirt, a silk blouse, and had a cardigan tied around her neck.

It was almost as if she had been sculpted to resemble the oddly athletic but sturdy women from the paintings.

"Detective Nyquist," she began in that same weird accent. "I'm—"

"I'm here to see whoever is in charge," he said. "It's urgent."

"I'm sure we'll get to everything in due time," the woman said. "Nothing—"

"You have two dead bodies in your forest. The forest's programming is disrupting our investigation. Unless you people want the club's management to be indicted for conspiracy to conceal evidence in a felony investigation, you will take me to whoever is in charge immediately."

The woman's mouth was still open, as if she couldn't close it until she completed her thought. Finally she did shut her mouth, and she nodded.

"You'll want to see Director Jaeger. He's in his study."

She spun on her flat shoes as if they were designed for that, then marched down the carpeted hallway.

Nyquist followed, feeling more and more uncomfortable. The dark wood walls were covered with two-dimensional reproductions of those hunting scenes he remembered from school. The carpet was green and everything from the real potted plants to the upholstery was accented with a deep red.

The hall opened into a sitting area, complete with fireplace. A fire burned in it, and Nyquist hoped that the damn thing was fake. He had no idea what kind of permits it would take to waste real wood and pollute the air in the dome the way that smoke from a real chimney would.

The woman swept her arm toward the couch in front of the fire. "Director Jaeger will be with you in a moment."

"It better be fast," Nyquist said.

She nodded and disappeared through some more wooden doors.

Two large white dogs lay in front of the fire, and it took Nyquist a moment to realize that they weren't sculptures. The dogs watched him, their chins resting on their front paws, but their bodies were alert, as if they could attack at any moment.

He had encountered dogs only a few times in his life—the permits to keep domestic animals in Armstrong were prohibitively expensive—and he had never liked them. He always felt as if they were only seconds away from real violence.

"Detective Nyquist."

Nyquist turned. A short man with a bald head was walking toward him, hand extended.

"I'm Edvard Jaeger. How may I help you?"

"By taking me somewhere private," Nyquist said.

"This will be private enough. My assistant will put up screens."

Nyquist hoped that would be enough. "Two street cops came in here almost half an hour ago to request that you shut down every bit of equipment in the forest outside the club. Nothing has been shut off."

Jaeger folded his small hands in front of the brown vest he wore over matching brown pants. Beneath the vest he wore a white shirt. The outfit, which was supposed to make him resemble the athletic men in the paintings, only served to show how small he was. "That system as you call it is our security. We cannot shut it off without express permission of the board of directors."

"Get it," Nyquist said. *"Now."*

"I have put in a request," Jaeger said. "It may take as many as two days to get a response. Some of our board members aren't on the Moon—"

"I don't care," Nyquist said. "Shut it down now or the City of Armstrong will shut it down for you."

Jaeger reached into his breast pocket and removed a small plastic card. He handed it to Nyquist. "These are our attorneys. Please take up any problems you have with them."

Nyquist shoved the card into the pocket of his coat without looking at it. "Have you ever heard of Ki Bowles, the investigative reporter?"

"Don't threaten, Detective. As I said, if you need to—"

"She's one of the dead people in your forest. This is going to be a media nightmare, and I'll make it worse, starting now, if you don't shut this whole thing down."

Jaeger bit his lower lip. For the first time, he looked rattled. "I'm afraid I don't have the authority—"

"Who does?"

"No one on the premises."

"I don't care about the authority," Nyquist said. "Show me the system and I'll shut the damn thing down."

"You need codes and permissions and everything in the proper sequence. Otherwise it triggers the system and we go into lockdown. I'm not trying to be difficult, but I truly am unable to help you."

Nyquist studied him. Jaeger did seem nervous. Nyquist actually believed him.

"You can arrange it so that my links work here, can't you?" Nyquist asked.

Jaeger nodded.

"Do that, at least."

Jaeger bit his lower lip, then turned to the woman who stood near the back of the room. He waved a hand. She disappeared through the doors.

There was momentary static and then Nyquist heard the familiar (and much missed) white noise that indicated his links were up and running.

He sent an urgent message through them to Andrea Gumiela.

The Hunting Club won't shut down its security system. The system is destroying evidence and hampering our investigation. I need high-level help here to get these bastards to cooperate.

Gumiela sent a message back immediately, the fastest Nyquist had ever heard from her on anything.

I'm already working on it, but I'm having trouble as well. You might want to go to your girlfriend for help. The only person who can override elaborate private security systems is the Moon's Chief of Security.

Nyquist sighed. He didn't want to go to DeRicci for help. But he also didn't want to fail at this investigation because the Hunting Club was run by a bunch of anal assholes who believed their security was more important than anything else in the city.

Will do. Nyquist sent. Then he turned to Jaeger. "Is there a private room I can use to send a visual message?"

"My office," Jaeger said. "Follow me."

He led Nyquist through the double doors into an even darker room, filled with hardbound books and another fireplace. Yet another dog rested in front of this one as well. It raised its head as Nyquist entered the room.

"Take your time," Jaeger said.

That was the thing: They didn't have time. Nyquist was

about to tell the man but Jaeger had already left the room. Nyquist stared at the only blank wall.

"On-screen," he said, hoping that would bring up a visual link. It did.

He gave it DeRicci's private address, unable to shake the feeling that he was asking her for help on his first investigation back because he was no longer competent enough to handle his problems on his own.

4

Flint's office was in the oldest section of Armstrong. The dome here had been replaced half a dozen times, but it still didn't function properly. Its surface was scratched and dark, although right now it was supposed to show Dome Daylight.

In this section of Armstrong, Dome Daylight was more like Dome Opaque Light—the cloudiness from the ancient materials made the fake sunlight seem like something far away instead of built into the dome itself.

The filtration systems didn't work well, either, so the entire neighborhood always had a thin layer of Moon dust. Sometimes the dust was worse than others, and fortunately this was not one of those times.

Flint and the rent-a-lawyer who shared the building with him had contacted the city a few months ago, requesting filtration repairs, and had actually gotten them. Now, instead of slogging through a few inches of dust, his feet slid against a barely noticeable coating.

His office building was one of the original buildings from Armstrong's first settlement. The building was made of permaplastic—probably the most indestructible material ever invented. But it had seen better days, and repairs took approval from City of Armstrong Historical Oversight Committee.

He didn't want any of those people near his office, so he never requested any repairs. He let the exterior lapse into a dust-covered shambles. But the interior was state of the art. He had violated he didn't know how many codes when he covered the walls with a Moon-made material that didn't allow dust—or information—through its thin membrane surface.

He'd attached modern lighting, an up-to-date environmental system, and the latest netfiber equipment throughout.

And he had done all of that in the last few months, since it became clear that Talia would be in this place at least a couple of times per week. He didn't want to expose her to old decaying permaplastic chemicals or to Moon dust seeping through the filtration system or to any one of a dozen environmental hazards that he suspected the old place had.

Not to mention the fact that he had to upgrade everything when he realized his daughter was as gifted with computer systems as he was. He needed up-to-date firewalls and equipment that was beyond her level of expertise.

He never let her work on this system. In fact, he had actively worked to lock her out of it. He had programmed the system to shut down if she touched it—it recognized her DNA, and the moment she made contact with any part of the machine, it would turn off. No warnings, no nothing.

Flint knew she would work with gloves and with other devices, so he set the system so that it would go on alert every time she entered the building. If she spoke directly to the computer, she would initiate a longer series of shutdown procedures.

He found he needed that longer series because sometimes she was there with him, and he hated it when the system shut down while he was working on it.

Like it could now, if he wasn't careful.

Talia stood in the middle of the room, like she always did when he brought her here. He had warned her from the beginning that this was where he worked, that everything here was confidential, and that she was in the office only as a courtesy.

If he ever found her tampering with the systems, he would make sure she couldn't enter the building again.

He might have stated things too harshly. She always stood with her arms clasped around her waist, looking awkward and a bit frightened.

He moved a second chair near his desk. "Go ahead and sit down."

She did, keeping her back rigid. The chair wasn't that comfortable—it was made of a hard plastic—but it couldn't hurt her. Sometimes she acted like it could.

He went around the desk to the upholstered chair that he had splurged on. As he did, he touched a corner of the desk, ordering it to keep its fake wood look and to mask its pop-up screens. He didn't want Talia to see any of the information he planned to look up.

For the moment, though, he didn't look up anything. He sat down and leaned back. The chair squeaked beneath his weight.

"Okay," he said. "First you need to tell me how you found the others."

He couldn't call the five clones sisters, as she had. He wasn't sure how to think about them.

He wasn't sure whether he was ready to think about them at all.

"I didn't find all of them." Talia still had her arms wrapped around her stomach. She looked scared.

She'd had some time to think about what he said, and she seemed even more uncomfortable than she had before.

"Maybe you could tell me what's wrong with looking for them," she said. "I mean, Mom's dead. That court ruling was against her, right?"

Talia was referring to a court ruling that Flint had found out about only recently. His wife, Rhonda, had invented a nutrient-rich water that, when tested on another planet, had accidentally destroyed a colony of young Gyonnese.

The Gyonnese were part of the Earth Alliance, and they brought the case before a Multicultural Tribunal. Under Earth Alliance law, anyone who broke a law on a particular place was subject to the laws of that place.

Under Gyonnese law, Rhonda Shindo was guilty of mass murder.

The punishment was also Gyonnese—and considered the worst it could give out. She had to forfeit any and all children to the Gyonnese for the rest of her life.

But the Gyonnese had distinctions between real children and false children. Real children were children like Emmeline—what the Gyonnese called the Originals. Talia was a false child, a clone, a duplicate, and therefore beneath the Gyonnese's notice.

"I mean," Talia was saying, "the Gyonnese got to take her real children as a punishment to *Mom*, right? And if she's gone, they can't punish her anymore."

"I'm not sure," Flint said. "I'm not an expert in Gyonnese law, which is what prevails here."

"But they don't consider me a real child," Talia said, her voice trembling. "They would never take me. Why would my searching for my sisters put them in danger? They're not 'real,' either."

Flint rubbed his chin, then tapped his thumbnail against his teeth. He wasn't quite sure how to explain any of this. But he was going to have to try.

"I've worked around Earth Alliance laws for more than a decade now," he said, "and they're difficult and nuanced at best. The thing to remember—and it's the hardest thing to keep in mind; it's the thing that makes this so complicated—is that the only reason the Earth Alliance works is that each member agrees to live by another member's laws whenever the first member is in the other member's territory. Humans are the worst at doing this. We don't like laws we don't understand."

Talia had slid her arms away from her abdomen. She had crossed them over her chest instead. "I studied this stuff in school."

"I know," he said, "but I've lived it. This aspect of the Earth Alliance is why I became a Retrieval Artist."

She frowned at him. "What do you mean?"

He wasn't sure he could describe those last few weeks he had spent as a detective, when he was going to have to give up children for the crimes their parents had committed. He couldn't give those children to alien governments, knowing the children's humanity would be broken, and they would become crazed things without much of a life.

"You know the stories," Flint said. "You've heard them all your life. Disappearance companies were invented so that children wouldn't have to pay for their parents' crimes, especially when the crimes were minor or nonexistent by human standards, such as stepping on a flower or walking next to a prohibited riverbank."

"I don't know your story," she said.

And she didn't. So he told her, in a truncated way, about those last few weeks, about the baby that would have gone to the Wygnin, the children that he had found in a transport, sobbing for their parents, and the woman who had given herself up for them, so that they wouldn't suffer for something she had done.

When he was done, Talia stared at him.

"You became a Retrieval Artist because you didn't want to be a detective anymore?" she asked.

He sighed. It wasn't quite that simple. "When I was a detective, I was sworn to uphold the laws of Armstrong. Those laws function within the laws of the Earth Alliance. If a court decides—as it did with your mother—that her children would be sacrificed because she had broken another species' law, then I would have to sacrifice those children, if I found them. Do you understand?"

"No," Talia said. "So why find the people who Disappeared?

It seems to me that they had escaped, and you shouldn't want to get them back."

"Most of the time, I don't," he said. "Most of the time I turn down clients."

"So when do you take them?"

"When the laws they've supposedly broken no longer apply. When the charges are withdrawn. When they've come into an inheritance or when there's a true family emergency, something they need to know about. Even then, I don't always bring them back to the society they disappeared from. Sometimes I just notify them, and let them decide what to do. Often they've built a new life that they don't want to lose."

"Like Mom," Talia said.

"Your mother didn't Disappear," Flint said. "She was protected by a strangeness in Gyonnese law."

"The real child thing," Talia said.

Flint nodded. "The real versus false child attitudes that the Gyonnese have."

"Humans have that attitude, too," Talia said.

"Not like the Gyonnese." He folded his hands over his stomach, pretending a relaxation he didn't really feel. "Do you understand what happened with your mother? Why she did what she did?"

Talia shrugged. That had been the answer she had given him from the beginning. Maybe she didn't understand, not on a deep level. If she understood, she wouldn't have searched for the other clones.

"All right," he said. "Let me tell you this as I understand it. And remember, I learned about it at the same time I learned about you. I never got a chance to ask your mother about it before she died. I'll never know the whole story."

"Me, either," Talia muttered. But she watched him warily, clearly waiting for him to continue.

"Your mother," he said, "started working for Aleyd Corporation when we were married and living here in Armstrong."

"You weren't a police officer then," Talia said.

"No, I worked in computers," Flint said.

She started. Apparently he hadn't told her that.

"Your mother was a brilliant researcher who specialized in biology and chemistry. She was the up-and-coming genius in the family, not me."

He smiled at that memory.

"We didn't realize the toll it would take on us. When she got pregnant with Emmeline, we figured we had good jobs and we'd be able to raise a nice-sized family. We—or maybe it was just me—weren't much more ambitious than that. Kids, a nice house, good jobs, a good life."

He shook his head. He had come a long way from that man. He could barely remember what it was like to be him.

"Your mom got so busy at work that by the time Emmeline was only a few weeks old, I became her primary caregiver. I did almost everything for the household. It got so that Emmeline wouldn't even go to your mom when she came home from work."

Talia hadn't moved. She was rigid, but attentive, as if this part of the story was the most important part.

"I didn't know that your mom was working on this top-secret project for Aleyd. It was a nutrient-rich water that was like a high-end fertilizer, only supposedly better, something that could be brought to arid, water-poor places like this Moon, and make the growing cycles more productive."

"That's the crap they tested on Gyonne," Talia said.

"Yeah," Flint said softly, deciding not to reprimand her for her language. "That's the stuff."

"The stuff in the holo," she said.

He nodded. When Rhonda had been kidnapped, her kidnappers had left a holo in the house. Talia had seen the holo. It had been devastating, detailing Rhonda's crimes in a horrifying manner.

"I know all of that," Talia said. "About her convictions and how the Gyonnese don't consider me a real child. That's how she could raise me."

"That's right," Flint said. But he didn't think that Rhonda had created Talia just for the sake of raising a child.

He had a hunch—one that he couldn't prove—that Rhonda had created the clones to substitute for Emmeline when the Gyonnese came to collect on their debt.

Only Emmeline died, and the Gyonnese were never able to collect. Because they believed her to be the real child.

The others didn't count.

"Okay," Talia said, "here's what I don't get. You said I was incautious, that I might hurt the others by looking for them. But I don't see how that's possible. I mean, the judgment was against Mom, and it didn't apply to me or the other five because the Gyonnese don't consider us real children. Emmeline is dead. So I don't know how I could be endangering anyone."

Flint took a deep breath. This was where it got tricky.

"We're in the realm of supposition now," he said. "And in my job, I have to suppose. I have to look at worst-case scenarios because if I don't, people will die."

"So you're going to make stuff up?"

He shook his head. "You're looking at the upside, the logical upside, of the case against your mother. You're assuming that the Gyonnese react the way humans do and will now realize that they'll never get their vengeance and no one will be punished for those crimes."

"You think they were crimes," Talia said softly.

He had never discussed it with her, not like this. He'd made sure she understood the holo, that she knew about the court case, that she knew who had ordered her mother taken and why.

But he had never discussed the case, not like this.

"Yeah," he said, "I think they're crimes."

"But Celestine Gonzalez, she said that the Gyonnese should understand that humans don't consider this a crime at all."

He frowned at the mention of one of the lawyers who had worked for Rhonda. And for him, after Rhonda died. Gonzalez, who had taken a liking to Talia, had helped Flint adopt her before he brought her back to the Moon.

"Why did she say that?" Flint asked.

"Because the larva weren't grown yet. They were just, you know, things. And there was no difference between them and the ones that split off. So why not just call the Seconds an Original, and not worry about it?"

Flint stared at his daughter. He couldn't believe that Gonzalez had said that to her, to a cloned child. He suspected that Gonzalez hadn't been that explicit—or if she had, she had been discussing a point of law.

The woman had been very careful to guard Talia's feelings the rest of the time.

This was where the path he was on—the new parent path—seemed even more treacherous. What would be best for Talia? Telling her the truth? Telling it harshly? Or glossing over this part of the conversation and letting her come to the realization on her own?

"Tal," he said gently, "think about what you just said."

"It's not like cloning," she said. "It would be like the destruction of the fertilized eggs. They hadn't developed into a person yet. No one knew them. They didn't have experiences, so they weren't different from each other. They were just biological matter."

"So we believe," Flint said. "And not all of us believe that, either. But the Gyonnese are different from us. And who's to know if the Originals aren't somehow different from creation from the Seconds and Thirds?"

Talia bit her lower lip. "So you think Mom really killed entire families?"

Flint nodded. "But not deliberately, and not alone. That's where the Gyonnese make their mistake. The corporation is liable and so is everyone along the decision-making chain. I'm sure your mother wouldn't have wanted that water tested on a windy day. I'm sure that she would have been cautious, if she had been on-site, to make certain nothing went wrong."

At least that was what he wanted to believe, on his best days. On his bad days, he wondered whether Aleyd hadn't been testing the nutrient-rich water as a weapon—a seemingly innocuous weapon that could be "accidentally" deployed when the wind blew in the wrong direction.

"It was an accident?" Talia asked.

"Sometimes terrible things happen," Flint said, "and we can't do anything about them."

"Like Emmeline's death," Talia said. "She would have had to be punished for what Mom did."

"She would have had to live with the Gyonnese," Flint said. "I've never learned what that meant, how they would have raised her, how they would have treated her. The punishment, in their mind, was that your mother wouldn't ever see her children again."

"But Mom's gone. So how can she still be punished?"

"She can't," Flint said. "But the Gyonnese never got their punishment. They can't revive the case—thanks to all the treaties that exist within the Earth Alliance. Once a judgment is rendered, it's either appealed or it stands. Your mother's judgment was appealed, and the appeal was denied, so it stands. The Gyonnese can't go after someone else now."

"But if Emmeline were still alive, they could take her?" Talia asked.

"I don't know," Flint said. "I'd have to be an expert in Gyonnese law to give you an answer on that."

"Someone can answer it, though," Talia said.

"I'm sure," Flint said.

"So you think that maybe she's still alive?"

His heart jumped. He hoped that reaction hadn't shown on his face.

But Talia didn't seem to notice. She was still talking. "Like maybe Mom concealed her with the other clones? Or Disappeared her?"

"No," Flint said, although he thought it was a distant possibility. "I'm much more concerned about the fact that the Gyonnese paid to have your mother kidnapped."

"What do you mean?" Talia asked. She clearly hadn't thought of this before.

"The judgment had been rendered. The case was settled. They had no right, under Alliance law, to interview her, let alone take her away from Callisto."

"It was an illegal act," Talia said.

Flint nodded. "Which is why they hired a Recovery Man. A Tracker wouldn't bring her to them because she hadn't done anything wrong. Retrieval Artists don't work with alien governments. We work only with humans."

And only to find true Disappeareds. No one Flint knew, not even the most unethical Retrieval Artists, would have taken the Gyonnese case.

"Recovery Men kidnap people?" Talia asked.

"Usually they don't work with sentient creatures at all, be they human or Disty or any other species we know of. They might take a plant or a creature everyone believes to be un-intelligent, but even that can be stretching it. Usually Recovery Men specialize in rare artifacts."

"Why would he take the job, then?" Talia asked.

Flint shrugged. They might never know. He'd received word from Detective Zagrando on Callisto that the Earth Alliance authorities had made some kind of deal with the Recovery Man, and had let him go.

Zagrando had been angry: the Earth Alliance authorities hadn't even asked a lot of questions about the case. They seemed to want the whole thing to go away.

"The Recovery Man's not the issue," Flint said. "The Gyonnese are."

"What did he say? Why did they hire him?"

Flint did know the answer to that. Zagrando had given him that information shortly after Flint had returned from Callisto.

"He said they believed they could use your mother to show the illegality of human behavior with regard to Earth

Alliance law. He mentioned bringing down the Disappearance Services, but the authorities believe that the Gyonnese were going to use the cloning and the tacit approval of Aleyd Corporation, not to mention the Earth Alliance itself, to show how corrupt the system was."

"Why didn't they just indict her or whatever it is that lawyers do?" Talia's voice was getting tight. She was clearly getting upset.

"The Gyonnese believed no one would bring charges. And they might have been right. At that point, Aleyd might have used their own internal Disappearance Company to help the two of you Disappear. Or they might have tied up everything in court until you and your mother were long dead."

Talia frowned. "I still don't know why this is important, why it means I might have done something wrong."

"I never said you did anything wrong," Flint said. "But you hadn't looked at all the possibilities. The Gyonnese are looking for a test case. They believe your mother committed a heinous crime against them—"

"You believe it, too," Talia said.

She sounded accusing. But he wasn't going to lie about how he felt. And he wasn't going to soften Rhonda's actions any more than he already had.

"What happened in that larval colony," Flint said, "was one of the defining moments of Gyonnese culture. The Gyonnese don't want to let it go. With your mother gone, they might go after her heirs."

"Heirs," Talia repeated.

"You, for one," Flint said.

"And the others?" Talia asked.

"Under Earth Alliance law, the other clones aren't able to inherit from your mother's estate." Technically, Talia wasn't, either—Rhonda had never given Talia full legal status as a child, like Flint had done. But he hadn't told her that.

Nor had he told her that he had a team of lawyers working on her inheritance.

"So they're not legal heirs under Earth Alliance law," Flint said. "But the Gyonnese might think them useful. All six of you would be a great visual example of the way to circumvent the rule of law, with you sitting side by side in some Multicultural Tribunal Courtroom. It would be hard to argue that your existence wasn't a deliberate attempt by your mother to avoid punishment."

"But she's not here—"

"I know," Flint said. "But she isn't really the case. She's an example. And the Gyonnese could go after her, after Aleyd, and after the entire system. Right now they just have you. But if they find the others, they'd have an emotional core to their case that would be almost impossible to fight."

Talia's frown had deepened. Flint could almost see her imagining herself sitting with five older versions of her DNA, sisters, as she called them, and they would probably be as different as sisters. They would look alike, but dress differently. They would speak with different accents or even in different languages. They would have different ways of looking at the universe.

And yet it would be impossible to deny that they had come from the very same stock. And five of them would be the exact same age.

It would be a devastating visual example of a human's attempt to go around Earth Alliance law, with a wink from all the human governments and corporations.

"You think that's what the Gyonnese are going to do?" Talia asked.

Flint shrugged. "For all I know, they put this entire case away when your mother died. But what if they didn't? What if they were waiting for something? You're not enough by yourself. You could have been an accident or a selfish moment on your mother's part. You were created after the case was settled and your mother knew the Gyonnese wouldn't take you. If there was only you, a good lawyer, like one of Aleyd's, might have a fairly easy time of keeping the Gyonnese case out of a court."

"But the six of us are too much evidence," Talia said.

Flint nodded. "And there's one more thing to think about. You grew up with your mother. You were shocked when you learned about all of this. It's had an impact on you that I can't begin to understand."

Talia looked down.

"But I'm assuming these other girls know only that they were adopted. If they even know that. They don't know they're cloned. They don't know where they're from or who their biological parents were. They don't know any of this history. Suddenly you appear and then there's this court case, and they're an example. If things go horribly wrong, they might even be punished for Rhonda's actions all those years ago. It would be as bad as what happened to you. Maybe even worse, because you at least knew her. You loved her. To the other five, she's just a name. A woman who had done something wrong and might have used them to get herself out of it."

"Oh, man," Talia said, still looking down. "I didn't know."

"I know," Flint said. "And like I said, this is all supposition. I'm trained to look for the worst case. Best case is exactly what you said in the beginning. Your mother is gone, so the Gyonnese no longer have any interest in our family."

"You don't think that's what's going to happen, though, do you?" Talia asked.

"The fact of your mother's kidnapping bothers me more than anything," Flint said. "It means that as of six months ago, the Gyonnese were still trying to prosecute this crime in a way that'll satisfy their people."

"And you think they're going to keep trying," Talia said.

"I hope not," Flint said. "But we have to be prepared for it."

"Are we?" Talia asked.

He nodded. "I've already got some plans in place for the two of us. I hadn't counted on five other viable clones."

Talia raised her head. "Maybe the Gyonnese won't find them. Maybe they're not looking."

"But if they are," Flint said, "I need to know what you did."

That guarded look returned to Talia's face. "What do you mean?"

"To find the others. I need to know how you tracked them down."

"It wasn't hard," she said, "once I knew what to look for."

"Walk me through it," he said.

"Why?" she asked. "Won't that get their attention?"

He smiled gently at her. "I'm good at what I do. I'm hoping we have the time to cover the tracks you laid."

"And if we don't?" Talia asked.

His smile faded. "We'll find out soon enough."

5

Noelle DeRicci sat at her desk, watching the screen she had called up in the middle of the room. The screen covered her floor-to-ceiling windows and stretched from the comfortable chair on the right side of the room to the large green tree-thing on the left.

The screen itself was clear, which made the images look like they were acted out especially for her, on the white carpet that she still hadn't managed to get rid of.

In the center of those images: Ki Bowles, looking smug, not knowing what a disaster faced her at the end of the story. Bowles was standing in front of the Armstrong City Complex, her strawberry hair setting off those goofy tattoos that covered her nasty face.

"Given her history with various alien cultures," Bowles was saying, "many have asked if we should trust Noelle De-Ricci to handle all of the Moon's security."

"Many," DeRicci snarled. She always snarled at this point in the story. "Meaning *you*."

She knew she should shut the vid off, but she couldn't. The damn story was back, and even though the media cited it as the source of Bowles's disgrace, they still reran the damn thing.

DeRicci had already gotten calls from the media center, asking how she wanted to handle this.

But she was older than she had been when Ki Bowles first attacked her. Older, wiser, and used to inane media coverage, no matter how hurtful.

DeRicci had told the media center that the only comment they should issue was this one: *The story that Ki Bowles is covering has nothing to do with the United Domes of the Moon or its security chief. Our comments on the discredited story that got Ms. Bowles fired six months ago are all on the record. We have nothing to add.*

DeRicci figured that would have to do.

Still, she was wallowing. She didn't have to watch this. Technically, she had won this battle. Bowles had been fired over this story, her career in tatters.

Yet she was back, with some kind of sensational piece about the law firm Wagner, Stuart, and Xendor, which created its own problems for DeRicci's office.

DeRicci's boss, Cecelia Alfreda, the governor-general of the Moon, had once worked for WSX. She still kept them as her personal attorneys.

DeRicci hoped that someone would find a way to discredit Bowles's latest story. Otherwise the media center would have a lot more to do than defend DeRicci against ancient charges. It would have to defend the governor-general against whatever scandal Bowles thought she had uncovered.

Finally DeRicci waved a hand. "Off," she said to the office system. The images on the screen winked out, and then it disappeared, leaving the windows unblocked for the first time that day.

DeRicci stood. She loved the view from those windows. She believed it was a view of consistent triumph. Nearly two years ago, an unknown bomber had tried to destroy the dome. The bomb had opened a hole in a section of the dome, and had ruined an entire neighborhood of Armstrong.

That had been one of the last cases DeRicci had worked

as a detective. She had never caught the bomber—no one had. Most people, including her, believed that the bomber had died in the explosion.

DeRicci used that view to remind herself that not everything had an answer. And even so, people, the city, the dome, the Moon itself, could recover from unanswerable—and catastrophic—events.

She needed to remember that she was in charge of security—not just for Armstrong, but for all of the United Domes of the Moon. She needed to protect the entire place against the unknown and the unimaginable.

And that did not include Ki Bowles.

Bowles was known and, unfortunately, easy to imagine. She wasn't that easy to ignore, however.

DeRicci's desklink chirruped. She sighed. She had shut off most of her personal links because of the revival of the Bowles story, leaving only the emergency links and contact information for the people who worked with her directly.

The chirrup sounded again. It had to come from someone who wasn't on her approved list.

She slammed her palm onto the desk, activating her side of the link. A face she didn't recognize appeared on the desk's edge.

"I'm sorry to disturb you, sir," the young woman said.

"Apology accepted," DeRicci said.

She was about to shut the connection down when the woman said, "But there's a Detective Nyquist trying to reach you. He says it's important."

DeRicci frowned. Bartholomew Nyquist was on her approved list. In fact, he was at the top of it.

"What the hell is he going through channels for?" DeRicci asked.

"I don't know, sir, but—"

"The question was rhetorical," DeRicci snapped. "Put him through."

The woman's image vanished, replaced by Nyquist's

rumpled face. He looked tired and sad. DeRicci had gotten used to tired, but sad was something new.

DeRicci braced herself for some kind of bad news.

"Noelle," he said, his voice soft. "I'm at the Hunting Club."

"The Hunting Club?" She smiled. He hated that place. She'd made the mistake of taking him there when he got out of the hospital, and that was when she learned how few pretensions he had.

Nyquist didn't care if he was seen. In fact, he preferred not to be seen. He wanted to live his life, do his job, and spend time with the people he cared about.

Which, fortunately, included her.

"Yeah." His tone made it clear that he wasn't happy about being at the club. "I'm investigating two murders, only I have a problem."

It took her a moment to realize this was a professional contact, not a personal one.

"Something I can help you with?" she asked.

"Oddly, yes," he said. "This stupid place needs to have its board of directors sign off every time the security system gets shut down. And I don't have the time for that."

"What's the problem with the system?" DeRicci asked.

"It's destroying my evidence," Nyquist said.

"But you have to realize that the Hunting Club's security is there for a reason," DeRicci said. "The rich, powerful, and famous of Armstrong—"

"Need the privacy and the protection from I don't know what kind of threats." He shook his head. He'd obviously heard that argument already today. "But somehow someone managed to breach the system anyway and kill two people. And I won't find out why unless the system gets shut down."

While she could empathize with his dilemma, she didn't entirely understand it. "Why are you telling me this?"

"Because, I'm told, the only person who has the authority to shut this system down is you."

"Oh." She let out a small breath of air. Of course she had

the authority. She had the authority to shut down the entire port under the right circumstances. She could even shut down the environmental systems in the dome if she believed they'd been tampered with.

But as the governor-general had told her, that belief had better be damn solid, because if DeRicci was wrong, she'd lose not just her job, but probably any rights she had to live in Armstrong.

"You can, right?" Nyquist asked.

"Yeah, if there's some kind of domewide threat or proof that we need to get into the club to ensure the survival of everyone in the United Domes. I don't think a murder investigation qualifies."

"Of course it does," Nyquist said. "You just told me why. The rich, powerful, and famous in Armstrong spend their leisure time here. This system has been breached, and they're all vulnerable to attack until we learn what caused the problem."

"So shutting down all protection is better than marginal protection?" she asked. "You want to tell me what kind of logic that is?"

"We'll do it before the crimes hit the media," he said. "All we need is half an hour, maybe less. If you could do that—"

"I can't, Bartholomew," she said. "Much as I want to."

"It's within your discretion, Noelle," he said.

"Yeah, and it doesn't fit into the guidelines for an emergency shutdown. Unless someone really important died. It's not the governor-general, is it?"

"No," Nyquist said.

And he didn't add any more. He wasn't going to tell her who the victims were.

Which made her nervous. He had a reason for not telling her and it couldn't be the open link.

"What if I got the head of the Hunting Club to tell you that he approves the shutoff?" Nyquist asked.

DeRicci shook her head. "I can't. I'm sorry."

He cursed. "Well, it was a long shot," he said, and signed off.

She remained at her desk for a long moment. She hated disappointing him. But he had to learn that he couldn't use her position to help his investigations.

Not that he'd ever really tried before.

But her curiosity was up now. Who could have died at the Hunting Club? Why would anyone think it was a murder? And how could anyone murder someone in a place with more security than the rest of Armstrong combined?

She leaned back in her chair, wishing she was still investigating crimes. She liked her new job most of the time, but it didn't resolve that need she had to have her curiosity answered.

She was half tempted to shut down the system anyway. Then she stared at the empty white carpet in the middle of her floor.

Right now she didn't dare do something that smacked of favoritism, even if no one really cared. If Ki Bowles found out about it, she'd use it to question DeRicci's abilities again.

Damn that woman. DeRicci hated being examined this closely. She hated looking over her own shoulder, questioning her own decisions.

But she would do that as long as that horrible story played.

She hoped something would come along—something bigger—that would allow that ancient history to disappear into the natter that composed most of the entertainment programming.

But she doubted that would happen, at least not for a while.

So until then, she had to be careful.

Until then, she had to do everything by the book, and hope that no one—and no investigation—got seriously hurt in the process.

6

Talia wanted to leave her dad's office. She just wanted to run out the door, through this horrible messy part of Armstrong, and down the deserted streets. She didn't want anyone to look at her, and she didn't want to look at them.

She just wanted to disappear, vanish out of the universe. She didn't want anyone to think about her, and she didn't want anyone to care about her.

She certainly didn't want her dad to look at her again, not with that sharp assessing glance he managed, the one that saw her better than her mother ever could. With one look, it felt like he could see all the way down to her soul.

If clones had souls.

Talia brought her legs up to her chest and hugged them. She hated this office. It was too plain. Her dad had upgraded the place since she came to Armstrong, and he said he'd improved it.

If this was an improvement, she didn't want to know what it had looked like before.

"So, tell me what you did, Talia," he said in that gentle voice.

She'd only heard him use that voice with her, not with anyone else. His voice was harsher with people who wanted something from him, and softer with people who seemed to know him.

But he was not gentle. Except with her.

Talia put her cheek on her knee. She wished he hadn't told her anything—not about Mom or the Recovery Man or the Gyonnese.

Especially not the Gyonnese. As she was listening, she was actually feeling sorry for them.

For what her mom had done.

And that confused her. Shouldn't she be loyal to her mom? Shouldn't she believe in her mom no matter what?

"Talia," he said again. "I'm not mad. I just want to figure out what happened."

"I know," she said without looking at him.

"So tell me what you did."

It was so embarrassing. And sneaky. Stuff that wouldn't have bothered her back home. It made her feel kinda dirty now, like she'd been bad or something.

"I guessed," she said. She still wasn't looking at him. It scraped her cheek to talk from this position, but she wasn't going to raise her head. She wasn't going to move.

"What do you mean?"

She sighed. This was the hard part. She hadn't been thinking that clearly when they moved to Armstrong. She didn't want a dad. She didn't want this dad. Her mom had told her some things about him, and while some of them were good—*You got your looks from him, you know. That's why you're so pretty*; or *You have his talent with computers. I guess I shouldn't be surprised at how smart you are*—most of them weren't.

Like the way he wouldn't come visit her. (How could he, when he didn't know she existed?) Or the way he never acknowledged her birthday. (She didn't have a conventional birthday, but she didn't know that then.) Or that he made it clear that he didn't want her or her mom. (Which was the biggest lie of all.)

But it took Talia a long time to lose those lies. Because losing them meant losing even more faith in her mom.

Her mom, the mass murderer.

"What did you guess?" her dad asked.

He wasn't going to stop questioning her. He wasn't going to let this go. And that was an annoying part of him.

When he had something he needed to know, he didn't let up until he knew it.

Talia sighed and put her feet on the floor. She rubbed her sore cheek, still not meeting his gaze.

Instead she looked at the edge of the desk—the desk that hid she didn't know how many computer screens and how much information, the desk that he wouldn't let her touch, not even after six months of begging and trying to prove herself worthy.

"Well," she said, "I got the stuff from the city about me. And I thought about it for a while, about the viable line thing. Then I did the math. If Mom was going to make clones to get her out of that lawsuit, she had to start them before Emmeline was born or she had to fast-grow them."

Her dad started. He hadn't thought of that, clearly. And that surprised Talia. She figured he thought of everything.

"It's illegal to fast-grow," he said. "There's too many problems. Most of the clones don't develop."

"That doesn't stop people," Talia said. "There's some places that deny they do it way too much. They gotta be doing something."

"So you checked them out," her dad said.

"All of them. I only found Speidel. You know, the one that made me. Speidel doesn't have the technology to fast-grow."

He nodded.

"Then I looked through all of Mom's records to see if there was billing from any other cloning company." Talia had taken all of her mom's stuff, as much as she could, anyway, and had left it in the open in her dad's apartment, figuring he could look through it if he wanted.

He kept walking around it all as if it were toxic or something. As though he didn't want to know.

Maybe she should have taken a hint from that.

"I couldn't find anything, which I thought was kinda weird," Talia said. "So I looked to see if the records went back that far. They kinda did, but they didn't. Like there wasn't legal bills—"

"Aleyd paid the court costs," Flint said.

"Yeah, I figured that out," Talia said. "So I figured, okay, what if Mom didn't pay for the clones? What if Aleyd did?"

"Good reasoning," her dad said.

Talia felt her cheeks warm. His compliments meant something. Mostly because they weren't idle. But she didn't want him to know that.

She didn't want him to know much about her, really. For a while, she'd thought she wouldn't stay, that she'd get emancipated or something. But after a while, she realized that idea was kinda dumb. He did care about her. And she liked him, even if she wasn't going to tell him that.

"What did you do next?" her dad asked. He wasn't going to let this go—and this was the part she didn't want to tell him. Everything from here out.

She straightened her shoulders. "Well, most corporate stuff is supposed to be public record unless it goes through attorneys, right?"

"Right," her dad said. "Even though it isn't always. Not everyone follows the rules."

"I figured with all the lawsuits going on, Aleyd would pretend to follow the rules. No shady stuff to make the charges worse or anything."

Her dad nodded.

"So the next time you and me went to Oberholst, Martinez, and Mlsnavek—"

Those were the lawyers that her mom had told Talia to contact if there was ever any trouble, the lawyers her dad ended up hiring to help him adopt Talia because they were already in place on Callisto when he found her.

When Talia first moved to Armstrong, she and her dad had to see those lawyers a lot, especially Celestine Gonzalez, who handled the closing of all her mom's affairs.

Talia said real fast, "I checked in their computer system and I found some bills from the right time. Well, kinda the right time. I figured fast-grow, but these were from—"

"You what?" her dad asked.

Her cheeks heated even worse. He didn't miss anything. Her mom might have missed the part about digging into Oberholst, Martinez, and Mlsnavek's files because she would have heard the fast-grow part. But her dad was methodical. He didn't seem to miss anything.

"You broke into a law firm's computer system?" he asked.

Like he hadn't done anything like that. She knew about the files he had from that other law firm, the ones he and Maxine Van Alen were giving to that pretty reporter woman. But he didn't know Talia knew.

It was just that she paid attention to everything because if she didn't, then she might miss something—and she'd missed so much growing up that she didn't want to make that mistake again.

Not with anyone.

Especially someone she wanted to trust.

Like her dad.

"I didn't exactly break into their system," Talia said. "I just looked at stuff I wasn't supposed to."

"That's breaking in," he said.

She shook her head. "I had permission."

He frowned.

"Seriously." She sat up, feeling animated. She was proud of this part. "Nobody thinks anything about a kid in a waiting room. Especially if you behave and have a handscreen for homework and are dressed real nice. Y'know, you say please and thank you a lot, and you smile at the people who talk to you and you're just friendly. Y'know?"

He didn't say anything. She recognized the expression. He was going to wait her out.

She hated that.

"Anyway," she said, wishing this was over, but not knowing how to completely get out of it without telling him the truth, "I asked one of the associates if there was some public computer I could use. I knew there wasn't. But I figured she'd set up some kind of firewall that I could get through on some computer. I said I needed to check some references that weren't on the public links for this homework assignment I had."

The left corner of her dad's mouth twitched. He was trying not to smile. That lifted her spirits a little.

"So she takes me to this bank of screens in this room off the waiting area. Turns out it's what they call the law library, and theoretically, none of the computers are networked with the firm's computers. But they are because they wouldn't have a link access otherwise. I did my homework, then looked at their billing records from Mom's time just to see if they paid some cloning place. And they did. Only it was a month or two before Emmeline was born."

Her dad let out a small sigh and stood, turning his back on Talia. For once, she didn't take it personally. She saw the look in his eyes just before he moved. It was a combination of hurt and anger.

He was really furious with her mom, but he'd never said that. It made sense, though. If everything he said was true, and it sure looked like it was, Mom had lied to him more than she had lied to Talia.

He kept his back to her. He didn't say anything, and she didn't like the silence.

If he was going to be mad, he might as well know the worst of it.

"That was about the time the Earth Alliance found out about the deaths in the larval colony," Talia said.

"I know." He ran a hand through his hair. The curls

sprang back up like they were specially programmed or something.

"So, I think, you know, she might have planned stuff." She didn't want to think about her mom that way, and she couldn't stop thinking about her mom that way.

It pissed her off and made her sad and worried her all at the same time.

"We don't know her plans for certain," her dad said.

"Yeah, but we can guess—"

He shook his head as he turned around. "The billing records were Aleyd's, not your mom's. In the last stages of a pregnancy, there are a lot of opportunities to collect DNA. She went to Aleyd's doctors because it was a free service. For all we know, they're the ones who set this up."

Talia swallowed, and to her surprise, her eyes filled with tears. She wiped at them angrily. She had thought for so long that her mom had done this, that this other interpretation felt like a gift.

"Would they do that?" she asked, her voice shaking.

"Yeah." His voice was clipped. She could follow the thought. They'd set up the clones and substitute one for the real child at birth. Who would know? Who would check for a clone mark, particularly if it was as well hidden as Talia's was?

"She had nothing to do with it?" Talia asked.

"Probably," he said. "We'll never know for sure."

But they could, if they broke into all the records. And he knew how to do that. Talia didn't, not yet, but he could. He was really good and really smart and maybe he would do it now that he had a reason.

He sat back down. "You checked the billing records and found this company. Then what?"

"You gotta realize this was during all the meetings you had with Ms. Gonzalez. I didn't do it all at once. I was afraid they'd catch me."

"They didn't, did they?"

She shook her head. "I was careful not to dig too hard,

and I didn't use the same machines all the time. Besides, if someone asked what I was doing, I was gonna say I didn't know and I'd take my hands off the computer and pretend like I got in there by accident. Because, y'know, when you're a kid—"

"I know," he said. The smile was gone. "What did you find?"

"I couldn't find all the records," she said. "I wanted to cross-check with Disappearances, but I couldn't get into those files at all. They weren't accessible. I'm not sure they exist."

"If Oberholst, Martinez, and Mlsnavek has access to a Disappearance Service, they let the service keep the records. If they have their own, they destroy the records. It's the only way a Disappearance Service can properly function. No questions, no answers, no history. It's better that way. And it makes it hard for me to do my job."

She suspected as much. But she hadn't known for sure. "I wasted a whole afternoon trying to track that down. Then I got this brilliant idea. You gave it to me, actually."

"Me?" he said, sounding surprised.

"You wiped away my clone status when you adopted me. I'm a real person under Armstrong law now, and I'll inherit and stuff if you want me to, but I can call myself your daughter and nobody asks about it or wants to see that mark or anything."

"That's not the only reason I did it, you know," he said.

She frowned at him. She didn't want to hear the other reasons. "I needed to be legal. That's what you did."

"You're my child," he said. "I'm not a Gyonnese. You were raised by my wife and your DNA comes from both of us. That some scientist took that DNA from another child of mine doesn't matter. I wanted to acknowledge you as my daughter. The rest of it was just bonus."

Her cheeks were hot again. He'd made that speech before, especially early on, and she'd always thought he was just trying to charm her. But over the last few months, she'd started to realize that he didn't value charm much. He liked real people with real emotions and he valued honesty more than anything.

So maybe he was telling her the truth.

"Anyway," she said, not certain how to respond, "I got to thinking about the five of them and how they'd just kinda vanished, and if they hadn't Disappeared, then maybe they were put somewhere for safekeeping and when the case got settled, they weren't needed anymore, so they became real like me."

He was frowning. It didn't seem like he completely understood.

"You are real," he said, "with or without my adopting you."

"No," she said. "I'm a clone, not a full-fledged human."

"You were a human being without parents or family," he said. "That was how the law saw you. Otherwise you were covered under every single law that applies to human beings."

"What-*ever*," she said, waving a hand. "I got thinking that maybe after the court case, the five got adopted. And that Oberholst, Martinez, and Mlsnavek, being a law firm— and my mom's law firm besides having ties with Aleyd— would handle those adoptions."

"Logical," her dad said. "I should have thought of that."

"You couldn't've found out," Talia said. "These aren't public records."

"They are in Armstrong."

"But not in the Earth Alliance. It varies from community to community."

He nodded. He must have known that. He just hadn't thought that the five had left Armstrong. He thought they were here, and he wasn't willing to look for them? That struck her as strange. But she wasn't going to get sidetracked, not when she was almost done.

"I found two," she said.

"Two adoptions?" he asked.

"Yep," she said. "Two adoptions at the right time period of two little girls. They were the same age—the right age, seven months younger than Emmeline. Oberholst, Martinez, and Mlsnavek doesn't handle a lot of adoptions, so these really stuck out. And it was weird. They didn't handle the kids. They handled the parents."

"And you assumed that these were two of the five?"

She bristled. "I didn't assume anything. I wrote down the names and tracked them through public records. I found images."

"Of the girls," he said.

She nodded, then bit her lower lip again. It was bleeding. She had to stop that. It was a nervous habit that her mom always wanted her to quit, and it had gotten worse since her mom died.

"They look like me," she said softly.

"Yeah," he said. "They would."

Her heart was pounding. She'd admitted the worst to him, and he wasn't reacting. He wasn't saying much at all.

"I only found two," she said because she wasn't sure he understood. "I never did find all five."

"Good," he said, but he sounded distracted. He was thinking, probably going over everything she had told him.

"The information links that I found, the important documents, they're only in Oberholst, Martinez, and Mlsnavek's system. I didn't do that on a public research board."

"But you looked for those names on a public board?" he asked, and there was something in his face—a stillness, a worry, a hesitation. She wasn't quite sure what it was, except that it made her nervous.

She wanted to lie to him, because she knew the real answer would piss him off.

"Yeah," she said. "But it wasn't like they were the only things I looked at on that board. I did schoolwork and I looked up some old friends from Valhalla Basin and I looked up some kids I'd met in school here. It was all jumbled up."

"That might help," her dad said. "After you found the images, did you look up more information on those families?"

Every week until she got passage on the first ship. Was she supposed to tell him that, too?

Probably. It was probably what she needed to tell him.

She sure didn't want to.

"I wanted to know if they still lived at the old addresses," she said.

"And?" he asked.

"If they had other kids," she said.

"And?"

"If they were in touch with Oberholst, Martinez, and Mlsnavek or with Aleyd or with Mom."

"Were they?"

"One of the men who adopted one of the girls, he works for Aleyd."

Her dad let out another one of those gusty sighs. "And the other family? Does it have a tie?"

"Not like that," she said. "Nobody works for Aleyd anymore."

"But they did."

She nodded. "Both parents. They're retired now, doing artsy stuff, I guess. They got some big payout."

He swore. She'd never heard him sound so upset before. Her heart pounded. "I screwed up, huh?"

"No," he said, "it's not your fault. I would have figured that Aleyd would have covered its tracks better."

"What do you mean?" she asked, feeling confused. After all, he had been the one who was worried she'd started a trail. And she had, from the look on his face. Only she expected him to yell at her, and he really hadn't yet.

"You'd think if they were going to find homes for the other five, they'd have done it with families not connected to Aleyd."

"Maybe they did," Talia said. "I only found two. That means there are three more out there."

He nodded, but the nod seemed abstract, like he was thinking about something else.

"The problem isn't you," he said. "The problem is that they didn't think. They were looking short term, at the trial and the possible punishment. Then when the case got settled, they let two of the couples adopt. They probably had couples that Aleyd knew it could control fostering the children just in case one of the children had to go to the Gyonnese."

"Ick," Talia said. They could just as easily be talking about her. "Who would do that?"

Her dad gave her a flat look. It was almost cold. He didn't answer her.

Probably because she didn't need the answer. She had it.

Her mother would have.

Did, in fact. If her dad hadn't shown up and hired all those lawyers, Talia's legal guardian would have been Aleyd Corporation. A condition of employment was that kids whose parents died while working for Aleyd could become wards of the company.

Maybe it wasn't her mom's carelessness that put Talia in that position like everyone assumed. They just figured Mom hadn't done the paperwork to protect Talia. Maybe Mom had done that intentionally.

Or maybe that had been a condition of Talia's creation.

A headache rose from her shoulders, through the back of her neck, and into the base of her skull. Her eyes stung.

"What are we going to do?" she asked.

"You're going to walk me through everything you found on the public links," he said. "And then I'm going to see if anyone Tracked your trail."

"If they did?" Her voice shook just a little.

"Then I'll see if I can figure out who the Tracker was, and see how much danger the two are in."

"And if no one Tracked it?" Talia asked.

"I'm going to wipe out the records as best I can. They

can't go away completely, but I can make them invisible to the casual scan."

Talia swallowed hard. The headache was getting worse. "Will that solve the problem?"

He looked at her again, and this time his gaze softened. She had the sense he felt sorry for her.

"All we can do," he said, "is hope."

7

Nyquist walked down the freshly raked path, feeling a frustration deeper than any he'd felt in years. DeRicci had probably been right to be cautious—her job was all about balancing politics with safety, and if someone else had been attacked in the Hunting Club while the security was off, then she would have been blamed.

But the problem was that someone had been attacked on the Hunting Club grounds while security was *on*. And no one seemed to care except him.

He wasn't media savvy enough to know what the reaction would be when the press found out that the security hadn't worked right. He didn't know whether they'd belatedly come to Ki Bowles's defense or they would argue that the exclusive club wasn't so exclusive after all.

It really wasn't his concern, unless it hampered his investigation.

Like the damn security procedures did.

The air in the fake forest smelled of real pine. He sneezed, wondering how much of the evidence he'd needed had already been recycled and recast as that lovely piney smell.

He tugged his coat tighter and stepped between the trees.

All four techs were crouched over the two bodies. Apparently the search for more bodies had ended.

"You didn't find anyone else?" Nyquist asked without saying hello.

"No." Adyson Owens was working around the face of the second victim, the man.

"We got a real problem here." Hadassa Leidmann stood up. She peeled off her gloves and put them in her evidence kit. Then she removed two more gloves and held them while she stepped around Bowles's body to walk to Nyquist. "We're losing evidence by the second."

"I tried everything," he said. "We can't shut the system down without some kind of order from God."

"You'd better get it," she said, "or we're not going to be able to do a thorough investigation. And, provided we get enough that you can make a case against someone, you won't have enough to hold up in court."

He walked over to Bowles and crouched beside the body. It looked cleaner than it had when he arrived. "You've made recordings of the scene, right?"

"One of the team is recording everything, all the time. We have to show the deterioration of the evidence. Unfortunately, that's not going to help convict anyone. That'll just help with the defense."

He nodded. He understood. But he wasn't so much interested in a conviction at the moment as he was in catching whoever did this.

"We're not going to get this shut down in time to do any good," he said. "So do what you can."

Leidmann nodded and crouched beside him.

"We have a few things," she said. "We know that she died before he did, but not much before. We figure from the angle of the wounds on her stomach and on his arm that he was holding her against him when those wounds happened. It was almost simultaneous."

"Her back against his stomach?" Nyquist asked.

"Yeah. It doesn't work any other way. And we did get

enough trace off those wounds to show that they happened at about the same time with the same weapon."

"That's not a friendly position," Nyquist said. "You don't hold someone's back against your front with a hand around the waist very often."

"Oh," Leidmann said, "sometimes you do. You might both be listening to a concert or talking to someone. The person in front, the smaller person—in this case, Bowles—would lean against the taller person and that person would put his arm around her waist. Sure. I've seen it."

Nyquist had, too. He'd even done it once or twice, but that didn't make it something people usually did along a wooded path, with no entertainment in sight.

"You think these two knew each other?" he asked Leidmann.

"Impossible to say from any evidence we've found here," she said. "I suspect that'll be your job."

"Do you have an identification on the man?"

"No," Owens said. "We've checked his ID chips. They're clean."

"Clean?" Nyquist asked. He'd never heard of anything like that before.

"Yeah," Owens said. "I'll have to check in the lab, but right now the reading that I'm getting is that they're new. They're the kind of chips you'd find in a hospital, the kind you'd set just before you put it into a newborn."

"These haven't been set?" Nyquist asked.

"Not that I can tell. But they might just be an upgrade that got erased. I'll be able to tell with the right equipment."

"Have you checked Bowles's ID chips?" Nyquist asked.

"No," Owens said. "There's no need. We all know who she is."

"Do it anyway," Nyquist said.

Owens shot him an irritated look and started to move toward Bowles's body. But Leidmann waved him away.

"I'll do it," she said.

She took out a small handheld and ran it over Bowles's

left hand. Then she frowned, and ran it over Bowles's right hand. Finally she ran it along Bowles's entire body.

"Nothing," she said. "Clean."

"No identification?" Nyquist asked.

"None."

"Could something in this security system be wiping the identification chips?" Nyquist asked.

"That would be counterproductive," Owen said. "That would mean everyone who went to the Hunting Club would have to reset their identification chips."

"Most people don't lie on the ground for a long period of time," Nyquist said. "Not even during the so-called hunts. Both bodies have had prolonged contact with the same system that cleans up the dirt and smoothes the grass—"

"And absorbs small particles," Leidmann said.

"It's possible," Owens said. "But why would it have that function?"

"Think about it," Nyquist said. "If you're some kind of Gossip reporter and you hide behind these fake trees or rig up a camera behind one of the expensive rocks, the security system would wipe it clean as a matter of course. The work you meticulously gathered over a prolonged period of time would vanish, and you wouldn't know until you went back to the studio."

Owens cursed. "I'll bet you're right."

"There are systems like that," Leidmann said. "Sometimes they erase, but sometimes they mine and store. Same with the security system itself. Our trace might show up in some kind of storage bag. The problem would be proving that it's the stuff from this crime scene and not from some other part of the so-called forest."

"I'm sure we can get a court order for all of that," Nyquist said, "and it'll be better coming from you guys. You're the ones who process the evidence. It won't look like you have a vendetta against the club. It'll just look like you're trying to get as much evidence as possible."

Leidmann raised an eyebrow. She looked amused. "Do you have a vendetta against the club?"

"I'm sure I will by the time this investigation is over," he said. "Anything else you can tell me?"

"They died about the same time," Owens said. "They were killed with the laser knife that we found. It had Bowles's initials. It seemed to come from her bag. The bag itself didn't have much. A scarf, the laser knife, and a hand-held, which I think is weird considering how many chips she has that link her to various systems. She has independent cameras on her hands, in the corners of her eyes, and dotting her tattoos. There are other chips on her that record sound, some that do entire holo imagery—she's a walking spy system."

"And all of that shuts down in the Hunting Club?" Nyquist asked.

"Yeah," Owens said. "It gets shut off just like the emergency links. That's automatic."

"Which makes you wonder what she was doing here," Nyquist said.

"Probably being seen," Leidmann said. "She had that story run last night. It was a big comeback for her."

"Story?" Nyquist asked. "I wasn't watching yesterday."

"Something about Wagner, Stuart, and Xendor," Leidmann said. "I didn't pay a lot of attention because I felt like it was just a rehashing of stuff anyone who paid attention already knew."

The hair rose on the back of Nyquist's neck. The case he'd nearly died working had involved Wagner, Stuart, and Xendor.

"That seems like a huge coincidence," he said.

"What?" Leidmann asked. "That she did a big story? She specializes in big stories."

"She hadn't had one for more than six months," Nyquist said. "Then her big story, her comeback story, is about WSX? And she dies the next day."

"It wasn't supposed to be one story," Leidmann said. "I

remember that. It was the first in a series. You probably should watch it."

Nyquist couldn't suppress his shudder. "I probably should," he said.

8

Justinian Wagner's office was as black as his mood—which, he knew, was normal. The place was designed to mirror his moods. But he'd never seen it this dark. His desk was black, the carpet had turned black, and even the skylight that opened to the dome was closed.

He supposed he could shut off the mood-matching feature, but that seemed like too much work. Besides, it would be a nice warning to any assistants who tried to contact him.

Now might not be the best time.

He smiled grimly at the understatement. There was no best time, not anymore. He'd watched Ki Bowles's piece on his law firm for the fifteenth time in the past twenty hours, and he still didn't know where she'd gotten the information.

He had associates scrambling to find out who had given out confidential files. He had his best computer techs searching for a smooth backdoor hack into the firm's systems, and he was going to have to use another tech to sweep his own private systems.

The story was too good, the facts too accurate. Bowles clearly had had access to confidential materials. Her interviews with former employees seemed to back up her conclusions, but no one—not even the other partners—knew everything that she had brought up in that first five-minute segment.

Or they hadn't known it until six p.m. last night when the first installment ran.

Bowles was planning to run a dozen other installments or more, all on WSX, all about its practices and its misdeeds.

He was doing everything he could to stop her—an injunction on airing the piece further, a lawsuit alleging slander, and a third alleging fraud designed for personal gain. He didn't just file against her, he filed against Upstart Productions and the various networks that aired the first story, adding criminal conspiracy to their charges—although that would be difficult to make stick.

By the time that last charge went to court, he had to find proof or withdraw the charges. Because if he accused them of criminal conspiracy without actual proof of a theft or malicious intent, all he was doing was confirming what she had reported.

He'd worried about that from the moment he filed the charges, which was one reason why he hadn't filed the criminal charges against Bowles.

At least, not yet.

He clasped his well-manicured hands behind his back as he walked toward the center of the room. He'd frozen the image of Bowles as she sat behind some cheap desk. He'd left the image as a 3-D hologram, one that was slightly see-through as all net-provided holograms were, so that no one would confuse them with the real thing.

She seemed slight and a bit overdressed. The tattoos across her face were beautifully drawn for something that cheap, and her multicolored hair accented them perfectly. She wore no jewelry at all, which surprised him.

She seemed very comfortable with her little truth-telling mission, as if she wasn't afraid of the consequences of her so-called investigative journalism.

He was afraid. He had made certain he was unavailable

all day. The senior partners would meet in two hours, and he wasn't sure what he could tell them.

Wagner walked around her image, as if in studying the posture of something filmed hours, maybe days, ago could give him an insight into this woman.

This first story was mostly allegations and tantalizing tidbits, with just enough documentation to show that Bowles was serious. The problem with the story was the promises Bowles made for future stories.

She had, in just a few words, outlined WSX's longstanding relationship with Ultre Corporation. Ultre had been one of the first businesses to work with Wagner's father, back when WSX was a new law firm. Most of the other clients had come from Wagner's mother. She'd been the prime breadwinner when the law firm was founded.

Bowles didn't mention that. She did talk about the solar arrays that Ultre had placed on Mina, the arrays that had ended up malfunctioning and costing the lives of two dozen Ultre employees. She mentioned the settlement that, considering the easy-to-prove liability for Ultre, had been more than fair to all concerned, the payouts to the families of the victims, and the legal fees that Ultre paid.

She also provided evidence—mostly testimony from forensic accountants who followed what she called "a clear document trail"—that the victims all had lawyers from a firm with tight connections to WSX. In fact, that firm, which advertised itself as the only privately owned, human-focused law firm on Mina, was a satellite company of WSX. The ties were so hidden that no one would ever have been able to find it, but the firm's partners knew. And they had consulted with WSX before any settlement had been made.

Which was illegal under Earth Alliance law.

Wagner stopped next to the image of Bowles. Illegal, but no longer prosecutable. His father had made the arrangement. The money from the Ultre deal had gone into building WSX into the firm it was now. When that deal had been completed, Wagner had been less than a year old.

His parents were dead. Xendor was no longer an active partner, although the name remained on the door. Wagner could easily defend himself and his firm against these charges. But they weren't the only ones. They were the beginning of a very, very long list.

The fact that Bowles listed several other names on that list frightened him.

And he didn't scare easily.

He had taken action, but he wasn't sure it was the right action. The allegations would remain. He had noticed that with the Bowles's story. Other networks had picked it up and folded it into a story on Bowles herself—her firing from InterDome Media six months ago, the ill-advised piece she had completed on Noelle DeRicci, which ran as DeRicci had saved the Moon from one of the worst disasters it had ever faced, the previous award-winning stories and triumphs that had marked Bowles's career before the DeRicci piece.

A few networks had even run stories on Bowles's past, how she hadn't come up through the normal channels. Her training had been in art history and that, the dumb reporter had maintained with an air of authority, had given her the ability to sift through details to find the one important piece of information hidden in plain sight.

The problem was that nothing about WSX was in plain sight. Wagner ruthlessly controlled his firm's image. He knew what information was out there on the public links about his firm.

He knew what former employees could say with authority and what they could suppose. He had worked very hard, first with his father and then after his father left, to make sure that no one knew as much about the firm as he did.

Not even the other partners knew which "privately owned, human-focused" firms throughout the known universe had ties to WSX. The more limited the knowledge, the more he could control it.

The files on the firm's business had layers upon layers. Some never left his private system at all. Others were buried in a code that only the most savvy could find—and then, only if they had months to sift through and the expertise to understand both computers and the law.

Bowles, for all her pretense at intelligence, didn't have either expertise. And even though she had been out of work for six months, she didn't have the patience or the kind of mind that would allow her to sift through those details and see the pattern, no matter what some stupid network talking head said.

Bowles had assistance. A lot of it. And she'd been smart enough to protect her sources. She had a raft of lawyers, some copyright and trademark lawyers, some business lawyers, some civil attorneys. She had started with Maxine Van Alen, who was one of the few attorneys in Armstrong smart enough—and courageous enough—to take on Justinian Wagner and win.

Van Alen had a grudge against him. She understood how he worked, too. She would have built the tightest firewall around the information in her firm that any firm could assemble.

He'd tried to break through her firewalls before, first on a Disappeared case, and then when she represented Miles Flint, and he hadn't been able to.

If she had known that Bowles was taking on WSX, she would have built an even tighter firewall.

Maxine Van Alen wasn't the doorway into Bowles's sources. But the other attorneys might be.

He would see what they knew. And he would see whether he could get an advance screening of the next two or three stories.

With the right amount of money and a few softly voiced threats, he should be able to see what he was up against.

Because if Bowles actually had what she said she did, she had the ability to destroy WSX. Not through negative public opinion or even through the courts.

But through the clients. They would believe—they would

know—that WSX sometimes (often) manipulated them into a deal that would work better for WSX than anyone else.

So far, the firm had been able to keep such deals secret.

But that wouldn't last.

One story could exist out there and over time, it would become little more than a rumor. But another story, then another, with other reporters chasing the information or just repeating it, would make the damage substantial.

WSX would survive, but it would be reduced to a standard law firm, not one of the most powerful entities in the Earth Alliance.

Justinian Wagner didn't want to head a standard law firm. He liked the power he wielded. Six months ago, when his parents died and his brother Disappeared, he had guaranteed that he would be the most powerful man in Armstrong.

He'd never thought he could lose his power base by losing the influence his law firm had.

He'd never thought of that.

Until last night.

When he first watched Ki Bowles.

9

Before he could find and watch the report Ki Bowles made before her death, Nyquist had to report to the First Rank Detective Unit. His boss, Andrea Gumiela, had sent him several urgent messages through his links, which he got the moment he stepped outside the Hunting Club's protective grounds.

She wanted to know how the investigation was proceeding. Then, when Nyquist hadn't answered any of her urgent messages, she demanded to see him the moment he left the grounds.

Normally, he would have sent a message across his own links, explaining the problem with the Hunting Club and asking her to wait. But this wasn't a normal case.

He needed Gumiela, not just because he was freshly back to work, but because she liked handling the media. And the media would be all over this case.

The unit was on the fifth floor of the First Detective Division, not far from the City Complex. The law enforcement buildings surrounded the City Complex like a protective ring, with all of the divisions having their own buildings.

Gumiela's office was in the center of the First Rank Detective Unit. Many of the newer detectives had offices—or, more properly, cubicles on this floor, and she had learned that to control them, she had to be in the center of them.

So she moved her office from a lush suite on the top floor to several large central offices in the middle of the First Rank Unit. She no longer had a spectacular view, but she controlled her troops better.

Nyquist stepped inside the unit, wincing at the smell of burnt coffee. During his rehabilitation, DeRicci had given him a taste for real Earth-grown coffee. Her job paid ten times his, and because of that—and because she had been a detective herself once—she indulged herself in all kinds of luxuries.

Nyquist couldn't care about most of them, but he could do with some real coffee now.

He stopped at the common table, put some money in a nearby jar, and helped himself to the crap that passed for real in the detective unit. Then he grabbed a large handful of crackers, knowing they would probably be all he'd get to eat for hours.

He was chewing on them as he rounded the corner into Gumiela's office.

Because the office had subsumed three smaller offices, it had an odd octagonal shape. Initially, there had been no windows, but Gumiela had had a few installed. They overlooked the main detective unit, where the newbies sat at their barely private desks, trying to overcome the caseloads that would destroy a more experienced detective.

Gumiela watched her entire squad closely. DeRicci had hated her when she worked for her—and still held a grudge. Nyquist didn't like the way Gumiela micromanaged, but he realized somewhere along the way that Gumiela was the best chief of detectives the city had ever had.

The case closure rate since she had been promoted had gone up, the crime rate down, and the number of career criminals removed from Armstrong's street staggering.

Whether or not Nyquist agreed with Gumiela's methods, they certainly got results.

But that didn't mean he had to like the woman. She was thin and tall and constantly nervous. She moved more than she sat, and she stared at people when she should have put them at ease. One on one, she had few social skills, but she could handle the media very well.

She had probably known Ki Bowles better than anyone else.

When he entered the office, he found Gumiela standing near one of the windows. She was wearing one of her trademark short skirts, which revealed her only good characteristic—a fantastic pair of legs.

"It's about time," Gumiela said as she turned toward him. Her eyes had deep circles under them. She had pulled back her shoulder-length hair into a bun, which only accented the exhaustion on her thin face. "Close the door."

As he did, he forced himself to take a deep breath. He promised himself he wouldn't get defensive, but her first words had provoked a defensive reaction in him. He just wouldn't act on it. Not yet.

"We need to stay ahead of this," Gumiela said. "Someone is going to leak this story, and then we're going to have more media than we know what to do with."

He turned around slowly, making each movement deliberate. "We can't afford media involvement yet. We're having trouble with the case."

"We can't avoid media involvement," she said. "One of their own has died."

He shoved his hands in his pockets. "They don't know that yet."

"But it'll only take a few hours for someone to leak it." Gumiela walked back to her desk and sat on the corner of it, crossing her long legs, and tugging her skirt over her thighs as she did so.

"The Hunting Club swears no leak will come from them," Nyquist said, "and I believe them. They exist because of their discretion."

"That won't stop someone from our offices from releasing it," Gumiela said.

He looked at her sharply. Had she already done so? And how did he ask that question without offending her?

"And no, I haven't done it yet," she said as if she heard his thoughts. "I needed to talk to you first. But I also need to stay ahead of this story. If the media get to it first, then we're all in trouble. We'll be chasing after their leads instead of them chasing after ours."

"We don't have any leads," he said.

"Excuse me?" She slid off the desk and stood up as if she was going to threaten him.

"It takes an act of God to get the Hunting Club to shut down its security system, and apparently two murders on its highly secure property is not enough to be considered an act of God. The system shuts down links, as you well know, including emergency links, which violates half a dozen city ordinances as well as probably some United Dome of the Moon laws, and to make matters worse—"

"It shuts off emergency links?" she asked.

He nodded.

"That's why I couldn't raise you?"

"And why I think our victims couldn't get the help they needed even though it was only a few meters away."

Gumiela's lips moved in a calculated smile. "So there will be some civil lawsuits against the Hunting Club."

"Probably," Nyquist said, "but that's for the families to decide. The lack of emergency links—"

"Might be one of the reasons the killer or killers chose those grounds as his killing field. What did the witnesses say? Anything about someone leaving that forest?"

"I never saw a witness," Nyquist said. "This is the first I've heard of one. Which is indicative of the case, and not the worst thing I've encountered today. The Hunting Club—"

"The information should be on the police links," Gumiela said. "I thought you had the street cops working for you.

One of them tried to contact me from inside the Hunting Club—"

"And I wish he'd reached you," Nyquist said. "The Hunting Club's security system rakes its grounds every thirty seconds. We lost all our trace."

"Lost it?" Gumiela crossed her arms.

He nodded. "The Hunting Club wouldn't shut down the system. By the time I got there, at least half the evidence was lost. By the time the techs got there, most of it was gone. I finally gave up trying to shut anything down. It was a waste of time, since the evidence was already destroyed."

"So you believe the Hunting Club had something to do with Bowles's death?"

He hadn't thought of that. He hadn't thought of many possibles, not yet. He'd been too frustrated by everything that faced him.

"I don't know," he said. "I lost a lot of valuable information and a lot of valuable time. I may never know who killed Bowles or why because of that damn security system."

Gumiela looked toward the windows. He recognized the movement. She did that when she was pretending to come up with a new thought. When she actually came up with one, her eyes lit up and she leaned forward. When she pretended, she looked away.

"Maybe we should put someone else on the case, then," she said.

"And what?" he snapped, not caring whether he offended her or not. "Give them less to work with? I at least saw the bodies. I was able to examine them along with the techs and take some conclusions from positions and the order of the wounds. Someone new would miss what little we have."

Gumiela shrugged one shoulder. "I'm not sure you're up for this, Bartholomew. You just got back."

"I know." He made himself take a deep breath, trying to stay calm. "I think I bring more than just my years of expertise, my judgment, and my observation of the crime scene to this case."

"Oh?" She slid back onto the corner of the desk, crossing her legs again. This time she didn't tug on the skirt and it rode slightly up her thighs. He tried not to look. He hated it when she tried to distract the male detectives with those fantastic legs.

"I've met Bowles," he said, "and I've seen her in her home. In fact, I saw her when she was the most vulnerable, right after she had been fired. I have a sense of the woman, not just the media star."

Gumiela finally tugged at the skirt. She wasn't looking at him, which was a bad sign.

"And then, just before I left, one of the techs told me that Bowles had just run her comeback story last night. That story—and the series it was supposed to start—is about corruption at Wagner, Stuart, and Xendor."

"I know," Gumiela said. "That's one of the reasons I'm thinking about taking you off this case."

He shook his head, biting back hasty words. He didn't want her to think he was desperate—although he was beginning to believe that he was.

He hadn't realized he wanted the case this much until he started into this conversation.

"It's precisely why you shouldn't take me off the case," he said. "I've met Justinian Wagner several times. I got injured trying to save his father's life. That should open several doors that other detectives would find closed."

Gumiela smiled. "Justinian Wagner? The man everyone believes hired the Bixian assassins to kill his father? Why would he want to talk with the man who nearly thwarted him?"

"Unlike some of the other senior detectives in this department," Nyquist said, "I never spoke to Wagner after his father died. I never let him know that I thought he'd try to have his father killed."

"Yet you're the one who saw him just before the assassins took out his father and figured out where they were going to go," Gumiela said.

"I already knew where they'd go. I just let Wagner tell me where his father lived. The man thinks he's smarter than I am. That's an advantage for me."

"Have you ever thought that perhaps he is smarter?" she asked. "After all, he's never been charged with the murders of his father or his mother."

"That's not a failing of our department," Nyquist said. "That's a failing of the Earth Alliance. We have no way to find out who hired the Bixian assassins. We can only guess. They operate outside the law, and any records we could find, we're not entitled to because of the various Earth Alliance agreements."

"I still don't see your presence as an advantage," she said. "I think your emotions will be too involved."

"Because Wagner hired the assassins?" Nyquist asked. "You think I'll go after him?"

"Won't you? Isn't he a prime suspect, given what Bowles did yesterday?"

"First, I don't know what she did yesterday. I came to see you before I watched her pieces on WSX. Second, I never make up my mind about the case until I've studied the evidence."

"But now you say there's no evidence to study."

"There's very little to study, at least at the scene," Nyquist said. "Which makes my reason for talking to you all the more important."

"I thought I'm the one who called this meeting," Gumiela said with a slight smile.

"You are." And he didn't want to add that he might have stalled the meeting if he hadn't thought he could get something out of it. "But I had an agenda when I walked through that door."

"Staying on the case," Gumiela said.

"Honestly, I never thought you'd take me off it," he said. "I'm surprised you're considering it."

She brushed that off as if he hadn't spoken. "What, then?"

"I don't want you to make an announcement to the press for twenty-four hours."

"I can't hold them off that long."

"The longer you hold them off, the more evidence I can gather," he said. "They won't be watching my every move. They won't be speculating on all those Gossip shows why I'd driven down Street A versus Street B or why I spent three hours inside Bowles's apartment or talked to an old college professor. I'll have the benefit of surprise with the interviews and the ability to collect some evidence that might disappear if the press tramples it or gets to it first."

Gumiela frowned. "I don't know how to forestall this. It's going to leak."

"So send the press in the wrong direction," he said. "Say that the two victims are impossible to identify with any certainty. Blame the Hunting Club and talk about the fact that no links or cameras or any equipment can be used on their grounds. Believe me, that'll get the press busy. They hate the Hunting Club restrictions because those things are aimed at the press, not at the rest of us. And now they've backfired. Two people are dead."

"Two hard-to-identify people," she said slowly.

He nodded. "The evidence at the scene gave us one name, but we have no way to confirm. Because the Hunting Club security system destroyed evidence, and the bodies were too marked up for precise on-scene identification."

"We never release names without a coroner's okay," Gumiela said. "We don't do official on-scene identifications."

"We know that," Nyquist said. "They don't. Give them some things to run after, give them some stuff to chew on, and that'll send them away from me."

"You're not going to go after the Hunting Club?" Gumiela asked.

"Later maybe," he said. "Right now the techs are getting all they can from the grounds and, I hope, from the security system's filters. But that's half-assed at best. I want just twenty-four hours to get ahead of them."

"I can give you twelve," Gumiela said. "That's how long I can fake not knowing for certain who our victims are."

Nyquist smiled for the first time. "Twelve is good enough."

10

The two clones Talia found had Flint's curly blond hair. He should have expected that. Talia had his hair, after all, and his blue eyes. But he wasn't quite prepared for the reality of them, which was probably why he'd been thinking of them as "clones" instead of "girls."

They were girls. He'd put up images of both of them on the screens that rose out of his desk. He hadn't made those images into holoimages—he couldn't quite handle a 3-D representation of two more of his children.

Two more matching children.

Talia sat beside him behind the desk. She'd had to wait until he'd opened several systems, and then she had walked him through the steps she'd taken to find these girls.

They didn't quite look like twins. One wore her curly hair short. It exploded around her face, which was narrower than Talia's. Apparently in the next twenty-nine months, his daughter would lose the last baby fat and would look more like a woman.

This daughter—her name was Gita Havos—had sparkling blue eyes and a pleasant expression as if she were sharing a joke with someone just off camera. Those eyes had a sharp intelligence, and the mouth had a wry turn, which suggested just a trace of self-awareness.

Or maybe he was reading too much into it.

She wore a black coat and a silver necklace with matching earrings. They looked expensive to him, as did that wayward hairstyle. He got a sense of a self-confident, happy girl who was ready to face her future.

All that from one image. He knew if he asked Talia, he would find more. He wasn't sure he was ready for them.

The second girl, Kahlila El Alamen, had somehow straightened those blond curls. She had tamed her hair and grown it long. She had pulled it away from her face with some kind of clips, and the clips managed to hold the waves that she hadn't quite been able to get rid of.

The hairstyle accented the leanness of her face. She was thinner than the other two—her cheekbones and her chin stood out in sharp relief against her generous mouth. He glanced at Gita, because he didn't want to check against Talia. The mouth would look bigger when there was less flesh on the face. He hadn't realized that his daughter had her mother's mouth—wide and angular, like a slash across her face.

This girl, Kahlila, wore a shirt with a ripped collar and no sleeves. The collar's ripping was too even to be anything but an affectation, and the lack of sleeves showed off beautifully drawn tattoos on her biceps. Those biceps were well formed. Kahlila, unlike her—what was Talia's term? Sisters?—was some kind of athlete.

"Well?" Talia asked.

Apparently he'd been studying them too long, and he'd been too quiet about it.

"I never expected to see them," he said because he didn't know how else to respond. He wasn't sure how he was feeling. His stomach was knotted, his heart was pounding, and he had to remind himself to breathe.

Beneath all that, he was furious at Rhonda for doing this to him. For denying him not one child, but six. He had told her before they married that he wanted a family. They'd planned on two children, but six would have been fine.

Or one.

"We could meet them," Talia said.

He glanced at her. Her face seemed different from theirs. He wanted to believe that it was the twenty-nine months' difference, or the baby fat, or the expression, but it was none of those things.

Talia had become more than the sum of her features. She had become more than her looks, more than her creation, more than her inheritance. She was her own person and would be forever, at least to him.

"You know we can't." He tried to keep the disappointment from his voice. All of that conversation earlier, and Talia still suggested this? Hadn't she understood the stakes?

"I don't mean now," she said, a bit defensively. "I mean when you think it's safe. Like when they're twenty-one or something."

He blinked, turning away from his daughter—the only daughter he would probably ever be able to acknowledge—and took a moment to catch his breath.

"I'm not sure it would ever be wise to see them," he said. "We don't know—"

"We can't always be cautious," Talia said.

"Yes, we can," he said.

"But it's not fair to them," she said.

"To them?" he asked. "Do they really need to know what happened here on Armstrong? Aren't you saying it's not fair to you?"

That generous mouth, the one he hadn't really noticed before, thinned. She pressed her lips together, as if she wanted to yell at him, and then she finally rubbed her chin.

She had never used that gesture before. She had picked it up from him in just the past few months.

"Maybe I am saying it's not fair to me," she said after a moment. "But what if they want to know where they came from?"

"That's not up to us," he said.

She made a disgusted noise. "Can't you at least humor me? Can't you say, 'Tal, we'll revisit this when you're twenty-one,' or something like that?"

Her comments suddenly made him calmer. She planned to stay with him. She wanted him to make plans for her twenty-first year. She expected them to stay together.

The very idea, expressed so casually, pleased him more than he could say. Until that moment, he wasn't sure whether Talia wanted to remain near him for the next six months, let alone the next eight years.

"We can talk about it then," he said, hoping she would forget he said that. He had a hunch she wouldn't. It was too important to her.

"Promise?"

"I promise we'll talk about it," he said.

She sighed. Eight years had to seem like an eternity to her. Eight years ago, she had been five, and living with Rhonda, without the father who had "abandoned" them.

She squared her shoulders and faced the images before her. "Did I make a lot of mistakes?"

"We can cover your tracks," he said. "I've already covered a lot."

"Good."

He looked at the images. He understood Talia's desire to meet these girls. He felt something similar. He'd downloaded information about their families and had to stop himself from reading with great interest.

All he knew was that Gita Havos's parents were the ones still working for Aleyd. Kahlila El Alamen's had quit to become some kind of artists.

Kahlila's parents lived on Earth—Talia had been going to see them when she had been stopped. Gita's lived in a small Aleyd-owned community on Mars.

"It's addicting, isn't it?" Talia asked him.

He made himself look away. With a touch of the finger, he made both images disappear.

"It's all about the possibilities," he said.

She frowned at him. "What do you mean?"

"Right now, all five of the others are possibilities, to both of us. Different versions of the baby I lost. Different versions of yourself for you."

"I don't think of them as me," she said.

"I understand that," he said. "I phrased it wrong. They're living a 'what-if' for you. What if you hadn't been raised by your mother? What if you'd been adopted by one of these two families? Would you have turned out exactly like Gita and Kahlila? Or would you have been different yet again?"

"You think I'd've been the same?" The question was hesitant. He thought he heard fear in her voice.

"No," he said. "I think we're the sum of our actions. Yours would have been different from theirs from the beginning."

"Because I'm younger," she said.

"Because you're you."

She looked at him sideways. "We're exactly the same. The five of them and me. We're just—what did you say? Parts of the baby you lost."

"None of you are the child I lost," he said. "She was very different. She probably talked at a different age, and found different things interesting. She spent most of her time interacting with me. None of you had met me. Your interactions with me are very different than they would have been if I had raised you."

"But Mom was there for me."

"Your mom was," he said. "But not for Emmeline. She barely knew your mother."

"That's just environmental."

"Maybe," Flint said. "One thing I know for certain. All six of you do not share Emmeline's consciousness. You don't even share each other's. You have different thoughts, different desires, and different interests. By definition that makes you different people. You didn't even know the others existed until the Recovery Man told you, right?"

"How could I?" she asked.

"Some twins describe the feeling of being 'connected' to each other. They know what the other is feeling even if they're several kilometers apart. Did you ever have that feeling?"

Talia shook her head. "Maybe because we're clones," she said bitterly.

"Maybe," he agreed. "But not because you're inferior. But because you had no knowledge of each other. Identical twins share a womb. They spend nine months together even if they're adopted out to different families. The twins know on a subconscious level that there's another person out there, a person they were once close to. You weren't close to the other five. You never met them, not even before you could remember. I don't think they have any knowledge of you, either. Or of each other."

She brightened at that. "You think that's true? Or are you trying to make me feel better?"

He sighed and ran a hand through his curls, the curls all of his daughters—all six of them—had in one degree or another.

"One thing I can promise you," he said. "I will never lie just to make you feel better. I might have to in order to protect you, but I won't do it casually. I will always do my best to tell you the truth."

"Even if it hurts?" she asked. That needy tone was in her voice again. Rhonda hadn't told Talia any hurtful truths. Rhonda had left that to her lawyers and her adversaries and her ex-husband.

And Talia was bright enough to know that.

"Even if it hurts," he said. "It's better to get it out of the way than it is to protect your feelings."

"Why?" she asked.

He sighed. "Because it might grow into something bigger. And the bigger a lie gets, the more hurtful it becomes."

"That's for sure." Talia looked at the now-empty screens. "You think they have any idea they're adopted?"

"Maybe one or two of them know," he said. "I wouldn't think all of them do."

"You think they ever wonder about their real family?"

"Yeah," he said. "I do."

"I'm going to keep wondering about them," she said almost defiantly.

He put a hand on hers.

"Me, too," he said softly. "Me, too."

11

Nyquist pushed open the door of Bowles's rented studio. The techs had finished with the main room. He wasn't sure what he expected them to find, but he'd had them go over the place anyway. Since the Hunting Club had denied him his crime scene evidence, he'd take evidence from other places like this studio, and see what he could come up with.

He fully expected to come up with nothing. Bowles had died in the Hunting Club's fake forest and she might not even have been the main target. The other man—still unidentified—might have been the focus of the killer, and Bowles might have been in the wrong place.

Nyquist couldn't work on the other man until the identification was complete.

So he was going to focus on Bowles.

The studio looked exactly like it was supposed to—a small, rented space that somehow had to mimic the big production places like InterDome.

Most of InterDome's techniques could be done on handhelds and on personal links, but some of them were difficult to reproduce—especially in holoproduction.

He had worked enough cases—and done enough interviews—to learn that much.

The door to the building opened directly into the studio. A production desk, which reminded him of nothing more than the cockpit of a space yacht, sat in the middle of the room. Nearly empty shelves stood behind the desk, and in front of it, a window that opened into an empty room. That room had sound dampeners on the wall, ceiling, and floor, and a door to the left.

He'd seen rooms like it before: They were used for holo-production. Only more sophisticated places didn't have visible sound dampeners on the walls. They had clear screens that could be made to show any image at any time—a way of presenting a holoreporter as if she were standing in Wells City on Mars when she was actually here, reporting "live."

A small bathroom opened off the studio. He went in, and was surprised to find another door. That opened into a dark space. He requested a light, and nothing came on, so he fumbled against the wall. Still nothing.

He went back into the studio and looked at the production desk. On one corner were the environmental controls. They were labeled for the three other rooms, including the back, which was marked as VIEWING ROOM.

Of course. She used it to watch what she had completed.

He shoved his hands in his pocket. Most studios were smaller spaces in large media conglomerates.

The studios themselves were often smaller than this, but better appointed, and crammed with listeners, engineers, and supervisors.

This one felt lonely.

He wondered whether Bowles had noticed that or she had liked the solitude. He knew that some investigative reporters worked alone, even at places like InterDome, because they didn't want to be scooped.

There had to be preventive equipment here, too, although—he was surprised to note—his links (even the unimportant ones) remained on.

He sat in the overstuffed chair and felt it mold to his

body. A luxury in a place that didn't seem to have any. He whirled the chair around and studied those empty shelves.

What had she planned to put on them?

Or had she planned to put nothing on them?

They weren't built in. They had been moved here, and they were an unusual feature.

He got up and walked to them, and that's when he saw a single jewel case holding a tiny chip. The case was marked THE FIRST — COMPLETE, and he finally knew what he was looking at.

She had planned to use the shelves to keep track of every story she had done here. Which seemed more pretentious than it should have, even for Ki Bowles.

A single jewel case could hold a hundred chips, and the jewel case pretty much disappeared against the wall of the shelf. She could have put tens of thousands of stories here and not taken up more than two shelves.

It was a waste of space, and in a place like this, that seemed out of character. He grabbed one of the shelves and started to muscle it aside.

To his surprise, it slid on its own track, moving toward the wall. The other shelf did the same, blocking the door.

He didn't care that he was trapped in here. What pleased him was the screen behind the shelves. The screen with its touch-control features and the large keypad beneath.

The production desk might have been the center of recording for the studio, but this was the mixing board, the storage unit, and the place where Bowles did her thinking.

He could tell that just from the diagrams that opened without his even asking. The diagram flowed, like a two-dimensional genealogy chart.

He squinted at it. The labels were small, but he could read them.

She had diagrammed a conglomerate, with all its corporate holdings. Each holding had subcorporations as well, and what appeared to be several small businesses.

She hadn't written names anywhere, just the type of

business: corporation, subcorporation, affiliated business. She had made arrows that ran from a corporation to an affiliated business of another corporation. Some of those arrows then went back up to the conglomerate.

He didn't understand those arrows at all.

Nor could he tell just from the diagram which conglomerate she was illustrating. He supposed that information would be in her files somewhere, along with the reasons she had for doing this.

He tapped the dedicated link on his thumb to tell the techs to come back into the studio. But the link was blocked. He searched for his internal links and found all of them blocked as well.

He couldn't access anything except the emergency links.

He felt a momentary irritation. Then he stepped back to see if all of his links worked near the production desk.

They didn't.

When he had moved the shelves, revealing Bowles's true workstation, he had activated the link blocker. In spite of himself, he smiled.

That was just plain brilliant.

He stepped forward again and pulled the shelves toward each other. They slid easily and then clicked as they locked into place.

Then he heard the white noise as his links reconnected. He tapped the dedicated link on his thumb again, and this time, one of the techs answered.

"I need the team back in here," he said. "You won't believe what I found."

He signed off, grabbed the chip from the top shelf, and opened the viewing room. While the techs worked the new area, he would watch Bowles's last production—and see whether anything in it had gotten her killed.

12

Maxine Van Alen sat behind her desk, folders scattered in front of her. The company she was suing had so much money they could waste it on expensive paper bindings for their annual reports. And, in case anyone missed the we're-wealthier-than-the-rest-of-you-idiots message, the files were labeled in gold leaf.

She wore a pair of jeweled half-glasses frames halfway down her nose. A matching jeweled chain kept the frames around her neck when she didn't want to wear them. Her earrings and rings also matched.

Otherwise she was wearing all black today, from the thin silk tunic that ran over a pair of matching pants to her black hair and black fingernails. She'd debated making her eye color black today as well, but she opted for bright blue instead, matching the sapphires in the jeweled chain.

She flicked off the glasses and let them fall against her chest as she sorted the expensive folders in front of her.

Then one of her links activated. Her assistant, a slender dark-haired man, appeared in the lower corner of her left eye.

"I know you didn't want to be disturbed," he said, "but I'm being told this is an emergency."

The passive construction was unusual for him. She was about to say that when someone knocked on her office's frosted glass doors.

No one ever touched those doors. She had designed a system where the doors rose into the walls, revealing her private waiting room. Usually she kept the doors open, closing them only when she was doing something important or meeting with a client inside her office.

The doors looked fragile and expensive, and no one, not even her assistants, touched them without fear of breaking them.

"What the hell is going on?" she asked her assistant as she stared at the shadow behind the opaque glass.

He looked panicked. "I told him to wait. I'm sorry. It's really important—"

"Doors open," she said as she severed the link. A man she had never seen before stood in the waiting room, his fist up as if he planned to knock again. He was stocky and balding. His clothing was dark and cheap, and, as far as she could tell, he had no enhancements. From his look alone, she could tell that he couldn't afford her.

"I was told I should wait but I don't think I should," he said, his voice shaking. "I figured you needed to know right away, Ms. Van Alen. I'm afraid maybe I listened to your assistant too long. It's been over an hour. . . ."

His voice trailed off and he finally stopped talking. She grabbed the earpiece on her fake glasses and moved them to the edge of her nose again.

"Do I know you?" she asked.

"No, ma'am," he said, slowly bringing his fist to his side. He still stood outside the doors, which had long since disappeared.

"Then I'm not sure why you're here," she said.

"My company was hired by your firm to run security for Ki Bowles." His voice started to shake again.

Van Alen cursed. "Come in here."

"Yes, ma'am." He stepped across the invisible threshold

as if the doors had vanished into the floor instead of the walls and ceiling.

"Doors down," she said, and stood as they eased back out of their pockets. She crossed to the front of her desk.

The man was so distracted he didn't seem to notice her presence at all. That was unusual. Even the most upset clients always stopped to look at her.

"If there's a problem," Van Alen said, "your boss should be talking to me."

"My boss is dead," he said. "I found him just before I came here."

She frowned. She'd worked with Roshdi Whitford for more than a dozen years. "What do you mean he's dead?"

"Someone killed him," the man said. That shaking had grown worse.

"Someone killed the head of the best security firm in Armstrong?" she asked.

Then she activated her link. She sent a private urgent message to Whitford. Her link beeped, then went to an automated request to contact one of the other top members of Whitford Security.

In all her years of dealing with Whitford, she'd never been given a brush-off message before.

"Yeah," the man in front of her was saying. "Someone killed him."

"Do the police know?" she asked.

"I thought it was more important to reach you," he said. "It might be related."

Related? She wasn't sure what he meant. Related to what?

Still, before she got too deeply into this interview, she sent a message to her assistant. *Get Roshdi Whitford for me. It's an emergency. I need him and only him. If he doesn't respond, send someone to find him.*

"You thought what might be related?" she asked the man.

"His death and Ki Bowles's death."

Van Alen leaned against her desk. "Ki Bowles is dead?"

"It's not on the news yet?" The man let out a gusty sigh that sounded like relief. "Then I am here quick enough."

"I don't know if it's on the news," Van Alen said. "I don't monitor the news while I'm working."

She rounded her desk, touched the top, and activated a search for the latest news stories on Ki Bowles. She got a written listing—something that the system defaulted to whenever someone was with her in the office—of all the current stories on Ki Bowles.

All of them were about the WSX piece that had run the day before.

"It's not on the news," Van Alen said slowly. "You'd better tell me first exactly who you are and what's going on."

He clasped his hands in front of him. He did seem to have a lot of muscles under those cheap dark clothes. Maybe she had underestimated him. Maybe he did have enhancements and maybe they were all for strength and agility instead of looks and grooming.

"My name is Pelham Monteith," he said. "I've worked for Whitford Securities for almost twelve years. You can check."

"I will," she said, and ran his name through one of her internal links. "Go on."

"I was assigned to Ki Bowles," he said. "I was with her today."

"Yet you say she got killed?" Van Alen wasn't quite following this. She wasn't certain whether or not she was being conned—and if she was, why? How did this man know that she had professional ties with Bowles, unless he worked with Whitford Securities?

"It was such a mess." Monteith looked almost green. Would a professional security man become queasy when talking about a death?

"What do you mean?" Van Alen asked.

Her assistant appeared in the lower corner of her left eye again. "I'm sorry to bother you," he said, "but no one seems able to find Roshdi Whitford."

"What?" Monteith had to have realized she was getting a message through her links—she probably had that glazed expression most people got when they were concentrating on the link instead of the person in front of them. "What's happening?"

"That's what I want you to tell me," she said as she sent a silent *Just a minute* to her assistant. "Where did you see Roshdi Whitford?"

"At his house. He's inside his house." Monteith's voice was shaking again.

Have someone check his house, she sent silently to her assistant. *Now!*

He vanished from her vision.

"You said Bowles's death was a mess? I don't understand." Van Alen almost reminded him that today was the most important day of their contract, but if he was a fake, then she didn't want to give him too much additional information.

Which reminded her to check the identity confirmation through her links. The first layer of confirmation had been completed. On the surface, it seemed, he was Pelham Monteith and he had been a stellar employee at Whitford Security since his hire twelve years ago.

"Since that piece ran," Monteith said, "we've had large teams guarding her. We'd have some check out the places she was heading and clear them, others going with her to wherever she was supposed to be, and some trailing to make sure no one else was."

Van Alen crossed her arms. She stopped herself from nodding because that would confirm what he was saying, and she didn't want to seem like she was agreeing with him, not yet.

"She went to InterDome Media this morning, and when she left—"

"InterDome?" Van Alen felt cold. Bowles wasn't double-crossing them, was she? They had a deal, a legal contract that was as ironclad as entertainment and business contracts got.

Van Alen knew that for certain. She'd drawn up the document herself.

"I don't know what she was doing there," Monteith said, "but she seemed happy when she left."

Van Alen frowned. Just then the search program ended. She got another confirmation, this one from more secure sources, that Monteith was exactly who he said he was.

"What happened next?" Van Alen asked.

"She wanted to have lunch at the Hunting Club. She wanted to show off, I think. That's what she said when she let us know that was the next destination."

"How did she let you know?" Van Alen asked. "Via link?"

"We have a secure link. She used that."

Van Alen knew about the secure links. She also had the most tech-savvy person she knew, Miles Flint, try to break into Whitford Security's secure links. He couldn't, at least not on his first try.

"So you went to the Hunting Club," Van Alen said.

"We sent a team ahead," Monteith said. "I wasn't on the team that was with her. I was trailing."

"And?"

"She and one of the guards got slaughtered in the forest."

"What?" Van Alen couldn't stop herself from blurting out the word. "How is that possible?"

"I don't know." He swallowed. "I really don't. But she couldn't send to us for help because the Hunting Club shuts down all link access."

"Not emergency," Van Alen said. "That's illegal."

"Even emergency." His voice was soft.

She felt the color leave her face. How many times had she eaten there? Dozens? A hundred? She never would have gone if she knew that she didn't have emergency link access.

"They were attacked in the forest?" Van Alen asked.

"How is that possible? Doesn't the Hunting Club itself have security?"

"I don't know," he said. "I entered the forest about five minutes after she did."

He paused. He was even greener than he'd been before. He put a hand on his stomach.

"I'm—I'm sorry," he said. "I've never lost anyone before. And now two—"

"You were protecting Roshdi Whitford as well?"

"No," he said. "I meant Ki Bowles and Enzio."

"Enzio?" Van Alen asked.

"Enzio Lamfier," he said. "He's the guard who was killed."

"You found them," she said.

He nodded.

"And what did you do?"

"I backtracked until my emergency links worked, then sent a help message. Some street cops were nearby. They showed up and I said something bad had happened in the forest."

"You didn't tell them what it was?"

He shook his head. "I went to tell Roshdi. I figured he had to know because there was a failure in the system somewhere and he would find it. He had to find it before the police even started to work on this."

She nodded. That was standard for a good security company. They didn't want to be well known, especially to the authorities. But they also didn't want to interfere with an investigation.

"But he wasn't at the office," Monteith said. "And our system told me he hadn't shown up yet, which wasn't unusual. Sometimes he worked from home. So I headed there. I didn't want to send anything on the links."

"Even though they were secure," Van Alen said.

"I don't know if they are." He sounded terrified. "I mean, Bowles told us where she'd be and now she's dead, and that might've come through the links, right?"

Van Alen didn't know. She could already think of a dozen ways the system could have been compromised.

Except for one.

"You've never lost a client before, right?" Van Alen asked.

"Not to my knowledge," Monteith said.

"Shouldn't her guards have kept her alive at all costs?" Van Alen asked.

"That's the thing," Monteith said. "We're missing one guard."

Van Alen let out a small breath. "Missing?"

"He might be deeper in that forest, but I don't know. We'd cleared the area before she arrived. At least, that's what I was told before we even sent her there. No one should have been in that forest with her, except her guards."

And now, if Van Alen could believe Monteith, one of those guards was dead and the other was missing.

She didn't like any of this.

Then her assistant appeared in the corner of her left eye.

"They found Roshdi Whitford," the assistant said.

She sighed. She had been expecting this.

"He's dead," the assistant said. "Murdered. The police are on the way."

She held up a finger, stopping the conversation with Monteith. Then she bent her head so that she could concentrate on the conversation with her assistant.

Where is he? she asked.

"In his house."

Thanks, she sent as she severed the connection.

She raised her head and looked directly at Monteith.

"So who killed Roshdi Whitford?" she asked.

Monteith shrugged.

"How did you know to come to me?"

"I headed the teams," he said. "My emergency contacts for this case were Whitford first, which is normal for all cases, and you second, which isn't normal. Usually the secondary contact is some kind of money manager or something, not an attorney."

"And that made you assume I'm paying for the contract on Bowles?"

"Aren't you?" he asked.

Van Alen didn't answer. Instead she swept her right hand toward the nearest chair.

"I've treated you poorly," she said. "Have a seat. I'll be right back."

As she walked out of her office, she linked into her own security system and had barriers placed over her desk and on her computer systems. She also made certain that all of the links inside the office were shut down, so he couldn't contact anyone.

She waved the opaque doors closed behind her and had them lock.

Then she walked through her waiting room, and down the corridors to her assistant's desk. He was pacing behind it, a thin dark-haired man who'd always seemed a bit too nervous for her tastes.

He jumped when he saw her. "Ms. Van Alen."

"Let me use your outside system," she said as she moved him away from his desk. She didn't want to use an internal or external personal link in case Monteith had used some high-tech way of piggybacking on her system.

She knew such things were possible—she'd learned a lot in the six months she'd known Miles Flint—but she didn't know whether men who worked for security outfits like Whitford's were capable of it. She wasn't going to take any chances, either.

She sat behind her assistant's desk. He hovered over her, making her even more nervous than she was.

"Go to my waiting room," she said. "Make sure nothing's happening inside my office."

"Should I go in?"

"No," she said. "Monitor it using the waiting room's systems. And make sure he doesn't leave."

"All right." The assistant walked around the desk, looking at her as he did so. He bobbed his head once, then hurried down the hall.

She tapped the system in front of her, going through several layers until she reached the address she wanted.

Even the Detective Division at the police station had its barriers. She got some sergeant who monitored all the higher ups' links.

"Maxine Van Alen for Andrea Gumiela," she said. "It's an emergency."

"Chief Gumiela isn't speaking to anyone right now," he said. "If it's a true emergency, I can put you through to the help line."

"Tell her that I need to talk to her about Ki Bowles and the Hunting Club. Now."

He blinked at Van Alen; then his image disappeared. Not five seconds later, Gumiela's image appeared.

Van Alen had worked with Andrea Gumiela dozens of times, sometimes off the record. Gumiela was known as a hard-ass particularly in her department, but she'd also helped half a dozen families Disappear by sending them to Van Alen on their way to the precinct to be booked.

Technically, Gumiela had broken the law she'd been sworn to uphold, but Van Alen never said anything and neither did Gumiela. In fact, Gumiela never asked after the families, either.

Van Alen admired that. She also admired Gumiela in court. The woman was ferocious on the witness stand, one of the few in the Detective Division that Van Alen couldn't beat on cross.

"What is this?" Gumiela asked.

"Is this link secure?" Van Alen asked.

"Secure enough," Gumiela said.

"I have a man in my office who claims that he was a bodyguard to Ki Bowles, and that she and another bodyguard were killed in the forest of the Hunting Club today. I assume he's telling the truth?"

"I can't comment," Gumiela said in her flattest tone. But her eyes had widened ever so slightly. That was a confirmation of sorts.

"He also claims to be the one who found her, and let some street officers know. He is the one who originally found Roshdi Whitford dead, but he never called that in, either."

Gumiela raised her chin. She didn't say anything. She couldn't.

"He makes me nervous," Van Alen said, "and he's not a client of mine. I have a hunch you're going to want to question him. If his stories check out, he's probably an important witness for you. Or a suspect."

Gumiela was smooth. She didn't confirm or deny any of this. "Why did he come to you?"

"He knew that Ki Bowles spent some time in this office recently," Van Alen said, just as smoothly.

"As a client?"

"You know I can't tell you why most people come here, Andrea," Van Alen said.

"Yet you're giving up this man. What's his name?"

"Pelham Monteith. He says he works for Whitford Securities."

"What don't you like?" Gumiela asked. She didn't finish the question, probably purposefully leaving it open-ended so that Van Alen could choose how she was going to answer.

"If he's telling me the truth," Van Alen said, "then he found three dead people and didn't remain at any of the scenes. As an officer of the court, I'm duty bound to make this information known."

"It's interesting how you pick and choose what is your duty, Ms. Van Alen," Gumiela said.

Van Alen smiled. "I'm not the only one," she said, and signed off.

Then she leaned back in her chair.

What a mess.

She had expected Bowles to get threats the moment the

first story appeared. She even expected Justinian Wagner to try something—and maybe succeed.

Flint and Bowles and Van Alen were under no illusions. They all knew that Bowles was risking her life with this series of stories.

Bowles had found it exciting.

Flint thought the risks could be minimized.

Truth be told, Van Alen thought the same thing or she never would have been connected to it.

She also thought Justinian Wagner was a cautious man who turned to murder as a last resort. He had a lot of legal means of stopping Bowles before he tried something illegal.

And even then, Van Alen expected threats first.

She rubbed a hand across her forehead. Her little finger caught on the half-glasses and she flicked them off her nose in disgust.

She had started to admire Bowles. The woman had a relentlessness that Van Alen could identify with, and a ruthlessness that Van Alen shared.

Flint had been right when he had chosen Bowles, although Van Alen hadn't been certain of that in the beginning.

But this whole scheme had backfired too quickly. Van Alen was frightened for the first time in years.

She took a deep breath and got a grip on herself. Fear was counterproductive. It always had been. It caused people to make mistakes instead of solve them.

She needed to solve this one, and she had to act quickly.

She'd done the right thing in contacting Gumiela.

Now Van Alen had to protect herself and her firm.

She stood, accessing one of her secure personal links.

She needed to get a hold of Miles Flint—and she had to do it fast.

13

Even though he left the door to the viewing room open, Nyquist felt as if he were surrounded by Ki Bowles. The illusion drove him slightly crazy.

She seemed to be sitting at the table inside the main studio, just a few meters from him. Her black, silver, and red hair was perfectly coiffed and she wore some kind of matching outfit that served to accent her tattoos.

Her voice filled the room, but the story she told seemed too vague to be important—at least to him. It was all innuendo and hearsay, nothing that would hold up in court, although she promised hard evidence in future pieces.

Nyquist knew that news had different standards of proof than the law did—witness how many people were found guilty in the press and never made it into a court of law—but he found himself wishing she had shown him more.

Making him wish for more was probably what the story had been designed to do. But he didn't see anything that would kill her, not even in the tidbits that the story presented. They were too small, and he felt like he'd heard a few of them before.

Maybe something that Bowles hinted at in this story or

something that she mentioned in passing had more significance than Nyquist realized.

He leaned back in the small chair that sat in the center of the room and stared at Bowles as she recited the names of the people she had spoken to.

He would have to retrace her steps on all of this, see if these people as well as this so-called deep background that she had had explosive information in it, the kind that would make Justinian Wagner careless, the kind that would get him to kill before he explored other options.

Of course, if Wagner was behind the death, then that meant that Bowles's killer was a hired assassin. Wagner would never do the work himself.

And Wagner would need time—from the moment he learned of Bowles's stories and how harmful or inflammatory they would be to the moment of Bowles's death—to hire the best in business.

Nyquist put Bowles's report on loop—he wanted the words to become second nature to him—and then he stood. His knees cracked as they had done every day since the rebuild. The sound still startled him, and reminded him he wasn't quite the same man as he had been just a year before.

He stepped back into the studio. One of the techs was pulling the shelves closed.

"Find anything new?" Nyquist asked.

"Just Bowles's fingerprints," the tech said. "I'm not sure anyone else knew about this thing until you came along."

"What makes you say that?" Nyquist asked.

"Her fingerprints are on everything from the back of the shelves to the plastic tabs holding the screen in place. I think she put it up, and we might be able to find that in the studio's security system, especially if it recorded what was going on in here as a matter of course. We're going to need some computer techs to dig into this."

Nyquist wasn't surprised that Bowles wouldn't trust anyone else with her secret information. "Were you able to back up those files she had behind the shelves?"

"What we could access," the tech said.

"You think there's more?" Nyquist asked.

"We don't know," the tech said. "There could be. But there might not be. Do you know how tech savvy she was?"

"She used to work for InterDome as an investigative reporter. I know she did a lot of her own on-screen work. Does that make her tech savvy?"

The tech shrugged. "I'm not a specialist in media systems. That's why we're going to send someone else down here."

"Well, can I poke around back there and see what she was working on?"

"I suppose," the tech said in a tone that meant he really didn't care.

"I mean, will I destroy anything by doing so?"

"I have no idea. I might have destroyed a few things myself in looking through the files. But that would require a level of sophistication that didn't seem evident in the setup."

"Meaning what?" Nyquist asked.

"Meaning if she knew how to hide information within her own systems, would she have set up the shelf units?"

"Good question." Nyquist wasn't sure of the answer to that, either, although he was inclined to say no.

"What I kept telling myself as I looked around in there," the tech said, "was that most everything in any computer system is retained, even when it's deleted, and the best techs can always retrieve deleted information."

Nyquist glanced at the screen over the tech's shoulder. "Do we have techs that are that good?"

"We have a few."

"Can you make sure one of them works on this case?"

"Absolutely," the tech said. "We're going to need our best team on it, anyway, given the level of scrutiny we'll all go through."

"Because it's a media case," Nyquist said.

"Yeah." The tech picked up his kit. "I've only worked one

other media case, and I vowed I'd never take lead on another one."

"Is that why you're handing over the computer to a different tech?" Nyquist asked.

The tech shook his head. "I'm not lead on this for our department. Leidmann and Owen are splitting it. They hope that with two of them one will avoid the inevitable firing."

And then he let himself out the main door.

Nyquist watched him go. The inevitable firing. He hadn't thought of that until now. People always lost their jobs in a media case. What was standard operating procedure often became "sloppy police work" under the eye of some inept reporter.

The problem was that the department didn't dare defend "sloppy police work," even if the work wasn't sloppy. They had to get rid of the offender to reassure the public that the department was doing everything that it could.

Maybe that was why Gumiela had put him on this case. She had needed a potentially expendable officer and he was the one. She had also known that it wouldn't hurt his pension or his medical benefits.

He stared at the door for a moment, not sure how he felt about that. Then he realized he couldn't worry about it.

He'd worked high-profile cases before and survived them. He would survive this one.

And if not, then he would offer to resign.

He pushed the shelves aside and stared at the diagram on the screen. It was clearly the family tree of a conglomerate. Somewhere in the middle of Bowles's report, he had found himself wondering whether that diagram had belonged to Wagner, Stuart, and Xendor.

If what Bowles had said was true, then she had probably done the same kind of diagram for WSX. Which firms branched off from it, which ones became hidden assets, which ones were publicly known affiliates.

The diagram in front of him could be for the Ultre Corporation, which she had mentioned in her report. Or for

Gramming Inc. or Environmental Systems Inc. or anyone of a dozen other clients of WSX.

Or for a conglomerate not associated with WSX at all.

He had no real idea what other work Bowles had been doing. All he knew was that InterDome had fired her six months ago, and then she reappeared with this rented studio and a several-part story on the Moon's largest law firm.

He didn't know whether she was working on other stories. He didn't know who paid her salary. He didn't know anything about her personal life.

He had to be careful not to get too focused on WSX. Otherwise he would be guilty of sloppy police work.

Rather than poke around in the information on that screen, he decided to look through the studio one more time, while he waited for the high-end computer techs. Let them find the files and hidden information.

Then he would compile it and see if it related to his case.

Or if he just wanted it to.

14

So far, Flint wasn't finding any evidence of anyone piggy-backing onto the work that Talia had done. No one, it seemed, appeared to be looking for the other five cloned children.

He couldn't be certain, of course. He was only using the files that Talia had created, and he was only about an hour into his work.

Talia had moved her chair beside his so that she could watch what he was doing. He hadn't let her see how to log in to his systems, but he was explaining to her how he worked without creating yet another trail.

Any normal thirteen-year-old would have lost interest within fifteen minutes. But Talia appeared to be fascinated—and not just because she was watching him use the forbidden computer system.

She had a knack for this work, and an interest in it that hadn't been tapped—at least, not by him, and certainly not by Rhonda. From everything he could gather, his ex-wife had discouraged her daughter's interest in computers, patterns, and systems, probably because it all reminded Rhonda too much of Flint.

Or maybe he was giving himself too much credit. Maybe

Talia's growing expertise in hunting out information had terrified her mother. Since Rhonda had lied about everything, she probably had been afraid that her daughter would uncover some kind of anomaly, and then start asking the wrong questions.

Now Talia was asking the questions of Flint. And he really didn't have a lot of answers.

So it felt good to explain how to dig without leaving a trail.

He was about to switch to a new screen, going into the history files for the Havos family, when one of his links cheeped.

He stopped and shrouded the screen in front of him.

"Sorry, Talia," he said. "I'm getting a personal communication."

She glared at him, then stood and walked across the room. He didn't move the contact onto one of his screens. Instead he instructed the link to place the image in front of his vision. He would use the privacy function.

He expected to hear from a potential client. That was usually how these messages found their way into his office.

Instead, Van Alen appeared across his vision.

She was wearing all black except for a very ugly pair of half-glasses that were supposed to be some kind of accessory. They made her face seem too round.

She leaned too close to the screen she was using to communicate with him.

"Miles, we have a serious problem." She wasn't using a personal link. She was actually talking to him through a screen somewhere. He could see a wall and artwork behind her. She was using the system at her assistant's desk.

"Brace yourself," she said. "Ki Bowles is dead."

What? He almost spoke out loud. He must have made a noise because Talia looked over her shoulder at him. He smiled at her and turned slightly in his chair. *How do you know this?*

"It's complicated," Van Alen said. "Get down here. The police will be here shortly."

I'm not talking to the police, Flint sent.

Van Alen looked over her shoulder, as if she was worried that someone was watching. Then she glanced at him again. "You won't have to unless you want to. You're going to be coming in as one of my clients, and I'll have to take the meeting. I've already put you on the books."

Maybe I should wait, he sent.

"I don't think so. The news hasn't been released yet. When it is, our hands might be tied. So get down here. Now."

She winked out of his vision. He blinked a few times. He wasn't used to being told what to do by anyone. That hadn't happened since he quit the force years ago.

But he trusted Van Alen. She had helped him when no one else had, and she was his partner in the attempted destruction of WSX. So he needed to listen.

First, he had to shut down the system he was running. He glanced at his daughter. She still had her back to him, her arms crossed.

"Talia," he said. "I have an emergency meeting."

And she was going to have to come with him. He didn't dare leave her, especially since he didn't know how or why Bowles had died.

Although he had his suspicions.

He carefully shut down the system, then stood and put his hand on his daughter's arm.

"You're going to have to come with me," he said. "We'll finish this later."

"I can finish," she said. "I know enough now."

He smiled. "Not quite. But thank you."

He led her out of the office building into the dust-covered street. It was empty.

"Stay close," he said as he double-locked the doors.

"Is something wrong?" she asked.

Everything, he thought.

"Not really," he lied, and then winced, remembering the promise he had made her just that afternoon. He wouldn't lie to her if at all possible.

Well, he'd find out what was wrong first, and then he'd decide what Talia needed to know.

And he hoped she wouldn't have to know anything.

15

Savita Romey stood in the living room of Roshdi Whitford's house, hands in her pockets, special liners on her shoes and pants. The house smelled of blood. This wasn't a murder; it was a slaughter.

Romey had caught the case only fifteen minutes before. She'd been about to leave after completing an extended series of reports on the past five cases she'd worked. She'd closed all five in record time, and her boss, Andrea Gumiela, wanted to use Romey's work habits as an example for the younger detectives in the squad.

It didn't matter that Romey had argued that her methods were the same as everyone else's. Nor had it mattered when Romey claimed she wasn't good at writing reports. Gumiela had given her a choice: Either write the reports or spend the next year training the current crop of detectives.

Romey wrote the reports.

She'd hoped for a week off after that. She didn't lead the rotation, and she hadn't had a day off in nearly a month. By all rights, she should have been at home in bed by now.

But Gumiela had contacted her on the way. *It's an important case*, Gumiela had said. *We need it closed fast and we need someone who can be discreet.*

Romey wasn't sure whether anyone on the squad lacked discretion, but she wasn't going to say that to her boss. Instead, she programmed the address Gumiela had given her into the air car and found herself here.

Fortunately the techs had arrived first. The victim, Roshdi Whitford, owned the best security company in Armstrong—or what had been known as the best security company in Armstrong. Romey now had her doubts. She had a hunch everyone else in the city would share those doubts when the news of Whitford's murder emerged.

Romey's identification chip, like every other chip given to police and emergency services, was supposed to open every door in the city.

But it didn't open Whitford's. She had to contact one of the techs to let her inside.

The techs had gotten in courtesy of one of Whitford's employees who had shown up just before them because his boss wasn't answering a page. That employee was now in a squad, waiting for someone to question him.

Romey would do that after she got a sense of the crime scene.

The house itself was made of some kind of concrete. The exterior walls were nearly ten centimeters thick, and one of the techs told her that the entire place would survive the collapse of the dome when most other buildings in Armstrong wouldn't.

There were no windows that she could see, although one had appeared on the door when she crossed the threshold. She'd seen windows like that before—they were formed only when needed. Since she needed to see out all the time, living in a place like this would drive her insane.

The interior walls were about half as thick as the exterior walls, and made of the same materials. With the doors closed, no one could hear what was going on from one room to the next.

But the doors were open, and sound traveled against the concrete walls, echoing down the corridors. She could hear the techs talking in the kitchen as they examined the room. She also could hear the beeps of someone's link as he asked for help from some security expert in the tech team.

She didn't need a security expert to know what had happened. Somehow someone had breached this fortress and slaughtered Roshdi Whitford. The place was locked up solid when the employee arrived, but until Romey understood how the security system worked, she wasn't going to assume this was some kind of locked room mystery.

Whatever happened here, it was clear that whoever killed Whitford had known how the house's security worked. Which made it an inside job—unless Whitford was incautious enough to post the specs of his personal system on some kind of database.

She doubted a man with his reputation would be incautious about something like security system specs. Especially when most security companies in Armstrong trademarked their own systems and maintained a proprietary relationship with their equipment—and their customers.

Romey stepped around the most uncomfortable-looking couch she'd ever seen and into the living room proper. Occasional tables were scattered in what seemed like a haphazard pattern. Each table, however, did have a chair beside it, and some kind of lamp built in.

"Is the security system shut down?" she asked one of the techs as he passed by.

"No, ma'am. We haven't figured out how to do that yet."

"Figure it out." She didn't want to broadcast the details of their investigation to whoever could hack into the security system. "And tell Central that they need to establish a security system of their own. I'll brief them later as to what kind we need."

Certainly she wouldn't do so in front of whatever recording equipment existed in this house.

Blood spattered along the tile floor. She would have expected carpet—easier to hide more security doodads. But the floor itself had some kind of mosaic pattern. It took her a minute to realize that not everything that looked like blood was.

Some of the red and black that she saw was a pattern in the tile. A design that caused an optical illusion and, if she stared at it long enough, made her dizzy.

Maybe she had been wrong about the tile and the carpet.

"Make sure," she said to the tech even though he was now leaving the room, "that whatever security team looks at this system looks at the tile as well."

A pattern that fine could hide anything: cameras, chips, money, information. She wanted everything from this house, and she wanted it as quickly as possible.

She checked the clock on her internal system. She'd already been here half an hour. She'd promised her son she'd be home in time to share dinner with him and his little brothers. She hated to renege on that.

She wondered how she'd be able to supervise this crime scene and manage a dinner with her family.

That was the problem with this job. She had taken it for the intellectual and financial promotion, but it was costing her in the one place she couldn't afford: time with her kids.

At least, at fifteen, her oldest could handle most of the emergencies that came up.

She'd give the scene another half hour, then she'd grab some takeout and run home for a quick dinner. She needed to touch base with the boys maybe more than they needed time with her.

She'd be back on scene before anyone got a chance to miss her.

The body itself was sprawled in the middle of the tile. No furniture was anywhere around the body and, oddly, none of the haphazard pieces looked like they'd been moved to accommodate it, either.

If Whitford had fallen where he stood, shouldn't he have hit something other than the floor? Or did his terrible interior decorating skills somehow make him decide that a big gaping bit of nothingness in the middle of his living room somehow made up for the dozen occasional tables scattered around the edges?

He had landed on his back, his arms up near his face, his legs twisted, but open. He had been slashed in several places—all arteries—and judging by the blood flow, the killer had hit at least two arteries on opposite sides of the body at the very same time.

Just from the way that the slashes were made, Romey was guessing that there was more than one assailant or the assailant was using a kind of weapon that she was unfamiliar with.

Of course, that was if Whitford's killer had been human.

If the killer wasn't human, all bets were off. Even a windowless concrete bunker couldn't keep certain types of aliens out. Some of them might not even trigger perimeter alarms.

But she wasn't going to make any suppositions about the species of the killer. Not yet. Nor was she going to guess what exactly had killed Whitford.

To her knowledge, no one had seen his back. No one knew whether or not the body's position—and the blood— had been staged.

"When you're done with him," she said to another tech who was working the far end of the room, "make sure you get excellent recordings of what's underneath him."

"Underneath?" the tech asked.

"Don't you think it odd that there's no furniture in the middle of the room?"

"I think this whole place is odd," the tech said, and returned to her work.

That about summed it up. The whole place was odd. And Romey had only seen the foyer, one of the corridors, and this living room.

And the grounds. Which had more security than all of the government buildings and the port combined. She'd had to respond to dozens of alerts in her own internal systems just to override the estate's commands to shut off her links.

She crouched next to the body, careful not to touch it or the blood spatter near him.

"You gotta wonder," she said softly to him as if he were still alive to hear it, "if all this paranoia about the perfect security system is what actually got you killed."

She waited. Of course, there was no response.

Then she stood.

Whatever had killed him had done so with all the security in place. Would it have been easier to kill him without the security? Or did the killer like a challenge?

She had a hunch she'd find out.

16

Flint made it to Van Alen's office in record time. Two squads blocked the entry, so he parked in the lot and took the back elevator. On the way, he told Talia that if he caught her touching any computers in Van Alen's office, he would tell Van Alen.

"So?" Talia said defiantly.

"So you don't want to go head-to-head with Maxine Van Alen," he said.

"She won't get mad at me," Talia said as the elevator doors opened onto the main floor, "she'll get mad at you."

Then she stepped into the large reception area. Flint smiled at her back. She was probably right. He kept forgetting the way other people perceived children—the way he used to perceive them before Talia had come into his life.

Usually the reception area was full of junior associates, assistants, and young successful lawyers hurrying from one important case to another. People were constantly talking, and constantly moving.

But not now. The human receptionist—an affectation that Van Alen insisted on—was the only one in the large area.

"Mr. Flint," she said as she stood. "Ms. Van Alen is in a situation."

Not with a client or in a meeting. Flint found that to be an interesting choice of words.

"I have a meeting with her," he said like he was supposed to, "and I think I'm a few minutes late."

"I don't recall. . . ." The receptionist bent over the clear screen that rose from part of her desk. "Oh. You're right. It's marked urgent. I'm to send you right back."

Flint nodded as he headed toward the back. Talia walked beside him until they reached the reception desk.

The receptionist put her hand out. "I'm afraid only Mr. Flint can go back there."

"She's my daughter," he said. "She comes with me."

The receptionist's eyes widened just a bit. She apparently had no idea that Talia had come into Flint's life.

He tried to remember if he had ever brought Talia here before. Probably not. He usually came while she was in school. He didn't want her to know about this part of his life.

He didn't want her to know about a lot of his life and his work. She didn't need to. It put her in danger.

The back, which usually bustled as much as the front, seemed calm as well, but in a different way. Attorneys, assistants, and some clients stood in the corridor, arms crossed, staring down the hallway.

A man's voice echoed through the normally quiet area.

"Ms. Van Alen, please. Tell them. They can't arrest me. I didn't do anything wrong."

Then there was silence. Flint couldn't tell whether that was because Van Alen was answering or someone else was speaking.

Talia looked at him. Flint put a hand on her back and propelled her forward.

"Sir," one of the attorneys said, "I don't think you should go back there."

"Maxine's expecting me," he said.

He continued to walk past the associates. They all looked nervous. A few stepped aside as he passed.

The corridor narrowed before it opened into the waiting

area that was exclusively Van Alen's. Four police officers stood near the corridor, and more were inside Van Alen's office.

A man Flint didn't recognize stood near Van Alen's desk. He was beefy and red faced, and he looked scared.

Van Alen stood near the waiting room couch, staring into her office. Two more officers stood inside.

They looked like street cops. Flint didn't see a detective, which surprised him. He would have expected to see one, given what Van Alen had told him.

"You can't arrest me," the man was saying. "I'm in a law office."

"That doesn't give you immunity," one of the officers said. "Especially when the office is the one who called us."

"Is that true?" The man looked at Van Alen. "I came here as a favor to you."

She didn't say anything. Flint couldn't read her face. She seemed calm, but she often put on that demeanor when she was the most nervous.

Talia glanced up at Flint again, as if he should do something. He let his hand drop from her back and stepped around her.

"Maxine," he said as he walked into the waiting area.

Van Alen looked over her shoulder. For a brief second, he thought she seemed relieved. "Miles."

"I came for our meeting."

"We have a situation," she said.

"I can see that." He wasn't sure what she wanted him to do. Everyone faced him, though, as if he were the authority in the room.

The officers seemed uncomfortable. They probably weren't used to being in a law office. Considering their training, they probably weren't certain what to do. They knew how to handle problems on the street and in other businesses, but they had been taught to give too much respect to lawyers.

"I used to be a detective with the Armstrong P.D.,"

Flint said to Van Alen, even though she already knew that. He knew the cops didn't. "Do you want me to see what I can do?"

One of the officers said, "No offense, sir, but if you're no longer with the department, then we'll have to ask you to step back."

But Flint continued to look at Van Alen. "Maybe I can mediate. It seems like you're at an impasse here."

She looked from the officers to the man in her office.

"Give us a minute," she said to the police.

They stepped back. That, too, was part of the training and Van Alen clearly knew it. She went into her office and nodded at the officers. They walked out.

"Stay here, Talia," Flint said.

"Da-ad." She looked frightened. She had no idea what was going on and he wasn't going to tell her.

"The officers will keep an eye on you."

"But—"

He didn't listen to her protest. Instead, he stepped into the office with Van Alen and the man from Whitford Security.

"I don't need a mediator," the man said. "I didn't expect a lawyer to call the cops."

"Doors down," Van Alen said. She stood close to the doors, though, as if she didn't want to get near this man.

He smelled of sweat. His eyes were wild, but if he had found three bodies as he claimed, he had every right to be upset.

"You were on protection duty for Ki Bowles?" Flint asked.

The man glanced at Van Alen.

"It's all right," she said to the man. "It's Mr. Flint's money that hired your firm."

The man frowned. "Yes."

"What's your name?" Flint asked.

"Pelham Monteith."

Flint used his links to check the man's name against

Whitford Security's current public database, which he had downloaded as he headed to meet Van Alen.

It didn't take him long to find Monteith.

Flint cross-checked the name against the police databases that he could access with his own network.

"I check out, don't I?" Monteith said.

"I understand you left two crime scenes today," Flint said.

"I have a duty to my clients."

"Which you clearly failed at, considering Ki Bowles is dead."

Monteith flushed.

Flint's personal links found nothing about Monteith in the database, but he would check from his own system later. He had a way to get into the police records that he didn't want to try from here.

"Ms. Van Alen is right to call the police. You were wrong not to go to them in the first place," Flint said.

"You're saying that because you used to be a detective," Monteith said.

"I'm a detective who is now a Retrieval Artist," Flint said.

Monteith started. He obviously knew that Retrieval Artists worked at the edges of the law.

"Then you should understand why I don't want to go in," Monteith said.

"You'll go in," Flint said. "You'll let them talk to you. You'll answer all the questions you can about the deaths of Ki Bowles and Roshdi Whitford."

"And the other security guard?" Van Alen asked.

Flint looked at her, surprised. He hadn't heard of the other guard.

"He was Bowles's guard," Van Alen said. "He was with her."

"Enzio Lamfier," Monteith said softly. He seemed more broken up about his colleague than he was about Bowles. Which made sense. He had worked with the other man.

"You'll answer every question you can without violating your contract with Whitford," Flint said.

"Any talking I do to the police violates my contract," Monteith said.

"Not if it's what the client wants. I'm the client. You'll talk to them."

"What if they arrest me?"

"You'll do what any other suspect does. You'll call an attorney. I'm sure Ms. Van Alen can provide names."

"She's an attorney."

"She has a conflict of interest. She brokered the deal between me, Bowles, and your firm. She's not going to handle your case, nor will anyone from this office."

Monteith squirmed. Van Alen gave Flint a sideways smile. She could have just told him this was what she wanted him to do. Instead, she let him figure it out on his own.

Which was probably smart. She hadn't imparted any information across any link, and she hadn't done anything that someone could use against her in some kind of case that came out of this meeting.

"You guys set me up," Monteith said.

"That's not possible," Van Alen said, "since you came to me."

"Because you're on the list. That's where I'm supposed to go if something went wrong."

"If you couldn't find Whitford," she said.

He nodded, looking miserable.

"But you did find Whitford." Flint took a step closer. "Where was he?"

"In his house. In the living room."

"You went in?"

"We all have access," Monteith said. "He was dead. In the middle of the floor. Someone slaughtered him."

"Was the death tied to Ki Bowles's?" Flint asked.

Monteith shrugged.

"Was Enzio Lamfier usually on Ki Bowles detail or was he just there for the day?"

Monteith looked surprised. "How did you know that?"

"What exactly did I know?" Flint asked.

"That he was just there for the day." Monteith glanced nervously at Van Alen. "This is all confidential, right?"

"No," she said. "But I'm sure your lawyer can argue it anyway."

"Then I'm not saying any more."

"Yes, you are," Flint said, "or Maxine won't vet your attorney. You'll have the same representation as Whitford and if the murders are tied to the company instead of Ki Bowles, you might have some serious conflict of interest problems."

"What do you mean?" Monteith asked.

"How many of the other people on Ki Bowles detail were there just for the day?"

"Most of them," Monteith said. "We stepped up the numbers after she ran that news story."

Flint sighed. "Had most been moved as a permanent assignment or were you planning to rotate people in and out?"

Monteith looked at them both. "We were going to rotate people in and out. Sometimes assigning them the entire time makes them get lax."

"You were in charge of the assignments?" Flint asked.

"I was in charge of the people on the street," Monteith said.

"In the Bowles case only."

He nodded. "I wasn't going to be rotated in and out."

"Do you know of any threats to Whitford himself?" Flint asked.

Monteith shook his head. "But it wouldn't surprise me. We get threats all the time when we're handling big cases."

"How about any connection between him and Enzio Lamfier?" Flint asked.

"You mean besides the fact that they were both part of Whitford Securities?"

"Besides that," Flint said.

"No," Monteith said.

"I thought you guarded in pairs," Flint said.

"We do."

"So you were the second on Bowles?"

"That was Gulliver Illiyitch."

"Where is this Illiyitch now?" Flint asked.

"I don't know," Monteith said. "He should have been with Bowles and Lamfier."

"But he wasn't."

"But that doesn't mean he's not on those grounds somewhere."

"Alive?" Flint asked.

"I don't know that, either," Monteith said.

"Aren't you supposed to defend your clients?"

"Yes," Monteith said.

"Then shouldn't Illiyitch have been there?"

"Yes," Monteith said. "Something happened, I'm sure."

"You didn't check?"

"When I saw Bowles's body, I tried to let Whitford know. When I didn't reach him the normal way, I went to the business. He wasn't there so I went to his house."

"You didn't look for your missing guard?"

"I wasn't supposed to. I was supposed to follow procedure."

"What about Illiyitch? If he's still alive, what's his procedure?"

"Same as mine."

"So you don't know if he tried to contact Whitford."

"I don't know anything!" Monteith looked at Van Alen. "Really. I'm not lying about that."

"I know," she said gently. Flint looked at her in surprise. He wasn't so certain that Monteith was telling the truth. Then Flint saw her expression. She had no idea, either. She was just soothing him so that he would talk more.

Flint wasn't sure he needed much more. He had enough to start with. Maybe enough to get ahead of the police investigation.

"Go with the police," Flint said. "Cooperate. You'll be fine."

"I'll lose my job," Monteith said.

"You may have already," Flint said.

"Because I lost a client?" Monteith asked.

"Because your boss is dead. The business might go along with him."

Monteith moaned. He clearly hadn't thought of that.

"Doors up," Van Alen said.

They rose to reveal the police officers leaning against the walls of the waiting room. Talia was standing near one of the men, talking with him.

She looked relieved when she saw Flint.

He winked at her, then turned to the officers. "Mr. Monteith will go with you now. He's going to tell you what he found and what he saw. You don't need to put him in custody."

"We'll decide that," one of the officers said.

"We'll be sending an attorney," Van Alen said, clearly warning the officers that they had limited time with Monteith before someone official would arrive and end the questions.

"I'm . . . I'm going to go voluntarily," Monteith said from inside the office, although he hadn't moved forward. "I'll tell you what I know."

The officers looked at one another; then one of them shrugged. Two walked over to Monteith and took his arms, leading him into the waiting area.

Talia watched with real interest, even though she still leaned against the wall. Flint had started toward her when one street cop held out a hand to stop Flint.

"What did you do?" the cop asked.

"Mediated, like I said I would." Flint kept his voice even.

"Should we take you along as well?"

"If you think it's necessary," Flint said.

The cop blinked at him. Van Alen was watching closely.

Talia had bit her lower lip, looking nervous. Monteith glanced at Flint.

The one thing Flint had forgotten to tell Monteith was to keep the identity of the paying customer quiet.

Well, Monteith was going to tell what he knew. If he told them that Flint was the paying customer, then he wasn't violating Flint's instructions, and it would be Flint's own fault.

"We need your name in any case," the street cop said.

"Sure," Flint started. "It's Miles Flint. I'm still pretty well known at the precinct. You can check with most anyone in the Detective Division. I retired from there about four years ago. My partner was Noelle DeRicci."

"She's the Chief of Security for the United Domes of the Moon," Van Alen said.

Flint wasn't going to mention that part. He was going to let the street cop find that out on his own.

"Oh," the cop said, obviously in awe. "I'm sorry, sir."

"No need," Flint said. "I told you. I do know my way around an investigation."

The other cops were leading Monteith down the hall. The remaining street cop nodded toward Flint, and thanked Van Alen for calling them. Then he followed his colleagues out of the law firm.

"What was that all about, Dad?" Talia asked.

Flint put his hand on her shoulder. She was so tense her muscles felt like wire.

"It's related to something I worked on before I met you," Flint said.

"What?"

He shook his head slightly. "I'm afraid it's confidential."

She rolled her eyes and crossed her arms. "Sure it is."

"I can vouch for that," Van Alen said. "Most anything that happens in a law firm is confidential."

"Except when some guy comes in here and confesses," Talia said.

"Mr. Monteith didn't confess to anything," Van Alen said. "He came to inform me that a friend was dead."

"So you called the police?" Talia asked.

"It turns out I was under a legal obligation to do so when I figured out that he had left two crime scenes."

"Is leaving a crime illegal?" Talia asked.

"It is if you don't report the crimes," Van Alen said.

"So he did break the law."

"In a minor way," Van Alen said. "All your father did was convince the man to talk to the police. I hadn't been able to."

"You'd think you could, being a lawyer and all," Talia said.

Van Alen smiled and then looked at Flint. "She's got your sense of irony and outrage."

"What does *that* mean?" Talia asked.

"It means," Van Alen said, "that you could grow into someone I could like very much."

Then she turned around and headed back into her office.

"Should we have that meeting?" she asked Flint.

"I think we are going to have to," he said. "Everything is different now."

17

The techs were already inside Bowles's apartment. Nyquist stopped in the hall and stared at the open door.

He remembered the first and only time he had come here. He had stopped in front of Bowles's security system, about to press a fingertip against the identification panel, when the panel insisted on a retinal scan.

He'd been pleased with that. He figured that Bowles had a security system that was good enough for her needs. Because he'd worried when he entered the building; he'd initially been afraid that there wasn't enough security in this place for someone of Bowles's level of fame.

Now her door stood open. Police line lasers marked an area just outside. Anyone who broke the beam would set off an alarm.

He put his hand through one of the beams, knowing that with his identification, the alarm would not go off. Then he stepped into the apartment.

None of the techs were in the living room, although two of Bowles's personal robots were, hovering as if they were distressed at the invasion of their personal domain.

The living room actually had a lived-in look: There was a blanket on the couch, over an indentation made by someone sitting there a little too often. An empty mug sat on an end table, and one of the nearby chairs had a handheld crossways on the seat, as if someone had set it down during a moment of distraction.

He distinctly remembered how uncomfortable the living room had seemed six months ago. Then he had the impression that Bowles never spent any time in it.

He walked past the hovering bots and down the hallway that led to the bedrooms. He hadn't been this way before. Bowles had never let him out of the living room. She'd answered his questions—looking uncomfortable at being the subject of the interview instead of the interviewer—and then she had ushered him out the door.

He felt odd going down the hallway now, as if he were invading her privacy.

The first room was an office. Handhelds, papers, books, and lots of jewel cases littered the floor, shelves, and desk. Another empty mug sat on the floor beside a sturdy ergonomically correct chair.

Only one wall remained clear. It had a slight blue tinge and it took him a moment of staring to realize that the wall was designed to be a backdrop to close-in reporting done away from any studio.

He'd need to make sure the team looked at all the handhelds and the computers in here.

Then he went down the hall to find a bedroom. It was the neatest room in the apartment, and it smelled musty. A bathroom opened off the back, with neatly folded towels and not a single personal item.

No one used this room. If he had to guess, he would assume it was a guest room—one that no guest had stayed in, or at least, had not stayed in for a very long time.

Finally he walked into the bedroom. It smelled of Bowles's perfume. The scent struck him as forcefully as she had. She still seemed alive in here, in the unmade bed, the three separate outfits resting on the sheets, and the matching shoes neatly placed on the carpet.

A tech was inside yet another bathroom. Nyquist peered in. It was Leidmann.

"Her bots didn't clean up after her, did they?" Nyquist asked.

To her credit, Leidmann didn't even jump at the sound of his voice. But she probably had the police line set to notify her whenever anyone else tried to enter.

"I already checked the programming," Leidmann said. "They were to clean surfaces and bathrooms and the kitchen. They were to make the bed, unless they had instructions otherwise, and they were to handle general maintenance, including washing her clothing, upgrading her wardrobe, and cooking small meals if she so desired."

"So why am I seeing handhelds everywhere and empty mugs beside tables?"

"Because the programming also specifies that they can't touch any work in progress. Since they're bots and not human assistants, they can't tell if a dirty mug is important to her work, so they just leave it until she tells them otherwise." Then Leidmann frowned just a little. "*Told* them otherwise."

"It almost seems like she's here, doesn't it?" Nyquist asked.

Leidmann nodded. "She spent a lot of time here."

"Or at least, she did after she got fired," Nyquist said, and told Leidmann what he had observed six months before.

"Well, this clearly became home base," Leidmann said. "She used this to stage everything."

Nyquist nodded. "What do you make of the bedroom?"

Leidmann grinned. "Still not married yet, huh, Bartholomew?"

"I was married once," he said, almost defensively. "Why?"

"When a woman lays three outfits across the bed, she can't decide what to wear."

"Yeah," he said dryly. "That's obvious."

"And what she is going to wear is an unusually important

decision, because on this day, she thinks someone will notice."

"You're saying she wore special clothes because she was involved with someone?" he asked.

Leidmann grinned at him. "You're a little too literal. I'm saying she believed she was going to have a big day today."

He frowned. "Didn't that piece run yesterday?"

"Yes, but she was going to face the reaction today." Leidmann touched the bathroom sink with the edge of a brush. "There's extra makeup in here, but none on the vanity or in the cracks along the floor like there would be if she always applied a ton of makeup."

"Even with bots cleaning up after her?" he asked.

"Especially with bots cleaning up. Makeup is the hardest thing to clean. Is that little pile of dust something that the woman is using to paint her face or is it just a pile of dust?"

"Most women don't wear makeup," Nyquist said. "And those that would have once upon a time now use enhancements."

"Ki Bowles was in a profession where the personal image constantly changed. She didn't dare get an enhancement that might outdate itself in a year or less."

"If the studio paid for it, she could," he said.

"And have some recovery time?" Leidmann shook her head. "You need to do some study of reporters. She didn't have the time to recover."

"It usually only takes a day or two."

"A day or two is too long, especially if some story is breaking. She needed to follow trends with a minimum of fuss."

"Seems like makeup would be a maximum of fuss," he said.

"To us, maybe. But it was part of her job. And she put some on this morning, again, for that big day." Leidmann touched the edge of the sink with a gloved hand.

"You feel sorry for her, don't you?" Nyquist asked.

"Yeah," Leidmann said. "I'm not finding any evidence of any other person here."

"We knew she lived alone," he said.

"But even people who live alone have evidence of the other people in their lives—holos on tables, two-D images on the wall, rotating images in little frames. Or gifts, something that doesn't quite fit—a toy, maybe, or a shirt that's the wrong color. Or messages on the household computer system. I'm not finding anything."

"It's that guest room that got you, isn't it?"

Leidmann braced her gloved hands against the edge of the sink and turned toward Nyquist so that she faced him directly. Her mouth turned downward.

He'd never seen her so disturbed, at least at an empty scene like this one—the one without the body.

"Why does she have a guest room?" Leidmann asked. "In anticipation of a guest that never came?"

That would be sad. He'd never seen the use for a guest room. When his mother had come after he went into the hospital, she stayed at his place for a few days. Then, when he was conscious enough to realize she was there, he insisted she get a hotel room—and he paid for it.

He supposed it was possible that Bowles kept the room for a guest that never came, but she didn't seem the type. Of course, he didn't know her all that well. He'd judged her on her media persona and the handful of encounters he'd had with her.

"Maybe a guest used to come, and stopped," Nyquist said. "Or several guests. I know almost nothing about her personal life. Does she have family? Was she married?"

"That's the whole point," Leidmann said. "There's no evidence of parents or siblings or college friends. No evidence of a boyfriend or a girlfriend or a pet. And certainly no evidence of a divorce."

"Except an empty apartment she never came home to," he said softly.

"Or maybe she was just a hardworking woman who had

never made time for a relationship in her life. It's not that unusual."

Nyquist peered at Leidmann. Was she talking about herself?

"Relationships take time." He was learning that with De-Ricci. She was one of the busiest professionals on the Moon, and he hadn't been busy at all until just recently. He'd spent a lot of time waiting for her, which irked him. He didn't want to be the kind of person who waited for anyone.

"You got techs coming in for the handhelds, right?" Nyquist asked.

"I got a tech for the household system," Leidmann said. "But I'm taking the handhelds back to the lab. There's something about the sheer number of them that has me intrigued."

Nyquist flashed on the diagram in Bowles's studio. "I'd look at them here," he said. "She may have them in their places for a reason."

"Like some kind of trail of information?" she asked.

"Maybe," Nyquist said. "I found some other information she'd been working on, and it was in the form of a diagram. We can't dismiss the idea that she liked patterns, and used them in her work."

Leidmann made a sound of disgust. "My teams are spread thin as it is. Two major murders in one day—"

"Two?" Nyquist asked. "I take it you're not just meaning the man killed with Bowles?"

"No," Leidmann said. "I'm talking high-profile murders. First Ki Bowles and now Roshdi Whitford."

Nyquist froze. He hadn't been monitoring his links since he was called to the crime scene. He'd downloaded the chatter, figuring he would run through it at the end of the day instead of letting it distract him now.

"Roshdi Whitford of Whitford Security?" he asked.

Leidmann nodded. Nyquist tapped a chip on the back of his hand. Someone had mentioned Whitford Security to him earlier in the day.

He searched through his notes. They were cursory—

something he usually improved when he returned to the office—but cursory was good enough.

Edvard Jaeger of the Hunting Club had mentioned that men from Whitford Security had cleared the place in anticipation of Bowles's visit. When Nyquist had asked to meet with them, he was told that the men were already gone.

He'd made a note to contact Whitford Security during the course of the investigation, see if he could get the men's names, and find out what kind of threat they were anticipating against Bowles.

But he couldn't wait now. He needed some information and he needed it fast.

"Excuse me," he said to Leidmann, and left the room. He went down the hallway to the living room, realizing as he did so that he hadn't inspected the kitchen yet.

It would have to wait.

First he had to get some questions answered, questions he was going to investigate when he was done here.

He linked to the coroner's office first. One of the lower-level examiners appeared in front of his vision.

"Who's handling the Bowles case?" he asked without preamble.

"Chief Examiner Brodeur," she said.

"Put me through."

For a moment, his vision was normal and then Brodeur appeared in front of it. He was wearing a drape over his clothing to catch spatter, and unlike most people when speaking on a visual link, he did not try to clean up.

He appeared to be leaning on a desk, peering at a screen rather than using his internal links like Nyquist was.

"I know, I know," Brodeur said. "You caught the Hunting Club case. We'll deal with it when you get back here. There's too much to discuss on a secure link."

Meaning he didn't want to risk leaking information, even on a supposedly secure link. Not that Nyquist blamed him. What it meant, though, was that Gumiela hadn't yet announced Bowles's death, which was good for him.

"I've just got one question for you," Nyquist said.

"Cause of death should have been obvious," Brodeur snapped, and Nyquist almost smiled. Once DeRicci had told him how much she hated Brodeur and his preemptory manner, but Nyquist found it amusing.

"At least let me ask the question first," Nyquist said.

Brodeur sighed. "Quickly."

"Have you identified the other body yet?"

"Not entirely," he said.

Whatever Nyquist had expected, it wasn't that. Brodeur was usually very certain of himself. "What does that mean?"

"It means our second corpse has history under various names."

"Which one came up first?" Nyquist asked.

"Enzio Lamfier."

"Which means nothing to me," Nyquist said. "Is he from Armstrong? Did he just come through the port? Was he a guest at the Hunting Club?"

"Those questions are for detectives to answer," Brodeur said. "But I do know that he has other identities as well. I'm just not able to confirm them as yet. You do know that we have a spate of celebrity bodies today."

"Spate?" Nyquist asked. "I thought only two."

"Two is plenty," Brodeur said. "In fact, it's too many. I have press everywhere, and I haven't even gotten the Whitford body yet."

"Do they know about our first victim?"

"No one's asked yet," Brodeur said.

"The second one—"

"Whitford?"

"No," Nyquist said. "This Lamfier or whatever his name is. In your initial scan, did you turn up any ties to Whitford Security?"

Brodeur nodded. "I thought you already knew that part."

"What part?" Nyquist asked.

"Apparently he was assigned as a bodyguard to our other victim. He might have died trying to save her."

"Might have?" Nyquist asked.

"The wounds aren't clear, and I've been too busy to examine them closely. Besides, I find these shadow identities suspicious, especially for a bodyguard. Now, may I return to my work?"

"Sure," Nyquist said, and shut down the link.

He remained in the living room for a moment, staring at the handhelds without really seeing them. Two people with ties to Whitford Security dead, as well as Bowles. And without stretching things, she could be seen as tied to them as well.

Obviously Gumiela hadn't thought of that or she would have contacted him when Whitford's body turned up. Nyquist needed to contact her, and then he had to insinuate himself into that investigation.

"Let me know what you find," he sent to Leidmann through his links. Then he left Bowles's apartment and headed back to the precinct, hoping that Gumiela was in a receptive mood.

18

Flint was too nervous to sit in Van Alen's office. He paced across the cream-colored carpet, skimming his fingers against the back of the upholstered chairs.

Van Alen leaned against her desk, watching him.

"We have to assume that Ki Bowles's death is linked to the story," Flint said.

Van Alen didn't move. "I know. I'm wondering if we did something wrong. We knew that she wouldn't be totally safe. I just never expected her to die."

"You knew it was a risk," Flint said, his fingers still skimming. "We talked about it."

"A risk is one thing," Van Alen said. "An actual murder is another."

Through the opaque glass, he could make out a coffee, blue, and blondish blur. That blur was Talia. He had asked Van Alen to set up the waiting room perimeter alarm and to shut off the room's external computers.

If Talia tried to go to another part of the office, the alarms would go off. If she tried to access one of the computers, she couldn't because there was no obvious way to hack in. Flint had updated the system for Van Alen six months before.

"We don't know if Bowles's death was random or if it was connected to the story," Flint said.

"We have to assume it was connected. Don't you think it odd that she died today of all days?"

"Yes," he said, "I do."

He stopped pacing and frowned at Van Alen. He had a sudden realization.

"She shouldn't have died so quickly," he said. "If Justinian Wagner was going after her, he wouldn't have done it like this. He would have tried to find out where she got the information first."

"Maybe he did," Van Alen said. "We don't know what happened just before she died."

Flint flopped into a nearby chair. "Thuggishness is not his way. He'd've tried to finesse it. Unless he already knew she was working on the story."

He was talking more to himself than Van Alen. But she didn't know that. She answered as if he were speaking directly to her.

"He had to know something," Van Alen said. "She corroborated the facts you gave her with some of his former employees."

"And the stuff they gave her was stuff they'd given other reporters," he said.

"So he killed her for the uncorroborated stuff? At least, the stuff that seems uncorroborated? Isn't that odd?"

"It's all odd," Flint said, "and yet I feel like I shouldn't be surprised. I picked . . ."

He let the sentence trail off. He wasn't going to admit to anyone that one of the many reasons he had chosen Ki Bowles to report this story was that he didn't like her. He had hoped it wouldn't bother him much if something happened to her.

But it did bother him. And not just because it had happened so much sooner than he expected, but because Bowles had done a good job.

"Miles?" Van Alen asked. "You picked what?"

He shook his head. He had forgotten he had spoken out loud. He didn't want Van Alen to know that he had picked Ki Bowles for more than her reporting skill.

He had picked her so that his conscience wouldn't get pricked if he had to ruin her life. Part of him saw this story—this long work on WSX—as revenge for the stories Bowles had done on him and on DeRicci.

And for the first time, he felt guilty about that.

But he had explained the risks to Bowles. She knew her life was at risk. She even knew that she might have to Disappear if things got really bad, although she had laughed at that idea.

He moved an arm onto the back of the chair and looked at Van Alen.

"We have some things to figure out," he said. "She let me know that she had completed several stories, and that she wanted me to see them. How many are here?"

Van Alen frowned as she worked to remember. "She dropped off two last week, including the one that Upstart had run. Then, this morning, she dropped off three more."

Then Van Alen sighed and looked down. "She was in a good mood."

He wasn't sure whether the good mood made things better or worse. "I'd better look at those stories, then," he said. "We have to decide if we want to run them ourselves."

Van Alen glanced at the opaque walls. He knew she was looking at Talia.

"Maybe we should stop now," Van Alen said.

He didn't turn around. He didn't want to see Talia out there, waiting.

He had put his daughter at risk, too, and he had never meant to. He hadn't even known she existed when he hatched this plot against WSX, to make them pay for everything they had done over the years.

The courts couldn't go after them. The police could do nothing.

This had been the only way to bring the firm down.

It probably wouldn't have put Justinian Wagner in jail, but it would have ruined his life.

Instead it took Ki Bowles's life and might damage Flint's. Or Talia's.

He thought aloud: "There's a tie to you just because Bowles was in and out of this office. We revealed another tie today to our friend from Whitford Security, so a few people, at least, know that I'm involved. If Justinian hears about my involvement, then he might figure out how Bowles got the information. Although he won't be able to prove it. Not that proof seems to matter to him."

"I don't see why he'd kill for revealing the firm's confidential files," Van Alen said. "He can sue both of us. He probably wouldn't win—we can successfully argue that those files were part of your inheritance from Paloma, and we can probably stretch that to mean that because she had them, and had given them to you, *she* had broken the confidentiality seal, not us. Not that it would matter. The resulting scandal would be as bad for my office as it would be for his."

Flint had purchased his business from Paloma. He had regarded her as his mentor until her murder. Then he had learned that she was Justinian Wagner's mother and the Stuart of Wagner, Stuart, and Xendor. He still felt betrayed.

"But that scandal wouldn't take care of me," Flint said. "I'd be fine. People already see me as operating on the edge of the law, anyway."

Van Alen tapped her forefinger against her lips. "Maybe we had more than we thought."

"We have a mountain of information. Ki Bowles wouldn't have reported it all in five years, let alone the— what was it? Ten?—stories she planned to do."

"No, no," Van Alen said. "I mean maybe there's something in those files that's worth killing for."

Flint shook his head. "First, you'd have to find out where the files are stored. You shoot the messenger, you'll never recover the information. No one's been here, right?"

"So far as I know," Van Alen said.

Flint remembered how Talia had accessed the files at Oberholtz, Martinez, and Mlsnavek. "You never linked our files to your computer network, did you?"

"No," Van Alen said, but Flint was already moving to her unnetworked systems. He had kept a backup of the files on one computer system that he made her swear she wouldn't use.

He turned on the computer (thinking it was a good sign that the thing was off), then searched through everything that had been accessed in the last six months.

Even though the search was rapid, he felt reassured.

No one had touched this computer except him.

"Are you finding anything?" Van Alen asked.

"No," he said. "And everything is just as I remembered it."

He knew these files better than anyone. Van Alen didn't, and Bowles certainly didn't. There was information in the WSX files that could bring down some of the most powerful politicians on the Moon. Even more that could implicate various corporations in all kinds of hideous scandals.

And worst of all, to his mind, was the way that WSX helped cover up truly heinous crimes, often to its own profit. That was the kind of information he had been feeding to Bowles bit by bit.

But they hadn't even gotten to the first bit, not really. Just some passing mentions.

Could those mentions have been enough to get Bowles killed? Enough to put a drastic plan into action, rather than have Wagner go through the usual channels as was his bent?

And if so, did that put Flint at risk? Or, more importantly, Talia?

He couldn't live with himself if he lost his daughter yet again. Anyone who looked at his past had to know that. It would be obvious.

Paloma had been right about one thing: Retrieval Artists shouldn't have connections. When she trained him in this new profession, she had told him that he was a perfect candidate. His parents were dead, he was divorced, and his child was dead, too.

No one could use his family as a blackmail tool. Paloma had warned him about friendships as well, but he'd had more trouble with that.

But Paloma hadn't separated herself, either. That was another lie, like her name. He had had no idea when he had bought her business that she had once been Lucianna Stuart, the woman who had started WSX, and he had no idea that she had a still living husband, whom she apparently still loved, and sons who ran the business.

He hadn't found out any of that until she died.

"It's odd," Van Alen said. "I'm usually not in a position where I say this, but I don't know what we should do."

"I don't, either." Flint shut off the computer and stood. "I don't think we have enough information."

"What do you mean?"

"Do you know much about Bowles's life?"

Van Alen shrugged. "She was single. She lived alone. She worked hard, and she was fired for doing her job—even if you don't like the story that she eventually came out with."

"Yeah," Flint said, "and what else?"

Van Alen opened her mouth to answer, and then closed it. "You'd think I'd know more," she said.

"Yeah, you would," Flint said. "Me, too. Considering how long I've known her and that investigation is part of my job description."

"You knew enough. You knew how she reported stories. You knew that she was an award-winning journalist, and that she was out of work. You also knew—how did you put it to me?—that she was utterly ruthless. That's all we needed."

"Yeah." Flint sat down in his chair. "But now that she's dead, I realize that's not enough."

"Meaning?"

"I have no idea if the WSX story is what got her killed. For all I know she had a stalker boyfriend or had trouble with the Gossip columnists or had made a dangerous enemy from a previous story."

"Who just happened to kill her now?" Van Alen snorted in disgust. "Come on, Miles. I thought you didn't believe in coincidence."

"I don't," he said. "But there are several factors at play here, and one is that Ki Bowles wasn't visible to the public for nearly six months. The thing that caused her death might be as simple as the fact that she became visible again."

"Oh," Van Alen said, and it was her turn to frown. She walked around her desk, pulled out the chair, and sat.

"I need to conduct an investigation of my own," Flint said. "I need to find out everything I can about this death and about Ki Bowles herself."

"The police can do it," Van Alen said.

"With limited information," Flint said. "Unless you plan to tell them about our scheme for WSX?"

Van Alen gave him a measuring look. "Point taken. Still, you won't have their resources."

He nodded. And the police no longer looked on him as one of their own. He'd burned those bridges. He still had some contacts in the department and a few old friends. He'd have to lean on them, as well as some of the back doors he'd built into the police database when he designed some of their computer security systems.

He hated using that a lot, though, because someday someone would close those back doors, and he wouldn't have access any longer.

"What about us in the meantime?" Van Alen asked.

"I'm sorry," he said, not quite following her.

"You, me." She paused just a moment, obviously for effect. "Talia. If we are in danger, any extra time you take is just going to keep us vulnerable."

"I guess we have to assume we're in danger," he said, and as he did, his heart started to pound. How would he investigate when he had Talia to protect?

"Maybe we should just leave Armstrong until this thing blows over," Van Alen said.

Flint raised his eyebrows. "You can abandon all your cases just like that?"

She gave him a sheepish smile. "No."

He could go if he had to, but he wasn't sure he had to. And there was one other problem.

"You know, if this is WSX, they have a long arm. And they're not afraid to go sideways. If WSX wants us dead, they'll kill us whether we're here or at the edges of the known universe."

"So better to stay here." Van Alen sighed. "And maybe hire a security firm?"

"Look what good that did Ki Bowles," Flint said.

"Then what do you suggest?" Van Alen asked.

"I don't have any suggestions." Flint had to stand again. The nervousness was back.

This time, he did look at the opaque windows. The coffee, blue, and blondish blur that was Talia had moved to a different couch.

He couldn't trust her safety to someone else. He had done that with Emmeline, and she had ended up dead. And he couldn't take Talia with him everywhere he went.

He'd given her a list of contacts in case anything happened to him. Noelle DeRicci. Bartholomew Nyquist. Even her mother's old attorney, Celestine Gonzalez.

But none of them were good enough to handle a crisis of this magnitude.

"I think," he said after a moment, "that we both need to be responsible for our own safety. If you feel better hiring someone, go ahead."

"What are you going to do?" Van Alen asked.

"Until I know that we're targets," he said, "I'm going to take care of myself."

"And Talia?"

"For now, I'll keep her with me." He didn't know what else to do.

"And if it turns out that someone is after us, too?" Van Alen asked.

"I don't know," he said. He needed time to think about that. He supposed all the options that he had once presented to Ki Bowles were now on his table.

He could hire guards. Or he could Disappear. Or he could find some kind of compromise—if he believed a compromise possible.

"Let me do the research," he said.

"Well, I'm going to act like I could die at any moment," Van Alen said.

"That's probably sensible," he said. He would do the same.

And he would tell Talia about the risks.

For now, that was the best he could do.

19

Sixty-five client contacts so far, and those were just the ones Justinian Wagner knew about. Of those sixty-five, three had pulled their business from Wagner, Stuart, and Xendor, threatening to sue the law firm if they weren't allowed to leave.

Six more had demanded copies of their confidential files sent over a secure link. Once they received those files, he knew, they would demand that the firm destroy the copies they held. It was a smarter, more organized way to fire WSX.

He remained at his desk, handling the most important cases from there. So far he had cajoled twenty of their top clients to remain.

He even had a speech: *At this point, it's just innuendo and speculation. We've already filed an injunction against Ki Bowles and Upstart Productions. They won't be able to run any more stories. We'll be going after her in court. Even if she has access to confidential material—and frankly, I have no idea how she could—then we shall get it back from her, whatever that takes, and enjoin her from ever speaking about it.*

And if that didn't pacify the client, he added this:

*No court is going to allow a law firm's confidential files
to remain in the hands of a reporter. The attorney-client
privilege is a sacrosanct premise of law throughout the
Earth Alliance. No court is going to allow that to be violated, no matter how the violation happened.*

A few clients hadn't been satisfied with that, and for
them, he played part of Bowles's report. The part where she
promised but did not deliver on what she would show.

*She probably got some of that from disgruntled former
employees who, by talking with her, have bankrupted themselves. She will get no more information, and we can only
assume that what she has is gossip and innuendo. Reporters
always magnify the importance of their evidence to make
their stories seem even more important. This reporter was
fired from her last position for improperly handling evidence
on a high-level story. She nearly brought down the Chief of
Security for the United Domes of the Moon at a time that
would have threatened the Moon's security just by doing so.
This reporter is a loose cannon. No one will believe anything she says.*

Except, so far, nine of his important clients, and probably
more who hadn't even contacted him yet.

Wagner put his head in his hands. The partners wanted a
meeting to figure out how to handle the crisis. He didn't. Not
yet. He was hoping he could cajole clients out of their anger
and fear.

Of course, to do that, he would have to cajole himself
first.

If Bowles did have access to the kind of confidential material that she claimed to have, then she knew a lot of harmful secrets—not just for his clients, but for WSX as well.
And no matter what he said about the woman, she was good
at her work.

He stood, his stomach queasy. The damage to his firm
had just begun. The sixty-five clients were merely the first to
respond. He had no idea how clients of the subsidiary firms

in the rest of the known universe were responding to this story—or how they would respond to future stories.

The cost to WSX's reputation was phenomenal, but the financial cost would be even worse.

And then there was the malpractice vulnerabilities, particularly with some of the cases his parents had handled.

Not to mention the criminal liability on dozens, maybe hundreds of cases.

He made himself breathe.

He hadn't lied to his clients. He could quash this.

WSX could survive rumors so long as they remained only that—rumors. His biggest worry was that in the public mind the rumors would become fact.

And once that happened, his firm would lose all of the power that it had ever had.

20

Fifteen minutes with her sons. That was all Romey had managed. She'd gotten home long enough to program a meal, serve it, take a bite, and leave.

Her sons were used to it. She doubted she would ever be.

She would have found another fifteen minutes if it weren't for Gumiela's apologetic message on her links.

I'm going to have to put another lead on your case. Seems your case might be tied to another, and he's already well under way in that investigation. Please brief him when he arrives at the scene.

Not only was the message vague; it was cowardly. Gumiela could have contacted Romey directly. Instead, she chose to leave the message—without the name of the new lead detective on the case. Now anyone could come in and claim Romey's case and she would have no say in it.

She had saved the message and scurried back to the scene, fortunately arriving before the new lead detective had.

The techs still weren't finished. Before Romey left, they had established that Whitford's was the only dead body in the house. No one knew yet whether Whitford lived alone or whether he had family.

She had planned to run an information feed on him while she ate and listened to her sons' tales of school, but she hadn't had time for that. And she didn't want the feed still running when she got back to the crime scene.

Tech vehicles littered the long drive leading to the Whitford estate. A few street cops guarded the scene, mostly shooing gogglers and the occasional reporter away from the area.

She got out of her own air car and trudged down the long path that twisted and turned its way into the estate. She already had the techs check out the path, knowing that everyone who visited this place would have to use it.

One squad, parked near the front gate, had a person in it. The employee who had let the techs inside. She felt a lurch in her stomach. In her haste to get home to the boys, she had forgotten her only witness.

And she wanted to interview this employee before the new lead detective came on the scene.

She opened the door on the front passenger side and sat down. A see-through screen rose between her and the witness, a young man with frightened eyes and blotchy skin.

"My links don't work in here," he said somewhat tearfully, which surprised her. "Can I at least let my boss know where I am so I don't get fired?"

He didn't just look young; he *was* young. Romey almost smiled. But she didn't dare. She didn't want to lose control of this interview before it really started.

"I thought that was your boss inside the house," she said.

"Technically." The boy—she couldn't quite think of him as a man, even though he probably had ten years on her fourteen-year-old—sniffled. "I mean, he's the boss of the whole company, but I've never met him before."

He ran a hand over his nose. At that moment, she decided to play this one motherly. She reached into her pocket and removed some tissue. Then she shut off the screen for just a moment and handed the tissue across.

He took it without touching her or reaching through the screen. That almost convinced her to keep the screen down.

Almost.

"What's your name, son?" she asked.

He sniffled again. "Parthalán Gimble."

She almost smiled again. The name was too much for such a sorry creature. "And what do they call you, Parthalán?"

"Lán," he said.

Of course. Maybe he was as hapless as he seemed. "Okay, Lán. Tell me why you're here."

"They put me in the squad and told me to wait. I've been here at least ninety minutes and no one's even checked up on me—"

"I know," she said soothingly. "I'm sorry. We've been dealing with the crime scene. We should have talked with you earlier. Do you need some food or a bathroom?"

He shook his head, but his cheeks flushed at the very idea of someone asking him those questions. He was an interesting choice for an employee of a security firm.

"When I asked why you're here," she said, "I meant why did Whitford Security send you here?"

"Oh." He wiped at his nose again with the tissue. "They needed a body on-site to see if the system was working."

Then his flush deepened.

"I mean, you know, a real person. I mean, like someone alive. I mean, oh God . . ." He buried his face in his hands.

Romey permitted herself a small smile, mostly because she couldn't help it. She hoped her sons would never behave like this in a crisis. She hoped she'd trained them better.

"Who sent you?" she asked gently.

"Mr. Lautenberg." Lán raised his head. The blush had faded, leaving his skin even blotchier.

"Who is Mr. Lautenberg?" Romey asked.

"My boss."

"What does he do?"

"I don't know exactly," Lán said.

Of course he didn't. "I mean, what's his job title?"

"Deputy head of operations, but the head of operations wasn't there and neither was anyone else of importance so Mr. Lautenberg, he had to make some decisions on his own, which he didn't like doing, but he felt it was necessary, so he was yelling at people; then he pointed at me, and I thought, you know, that was it. I was fired. But he didn't fire me. He sent me here. Which was a trick because there's no public transportation within two kilometers and I don't have my own car and I wasn't sure how to get here and I didn't have money for a taxi."

He took a breath, and so did Romey. "I take it Mr. Lautenberg doesn't talk to you very often."

"He's never talked to me." Lán's voice rose in panic. "That's why I have to let him know that I'm all right. I'll get fired, and this is the best job I've ever had. The pay—"

"I understand," Romey said, "and I'm sure he will, too. By now everyone at your company probably knows that Mr. Whitford is dead."

"*That* was Mr. Whitford?" Lán's voice rose even more, and then it cracked. Maybe he was younger than she thought. Maybe he had only five years on her eldest son.

"Roshdi Whitford," she said. "You didn't know?"

"I thought Mr. Whitford had killed some guy who broke in, you know? I didn't think it was him."

"You'd never met him?"

"No."

"Or seen a picture?"

"No."

"There's no image of the company's founder in its primary building?" Romey asked.

"There's no image of anything in there. It's like a fortress. You're not supposed to look at anything but your work. It's weird. But it pays good."

She got that. She was also relieved that she had ordered the Whitford Securities building locked down the moment she got wind of who had died.

"Okay," she said. "Tell me the events before you were sent here. You said this Mr. Lautenberg was yelling at people. Was this in the office or were you in a meeting?"

"*They* were in a meeting," he said. "I just came in with the lunch tray. We don't have bots, you know, because they can be tampered with. I guess no technology is really safe."

"I guess not," she said, deciding to wait to find out who "they" were.

"So there I was passing out the sandwiches and the special orders and he was yelling about how could this crisis happen and who let things get out of hand and where the hell were the two original guards and then he got some private message and he asked if anyone had seen Mr. Whitford today and no one had and then he frowned and he pointed at me and he told me to come here so that they could use their security system to track a real body. Those were his words. 'A real body.' I didn't say it to be insensitive or anything."

She nodded, trying to get a picture of what had really happened. "Do you think he knew something had happened to Mr. Whitford?"

"Why would he have sent me if he did? I mean, I'm the newest hire. There's no reason to send me. I'm not trained in anything. Like I know there's ways to go across the lawn here without activating too many cameras. It's the prescribed company route, but no one taught it to me. They wanted someone to mimic a nonemployee's route and I guess I'm the closest any employee gets to a nonemployee."

She almost smiled again, then caught herself. This poor boy. At least he was smart enough to know he'd been sent here because he was the least important employee in the firm.

"Let's back up for a moment," she said. "Was this a regular meeting that you brought sandwiches to?"

"No," he said. "It was an emergency meeting. I usually bring everyone sandwiches at their desk. It was kinda hard to find who had what because I go by desk, not by person—"

"And," she interrupted, not wanting to know the minutiae of his work, "when was the meeting called?"

"An hour, maybe, before I had to go in there?" He shrugged. He clearly didn't know.

"Do you know why it was called?"

"They got some ping."

"Ping?" she asked.

"From someone who was supposed to be working who wasn't? Or something. The higher up you go, the more regulated you get. If you're supposed to be on a job, you walk past the building, so that your company identification logs in. If you don't log in and you're supposed to be on some shift somewhere, like some building we're providing security at or something, the system pings the upper level."

It sounded elaborate. Romey frowned. "They had a meeting because someone didn't show up for work?"

"That happens," he said. "It's happened a few times since I got there. Usually the guy just gets fired, but this time, something went really wrong."

She nodded. "Were they trying to track him down?"

"I don't know," he said. "Everyone ran around for a few minutes, then Mr. Lautenberg called the meeting, and stuff went on in the meeting room that I didn't know about. I do know that no one wanted Mr. Whitford to know until we all knew—or *they* all knew, really. The rest of us would find out whenever."

"Right," she said. "Who was missing?"

He shrugged.

"Do you know what he was supposed to be doing?"

"Guarding something," Lán said. "I know that because they were really afraid. This could be big."

"And they didn't contact the company's head over it?"

"Not right away," Lán said. "But I got the sense that they were trying when I got in there, and then he wasn't answering, and everyone said that was weird, and then they got weird hits on the security system, and that's when they sent me."

If he was telling the truth, then this poor kid had no idea what the company had done to him. They had sent him here as a decoy, not just to see whether the security system was working, but also to see whether whatever had gone wrong was in any way dangerous.

Since they didn't use bots or other major tech, they had no choice but to send in lower-level employees. It was interesting that they had sent in a kid who had no training at all, probably because anyone with enough training would understand the dangers and behave accordingly.

"Did they think something had happened to Mr. Whitford?"

Lán shrugged. "I didn't know anything had happened to him until you told me."

"You called the police before you called your boss?" she asked.

He flushed again. "He was dead. I work for a security company. We're not the police. We don't investigate anything. I did the right thing, right?"

Probably not for the company. The poor kid would probably lose his job because he hadn't followed company policy. But for her . . .

"You did the right thing," she said. "You're amazingly brave. You waited here with the body until the police arrived?"

"No," he said, looking down. "I ran out into the yard. I didn't want—you know—to be close to it."

She nodded. If he ran around and the company's security systems were working properly, then they had known that he had called the police. They also had known that something had scared the poor boy.

He probably wouldn't get fired. He probably already *was* fired.

"Then when the police arrived, you let them in," she said.

"They just looked in the house, like I did, and called for some techs or something like that. They made me wait. When the techs got here, they had me open the door."

"I thought you didn't know how the security system worked," she said.

"Every employee has a passkey into any Whitford Security System."

"Any system?" she asked. That didn't sound very secure.

"Initially, yeah. Then it gets modified by position. The higher up you are, the more places you can go. Like there are places even in the Whitford Security building that I can't get into."

"And if clients have a Whitford Security System?"

"I can't get in. But some of my bosses can. And the operations guys and maintenance guys, they can. But they leave a trail so if something bad happens, then they'd get blamed, you know."

It didn't sound very efficient to her, but she wasn't going to trust the probably-fired almost-nonemployee employee. She would have someone else explain the system to her.

"Yet you could open your boss's front door?" she asked.

"He's the one who sets the level of security at his house," Lán said. "If he didn't want someone like me in there, he would have had a tighter security system."

She frowned. "You never told me how you did get here. You said you didn't have a car and there was no nearby public transportation and you couldn't afford a taxi."

He pressed his lips together. He had clearly done something he wasn't supposed to.

"I promise I won't tell your bosses," she said. And she wasn't lying. She wouldn't tell his bosses because his bosses wouldn't care.

"I got a friend to drop me here." He spoke quietly.

"And who is this friend?" she asked.

He still wasn't looking at her. "Jude Andreeson."

"Did Jude Andreeson come onto the property with you?"

"No!" Lán whirled his head toward her. "They might've been watching. I'd get fired."

"All right," she said, using her mother voice. Reasonable, yet demanding. "Where did he drop you off?"

"Up the street, far from here," Lán said. "I made him turn around so he wouldn't drive down the street."

She nodded. "How were you planning to get back to work?"

"I thought maybe someone would come for me, but if they didn't, I'd walk to the public transport."

"You figured they were watching you when you got here?"

"That was the whole point," he said. "They were afraid the system wasn't working."

"Do you know why?" she asked.

"Because they thought Mr. Whitford was here. There was no other place he'd be. Or maybe they tried to find him somewhere else or something. I'm not exactly sure. But they wanted—"

"A real body, I know," she said more to herself than him. Was the missing word in that phrase *live*? A real live body. She almost asked Lán how the system worked, then decided not to. He probably didn't know.

But if it wasn't registering a glitch in the system and it wasn't getting a reading of anyone alive here, wouldn't they have sent someone more experienced?

She smiled at Lán, making sure the expression was reassuring. "I'm going to need you here for a few more minutes. I'll send someone over to get your personal information and do a follow-up interview. Then you'll be free to go."

He nodded, even though he looked unhappier than he had before.

She got out of the car, closing the door, before she allowed herself a deep frown. The kid had raised a lot more problems than he had solved for her.

"Find the killer?"

Romey started. She should have noticed that a man was standing near the back of the squad, but she hadn't. Part of the reason was that the man had somehow made himself blend into his surroundings.

He was taller than she was, which wasn't difficult to be,

and he looked square, probably because the jacket he wore didn't taper from his broad shoulders. His blue-black hair was thinning, and his face was oddly lined, as if he had started to develop wrinkles and then they moved to a different part of his skin.

He also looked tired.

It took her a moment to recognize him. Detective Bartholomew Nyquist, surly and temperamental, with one of the best closing rates in the department until he nearly died trying to thwart an assassin last year.

"I take it you're the new lead on the investigation." She tried not to sound disappointed, but she doubted she was successful.

"Sorry," he said. "I hate taking over cases someone else has started, but it looks like your case and mine are related."

"Related means that I stay lead on mine and you stay lead on yours." Now she did sound bitter and she didn't mean to. Or maybe she did. She'd caught this case because Gumiela said there was no one better, even though Romey needed a day off, some time with her family, and some sleep.

Now, apparently, there was someone better.

"Okay," he said, "so I couched the language a bit. Our cases aren't just related. I think they're the same case. Which is why I'm here."

"You think?" she asked. "The chief said it was her idea."

"It was her idea after I explained the ties between the cases to her," he said. "Let me explain them to you, and then you can catch me up on what's going on here."

He rounded the car and held out his hand.

"Let's start, though, with a formal introduction. I know who you are, but you probably have no idea who I am." The words didn't sound fake. He truly thought she had no idea who he was. "I'm Bartholomew Nyquist."

She took his hand and shook it. "Savita Romey."

"You've done some great work," he said, letting her hand go. "I'm going to try to stay out of your way on this. I just need the information that being part of the investigation yields."

"All right," she said, not sure if he was now trying to smooth things over.

"And of course, you're going to have full access to my investigation as well." He smiled at her, then glanced inside the car. "Witness or suspect?"

"I'd almost say victim, but he's not injured," she said. "At least not that he knows about."

"Meaning?"

"I think he works for a company that knew he might die when they sent him out here."

Nyquist whistled. "That's a harsh accusation."

"Just my sense," she said. "But I have a hunch it'll be accurate."

"Do you work a lot on hunches?" he asked.

She felt her spine stiffen. "Is that a problem?"

He grinned. "No. I like partners who trust their gut. Too many don't."

She nodded. "I think I should warn you that I don't have a partner because the chief knows that I don't play well with others."

"Well," Nyquist said, "I'm working without a partner because I'm newly back from medical leave. I guess we buddy up on this case."

"I wasn't kidding about my predilection for working alone," she said. It gave her a little extra time with her family without the risk of being reported. It also streamlined her investigations.

"I understand," he said. "I've chased away a few partners on my own. I've never understood the need the department has to assign two radically different people to share assignments. I used to compare it to an arranged marriage."

"Is that what this is?" she asked.

His smile widened. "More like a shotgun affair. Does that work for you?"

For the first time since she caught this case, she grinned.

"Yeah," she said, finally taking his hand and shaking it. "An affair I can handle."

"Me, too," he said. "In fact, an affair's perfect. I'm not sure I want to face my case alone."

She glanced over her shoulder at the car. Maybe it was good to have backup when she went head-to-head with Whitford Security.

"Yeah," she said, deciding to maintain the metaphor. "Sometimes an affair is just the thing."

21

Six different reports in front of her, and all Noelle DeRicci could think about was how annoyed she was. Not just at the stupid rehash of Ki Bowles's old news story, but also at Nyquist.

He shouldn't have tried to take advantage of their relationship to get her to shut down security at the Hunting Club.

She had thought that when he went back to work he would not bother her that much. It had been hard while he was healing; he'd needed a lot from her, and she'd been willing to provide it, even though it meant she didn't get a lot of sleep. She had to be able to do her job, and see to him.

That request today did not bode well for the future of their relationship. If he tried to use her again, she would have to tell him that such behavior compromised her.

He'd hate to hear it, and she'd hate to say it. But she had to draw a line.

And what upset her the most was that the line would be at the expense of her relationship, not at the expense of her job, just like those lines had been in the past.

She leaned back in her chair. Did that mean she valued

her job more than Nyquist? That's what someone like Bowles would say.

Flint would tell her that a person had to take care of herself, and DeRicci was doing just that. He would also remind her that limits made relationships possible.

Of course, he hadn't had a relationship since his wife left, and that went so well for him, given that he now had a daughter he hadn't known about until six months ago.

So maybe DeRicci shouldn't turn to someone like Flint for relationship advice, even if it was just in her imagination.

She made herself focus on the reports. They had come to her desk for a reason. Half a dozen lower-level employees of the newly formed security department had reviewed them, and decided that they meant something.

She usually didn't read the lower-level employee analysis until after she looked at the problems herself—it kept her mind clear, and made sure she didn't focus on the area that the underlings had. Sometimes they didn't see the entire picture accurately, and she had to adjust things.

If she always looked at things from the employees' point of view, she would miss the central fact of some of the issues she faced.

At other times, though, her lower-level employees had been exactly on target.

She never knew until she looked at the raw data herself.

The raw data here was attached to the end of the reports. She rearranged the information so that she looked at the raw data, then at the originating reports—which came from outside her office, from someone who believed there was a security breach or some kind of similar problem—and then the analysis from the members of her department.

It took her a minute to understand what the raw data was.

The raw data concerned outside tampering with the Moon's public net.

She had never thought the public net very important. Even though everyone used it, from communications to watching vids and holos to getting information from news to personal messages, everyone also knew that the net was notoriously unreliable.

No one—except someone too poor to afford their own links (and that was hardly anyone anymore)—used the net for secure personal business. People used it for hurried communication (*Hon, I'm at the port. My links are down, so I had to use the public system. I'll be home in an hour*) to the most basic level of research (such as discovering the names of all the publicly listed companies in Armstrong that sold clothing) before using private services to search out more exclusive information.

Old news stories sometimes floated around the public net and so did old plays or programs, but even those had expirations or copyright limitations. Usually a net user saw only headlines or possible links for news stories, and entertainment options, available at a price for private download. Never the news or the entertainment itself.

So DeRicci was a bit confused as to why information concerning the public net had made it to her desk. She studied the data for a few minutes longer. From what she could understand, items had been removed from the public information network. And those items hadn't been removed from within the network itself, but from outside.

She frowned, trying to make sense of that. Technically there was no central home from the public net—not the way there was for the city government or for InterDome Media or even for the Human Library Project, her personal favorite because it tried to contain everything ever published by humans within this solar system.

As she understood it, people could take anything they wanted off the public net and they could delete anything, if they found out where its home base was located. They could then, if they had the time, delete all references to it.

If that piece of information had found its way into any of the Earth Alliance information networks, then the information might still exist in the Earth's public net or on Mars's public net. So information didn't just vanish.

And even if it did, she didn't understand why someone would present that to her as a security breach.

She tried the raw data again, trying to see whether she got a different understanding from it. She was hoping she had misread what had come before her.

But so far as she could tell, she hadn't misread it. Of course, she didn't do the close analysis her underlings did. But she should have some sense of what was before her, just by the information she was looking at.

And she got nothing different than the first time she went through it all.

Finally, in frustration, she gave up digging through the raw data and turned to the first underling's report. It concerned a block of information that had just vanished from the public nets. That block of information disappeared from backup systems as well, and if it weren't for some retired citizen who believed that all the information on the public net should be backed up on a private network (his private network), no one would ever have even known what the information was.

The information was a list of people who had come through the Port of Armstrong during one week over fifteen years ago. The port kept such information as well. In fact, the port's records should have been extremely detailed.

But the security analyst went to the port with a request for the information, and discovered that the port's records for that week were missing.

They had gone missing about two weeks ago, at the same time the information disappeared off the public nets.

DeRicci leaned back. Now she was beginning to understand. Someone was trying to cover up their entry (or exit) from Armstrong fifteen years ago.

Because they'd been charged with a crime now? Or because of some other event she didn't know about?

She opened a screen on her own personal system, the one that wasn't linked to anything, not even her assistant's system. Bowles and her ancient story were no longer important.

This was. And DeRicci had an idea how to track down that information without access to the port's records or the public net.

But first she was going to look at the other cases.

She was going to see what else she needed to know.

22

Flint waited until they reached his air car before he spoke to Talia. The car was in the VIP section of Van Alen's parking structure, off to one side.

He loved the VIP section because it scanned for illegal links. It also shut off all but the most common emergency links. Many of Van Alen's clients were people who believed they needed to Disappear, which meant that they were in some kind of trouble. They were tailed or watched or hounded. Over the years, Van Alen had put the best possible security in her VIP section.

He had parked the car in a corner near the jamming systems. He knew that proximity gave extra protection.

On this afternoon, his was the only car parked up here. It was a sleek, state-of-the-art model, a little larger than he liked. He had bought it after Talia had come into his life, and he felt that he needed something bigger and safer.

Of course, he hadn't expected to work much during the years he raised Talia, so he didn't think speed was as much of an issue as it had been just a few months before.

He was no longer sure that he was right.

Talia hadn't asked a lot of questions while they were still

in Van Alen's office. When they got into the elevator, she asked what the police wanted.

Flint had held up a single finger, silently asking her to wait, and looking pointedly at the walls of the elevator. He doubted anyone was listening in except maybe Van Alen's people, but he didn't want to take any risks.

He touched the driver's door and the car unlocked. Talia opened her door before he did, and slid inside, slamming the door so hard that the car shook.

She had had an interesting day—trying to leave, getting caught, having her research examined, and then accompanying him to Van Alen's. Talia was surly on the best of days, and this wasn't the best of days.

Flint got in beside her. He turned the environmental systems on, checked the logs to make sure no one had so much as looked at the car in his absence, and then turned to his daughter.

"I'm going to tell you something difficult," he said. "We have a problem and I'm not quite sure I know how to solve it."

Talia faced him, looking like the adult she would some-day be. He sensed she was flattered that he trusted her enough to tell her about this, even though she didn't yet know what he was going to say.

He couldn't tell her everything. In fact, he couldn't tell her much. But he had to tell her enough.

"You remember Ki Bowles?" he asked.

"Yeah." Talia had a slight frown, as if she were trying to stay ahead of the conversation, anticipating everything he was going to say.

"She was murdered this morning," he said.

Talia's breath caught. She blinked and then looked away.

He wondered whether he should have broken the news to her more gently. After all, her mother had just died—and that might have been a murder, although the Recovery Man who had kidnapped her insisted it was a suicide.

"Tal?" he said.

She nodded, then turned toward him again. Somehow she had gotten control of her facial expression, but her eyes held some fear.

"Maxine and I were working on a project with Ki."

"I know," Talia said.

He moved sharply, cutting off his own reply, which would have been harsh. He wondered if she had looked through his or Van Alen's files.

Talia must have sensed what he was going to say because she added somewhat defensively, "You told me, remember? When you introduced us that one time?"

He barely remembered. He had muttered something about working together and left it at that.

"I assume it was a dangerous project?" Talia asked.

"It might be the reason she died," he said.

Talia's lips trembled. She nodded, then looked away again. He put his hand on hers.

"I took on the project," he said, "long before I knew about you. Then when we came back here, you and me, I didn't really give the project much thought. It was just something that was under way. I should have stopped it then, and I just didn't think of it."

"You're in danger?" she asked.

"I don't know," he said. "The news is sketchy and I learned long ago not to act without all the facts. Ki Bowles had a life besides this project. Something else might have gotten her killed. It might even have been random."

"But you don't know that."

"I don't," he said. "And that's the problem."

She kept her hand under his. He could feel her trembling. This poor girl, who had lost her entire life, was just gaining a new one, and he was telling her that it was threatened.

"I have to investigate what happened to Ki."

"Isn't that what the police are for?"

"What we were working on is confidential," Flint said. "The police won't—they can't—have all the facts."

"Why not?" She turned toward him again. She looked

more like the terrified young girl he had first met than the woman she would be.

"Because," he said, not sure exactly how to answer this, "although our motives were pure, our methods may not have been."

"You broke the law?" Her voice rose. "You mean what the kids at school say about you is true?"

"What do they say?" he asked, not liking her distress.

"That because you're a Retrieval Artist, you're a criminal."

He smiled in spite of himself.

She pulled her hand away from him. "They say that. They do. And they mean it."

"I'm sure they do," he said.

"Is it true?" she asked.

"Retrieval Artists don't always follow the law," he said.

"That makes you a criminal."

"If you look at the universe in black and white, maybe," he said.

"Police look at the universe like that," she said. "Shouldn't lawyers? Shouldn't you?"

"Police don't always," he said, choosing not to answer the last question. "Some of my referrals have come from the police."

"You've done illegal work for the police?"

"And for the United Domes of the Moon." He sighed. "Sometimes it's the only way."

"And this thing, this thing that got Ms. Bowles killed, it was illegal?" Talia made it sound dirty.

"Not exactly," he said. "Technically, what we were doing was defendable in court."

"Which is what Ms. Van Alen says."

"Or she wouldn't have been involved."

"But it got Ms. Bowles killed."

"We don't know that," he said.

Talia glared at him.

"But right now we have to assume it." He sighed again. "I'm sorry, Talia."

"Sorry why? Because you're going to die now, too?"

He started. He hadn't thought of it that way. He'd only thought of the threat to her.

"No," he said. "Because this threat shouldn't even exist. I told you I was going to mostly retire until you were out of school. Part of the reason was to minimize the dangers of my job. I didn't want to deal with crises like this."

"Have you before?"

He nodded.

"A lot?" Her lower lip was trembling again.

"Enough," he said. "As a police officer, too. Being a Retrieval Artist isn't day-to-day dangerous like being a policeman, but it sometimes gets the wrong groups after you. And while I didn't mind that for me when I was on my own, I mind it now."

"So don't do it anymore," she said.

"I wasn't going to, at least until you were away from home. I don't need the money," he said.

She raised her eyebrows. He knew she had poked into his bank accounts. He had let her. She would never discover all the money he had, no matter how good she was. She only discovered the money that was in his surface accounts—the accounts he used for the next two years. His deep accounts, the base of his fortune, were scattered throughout the known universe, under various names—and in some cases, only under numbers.

"So I don't see the problem," she said.

"If Ki Bowles died because of this project," he said, "quitting won't help. If whoever killed her knows that I'm involved, then I'm at risk."

He paused, knowing this next part would be even harder to say. Because it would be hard for her, too.

"One of the ways that I'm at risk," he said gently, "is through you."

Her jaw snapped closed. Fear flashed through her eyes,

quickly replaced by fury. "What do you mean through me? You think they'll come after me?"

"They might."

"You think they'll hurt me to find out more about this project?"

"They could."

"God," she said, glaring at him. "I thought you were better than Mom."

He let the words hang for a moment. He liked the idea that she had actually thought him better than the woman who had raised her. But he had to address this issue and do it quickly.

"I didn't mean to do this to you," he said. "I honestly thought it would never come to this—and it might not. We might be overreacting. That's what I have to find out."

"How?" she asked.

"It'll take some research. But while I do it, I have to know you're safe."

"So hire someone to guard me," she said, her voice dripping with sarcasm. "Send to me to someone else. See if I care."

He almost smiled. She was still young enough to lack sophistication, not realizing how revealing her words were.

"Ki Bowles had security guards," he said. "One of them died defending her."

"Oh." Talia's voice got small. She crossed her arms. "So what're we going to do?"

He liked the "we." "I'm going to keep you close until I find out what's going on."

"And if it turns out that someone is after you?" she asked.

"And it's someone I can't easily deal with?" He shrugged. He didn't like the answer he was going to give her, but it was the only one he could come up with so far. "We'll probably have to Disappear."

"You're kidding, right?"

He shook his head.

"That's weird," she said, "and scary. When will we know?"

"Soon, I hope," he said. "So I'm going to need your help. You're going to have to stay at my side and be vigilant. If I tell you to sit still somewhere, you will. I'll never be more than a few meters from you. But I don't want you to know a lot about the project that Ki and Maxine and I worked on. It'll put you in too much danger. So if I tell you I can't explain any further, you're going to have to accept that. All right?"

She nodded. "Do I get a weapon or something?"

"No," he said.

"Then how do I defend myself?"

"With your emergency links and your proximity to me," he said. "This should only be for a day or so. We'll take it one moment at a time."

She nodded again. Her next question surprised him.

"Can I help?"

He frowned at her. She had great computer skills. She could dig and find information.

"There might be some things for you to do," he said. "But mostly, I need you to stay close. Can you do that?"

"Yeah," she said quietly. Then she turned toward him, that adult expression back. "Dad?"

"Yes?"

"You never told me. What happens if you die?"

"You're taken care of," he said.

"Meaning?"

"You get everything. My business, my home. My money. All of it." But he hadn't appointed a formal guardian yet. Right now the will simply gave Celestine Gonzalez and the staff at Oberholtz, Martinez, and Mlsnavek the right to appoint someone. Someone he hadn't approved.

"I don't want all that stuff," Talia said.

"I'm not planning on dying," Flint said.

"But you just told me your life is in danger," she said.

"My life has been in danger before, and I'm still sitting here."

"This kind of danger?" she asked.

"Worse," he said.

She frowned, clearly thinking about that. "More than once?"

"More than once," he said.

"And you survived." She said that more to herself than to him.

"I'm tough that way," he said.

She was silent for a long moment. He could see how hard she was thinking. It was as if her universe had shifted again.

He hated doing that to her.

"So," she said, "the only difference is me."

"What do you mean?" he asked.

"I mean, you can take care of yourself. You're afraid for me."

Sometimes he wished he could talk to Rhonda. Sometimes he wished he could ask her how she dealt with such a bright and intuitive child. Sometimes he wanted to ask how he was supposed to deal with her.

"Yeah," he said. "I'm afraid for you."

"And you can't trust someone else to take care of me," Talia said. "Not just because of Ms. Bowles, but because of the people at that day care center, the ones who were supposed to take care of Emmeline, the ones who killed her."

Out of the mouths of babes. At least he didn't wince at her crassness. "That's right," he said.

She was quiet again. He could sense her trying to come up with a solution.

"You should give me a weapon," she said.

"That just makes things more dangerous," he said. "I'd rather use your brain."

"For what?" she asked.

"Most of my job is research," he said. "and this might require me to synthesize a lot of information."

"I thought I couldn't know about the project," Talia said.

"But you can help me find out about Ki Bowles's private life," he said. "Maybe an old boyfriend killed her."

"We can only hope," said his daughter, and the sincerity in her voice—and the fact that he agreed with her—made his heart break.

At her age, his daughter shouldn't be that cynical.

And he was afraid it would only get worse.

23

DeRicci returned to the raw data from the reports she had been studying. She saw the same pattern the deeper she went into the data—information was missing—but she couldn't discern its significance.

Much as she wanted to stay ahead of her underlings on security topics, this one was over her head. She didn't have the technical expertise to examine the raw data here in a way that yielded an understanding of the potential security crisis.

The first report had highlighted information missing from the public records placed on the public net and from the port itself.

She flipped to the next report. It showed the same kind of lost information. Only this time, it was hotel records and banking statements—things that shouldn't have been on the public nets, anyway. She understood why those had vanished. Some bank or hotel had probably protested, and she was about to turn away from the report when she realized that this information had originated at the same time as the information about the port.

Little more than fifteen years ago.

She frowned.

The report told her that the banks in question as well as

the hotels had lost their records for that period. The hotels really didn't care—fifteen-year-old records of payment and who had stayed where didn't matter all that much.

But the banks were in a panic. They had approached a security consultant who was on retainer with DeRicci's office. He was supposed to bring anomalous information to the attention of low-level analysts.

It had been his find—the missing bank records—that had started a wider investigation.

Not every bank in Armstrong lost its records. Nor did every hotel. And it wasn't all records for that time period.

It was the transaction records, specifically in the case of the banks, the records that accessed off-Moon accounts.

Now DeRicci was starting to get worried. When she combined the information from reports one and two, something ominous started presenting itself.

Records of trips into and out of Armstrong had vanished, as well as hotel records and banking records from the same period.

If the information weren't so old, she would immediately issue a low-level emergency notice to law enforcement throughout the United Domes.

But the information was fifteen years old.

She wasn't sure how it mattered.

Except that someone had decided in the last few weeks that this information needed to be purged from the records.

Why was information fifteen years old worth tampering with?

More importantly, why was that fifteen-year-old information relevant *now*?

She didn't know. And she wasn't sure how she was going to find out.

24

Before Flint had left Van Alen's office, she had discovered that the lead investigator on the Bowles murder was Bartholomew Nyquist. She'd had to trade a few favors to get that information, but it had worked.

And the information pleased Flint.

He and Nyquist had worked on a couple of cases—not together, exactly, but in concert. They'd developed a kind of rapport. Nyquist had treated Flint well in a case in which Flint had been a suspect.

Nyquist had nearly died working on that case. And Flint had been with DeRicci when they discovered Nyquist's battered body. Together they had worked to save his life.

Flint had even paid for Nyquist's medical treatment, mostly as a favor to DeRicci, not because of any special fondness for Nyquist. And, if the truth be told, Flint had been impressed with Nyquist's survival skills. The man had used his brain to survive against a Bixian assassin.

To Flint's knowledge, Nyquist was the only human ever to survive a Bixian attack.

Flint considered all of this as he drove to Dome University's Armstrong campus with Talia in the seat beside him. He pinged Nyquist's links several times, with increasing frequency. He didn't want to leave a message that he had information on the Bowles killing, but he might have to, given that Nyquist hadn't yet contacted him back.

Talia was monitoring the news nets. So far, no one had reported on Bowles's death. And that was unusual. The woman was well known throughout Armstrong. Reporters should have been flocking to the story.

So far, Chief Andrea Gumiela had somehow managed to keep this death quiet.

That wouldn't be the case for much longer. Flint had to get to Nyquist before the news broke.

"What's at the university?" Talia asked.

"Open research nets," Flint said. "We can do a lot of untraceable work there."

He preferred a place called the Brownie Bar, but he hadn't been there much since Talia had joined him. The place served marijuana in its baked goods, and although it was perfectly legal for Flint to enjoy a brownie while Talia sat at the table, he didn't want her anywhere near that venue.

"Can't we just go back to your office?" Talia asked.

"We can," he said. "But I would rather make the research look general."

"I thought nothing can get traced back to you from your office," she said.

"That's the theory," he said.

"You don't believe it." Talia looked sideways at him.

"Let's just say it hasn't been tested to my satisfaction yet," he said.

He landed the car in the lot next to the university's law school. Over the years, he had acquired the special seal to park here. Although he wasn't going to tell Talia how he got that seal since it, like so much in his life, wasn't entirely on the up-and-up.

"What's this?" Talia asked.

She was looking at the law school, a black and chrome building to the side of campus. The building was one of the most structurally diverse on a campus filled with experimental buildings.

"They have a great research facility in there," he said as he got out of the car.

Talia got out, too. She shoved her hands in her pockets and made a slow three-hundred-and-sixty degree turn. She was looking for threats.

He felt guilty and relieved at the same time. She had taken his words seriously.

"Before we go in, let me try one thing." He walked a few meters away from the car and leaned against a signpost that announced the schedule for special lectures being held in the auditorium.

He sent a message to Nyquist:

I know about Bowles and I have some information to trade that you might not get anywhere else. Contact me immediately.

He marked the message urgent, and then turned to Talia.

She was leaning against the car, her arms crossed. She kept looking nervously from side to side.

His best-laid plans for her were ruined.

He never again wanted her to feel the kind of fear she'd felt when her mother was kidnapped. He'd planned on protecting her from as much as he could, including fear of physical harm.

Now he'd reintroduced that into her life.

He sighed and crossed over to her.

"Come on," he said. "Let me introduce you to terrible cafeteria food and the intricacies of legal research."

"Will we be safe there?" she asked.

"Safe enough," he said, and hoped it was true.

25

Savita Romey had been right: Roshdi Whitford's house looked like it had been built to survive the collapse of the dome. Nyquist walked around the first floor, careful to avoid any areas that the techs hadn't finished with yet.

The blood spatter surprised him. He hadn't expected so much from a single man. But Romey had had the techs do a preliminary test on-site, and their equipment said that the blood belonged to the same person.

Her theory that at least two arteries had been cut at the same time was one of the few things that made sense of the blood evidence. Her discovery, from the young employee in the squad, that anyone with the right pass codes could get into the house was disturbing.

They started their conversation after Nyquist took a look at this crime scene. Then they continued the conversation as they walked along the path around Whitford's house. The police security system didn't extend to the grounds, although the Whitford system did. It had been shut down, so when Nyquist and Romey talked outside, no one listened in.

He hoped.

Romey had already ordered a high-end tech to evaluate the security system. She'd also had it shut off, and a police system installed around the perimeter, afraid, she said, that the employees at Whitford Security might be monitoring the investigation.

Romey was methodical and she was thorough. Nyquist appreciated that.

He also appreciated the concentration she brought to his side of the case. As he told her about the deaths in the Hunting Club forest, she asked pointed questions about the evidence, the position of the bodies, and the weapon used.

It seemed that the weapons used in that crime and this one were similar.

Then he told her that the second body belonged to Enzio Lamfier of Whitford Security.

She let out a soft whistle. "No wonder you wanted on this case," she said. "Either Bowles got in the way of some Whitford-specific killing or Whitford and his man died because they were tied to Bowles."

Nyquist nodded. "That's two working theories. I'm hoping there are no more dead Whitford bodies around town, but I'm not even sure of that. Have you been to their offices yet?"

"I had them locked down," she said. "The staff remains until we get there."

"I suppose that's where we should go next," Nyquist said. "Unless there's more here that you need to see."

He was letting her remain in charge on the Whitford side of the case. If it became clear that Whitford was the target, then she could be the main investigator, no matter what Gumiela said. It was only fair. The responding detective had the right to close the case.

But if it turned out that this was, indeed, about Bowles, then he would take all the glory.

And all the criticism.

Romey tilted her head. She was one of those people who seemed to move whenever she got a message across her links. Apparently, her system hadn't shut down the way his had.

"Message?" he asked. "I thought all outside communication was blocked by the jammers across the property."

"But apparently not internal communication," she said. "That was one of the techs. They found something when they picked up Whitford's body."

She had told Nyquist before that she had suspected there was something under the body. There was no reason for the furniture in the main room to be so haphazard or the body to be left in that odd position.

She hurried inside. Even though she was significantly shorter than he was, Nyquist almost had to run to keep up.

The coroner's office had the body on a gurney. A slimy stain, vaguely human shaped, still covered the floor. And beneath it, a square etched into the tiles.

"That's not a design," said a tech that Nyquist didn't recognize. "It clearly opens. We ran some equipment over it. It's not part of the floor. It's hollow down there."

Hollow. Fascinating. Nyquist knew what order he'd give, but he waited for Romey to do it.

"You got everything you need from the floor's surface?" she asked the tech.

"Yeah," he said.

"Then let's open this thing."

The tech bent over. He reached around the edges of the square with his gloved hands, looking for a latch, and clearly finding none. He tapped nearby tiles, then reached into his kit for a crowbar.

"Before you ruin the floor," Nyquist said, "check with the guy examining the security system. See if there's some kind of command that opens this thing."

"It'll take forever to find," Romey said.

Nyquist just raised his eyebrows at her. She met his gaze, then shook her head and sighed.

"Check," she said to the tech.

He handed her the crowbar. She tried to hand it to Nyquist but he backed away. Instead, he walked over to the wall.

The concrete looked Earth-made, which meant it was heavy. A hollow floor couldn't sustain this kind of weight. So only that small section had to open.

It would seem unwieldy to hide the opening in the floor's design, then make the opening contingent on the security system. Not just unwieldy but dangerous as well.

If the security system shut down, anyone who had gone inside the hollow space would be trapped down there.

Nyquist looked at the concrete, trying to see a variation in its pattern. He found none. Then he looked at the tiles leading up to the wall, and he spied one raised edge.

He tapped it with his left shoe.

There was a rumbling sound as the floor inside the square dropped away.

Romey swore and stepped back. "What the heck did you do?"

"I found the automatic door opener," he said.

She came over to his side and stared at the raised area. "You realize you contaminated the evidence."

"Oh, I doubt it," he said. "They should have examined it when they examined the room."

"Then why didn't they find the automatic opener, as you call it?"

"Because they didn't step on it," he said. "They worked around it, like they were supposed to do."

He walked to the large hole in the floor. The center part of the flooring—the door, for lack of a better term—had lowered and landed on the floor below. The mechanism that allowed it to go down also formed a rather rickety-looking staircase.

Nyquist tapped the back of his hand and started recording this part of the investigation. Romey did the same.

"I'm going down there," Nyquist said.

"We should wait for the techs to come back," Romey said.

"I've been waiting too much in this investigation," Nyquist said. "I want to see what we have down here, and why someone felt it was necessary to put Whitford's body over this opening."

"You think it was a message?"

"I don't think it was a coincidence," Nyquist said.

He put a foot on the top step. He had been right; it was rickety. He eased his way down, making sure he kept his balance. As he got deeper into the hole, lights came on, and he heard the whoosh of an environmental system.

He also heard pinging, and it took him a moment to realize that was internal.

His links had come back on.

He stopped, about to shut them down, when he realized he had half a dozen messages from Miles Flint, the last of them urgent.

Nyquist's stomach clenched. All he and Flint had in common these days was DeRicci.

Nyquist paused so that he could access Flint's message. He didn't want to listen and go deeper into that hole at the same time. He was afraid he might miss something—on both counts.

The message had come from Flint's internal link. There was no visual attached to it, just Flint's distinctive inflections: *I know about Bowles and I have some information to trade that you might not get anywhere else. Contact me immediately.*

It should have surprised Nyquist that Flint was involved somehow in this investigation, but it didn't.

Ever since he'd met the man, Nyquist had realized that Flint knew more about most things than most people— including people who were paid to know.

And so far, Flint hadn't steered him wrong in an investigation. Although his behavior had seemed suspicious at times.

"You okay?" Romey asked.

Nyquist nodded. He moved the message aside—no matter how urgent Flint thought his knowledge was, it paled compared to this—and went down the last few steps, careful to keep his balance.

The room was the same size as the square. Obviously it was part of the bunker, made either to hide someone who was in danger or to store information.

Or both. The tile floor, with its bloodstains, seemed to cover a matching floor, but Nyquist couldn't be certain. The walls were made of the same concrete as above.

It bothered him that his links worked down here. The jammers should have kept all but the emergency links off— even with the security system down.

And it was colder down here than it should have been. The air smelled musty.

If this was supposed to be an area where someone could safely hide, the environmental systems should be top grade. Instead, they seemed to have failed.

"Find anything?" Romey asked.

"No," Nyquist said.

He looked around, examined the area above, then the floor again, but saw nothing unusual.

Finally he climbed out of the square hole and back into the main part of the living area. The internal pinging shut off.

"My links work down there," he said.

"They do?" she asked.

He nodded.

She peered down as if the hole held obvious answers. "They shouldn't work at all."

"I know," he said. "The air seems old, too. There's something odd about it."

"Let me look," she said, and before he could respond, she went down the steps.

He watched her reexamine everything he had looked at. She gently used her gloved hands to examine the wall, and then she crouched.

She leaned forward, and there was a bang. Then the floor rose and slammed into place. Only she didn't rise with it.

She should have. That floor covered the base of the hole, and she had been standing on that base.

"Romey?" he shouted. "You okay?"

She didn't answer. Or maybe she couldn't.

He sprinted across the floor to the automatic opener, but as he was about to press it, the bang repeated itself.

The floor fell open, and he heard Savita Romey laugh.

"This is brilliant," she said.

He walked back to the hole, as if she hadn't scared him to death.

He peered inside. "What the hell just happened?"

"The floor doesn't fall," she said. "It only looks like it does. It slides under another part of the floor. When everything closes, lights come on along the walls. It's yet another security system. Or maybe a storage area."

"Did your links work when it closed up?" he asked.

"Yeah," she said. "And you'd think they wouldn't. Someone can trace you through links."

"So maybe it's not designed to hide people, but things," he said.

"Or maybe it's malfunctioning," she said.

He sighed. "We need more techs."

"Everything about this case seems to be about techs," she said, "and I have a hunch it's only going to get worse."

26

DeRicci turned to the third report without looking at the raw data again.

So this time, she was surprised to find that the information was about power glitches in the Port of Armstrong.

The power glitches were minor, maybe two or three seconds long at their worst, just enough for a dimming of the lights and backup systems to start.

The port had enough of those glitches that it called in outside experts to examine the system. Those experts found nothing wrong with the port's systems, nor any reason the glitches should have happened.

Yet they had.

And the dates of the power losses coincided with the dates that the fifteen-year-old information vanished from the system.

Or at least, that was what it seemed like when computer records got traced. No one knew for certain when the information vanished.

It could have vanished ten years ago or during the week of the power glitches.

All the data stream told the researchers was that something in that data pool—where the information had been stored—had been either accessed or removed during that period of time.

Or, as one researcher noted, someone *tried* to access or remove the information during that period of time.

No one knew for certain.

DeRicci put a hand to her forehead. Her stomach was in knots. Something about this series of reports bothered her, and it wasn't just that the raw data was too technical for her to understand.

She could get someone whose expertise she trusted to look at the material.

What bothered her was that all of this seemed important, but she couldn't tell at first glance what the importance was.

Usually security breaches were pretty clear cut. A member of a species without access to the Earth Alliance had gotten stuck in holding at the port. A bomb threat against Gagarin Dome. A murder threat against the governor-general.

DeRicci had dealt with all of that and more, and while it might have seemed difficult while the case was ongoing, her understanding of the security breaches was easy.

She wasn't even sure whether this was important.

Although the loss of banking records and port records was troubling.

She turned to the last three reports and saw more of the same. Those reports, written by analysts farther up the food chain, tried to put the three disparate pieces of information together, to show why there could be a threat.

These were the kinds of reports she hated. And these three reports were the kind that had caused her to examine the raw data herself before reading reports.

Sometimes she thought the midlevel analysts were hired for their imagination, not for their knowledge. They could make up a threat where none existed or they could completely miss the real threat for some imaginary threat.

She skimmed these reports, seeing very little worthwhile in them except that the three separate analysts, working without contact to each other, were as disturbed by the preceding three information reports and the raw data as she had been.

Because during the time she'd been looking at the reports, she wondered whether the sense of unease that she felt had come from the resurrection of Ki Bowles's news story or the reports themselves.

That separate analysts who had nothing to do with each other had the same sense of unease that she had made her feel better.

Or worse, depending on how immediate the threat seemed.

DeRicci wasn't sure how immediate this threat was or wasn't.

Because she didn't know exactly what was missing.

And neither did her analysts.

They had tried to dig through existing files, but they hadn't found anything out.

She was going to do an old-fashioned investigation.

She was going to see exactly what information had vanished—and she hoped that would tell her why.

27

The problem with coming to the basement cafeteria in the law school, Flint realized as he slid into his favorite booth, was that he couldn't let Talia watch him log in.

The research setup in the cafeteria presupposed that whoever used the law school's networked systems had a university charge account. Flint did: He had set it up years ago, and he paid it anonymously. But the setup had been illegal—he'd just hacked into the system and invented an account.

And he didn't use that account for anything except entry into the cafeteria and charging food while he was here. To access the research network, he used stolen identifications from existing law students. Since they didn't pay for the research time, just the food in the cafeteria, he wasn't really stealing from them. He was just hiding his research under their names.

He hadn't thought twice about the system until this afternoon, with his daughter beside him.

"Check out the food displays," he said. "See what you want."

"It all looks plastic," she said.

It did. The law school cafeteria took up the entire basement of the law school not because the food was spectacular—it wasn't—but because the coffee and pastries were free. Law students could survive for months on coffee and pastries, and many did.

"Look at the menu, then," he said. "We have to order something every hour or so to keep the booth."

"That's a stupid rule," she said, but obligingly looked down at the tabletop. He used that moment to log in to the database using one of the stolen identifications.

Her hair had fallen over her face, but he could still see her frown. "This all looks awful."

"Oh well," he said. "Order something. We don't have to eat it."

"I'm not ordering for you. You can order for you."

"Fine," he said. "Get me coffee and some spaghetti."

He'd learned that the spaghetti was the least objectionable food in the cafeteria. Talia looked up, surprised at his choice, just as the log-in finished and the law school research network logo appeared on the beautifully backlit screen.

He had chosen this booth not just for its location near the serving trays (a location most students found to be loud and uncomfortable), but because the booth had large seat backs, making it almost impossible for anyone to spy on him while he worked.

Add to that the fact that the cafeteria used serving trays as their servers instead of humans or aliens, and this entire section of the cafeteria became one of the most private research spots in all of Armstrong.

"What're we looking for?" Talia asked.

"We're going to do a standard background run," Flint said. "But it's going to be a legal search."

"Which means what?" she asked.

"It means that we're doing the same kind of search a practicing lawyer would do. A lawyer might be looking for background on a witness or on a client. But each item has to come from a valid database."

Which hampered the search more often than not, but

Flint wanted accurate information on Bowles, so he didn't trust some of the looser research nets. He could always go to those later.

"Why does that matter?" Talia asked.

"The lawyer needs to have a reference for each piece of information. The lawyer doesn't want to be accused of obtaining information in a sketchy or illegal manner."

Flint could tell her these things aloud because the cafeteria was mostly empty. Midterms were just winding up. Two study groups sat in opposite corners of the cafeteria, arguing over various points. They were mixed—one group had humans and Peyti. The other were Peyti and Sequev.

Dome University's Armstrong campus had the most diverse law school in the sector. It also had the best reputation of any law school in the solar system.

The Peyti, who were known for their legal acumen, made it a point to study here. It had to be difficult for them. They had trouble with the oxygen atmosphere. Most wore complex breathing masks that they kept adjusting with their long fingers. Flint had seen more than one Peyti passed out during stressful weeks like midterms just because it couldn't breathe properly.

The Sequev couldn't look more different than the Peyti. The Sequev were eight-legged aliens not much larger than a small dog. In fact, in the Sequev/Peyti study group, the Sequev sat on the tabletop just so that they could hear the Peyti without asking them to remove the masks every time they spoke.

"Everything okay, Dad?" Talia asked, her voice filled with tension.

"We're safe here," he said, sliding back into the booth. So far as he knew, no one had ever been attacked in the law school, not even during the tense last weeks of the semester. It was difficult for nonstudents to get in. They had to have a pass, university identification, or be accompanied by someone with university identification.

Flint had his university ID. He also still had identification with his badge number on it, although he used that less and less. The Armstrong Police Department rarely updated its badge registry, and that had worked to his advantage so far.

A serving tray floated toward their table, hovering just above it. The tray carried two coffees and two spaghettis. Apparently Talia had gone for the same thing he had.

A little metal hand came off the bottom of the tray and reached to the top, grabbing the edge of a spaghetti plate, and sliding it off the tray. The tray wobbled for a moment, and Talia reached up to steady it.

"Don't touch it," Flint said.

She pulled her hand back.

"The things are precarious enough," he said. "You touch it, and the entire contents of the tray could end up on your lap."

"Has that happened to you?" she asked as she watched the metal hand drop the spaghetti plate onto the table.

"More than once," he said.

The hand managed to set the other plate near—not on—the first, and then put down the cups of coffee. It floated off before Flint could punch some extra time in the automatic pickup clock.

Midterms. He forgot. The cafeteria would be even more vigilante about people eating every hour or losing their seats.

"Okay," he said. "Ki Bowles. Why don't you see how much information this thing coughs up on her at the first request?"

"Me?" Talia squeaked.

"You may as well learn how to do research," he said with a grin, "since you're clearly so bad at it."

She stuck her tongue out at him, then leaned toward the screen.

"I set it up for no vocal commands," he said.

"So I what?"

"Open the touch keyboard at the bottom."

She did.

He took a bite of his spaghetti. It was too sweet and he doubted the cafeteria had used real tomatoes. The pasta was made from Moon flour, which made it stickier than pasta made with real flour. But he was hungry, and the food was adequate.

It took Talia a moment to figure out how to work the touch keyboard, but once she did, she had no trouble. The screen went dark for a moment, then came back with a list of legal citations.

"Wow," she said.

Flint leaned in. Wow was right. He'd expected date of birth, some kind of journalistic license, a few infractions like traffic tickets, but nothing like this.

"What is all that?" Talia asked.

"I'm not sure," he said. "Let's get this thing to organize the material by subject matter. Don't lose the original search, though. We might want to organize other ways, by date or something."

"Okay." Talia took a sip of her coffee, then touched her search parameters into the screen.

Flint's internal links beeped. Then Nyquist appeared in Flint's left eye.

"You alone?" Nyquist asked.

No, Flint sent back, using the nonverbal mode.

"Get somewhere where you can talk." Nyquist disappeared.

"I just got a message," Flint said. "I have to answer it. You'll be okay here. Make sure none of this material gets deleted, all right?"

"Can't I come with you?" Talia asked.

"You'll be able to see me," Flint said. "I'm going to the one corner of the cafeteria without a study group."

"I don't want you to leave me." Talia was clutching her coffee cup so hard that Flint thought she might break it.

"I'm going to be in the same room," he said. "Just a more private corner of it."

He got up before Talia could object again and walked

across the cafeteria to the pastry counter. Talia was right. The food inside did look plastic. He wondered how she'd been able to see that from so far away.

He slid into another booth and touched the screen. He knew how to hack into the university's secure system from here. He did so, then contacted Nyquist.

Flint used the privacy filter so that no one who happened past could see the screen. He kept the audio on low, so it would be impossible to hear outside the booth.

"This secure?" Nyquist asked as he appeared on the screen. He looked tired. There were deep shadows under his eyes.

There seemed to be trees behind him, but they weren't evenly spaced like the trees at the Hunting Club.

Flint couldn't quite figure out where Nyquist was.

"As secure as I can be in a public place," Flint said.

"How'd you know about Bowles?" No preamble, no niceties. Just the cop question.

"One of her security guards told me."

"What?" Nyquist looked startled. "Why you?"

"Because I was the one paying for her protection," Flint said.

"I thought you didn't like Ki Bowles."

"I didn't," Flint said.

"Then why would you pay for her security detail?"

"To keep her safe," Flint said. "And that's all you're going to get out of me until you give me something in return."

"One of her bodyguards was killed with her," Nyquist said.

"Tell me something I don't know."

"Along with Roshdi Whitford himself."

Flint leaned back in the booth. He wasn't sure how to play that. He knew that information, but it implicated the other guard.

But the guard was in police custody, so Nyquist would

eventually realize that Flint had known that bit of information before Nyquist revealed it.

"The bodyguard told me that as well," Flint said.

"Well, then you're ahead of me," Nyquist said. "This bodyguard have a name?"

"Pelham Monteith."

Nyquist nodded, as if he were making a mental note of the name. "So, do you have some other information for me?"

"In trade," Flint said.

"You know the department doesn't do that," Nyquist said.

"Of course you do." Flint leaned back in the booth. One of the serving trays came by and bumped him. He had to order to be here as well. "That's what informants are for."

"I can't give you anything," Nyquist said.

Flint pressed the top item on the menu in front of him, then punched in his number, not caring what he had just ordered. "Then we can't work together."

He moved broadly, as if he were going to sign off, when Nyquist asked, "Okay. What is it you want?"

"Leads when you have them in the Bowles case. I need to know if she's a random victim or if she was the target. I also need to know who targeted her."

"Why?" Nyquist asked.

"For the same reason I hired her protection," Flint said.

Nyquist frowned. "You in trouble?"

"I don't know," Flint said. "If you give me some information, I might be able to answer that question."

"What the hell did you involve her in? And why?"

"She's a good reporter," Flint said.

Nyquist's frown grew deeper. "You hired her for her skills?"

"Sometimes you take the best, even if you don't like their methods."

"For what?"

Flint grinned at him. "Think about it, Bartholomew. Then get back to me."

He was about to sign off when Nyquist held up a hand. "You're her source?"

"Of course not," Flint said. "How could I know anything about Wagner, Stuart, and Xendor?"

"Your closeness to . . ." Nyquist stopped speaking before he finished the thought. He finally put the information together. He knew that Flint had gotten some files from Paloma the day that she died. He also knew that Flint had never looked at those files.

Nyquist also knew that Flint hated Justinian Wagner, and was furious that no one would be punished for Paloma's death and the attack on Nyquist. They'd talked about it while Nyquist was still hospitalized.

Flint said someday Justinian Wagner had to pay for letting the assassins know where to find Paloma and her ex-husband, Claudius Wagner.

"You don't strike me as a revenge kinda guy," Nyquist said.

"You're right," Flint said. "I'm more a believer in justice."

Nyquist made a small dismissive sound. "Your justice might've just gotten a woman killed."

"Believe me," Flint said, "I am aware of that."

The serving tray appeared, covered with something that looked like a cross between vomit and peanuts. It smelled like green tea.

Flint made a face—he couldn't help himself—but let the serving tray place the food on the table. At least the stuff didn't smell all that bad. He just couldn't look at it.

"This stuff that you gave Bowles," Nyquist said, "is it—"

"I'm not saying I gave anything to Bowles," Flint said.

"You just said—"

"I just implied," Flint said.

"Oooo-kay." Nyquist spoke slowly, as if Flint were a crazy man. "This stuff you implied you had . . ."

"Didn't say I had it, either," Flint said.

Nyquist made that disgusted sound again. "This stuff

Bowles was using, this information, is there any way I can see it?"

"If she has copies," Flint said.

"You have to share something if you want information from me," Nyquist said.

Flint leaned closer to the screen. "I'm only going to say this once. Bowles and I made our deal before I found out about Talia. I need to know what happened to Bowles because . . ."

Nyquist closed his eyes, as if the realization just struck him. When he opened them again, his expression had some sympathy.

"I'll let you know if I think you're a target," Nyquist said. He paused, as if he were trying to figure out what to say next. Finally he settled on "Give me what you can, okay?"

"I will," Flint said, and signed off.

He sat in the booth a moment longer, staring at the vomit-covered peanuts. It had to be a Sequev dish. No human would eat anything that looked like that—at least, not voluntarily.

He shoved the plate away, and rubbed a hand over his face.

You didn't strike me as a revenge kinda guy, Nyquist had said.

Yet Flint was worried that his motives hadn't been as pure as he thought. He knew that Wagner wouldn't be punished for his parents' murder, so Flint had set this up, to punish the man in a way that would make him suffer the most.

That was a lot closer to revenge than justice.

Especially when you considered that it had gotten someone killed.

He sighed. It wasn't enough to tell himself that Ki Bowles had known what she had signed up for.

She hadn't, not really.

But then, neither had he.

28

Nyquist stood on the grounds just outside the Whitford estate, uncertain what to do next. Romey wanted to go to Whitford Securities—and she was right: Someone had to go there soon. There were employees to be interviewed, records to be examined, security systems to learn.

But, as usual, Nyquist's conversation with Flint left him unnerved. Flint always seemed to have a way of turning Nyquist's world around.

When Lucianna Stuart, aka Paloma, died six months ago, Miles Flint inherited her estate. This, despite the fact that she had two living sons, and an ex-husband whom, it turned out, she was still close to.

Justinian Wagner, the oldest Wagner son, threatened to fight Paloma's will in court, but after a few days Flint gave in. He said that Wagner could have anything from the estate that he wanted.

Flint even gave Wagner some disputed documents that, Flint said, washed his hands of the whole affair.

But now Flint had implied that he had more information on WSX than he should have had. And he implied that he had given that information to Ki Bowles, with the intent of bringing down Justinian Wagner and his empire.

No matter how much Flint denied it, a man only did things like that for revenge. Stupid fool, taking on the Wagners in any form.

Nyquist had already considered taking on the Wagners. He had been with Claudius Wagner, Justinian's father, when the Bixian assassins showed up to kill Claudius. Nyquist hadn't been able to save Claudius, but he had saved himself.

Claudius, who had been living under the name Charles Hawke, had taken his false name because some legal work he and Paloma had done had forced some victims of that work to hire Bixian assassins to kill Paloma and Claudius. Bixian assassins, while good at killing, weren't good at human legal systems; the assassins couldn't find any human who adopted a new name.

But Justinian had given Claudius's and Paloma's new names to the Bixians.

It was an efficient—and legal—way to make sure that assassins *someone else hired* took out his parents.

There was no way to prove malice or conspiracy to commit murder. There simply was no way to defeat the man within the law. Nyquist didn't care enough—even after the attack—to try something extralegal.

And he thought Flint would leave things alone as well. After all, Nyquist knew that Flint wasn't a killer. Or, perhaps put more accurately, Flint was a reluctant killer, like most police officers. He would shoot in the line of duty, but not out of cold blood.

This revealing background stuff, the stuff Bowles had hinted at in her first story, had to have come from Flint. And something in it was strong enough to bring down WSX—at least in Flint's mind.

And he might have been right.

After all, it could have gotten Bowles killed.

Which was what led to Nyquist's dilemma. The discovery of the connection to Whitford Securities made it seem as if Bowles had been an innocent bystander.

But now Nyquist's first theory was in play again:

Bowles's death happened because she had somehow messed with WSX.

He wanted to examine everything in Bowles's research files. Even though Flint claimed he couldn't tell Nyquist anything, he also implied that the information was there.

Which meant that Bowles had it.

All Nyquist had to do was find it.

Romey drove an air car out of the gates. She looked taller when she was driving a vehicle. She hovered only a few centimeters from the ground, and leaned out the window.

"Let's go," she said.

He shook his head. "I just got some information from an informant that leads me back to Bowles again. I'm going to dig into her files for a bit. Can you handle Whitford Securities without me?"

She grinned.

"Of course I can." Then her grin faded. "But you are going to tell me what your informant said."

"If it pans out," Nyquist said.

She gave him a sideways glance that was one part mocking and two parts disbelieving. And then she drove off without saying another word.

He pivoted and started back to the gate, where his own air car waited.

As he did, his links pinged.

Andrea Gumiela appeared before him, all head and neck against the gate itself. She looked even more frazzled than she had a few hours before.

"Your time is up," she said to him. "I don't know how they found out, but they did. The jackals have descended. And it's bloody out there."

It took Nyquist a moment to understand what she was saying. "The media knows that Bowles is dead?"

"Yep. And to them, that's a bigger story than Roshdi Whitford. They're going to be all over this, and all over you. I just wanted to warn you."

He sighed. "You told them about Whitford to throw them off?"'

"They already knew about Whitford," she said. "They were interested until someone found out about Bowles. The rumors spread, and then they became truth. It's all been in the last five minutes or so. I'm heading to the press conference now. The only choice you get is this one: Do you want me to release your name now as lead detective or do you want me to wait until tomorrow?"

"Tomorrow," he said. "So long as you think they're not going to suss me out, too."

"Who knows?" Gumiela said, brushing some hair off her forehead with one well-manicured hand.

"Well, tell me this before you go. Do they know that Bowles's death and Whitford's are tied?"

"Doubt it or they would have had more interest in Whitford. But I'm not sure. I'll know more after the press conference. Of course, they will, too." She gave him a tired smile. "And so the insanity begins. Have fun."

And with that, she vanished.

He rubbed his thumb and forefinger against the bridge of his nose, feeling some old scars that hadn't yet been lasered away. He liked the roughness between his fingers; he might request that those nearly invisible scars remain.

They reminded him that he was human and vulnerable, although on afternoons like this, he didn't need that big a reminder.

Then Gumiela reappeared against the gate. The size of her head unnerved him. He wished they had the kind of relationship where he could tell her to adjust her settings.

"One more thing," she said. "Are you and Romey headed to Whitford Security?"

"Romey is."

"You two fight already?"

"I have a new lead on Bowles," he said.

"Well, tell Romey there've been some blips in the power

grid near Whitford. Tell her I have no idea what that means, just that it's happening."

Then Gumiela vanished again.

Nyquist frowned. Blips in the power grid? The power grid was the most stable part of Armstrong's infrastructure. It had to be. It kept the dome running, and the environmental controls working.

If the power grid failed, the entire dome had backup generators that powered the dome for two days before it failed.

He tried to ping Gumiela but she had really and truly signed off this time. She was probably already in front of cameras, giving one of her spirited press conferences.

He would forward the message to Romey, and explain that he knew nothing. Then he would put it out of his mind until he saw DeRicci next.

She would know what intermittent power failures meant. She would know whether that was truly dangerous or just a maintenance problem.

Gumiela probably only noticed the whole thing because of the proximity to Whitford.

Nyquist sent a message to Romey, asking her to contact him as soon as she received it.

Then he went inside the gate and got into his car, knowing Bowles needed his full concentration—and not sure he could give her even half of that.

29

Justinian Wagner was just completing a holo meeting with the board of directors for one of his largest clients when his assistant broke into the conference room.

"You have to see this," the assistant said.

Wagner's breath caught. The assistant had just violated an entire set of company rules.

First, he'd barged into a closed conference with a half dozen people, all holographic reproductions, but still, there—a presence, even if they weren't actually on-site.

Then he had given Wagner an order—*You have to see this*—not a request, not an "excuse me." Just a "you have to."

And finally he hadn't followed protocol. And Wagner had made it a condition of the hire that everyone in WSX knew protocol. For some clients, protocol was more important than actual knowledge of the law.

He turned, about to rebuke the assistant—what was his name? Wagner couldn't remember. Every assistant seemed the same to him—when the young man did it again.

"Sir, please. It's important."

Better, but still not protocol. And what Wagner had taken for enthusiasm seemed more like terror.

He turned his back on the assistant, facing the group

before him. Their conference room—all teak and ma-
hogany—was superimposed over his.

"I do believe we're done for the moment," Wagner said.
"I thank you all for your time and your consideration. We
will find out what happened, and I can assure you nothing
like this will ever happen again."

Each board member made some reassuring noise.
The chairperson nodded, and then the conference room
winked out.

Wagner turned, about to launch into his own assistant, but
the young man was gone. The door was open, though, and
he heard voices from the outer office.

He stepped out, the rebuke on his tongue, and stopped
when he saw every screen in the waiting area activated, each
on a different newscast.

Conflicting images of Ki Bowles filled the screens. In
some she was young. In others, she had strawberry blond
hair. In still others she was bald and her tattoos—cheap but
attractive—stood out in strong relief against her cheeks.

He had to concentrate to catch any words.

". . . murdered in the grounds of the Hunting Club . . .

". . . despite the presence of a bodyguard . . .

". . . slashed almost beyond recognition . . ."

"What?" he asked, stepping closer.

Half the staff seemed to be in this room. The human staff,
anyway. The Peyti had no business in human affairs, and the
androids of course had no curiosity.

"What is this?" Wagner asked.

"Ki Bowles," said his assistant. "She's dead."

Wagner stared at the screens. On some images, Bowles
was talking in the background, sitting behind a desk. In others, she stood against various backdrops, including one just
outside the grounds of the Hunting Club.

No one showed the report he had memorized, the report
he had been dealing with all damn day.

"Dead," he repeated. The word didn't quite go in.

"Murdered," one of the young lawyers said with a little too much relish.

"By whom?" Wagner asked.

Collective shrugs around the room. But his assistant, who apparently had no fear of him, said, "They'll probably look at us."

The gasp around the room seemed to belong to no one and everyone. Wagner stiffened.

Bowles's last story was about WSX.

WSX was known for being ruthless.

His assistant was probably right.

"Nonsense," Wagner said. "If we were going to take action against this Bowles woman, we would sue her. In fact, we already have several cases started. At least that was what I ordered. I'm assuming each department stepped up."

Various heads nodded around the room. He didn't feel reassured.

His stomach ached. There was bile in his throat. He felt ill.

But he couldn't excuse himself, not yet. To do so would be to show weakness, and he didn't dare do that in front of his staff.

"We're being set up," he said.

"Sir?" His assistant came forward.

Wagner blinked. He hadn't realized he had spoken out loud. But he had.

They were being set up. First by Bowles with that horrible news story. Then by whoever killed her. People had short memories. The media had even shorter memories.

They would think that Bowles's death—which might have been just a mugging gone wrong—was tied to WSX.

What the public would think—what the media would imply—was that instead of going after Bowles legally, making sure she wasn't inventing the entire thing, WSX went straight to the worst option.

WSX didn't sue or take her to court.

WSX didn't try to destroy her in the media.

WSX had her killed.

Wagner cursed.

It had suddenly become less important to learn how Bowles had gotten her information and more important to learn how she died.

Wagner would have to use one of his in-house detectives.

But that might backfire as well.

He needed a plan. He didn't have a plan.

He was reacting to everyone else's plan. Everyone else's questions. Everyone else's fears.

People came to lawyers for rationality, for calmness, for cold calculating reasoning.

At the moment, he wasn't cold or calculating.

He was as panicked as his clients usually were.

He needed to think.

Wagner turned his back on the screens and headed to his office.

He needed to regain his rational self.

He needed to become Justinian Wagner, head of the biggest law firm in the Earth Alliance.

He needed to figure out exactly who was trying to hurt him, and then he had to hurt them back.

30

Flint returned to the booth. He surveyed the room before he sat down, and saw one of the Sequev sneak over to the table Flint had used to contact Nyquist. With one of its eight limbs, the Sequev grabbed the plate of food Flint had left, hiding the plate under its—armpit? Flint didn't know the exact terminology—as it scurried back across the room.

Otherwise there wasn't much movement. The human/Peyti study group seemed to be arguing, and the Peyti/Sequev group was using its own screen to check sources.

Flint slid into the booth. Talia was staring at their screen, her fingers threaded through her curls.

"This isn't what I wanted," she said, staring at the legal notations in front of her.

"What is it?" He had to get his head back into this part of the investigation.

"I don't know what it is," Talia said. "It's really technical."

That caught Flint's attention. Most legal documents, while written in legalese, were relatively easy to understand.

"What do you mean?"

"I mean, like, there's half a dozen injunctions here, and a lot of orders of protection and a few—I don't know—criminal things? And I can't tell if they're for Bowles or against her or what. It seems to contradict itself."

Flint's mouth opened. He hadn't expected a legal history that extended through dozens of cases.

"Each case is different," he said as he turned toward the screen. "She could have had an injunction placed against her at the same time that she had placed an injunction against someone else."

"Why?" Talia asked.

"Don't know yet," Flint said. "But I do know that such things are common in messy divorce cases. One party claims that the other is harassing them, the other party issues an injunction to prove that *they're* the one being harassed, so the first party does the same for the same reason."

"How do you figure out what's true?" Talia asked.

"I don't," Flint said, "at least not anymore. I had to a few times as a detective. It's not fun."

"Sounds weird," Talia said. "Weird" appeared to be her word for the day.

"It's annoying. Because usually no one is being harassed—except maybe the legal system."

He thumbed through the screen listings. For. Against. Plaintiff, Defendant.

He reset the search parameters, looking for cases where Bowles asked for the injunction.

"How does this help?" Talia asked.

"Watch," Flint said.

Three cases appeared, along with links to various other related cases.

In all three, Bowles had asked for an injunction against someone. All three someones had different names, and all three injunctions were issued at different times, but the reasons for the injunctions were the same:

She was being stalked.

"Here it is," he said, pointing to the relevant passages. "Someone was after her, as recently as last year."

Orders of protection, injunctions, and some stalking violations, but nothing solid or nothing that seemed solid. Except that one of the cases was scheduled to go to court in six months.

"Prosecuting a stalker," he muttered.

"What?" Talia asked.

"She pressed charges against someone under the harassment and stalking laws. It was going to trial relatively soon."

"You think the stalker got her?" Talia asked.

"It's a possibility." He pressed a side button and got the information on the stalking cases on a small chip that he could insert into his own systems. He put the chip in his pocket.

Then he switched to another search. He wanted to see why people had issued injunctions against Bowles.

"Shouldn't you be following the link on the stalker?" Talia asked.

"In a minute," Flint said.

He was staring at a series of injunctions and as he did, he realized that Talia was right; they were extremely technical. It took him a while to figure out that they were injunctions, not just against Bowles, but against InterDome.

Someone hadn't liked an investigation that Bowles had been conducting.

Several someones in fact.

He had thought there might be a couple of people who wanted Bowles dead. He just hadn't expected there to be so many of them.

And he hadn't even gone through the nonharassment, nonstalking, noninjunction cases.

"We need separate screens," he said to Talia.

"What for?" She apparently was thinking that he was going off to have another private conversation, leaving her alone again.

"There's too much material here, and we haven't even gotten to the public records. We have to go through all of it."

"All of it?" Talia asked. She seemed intrigued now.

He nodded.

"You think this stuff is important?"

"Until just now, Van Alen and I assumed that Bowles's death had to do with our case. But that's closing our eyes to all of this." He shook his head. "The woman had more enemies than anyone outside of politics."

Talia let out a small sigh of relief. "Does that mean we're safe?"

Flint looked at her, feeling the urge to lie, and realizing that it would do nothing more than make him feel better.

"It means we have a chance at being safe," he said. "But let's make sure before we relax our guard, okay?"

Talia flopped back against the booth. She tapped her fingers on the table.

"Okay," she said, as if this was all his fault.

Which, he suddenly realized, it was.

31

The Whitford Security offices were housed in one of the newest sections of the dome. The dome had been rebuilt here after a bombing almost three years ago. The building looked new, too, even if it was yet another concrete monstrosity with no windows.

The building had been locked down for most of the afternoon. Street cops and police security bots ringed the building's outside. A handful more guarded the parking lot.

Savita Romey parked her own car on the street in front of the building—if the street could truly be considered in front of the building. Even the building's doors were hard to see. The concrete exterior had some kind of weird paint or surface covering that made it reflect the colors being filtered through the dome.

Since the dome was still in Dome Daylight, the building itself looked yellow and Moon brown with just a hint of the blackness of space.

"Front door?" she asked one of the street cops. He handed her a small device that she could press her fist into before he answered. The device confirmed her identity.

And like a good cop on security detail, he actually

looked at the device before he pointed her to a corner of the building.

She thought she had seen the outline of the door near the end of the sidewalk, but his point was nowhere near that faint outline.

Still, she followed the man's gesture, and realized what she'd been seeing as she got closer.

What she had taken for the door's outline was really that, an outline etched into the concrete surface. She would wager there were two or three other outlines on other sides of the building.

She'd heard about the idea, but she'd never seen it in practice. Theoretically, a visible door outline at the end of a sidewalk would distract a perpetrator, and give whoever was inside a chance to either get away from him or secure the existing doors.

It wasn't until she reached the building's corner that the door revealed itself. Its outline appeared in the concrete, surprising her by covering the corner itself.

She shoved her fist against the identification node that opened at waist level. Lights revolved around the exterior of the node, a kind of wink-wink acknowledgment that the identification process was working.

But if it had been working properly, the door would have opened for her by now. What was really going on was that someone inside had seen her identification and had to approve the opening of the door.

Finally the entire corner moved away from her, revealing blackness inside.

For the first time since Nyquist had told her that he wasn't coming with her, she felt uncomfortable. Before she'd been elated that she was working on her own again.

But now she was going into a strange building with a dark interior, filled with angry security personnel.

She stopped, turned, and beckoned two of the street cops to join her.

They looked at each other, clearly surprised.

She was about to send a message to them on their links, along with a reminder that the detective controlled the scene, when they both ran toward her.

They were both men, both much larger than she was, although she would have wagered that the man on her left didn't have half of her strength.

"Sir?" asked the one on her right, clearly awaiting instructions.

"It's Detective Romey," she said, hating the whole sir designation. "You two are going to back me up. Have someone fill that hole you left in the perimeter."

The guy on her right started to head back, obviously to tell someone to take his place, when she caught his arm.

"Via your link, Officer . . . ?"

"Zurik," he said. "And this is Officer Novello."

He nodded toward the big guy still standing on Romey's left.

"Pleasure," she said in a dry tone. She hadn't meant for a full-fledged introduction. "Just follow me, keep an eye out for trouble, and do what I tell you."

"Yes, sir," Zurik said.

"Detective Romey," she said again. "Call me sir one more time and I'll put a notation on your record."

"Yes—" He caught himself before the "sir." She could see him try to substitute "ma'am" or some other honorific before he settled on— "Detective."

She nodded once and stepped inside.

The air smelled faintly of mint, which she knew was supposed to have calming properties. She found that interesting. The place was set up like a fortress and designed to repel an attack, no matter how small.

The street cops followed her, and the door closed behind them. At that moment, the lights came on full.

So the darkness was a twofold security design. It put the guest off balance and it prevented anyone standing outside the building from seeing in and noting the layout.

Paranoid. But smart.

She passed the first corner, which branched into a hall-way that turned left, and was looking for signage when a woman appeared seemingly from nowhere.

Romey had seen that trick before. There was a filter built into the hallway, and employees stepped through it, giving no hint of their presence—from sound to smell—until they just appeared.

"Detective Romey." Like most people, the woman was taller than Romey. She was also thinner, but the kind of thin that came from enhancements and not eating enough, not the kind that came from remaining in shape. "I'm to take you to our vice president in charge of operations."

"You're to take me to a conference room where you'll as-semble the staff," Romey said.

"We don't put our people in the same room," the woman said.

"Well, you do now," Romey said. "Find some place, put them there, and let them know I'll be coming to talk with them."

The woman stared at Romey, obviously confused by the order.

"Is there a problem?" Romey asked.

"I'm sorry," the woman said. "It's just that we're told not to do this under any circumstance."

"I'm not a circumstance," Romey said. "I'm the Arm-strong Police Department, and I trump any orders given by any boss. If your staff has trouble with that, I can send them all en masse to jail. Would that please you?"

"Our lawyers—"

"Are irrelevant," Romey said. "I'm not going to detain you people. I'm going to question you about Roshdi Whit-ford's death. Now, unless he died from some kind of con-spiracy involving every member of this company, most of your staff have nothing to worry about from me—unless you make sure they don't follow my orders."

The woman's eyes opened wide. Romey couldn't tell if she was communicating to someone higher up on a link or if she was just one of those people whose eyes got wider when she was surprised.

"I'll send the order," she said. "Come with me."

She didn't go through the filter. Instead, she walked to the next corner—this one on the right—and turned down the right-angled hallway.

Romey turned her head slightly and noted that her street cops were following. Good. She might need them.

"How many employees do you have?" she asked as they walked.

"Here or abroad?" the woman asked.

Abroad. That was a term Romey hadn't heard outside Earth.

"In the building," she said.

"At present . . ." This time the woman's pause was obvious. ". . . two hundred and fifty-seven."

"And how many are employed in Armstrong?"

"We don't give out that information," the woman said.

"What's your name?" Romey snapped.

"Um, Sally Juhl," the woman said.

"And your position here?" Romey asked.

"I'm liaison to the senior staff."

"The senior staff," Romey repeated. "I trust that includes Roshdi Whitford."

"No. He has his own assistants."

"Is that what a liaison is?" Romey asked. "An assistant?"

"No, I actually serve as a communications and business coordinator for the members of the senior staff. They're not allowed to hire their own assistants." She bit her lower lip, as if she'd said too much.

"Well, Ms. Sally Juhl, Liaison to the Senior Staff, you are now allowed to give out any and all information to me."

"I'm so sorry, ma'am," Juhl said. "I just can't. Almost everything we do here is proprietary."

"We don't care about your proprietary information. The owner of this company is dead. Doesn't that matter to you?"

"He warned us that that might happen," she said.

"Excuse me." Romey grabbed the woman's arm, stopping her from continuing down the hall. "What did you just say?"

"He warned us that he might die," Juhl said.

"When?" Romey asked.

"When he hired us. He said this is a cutthroat business. If we join it, we have to be willing to give a hundred-thousand percent. And that included our lives. He said that he was always ready to give his life. That's what made him good at what he did."

"Do you think he died protecting someone?" Romey asked.

"I don't know," Juhl said. "We're not allowed to know. That's what the officer who locked us down said. We know that Mr. Whitford is dead, that he died at home, and that we have lost two other employees although we don't know who they are yet, either."

At least the officer who closed the place down had done his job. Romey let Juhl's arm go.

"That's right, isn't it?" Juhl asked, absently rubbing the place where Romey's fingers had been. "We're not supposed to know, right?"

"The less you know the better I can interview," Romey said. She turned to Officer Zurik. "Send for some backup. I can't cover two-hundred-some-odd employees on my own. And get some techs in here, preferably ones who know something about security systems."

"Yes . . . Detective." He nodded, then stepped back, obviously planning to go outside to send the message.

"In here," Romey snapped. "We don't have a lot of time."

"Yes, sir. Ma'am. Detective. I'm sorry, sir."

Romey narrowed her eyes but didn't say anything. Instead she turned toward Juhl.

"Lead me to your colleagues," Romey said.

"I don't have colleagues per se," Juhl said. "I'm the only liaison on staff."

Romey wanted to shake her. But if Romey tried, she'd probably snap her like a brittle bread stick.

"The other employees," Romey said through her teeth. She'd already decided that some junior detective was going to interview this woman. Romey would probably kill her before the interview was done.

"Oh yes, right," Juhl said. "I think they've assembled now. Come with me."

And she finally stepped through one of the filters, holding the edge of it so that Romey could step inside.

Romey had a sense that Juhl could have done this at any point, taken them directly to the entire staff trapped inside the building, but had been stalling in the mazelike corridors, probably on someone's instruction.

Romey would find out who that someone was. Just like she was going to find out how this creepy place worked. And she was going to find out just why there were so many human staffers on the premises.

But most of all, she was going to find out what had initially caused the companywide paranoia, and whether it was related to Roshdi Whitford's death.

32

Rudra Popova still made DeRicci nervous. Even though they had worked together for almost a year now, Popova still had a look that could make DeRicci uncomfortable.

Part of it was that Popova was one of those brilliant women who also knew how to look beautiful ninety percent of the time. Add to that the fact that Popova had more formal training in security, analysis, and government than De-Ricci, and that had made both of them uncomfortable from the beginning.

DeRicci had to repeatedly remind herself that *she* was the Chief of Security for the United Domes of the Moon, not Rudra Popova. Popova was her assistant, and a damned good one.

But it still made DeRicci uncomfortable to watch Popova come through the doors to her office, looking well put together in a black dress and black flats that matched her long black hair. She clutched a pile of handhelds—and she looked frazzled.

Popova set the handhelds on DeRicci's desk.

"They're nut balls," Popova said. "All of them."

DeRicci nodded. Popova was referring to a small band of people who backed up the public information network onto private sites. Although to call these people a band was actually wrong. They didn't associate. Sometimes they even fought.

They were individualists. Some of them were very crazy, convinced that the changing information was filling up with lies that would eventually bring down the universe. Others were just paranoid, afraid that the changing information would cause the most valuable information to be deleted.

And a handful were archivists, who believed that information—whether it was accurate or not—needed a secondary backup in case something went wrong.

DeRicci had had Popova and a small team visit all of them, hoping to cajole the information from them. She wanted the records from that week fifteen years ago. She wanted to compare it all to what was available now.

"One guy wouldn't open the door because I was from the government. He climbed to the second story of his house and threw water on me, telling me to go away."

"Water?" DeRicci asked.

"I can't explain it," Popova said. "Then another guy deleted everything he had when he heard where I was from. He just destroyed it while I was standing there."

She sank into the nearest chair. "I hope this information is important."

It was comments like the last one, spoken in that superior tone, that had made DeRicci dislike Popova at first. Now that they knew each other, DeRicci realized Popova used that tone when she was the most uncomfortable.

"I hope it is, too," DeRicci said. "Which one of these comes from the archivists?"

"Those are the only ones I brought you," Popova said. "They don't save every site and they don't save every piece of information, so I tried to bring you the broadest range. I hope that's okay."

"It is," DeRicci said. "I might have to send you back out for the other stuff, though."

Popova shook her head. "Fortunately, I had enough

foresight to collect the information from the true crazies when I saw them. I marked their handhelds and I'll give them to you when you want."

"Not yet." DeRicci slid the top handheld toward her. She flicked on the handheld and watched information scroll along the tiny screen.

"In my absence," Popova said, "we got some more reports."

DeRicci looked up. Another crisis? Or was it just this one? Not that DeRicci was entirely convinced lost information from fifteen years ago could be called a crisis. To her, it seemed more like a curiosity.

One that might blossom into something more important.

"What?" DeRicci asked.

"You know those power grid flickers that we noted in the old reports?" Popova asked.

DeRicci nodded.

"We've had several in the past two days."

"What?" DeRicci asked. "How come no one brought this to me before?"

"Because they're not gridwide. They're isolated. Only certain parts of the infrastructure were effected."

DeRicci set the handheld aside. It continued to scroll. She should probably have shut the damn thing off, but she wasn't ready to just yet.

"We separated out the grid a few years ago," DeRicci said. "After the dome explosion, when we realized that it would be better to have parts of the dome with power."

"Then I should find out where these isolated grid problems were," Popova said. "That might tell us something."

"Do that," DeRicci said. "Look to see if any of the affected businesses from fifteen years ago were in these grid areas."

"All right." Popova headed for the door.

"And one more thing," DeRicci said.

"What?" Popova asked.

"Check the power glitches against police incident reports for the past week."

Popova raised her eyebrows. "Interesting," she said, and walked out the door, closing it softly behind her.

DeRicci looked at the handhelds, feeling more disturbed than she had all day. Something was wrong, but her information was incomplete.

And the incomplete information was preventing her from knowing how great the threat was—at least intellectually. On a gut level, she had a feeling she was discovering something very important, something she should have been paying attention to for a long time.

But she didn't yet know what that something was.

33

Flint had always known that Ki Bowles skirted an edge. He was just surprised at how close she had come to falling off it.

Even though he had been personally satisfied when Inter-Dome fired Bowles for her story on Noelle DeRicci, he had had the passing thought—never expressed—that InterDome had overreacted.

After all, Bowles was a well-known investigative reporter, with more awards than any other reporter on Inter-Dome's staff.

But those awards had cost the company millions in legal fees and damage awards. It seemed that every case Bowles had investigated had resulted in at least one police report, and sometimes dozens.

More than one subject of a Bowles story had filed harassment and stalking suits. Even more subjects had filed libel and slander suits. And one had filed a suit alleging restraint of trade.

Flint felt his stomach twist. Shouldn't Van Alen have investigated all of this before agreeing with Flint that Bowles would be perfect to hire to do the story against

WSX? Or had Van Alen thought that Flint had done this work?

Of course, he didn't know how many other investigative reporters had similar records. Maybe it was just a liability of the profession. Maybe the aggression that Bowles and her colleagues brought to bear against the subjects of their investigations provoked these kinds of reactions.

More often than not, the libel and slander cases got dismissed. The restraint-of-trade case went further than he thought it would, but it, too, got tossed for lack of evidence.

But the lower-level cases—stalking, harassment—a number of those got settled, not in criminal court, but in civil, with a rather large judgment to the plaintiff.

Flint had handled these cases because they were so technical, letting Talia investigate the stalking cases that Bowles herself had brought.

She had used InterDome's attorneys for those as well, going after people who sent her letters, followed her around the city, and in two scary instances, let themselves into her apartment.

That was when Bowles had upgraded her security systems, but she hadn't—oddly, Flint thought—hired a security team. Maybe InterDome provided one.

The stalking cases went on for years, with depositions and witnesses. The injunctions were violated on a regular basis, and each time, Bowles went back to court seeking higher and higher orders of protection.

In one notable case, Bowles had told the judge: *If you don't do something—imprison this guy or ask him to leave Armstrong—he'll kill me. He'll find me in some public park or some place and go after me and there won't be anything I can do about it.*

Flint downloaded that information as well. Then he went into the deeper tier of court cases. The defamation cases, the plagiarism cases, the breach-of-contract suits. They revealed an interesting pattern:

InterDome settled the defamation cases, apparently as part of its cost of doing business. It defended Bowles in the plagiarism cases, and always won.

It initiated the breach-of-contract suits itself against Bowles. She never answered in court, and the cases were dropped.

Flint would have to investigate to see if those were simply negotiation tactics for a new contract or if they were something else entirely.

"God," Talia said after their fourth plate of spaghetti—the last three having left the table untouched, "she lived a really messy life."

"Most people do," Flint said.

Although most people's lives weren't this messy. He was finding this wealth of legal information on Bowles reassuring. It meant that there were so many possible causes of her death that he didn't worry quite as much about his own case anymore.

But he wasn't going to relax. Not yet.

He didn't want to let down his guard and have something awful happen to Talia.

"It seems every time we look at this stuff, there's more," Talia said.

"And we've only been looking at criminal and business cases," Flint said. "There's nothing personal yet."

"I thought there wouldn't be," Talia said.

"Divorce decrees are legal documents. So are marriage certificates, if they were issued here in Armstrong."

"Do you want me to look for those?" she asked.

He liked that better than having her dig through the history of a stalker. "Yeah. Look for any marriages, divorces, domestic partnerships, or birth records with her name on them. Then let's get a sense of her family."

"You think that's more important than some stalker?"

He looked across the table at his daughter. He didn't want to tell her that most murders were simple things, caused by some trauma within the family.

"I think they could be as important as some stalker," he said. "And more than that, I think the more we know about Ki Bowles, the better off we all are."

Too bad he hadn't thought of that when he hired her.

Too bad he'd hired her at all.

34

Maxine Van Alen was prepping her closing arguments for a child custody case involving the daughter of a Disappeared when the lights in her office flickered—and went out.

Her computer network remained up, however, giving dim light to the rest of the room. The office network was on a secondary grid, one that had passwords and locks and all kinds of protections, things for which she once thought she paid too much and now knew she hadn't paid enough.

She reached for her desk, meaning to feel her way out of the room, when the lights came back up.

She stood, her hand on the desk and her heart pounding.

The lights had done that same thing two years ago when an explosion had blown a hole in the dome. But she had heard the concussion—and worse, she had felt it. It had knocked her to the ground, even though it was nowhere near her offices.

This silent flickering somehow bothered her more.

Before she called her assistant, she checked the screen that was connected to her office network. Nothing seemed different than it had before.

Which bothered her. Shouldn't it have been different?

Shouldn't something have shown up when the backup system kicked in?

She pressed a chip on her wrist. Her interoffice link flared to life, chirruping as it did.

"Find me the best tech we have in the office at the moment," she said.

Then she signed off before her assistant had time to say anything.

Van Alen walked around her office, checking for other problems. Her hands were shaking, which bothered her. Usually nothing rattled her.

But this had.

She looked at the nonnetworked computers, where Flint often did his research. They remained off.

She wasn't about to turn them on, not yet.

Then she went to the window, and peered out at the street below.

People continued to walk by as if nothing had gone wrong. She heard no horns or sirens or screams, like she had that day the explosion had rocked the dome.

She heard nothing at all, and she should have, if other places suffered something similar.

That uneasiness grew. Was this power loss unique to her building?

She touched her chip again.

"And send me the office manager as well as someone from maintenance. Someone human."

Maintenance had a lot of androids and bots, as well as a few college students who worked in the nonlegal areas, approved through alien student visas. She never let the aliens upstairs. They had no keys and no real knowledge of what went on up here.

She hoped.

Obadiah Mankoff, Van Alen's office manager, peeked around the raised doors. He was slender to the point of gauntness and no matter how much Van Alen fed him, he never seemed to gain weight. His hair was thinning, too. It was as if he couldn't acquire any more substance than he already had.

"No," he said, "I don't know what caused it. Give me some time and I'll figure it out."

"Nothing on the public news nets?" Van Alen asked.

"Nothing that I've found. It's only been about two minutes since we had the glitch, Maxine."

He could talk to her like that because he was the most efficient employee she'd ever had. He'd worked his way up from low-level maintenance where he started ten years ago to office manager just six months before—just after Flint went through his marathon sessions of research here in the office.

Mankoff had been one of the few upper-level employees who hadn't questioned Van Alen about the man she was keeping in her office.

She had liked that discretion. Mankoff treated everything Van Alen did as normal, even if it wasn't.

"I'm wondering if this is isolated to us," Van Alen said.

"Why would that be?" Mankoff asked.

Van Alen wasn't going to tell him about Bowles or the research or Flint's fears for all of their safety. But she was going to make sure Mankoff took this little light flicker seriously.

"Send someone around the neighborhood to see if the other buildings had an issue," Van Alen said. "And make sure that tech gets here."

"Did something malfunction?" Mankoff asked.

"That's the point. Something didn't malfunction at all," Van Alen said. "Didn't you notice? The office network didn't go down at all."

"It's on a separate grid," Mankoff said.

"Within the building," Van Alen said. "If the power went out in the neighborhood, everything should have shifted— even momentarily—to backup energy."

Mankoff's mouth opened slightly. He clearly hadn't thought of that. He'd been dealing with other things—probably panicked employees who, like Van Alen, had flashed back on the dome explosion.

"That is odd," he said. "I'll see what I can find."

"I want someone good with networks now," Van Alen said.

"Our best went out to lunch before the glitch," Mankoff said.

"Then send our second best and have our best come here when he gets back."

"All right." Mankoff slid out the door, hurrying away, obviously trying to get everything done as fast as Van Alen wanted it.

She went back to the window. Maybe she should contact Flint.

But he had enough troubles with that daughter of his, and conducting what he thought was a necessary investigation of Bowles.

Still, Flint knew computers and networks and systems better than anyone Van Alen had ever met.

And he did ask her to tell him if something went wrong.

She sat down behind her desk and used her personal link to contact Miles Flint.

35

Nyquist pulled up outside Paloma's apartment building, using one of two emergency vehicle spaces. He hit the car's police code, so that any passing police vehicle knew he had the right to park here, and then he shut off the engine.

Once, the buildings in this exclusive section of Armstrong had violated city codes by butting up against the dome. But rich people like Paloma loved the view. The dome side of the apartments overlooked the Moonscape, as if they were part of the dome itself.

Nyquist had nearly died here.

This was the first time he had come back.

He leaned back in his seat, trying to ignore the twisting feeling in his stomach. Flint had brought him back here. Flint and his hints that Ki Bowles's murder was somehow related to the murders of Paloma and Charles Hawke, aka Claudius Wagner.

Nyquist's stomach twisted even more.

He tried not to think about those last hours in this building. Sometimes he dreamed about them, though.

He'd been interviewing Claudius Wagner. Wagner had been a tall, athletic man with a mane of silver hair. He had a patrician look, and he'd used it, staring down his hawklike nose at Nyquist.

Nyquist had turned to go, and then he'd seen Wagner near the door, shaking his right arm as if it were on fire. The man didn't scream, even though the pain had to be intense.

For instead of skin, he had a Bixian assassin wrapped around the bone.

Bixian assassins looked like a rope, except when they were killing. Then they turned into a whirling machine. Their scales flared, acting like individual knives, severing the skin and arteries with ease.

In his dreams, that whirling thing would detach from Wagner's arm and twirl toward Nyquist.

And then he would force himself to wake up, his heart pounding.

His heart was pounding now.

But there was more than the dream. He needed to remember the case.

Once Nyquist became a victim of the same assassins that had killed Wagner, Gumiela had taken Nyquist off the case. At the time, he hadn't cared. He didn't want to think about it.

Instead, he wanted to concentrate on getting well.

So Gumiela had assigned a junior detective to the case, and that fact alone proved to Nyquist that Gumiela didn't want to follow where the trail led—to the head of WSX.

Initially, he'd been called to this place to investigate Paloma's death. It had taken him some time to realize that what he and the techs thought was a biochemical goo was the remains of a Bixian assassin. At that point, he also didn't know that the assassins worked in pairs.

Paloma had managed to kill one of them before the other killed her.

He shuddered. He'd managed to kill the assassin that had been attacking Wagner.

DeRicci told him that he eventually killed the other as well.

He remembered the fight in flashes. His laser pistol, the assassin being smaller than he expected, the pain, the pain, the pain, and trying to think through it, realizing if he didn't think through it he would be dead, then thinking he was dead, and DeRicci leaning over him, promising he would be all right in that voice people used when they didn't believe what they were saying, and then the hospital and more pain. . . .

He took a breath. He hated thinking about this. But if he was going to follow the leads in the Bowles case, he had to.

Initially, he had suspected Flint in Paloma's death. Paloma had been Flint's mentor and she had left everything to him in her will. Including some incriminating files from Wagner, Stuart, and Xendor, Ltd. Justinian Wagner had come to Nyquist, pretending an interest in finding his mother's killer, when really he had wanted those files.

Bowles had been part of that investigation, too. She had talked to Flint the morning that Paloma had died. Nyquist had found that strange because he believed that Flint and Bowles hated each other.

Had they been lying to Nyquist during the Paloma murder investigation? And if so, why?

He rubbed his fingers across the bridge of his nose, feeling the raised tissue from the thin, almost invisible scars.

Justinian Wagner had wanted files. Flint had inherited them.

When Nyquist had awakened in the hospital, he had asked about the case, particularly Wagner. Gumiela had said there was no evidence tying Justinian Wagner to his parents' murder, although they would continue looking into it.

And Flint had said . . .

Flint had said . . .

What?

Nyquist frowned. He had trouble remembering this, like he couldn't remember the beginning of the attack.

Flint had said . . .

That he had given the files to Justinian Wagner. That he hadn't even looked at them.

And Nyquist, not willing to think about the case anymore, had taken Flint's words at face value.

Even though Flint had lied to him before in other cases.

Now Ki Bowles was dead because she had confidential information. Flint had said he knew about that information.

Nyquist had understood during the conversation—even though it was all innuendo—that Flint had given Bowles the information that had jump-started her reporting, even hiring bodyguards to protect her.

Was he protecting her from Justinian Wagner?

Nyquist's thumb traced the scars all over his face. They really weren't visible anymore. He'd gone through so many surgeries. But they were still there, small raised areas that the doctors assured him would disappear with a few more surgeries.

Surgeries that would have been completely unnecessary if Justinian Wagner hadn't led the Bixian assassins to his parents.

Something about that . . .

Something about that day . . .

Nyquist made himself look at the building. Inside that building in one of the cheaper apartments, without a dome view, on a floor near Paloma's, he had nearly died.

But he'd been there for a reason, and that reason had not been to save Claudius Wagner's life.

It had been to talk with Claudius Wagner.

About files?

About assassins?

About the reasons Paloma died?

What had he said?

Nyquist closed his eyes. His head hurt. He hadn't allowed himself to remember this before, and he needed to.

He had to know now.

Nyquist clutched the edge of the seat, feeling the car's cheap cloth against his skin, using it to ground himself, like the hospital therapist told him to do when she had him talk about the nightmares.

He made himself recall. . . .

The apartment with the single chair and all the high-end entertainment equipment. An apartment of a man who lived alone and didn't expect visitors. A man who used stories and games to help the hours of his life pass, without doing much good work. Just playing, as if he deserved some kind of vacation.

Nyquist opened his eyes.

His heart was pounding, and his skin was clammy. He couldn't do this.

But there was no record of any of this. He hadn't written it into any file. Gumiela assured him it wasn't necessary and he hadn't cared. He'd been so badly injured, all he wanted to do was get better.

It had been the first time he'd failed to close the documentation on a case—even a case that remained open.

He'd let his situation—and the fact that the case revolved around the Wagners—lull him into thinking it was done.

And of course it wasn't.

Nyquist gripped the seat even harder. He'd stood up to two Bixian assassins—and survived. The first documented case of a human surviving a Bixian assassination attempt.

He'd had courage that day.

Yet it seemed that he needed more courage now.

Remembering it was harder than living it.

And, he reminded himself, he didn't have to remember the attack. Just the conversation with Claudius Wagner, before the assassins had slithered their way into the apartment.

Isn't it funny? The voice that appeared in Nyquist's head was Claudius Wagner's. *I would rather have given up my life and risk a hideous death than admit that I had anything to do with those cases.*

Cases. Nyquist didn't remember the cases or the files. He tried to make himself remember, and he couldn't.

What had the therapist said? Breathe. Relax. Come as

close as you can to sleeping. You'll find the memories. They exist. They're part of you.

But Nyquist had always resisted. He didn't want the memories.

Bowles and I made our deal before I found out about Talia. That was Flint. Flint, who seemed frightened for the first time since Nyquist had known him. Flint, who actually had something to lose now.

I need to know what happened to Bowles because . . .

Nyquist knew Flint had to figure that out. Because he thought he was the next target. And some killers—especially cruel ones, the motivated ones—thought that killing a man was less desirable than slaughtering his family and letting him live.

Nyquist shuddered.

Even if this weren't his first case back, even if he didn't feel an obligation to the dead—Bowles, Whitford, and the bodyguard, the man who had tried to defend Bowles—he had an obligation to solve this.

Flint had helped him. Flint had guaranteed the money so that Nyquist could have lifesaving surgeries.

Flint had told him that he would never ask for repayment—and Nyquist believed him.

But there were still unforeseen complications.

Like this one: *I need to know what happened to Bowles because . . .*

Because of Talia.

Because, Flint had been saying, *My daughter might die if I don't have that information. And you owe it to me.*

Only Flint was too classy to say that Nyquist owed him.

In fact, Flint might not have even thought of it—at least not consciously.

Have you ever seen the footage of the day care incident? Ki Bowles had asked Nyquist that day he interviewed her.

He hadn't known what she meant. *Day care incident?*

Flint's daughter was killed in a day care by one of the workers. Turns out that worker killed other children—

shaking them too hard—but it took a second visible death before anyone saw the pattern.

Bowles had been holding a mug of tea. If he closed his eyes, he could see her, as if she were still sitting across from him.

She swirled the mug because she was clearly nervous. He watched as the liquid would crest near the edge, then vanish again, never spilling, but always threatening.

That incident, she had said, *that's what started Flint on his journey from computer tech to Retrieval Artist. I think that journey has an ethical base. I think he tried to make things better as a police officer, then realized he couldn't enforce certain laws. So he became independent. I've talked to him. He's really firm about the way people should behave.*

She had been right. Flint was really firm about how people should behave.

They should protect children.

Flint couldn't protect his daughter because of his past. Flint had had no idea that his second child, the one that his wife had kept hidden from him, existed, and now he found himself in the middle of a mess, so he had come to Nyquist.

Nyquist, whose brain was refusing to remember its conversation with Claudius Wagner.

Although it seemed to have no trouble picking up memories of Ki Bowles.

I can't talk to you, Detective. I swore an oath. Claudius Wagner this time. Had he said that? Or was Nyquist's brain coming up with an excuse not to remember?

"What kind of oath?" Nyquist whispered.

Client confidentiality. I will tell you that we had the same client.

We. Nyquist frowned, almost opened his eyes. We. Claudius and—who?

I took over the account when she had to leave—and believe me, I was surprised at what I found.

Paloma. Or as Claudius probably called her until the day of his death, Lucianna. They'd hidden in plain sight because the Bixians didn't know Armstrong laws. They didn't understand that humans could legally change their identities and stay in the same area.

Nyquist almost opened his eyes as that information came back to him, then realized that he would break this, this slow trickle of memory.

A half-remembered conversation.

He leaned back, tried to relax even more. He wanted to picture Claudius Wagner, but all he got was that stupid entertainment system—a system he'd shattered with a shot from his laser rifle not an hour later.

The explosion—

The explosion had startled the second assassin and Nyquist had managed to move away from it. Somehow. Backing into the chair on his way to the kitchen.

The kitchen and a knife of his own.

He wouldn't be able to shoot when the thing latched on to him. He wouldn't be able to shoot, just slash and hope he killed it—hope he had enough time to survive.

Then a few things happened, Claudius Wagner had said, and Nyquist found himself feeling grateful. A different memory, one without the pain.

Some information leaked, Claudius Wagner had was saying. *Old cases resurfaced, old angers did as well, and suddenly I found myself subjected to the same treatment as Lucianna. We figured the name changes and the habit changes would be enough. And you know, they were, until yesterday.*

The man had been surprisingly honest. Nyquist hadn't expected honesty. He remembered that now. He had expected the same kind of creepy personality that Justinian Wagner had, the same kind of oily personality, the kind that shifted and moved with its moods—and tried to get you to do the same.

What do you think changed? Nyquist had asked.

I think someone offered my son the same deal I got offered. Claudius had spoken with great bitterness.

Nyquist didn't remember a deal. He needed to remember a deal.

"What deal?" he whispered because asking questions aloud had worked before.

I can't go into detail.

Be vague. He remembered now. He had promised himself he would try to find this information when he left Claudius's apartment. He would use the vague details to put together a real case. Somehow.

He'd done things like that before.

This client, Claudius had said, *is a long-term client, and this case is one of many. Lucianna kept most of her records and she didn't let me see the files, although she told me what was in them when I asked that year before I moved here.*

Here was the thing about the files. Nyquist knew there had been something. The entire case had been about files.

And Flint said he had given them back.

After making a copy?

This stuff Bowles was using, Nyquist had asked Flint, *this information, is there any way I can see it?*

If she has copies, Flint had said.

And where would she have gotten copies? Nyquist should have asked, but he hadn't.

He hadn't.

The client, Claudius was saying, *took some of Lucianna's advice, but not all of it. The circumstances happened again, in a different environment, but with the same results, and the client acted in the same way. Only the new case brought the old one up again, and stirred up anger . . .* He paused. *This can't be making sense to you.*

I'll figure it out, Nyquist had said. Only he never did.

He didn't have time. He nearly died. Then he forgot.

And then he got this case. And somehow it might be related.

So related that it frightened Flint.

Who had never seemed frightened before.

What if it was more than Talia? What if Flint's fear had

something to do with the cases that Claudius had talked about?

What if it had something to do with the files?

We managed to get some of the anger calmed, Claudius had said, *using extralegal means, very similar to what we had done before. And the result was the same as the ones before. The hurt party hired the Bixians at the advice of the previous hurt party.*

In other words, Claudius's firm had broken the law—done something horribly illegal, and the injured party had hired assassins—to go after Claudius and Paloma, the heads of the law firm.

Somehow the Wagners had found out about the threats to their lives.

And that's how you ended up here, Nyquist had said.

It's not so bad, really, Claudius had said, but he sounded wistful. That's what Nyquist remembered the most. How wistful the man sounded.

As if he had once been important and was no longer.

As if he once mattered and now he was just an old man living in a small apartment with a single chair and too much time on his hands.

Still, he had made the life sound as good as he could: *I can see my children. I can live my life. I find I don't miss the firm at all.*

At the time, Nyquist hadn't thought he was lying. But now he wasn't so sure. The man seemed like he missed everything.

And then his wife had been murdered.

He had to know he was next.

You said you were offered a deal, Nyquist had said, not knowing what was about to come, not knowing then that Claudius would die and Nyquist's whole life would change. *What was it?*

That I give up the client's files. Say that I advised them to take those extralegal measures. Admit my and the firm's

*culpability—not in public, mind you, just to the families—
and pay a steep fine.*

Steep?

*More money than you can earn in a lifetime, Detective.
More money than everyone on your force can.*

He had sounded so righteous. But that wasn't the question. Once again, Nyquist had asked the wrong question. He
should have said, *So you'd rather risk death than lose
money?*

Instead, he had said, *So you Disappeared rather than pay
out money.*

And that had made Claudius angry.

First of all, he said, *I haven't completely Disappeared.
Secondly, I was supposed to admit to both cases. I couldn't.
I only knew the one, and what little I knew of the other came
from a discussion with my wife. I'd have to allocute to the
details of both cases, and I couldn't, not without the files—*

Which your wife had, Nyquist had said.

Which she wouldn't relinquish, Claudius had said. *She
thought the allocution a very bad idea, even if it were supposedly confidential.*

She didn't think it would be? Nyquist had asked.

*She said we had an obligation to our client. She was right
about that.*

But?

Then there was nothing. For a moment, Nyquist panicked. Was that the end of the memory? He felt so tense. Was
that when Claudius had gone to the door and turned around
with that assassin covering his arm?

Nyquist felt vaguely nauseated.

He was sure there was more.

Something important.

Something he needed to remember.

We'd have to admit guilt, Claudius said as suddenly and
clearly as if he were in the car. Maybe he was. Maybe his
ghost was. *I would have had to admit guilt. And culpability
in a bunch of—*

He stopped himself. Nyquist remembered now. He suspected that Claudius wasn't thinking clearly, that he was truly upset or he wouldn't have made a slip like that.

But maybe the man had known he was going to die.

Maybe that was as close as he could come to confessing.

Then Claudius had sighed, and finished differently than he had obviously intended to.

Culpability in a major crime, he had said. *A horrible crime, if the truth be told. And what's worse is that these bastards hadn't learned from it. They did it again. So my guilt is compounded by the fact that they should have known better.*

A horrible crime. One that had been instigated by the Wagners. One that had caused an equally horrible revenge that Nyquist himself had gotten caught up in.

Had Bowles found that crime?

Isn't it funny? Claudius had said again. *I would rather have given up my life and risk a hideous death than admit that I had anything to do with those cases.*

The Claudius in Nyquist's memory had repeated that phrase, but Nyquist was certain the real Claudius had only said it once.

Was it important? Was that what this was all about?

Or was that the—what had the therapist called it?—the entry memory?

I guess I never believed anyone would find us, Claudius had said. *I guess I never really believed we'd be called to account. And here we are.*

Here we are. It seemed like he was here. Here they were, the survivor and the victim of a horrible attack, caused by a horrible crime.

Only just one of them had knowledge of what that crime had been.

A crime hidden in files.

Files Ki Bowles had threatened to reveal.

You said that your son received the same deal, said the Nyquist of his memory. And he wanted to rail at himself.

That wasn't the issue. It was clear that Justinian Wagner was behind everything. The issue was what was everything?

What had caused this?

What was in those files?

Nyquist wanted to ask the ghost of Claudius, but he couldn't. The man—or his shade—really wasn't here.

Just his memory.

And his memory answered the question that was actually asked: *Either they've done it again, which I doubt. I haven't heard news about it, and believe me, I watch. Or my son was told he could bring us in, pay the fine, and betray the client. Rumor has it that the client is looking for new attorneys. So my son had to be considering it.*

The vagueness had been frustrating then. It was even more frustrating now. Now that Nyquist couldn't verify the conversation, now that he couldn't be entirely sure that what he remembered as part of the conversation was truly part of the conversation.

Your son, he had said to Claudius, *was looking for a way out, one that didn't include vanishing.*

He had been guessing, missing the point again, focusing on Justinian instead of the files.

I think he was going for a half measure, Claudius had said. *I think he wanted the files. He'd hand them over, and maybe some money, and not admit anything. After all, he wasn't involved.*

The files again. Only Claudius had just said that Justinian would have turned them over. To the authorities? To the clients? To confess and allocute?

It wouldn't have mattered. If Nyquist understood the vagueness correctly, Justinian hadn't even been part of the firm when the "horrible crime" occurred.

"But you and your wife were," Nyquist said—aloud or in his memory he wasn't certain, and he really didn't care.

He did want the answer, though.

It can be argued by a good attorney that the real culprit here is my wife, said Claudius Wagner, who had been, by all accounts, a good attorney. *There is no proof in my files that I suggested anything other than the client do exactly as my wife advised them years ago. And if I had no records of what she advised them, then all that the attorney would have to say is that I added the sentence "because it seemed to work the first time." I had no liability. The firm had no liability. We'd gotten rid of the troublemaker by firing her, not killing her.*

But you didn't fire her, Nyquist had said.

It looked like we did.

Only she could have contradicted that, Nyquist had said.

She might have. Claudius had paused, then added, *My son is a good attorney.*

Just as his father had been. And what had Claudius just said? A good attorney could argue that the real culprit had been Paloma.

Nyquist was twisting himself around. He wasn't sure he understood Claudius's implications.

Had he asked?

"What do you mean?" he whispered.

Meaning, Claudius had said, speaking very slowly as if Nyquist were dumb, *it's better to have the files without the witness than the witness without the files.*

And there it was: the reason for Nyquist's conviction that Justinian had killed not just Paloma, but Claudius as well. In that conversation, just before Claudius's death.

Witnesses. Files. It was better to have the files.

Flint said he had given Justinian Wagner the files.

But what if he hadn't given Wagner all of them?

What if he had given some to Ki Bowles?

You think your son killed your wife? asked Nyquist the good cop who didn't realize he was about to be attacked by a Bixian assassin attempting yet another assassination of a Wagner.

I think my son covered his ass, Claudius Wagner had said, not without a little pride.

But he didn't get the files, Nyquist had said.

He will.

For the first time, Nyquist could actually see Claudius. The older man looked up, his gaze empty. His face so full of hurt that it seemed like he could barely contain it.

My son is a good attorney. He'll get what he wants.

Through whatever means necessary.

Maybe Justinian had thought the files destroyed. Maybe he believed they were missing.

Only Ki Bowles resurrected them, and Justinian Wagner wanted them.

He had killed before for those files.

Had he killed again?

36

Justinian Wagner had already dispatched two in-house detectives to see what kind of information they could gather about Ki Bowles's murder. He still hadn't tapped the rest of his Armstrong investigation team, however.

He felt he didn't have enough information to point them in the right direction.

Bowles's murder was about his firm. Someone was trying to destroy him. While he had dozens—maybe hundreds—of enemies, very few people in his life knew both his business and Ki Bowles's.

Which was why he was watching her news story about WSX again. He had to be missing something.

He was sitting at his desk with his own unnetworked system opened to the listing of all the files. Whenever Bowles mentioned a name or a case, he searched for it.

He was going to have his legal assistants make a list of all the people involved in each case. People or alien groups or corporations. He also wanted each case summarized—the core principle involved, and the means of settlement. Only he'd have some junior associates do that.

Then he would have a few partners scrutinize the cases for unusual activity. "Unusual activity" was the firm's euphemism for sometimes extralegal actions or, as Bowles would say, illegal proceedings.

What Wagner would tell Bowles now, if she were still alive, that legal or illegal sometimes didn't matter in this universe. Results did.

He would have thought she understood that.

He sent a message to the head of his detecting team. *I need a forensic accountant to examine Bowles's financials. Specifically, I need to know how she made her living in the six months since she left InterDome Media.*

That might give him who hired her. The amounts might also tell him whether or not Bowles had compromised what few ethics journalists had to tell the story that the person or persons who hired her wanted.

He got a message back. One word, which was all he needed.

Assigned.

Good. He'd have more assignments like that as the afternoon went on.

He wished he could hurry this, but he knew he didn't dare. He needed to be accurate, and as hidden as possible.

The police would probably blame him for Bowles's death as well. If they found that he was poking into her life after her death, they would think he had been looking for something when he had her killed.

He shuddered. He'd never hired an assassin in his life.

He'd let some information drop to the wrong source more than once—a lot of his former clients always had someone after them. And then there was his mother.

His mother, who had abandoned him and his brother, who had decided that her life was much more important than theirs.

His fingers clenched. He made himself turn his attention away from her, and then he stopped.

He hurried through the report, scanning it, not listening, until he got to Bowles's promises at the end.

"We will look at everything from WSX's relationship

with its individual clients, humans whose names you'll recognize, people who believe they're above the law, to the law itself. WSX has handled dozens of cases for the United Domes of the Moon. And then there are the corporate clients. From the various subsidiaries of Aleyd Corporation, arguably the largest corporation in this sector, to some questionable rulings in WSX's past, particularly those involving WSX's first big client, a corporation so deeply involved in this sector that everyone recognizes its name . . ."

Wagner froze her image after that quote. He hadn't thought much about what she said.

WSX's first big corporate client. *A corporation so deeply involved in this sector that everyone recognizes its name.*

He couldn't be sure which corporation Bowles meant. Information histories of WSX had mislabeled WSX's first corporate client many times, because informal histories had used news sources and interviews, not the client records.

WSX's first big corporate client was Environmental Systems Inc. Wagner's mother had brought the corporation into the WSX fold when she had become partners with his father. But she had continued to handle ESI, until she left the firm.

Then his father had handled them, passing them off to Wagner when he "retired."

Wagner's own files on ESI were incomplete. His parents had taken the incriminating files with them. He had gotten those files back when his mother was murdered.

The case that had ultimately gotten his mother killed was an ESI case. It was complicated, and he hadn't understood all of it himself, not until he got the complete files from Miles Flint.

Who had inherited them.

From Wagner's mother.

Miles Flint. Who had known Ki Bowles.

Wagner leaned back in his chair. He had had his computer techs go over and over the files, making sure Flint hadn't tampered with them or deleted any of them. The techs had reassured Wagner that Flint hadn't even looked at them, that the information Flint gave Wagner hadn't been copied or read or even touched since months before Paloma died.

Wagner scrolled through some old files of his own. The detective files he'd put together on Flint back when it became clear the man was too close to Paloma. Wagner had wanted information about the man Paloma had sold her business to.

He had wanted a way to destroy Flint, and he'd never quite found it. He hadn't had time to discredit the man with Paloma so he had hoped, immediately after his mother died and the terms of her will had become clear, to discredit Flint in the courts.

But there had been no need. Flint had cooperated, keeping his mother's money—which Wagner hadn't needed—but giving Wagner exactly what he wanted: all of the WSX files that his mother had kept in her ship, files she had stolen from the firm she started so that she could blackmail her entire family.

Wagner leaned forward. He could scan his own ESI files, but according to all he could remember, ESI hadn't broken any laws on any planet in the Earth Alliance since Wagner had become their lawyer.

The "questionable rulings in WSX's past" that concerned ESI had all happened when Wagner's parents ran the firm.

And all of that information had been in the files Flint had received from Paloma.

Wagner could sic the detectives on him, trying to find out for certain whether Flint had worked with Bowles to destroy WSX.

Or Wagner could talk to the man himself.

He slapped a corner on his desk, alerting his assistant. "I want the best security team we have in my office in three minutes."

"Yes, sir," the assistant said, wasting precious time. Wagner signed off before his assistant could say anything else.

Could Flint hate WSX enough to kill another human being?

Was the man capable of murder?

Wagner's mother never thought so. And Paloma wasn't fooled by many people.

But people changed.

Circumstances changed.

And when Wagner had been investigating the man who had inherited his mother's fortune, the word he'd heard the most was "ruthless."

Ruthless people took out anything that stood in their way. Including other people.

37

Flint was staring at a large group of files scattered across the screen when something screeched in his ear. He looked away from the screen, which illuminated the plate-covered table where he and Talia had been working, and stared at the new study groups sitting near the door.

Most of the groups were human although two were Peyti only. No one seemed to have screeched.

Then Maxine Van Alen appeared as a small hologram in the middle of all the plates.

Flint jumped.

Talia stared at him. "You okay, Dad?"

"I . . ." He'd never seen anything quite like it, at least not without a holoreceiver. "I think someone is trying to contact me."

"Damn straight," Van Alen said in a tiny voice that didn't quite sound like her.

"Let me move somewhere more private," Flint said to both Talia and Van Alen.

"I'll move," Talia said. "I've been sitting too long."

She stood before he could argue.

"Don't go far," he said.

She glared at him as if he had just said the stupidest thing ever, and he probably had. As afraid as she was of being hurt, it was clear she would stay within his line of sight.

"What the heck is this holoimage?" Flint asked Van Alen.

"Hmm?" She frowned. Then she looked down at something he couldn't see. "Oh. Must've been the glitch."

"Glitch?" he asked.

"We had a . . ." She wavered, disappeared, then reappeared as a free-floating see-through face where Talia had been sitting.

Flint found that a lot more disturbing than the tiny image standing on the table.

"Is your link secure?" Van Alen asked.

"Probably not," Flint said. "I'm in a more or less public place. I can contact you back."

She shook her head. "I don't think there's a need. I can talk to you when you get here."

"Is there a problem?" Flint asked.

"We don't know," Van Alen said. "I want you to check. We had a power flicker."

"Really?" Flint had seen power flickers during major emergencies, but never at any other time. It was simply too dangerous within the dome. "Nothing changed here."

"Oh dear," Van Alen said. "I'm beginning to wonder if it was isolated to our building. I'd like you to go through our systems and see."

Because she trusted him? Or because he worked for free? Or because she just needed some reassurance?

He dismissed that last thought. Van Alen was too self-confident to need reassurance.

"Unless this is a true emergency," Flint said, "I'd prefer not to."

"Given what we discussed earlier today," Van Alen said, "I'm worried. I'd like you to check our systems."

"Given what we talked about," Flint said, "and the work Talia and I've been doing, I've come to realize that there are dozens of other possible scenarios. All as or more likely than the one we came up with this afternoon."

He didn't like talking in code, but he felt it necessary, given the fact that the link wasn't secure.

"That is good news," Van Alen said.

"None of it is for sure. Just leads to explore. I can come if you think it critical."

"I don't know what to think," Van Alen said.

"Do you have any computer or network techs on-site?" Flint asked.

"I've sent for some."

"Let me send you a series of things they should look for. If they find even one of those things, contact me. I'll come running. Otherwise I'll be there as soon as I finish this research. How's that?"

Van Alen smiled at him. "Good enough, I think."

"All right, then," he said. "The list is forthcoming."

He would do it silently and send it through his more secure private link. Then he would return to the research on Bowles.

Van Alen signed off. Flint waved at Talia. She was standing near the pastries display, staring at it as if it were an excellent piece of art.

It took a moment to get her attention. When he did, she smiled at him, and came back so fast it seemed like she had run.

"Problem?" she asked.

"I have no idea," he said.

"Do we have to leave?" She sounded a little too hopeful.

"Not yet," he said. "Let's get back to work."

She sighed. He silently compiled his list and sent it to Van Alen. Then he returned to the screen that was filled with the downloads from public records all over the sector.

Bowles had lived an interesting life.

He was now going to see whether it had been interesting enough to get her killed.

38

An hour into the interview process and Savita Romey knew she was at a dead end. She'd spoken to at least twenty employees of Whitford Security, and none of them had the same information about anything.

Apparently information was as segregated as the rooms were, parceled out on a need-to-know basis, and sometimes not even then.

She'd set up in a conference room that had a program that assigned random pictures to the walls. If she wanted, she could set up the room to seem as if it overlooked the Grand Tetons on Earth. Or she could make it seem as if it were part of a ship hurtling through the solar system.

After testing the picture system, she decided on the blank white walls. They were less distracting, even though, after an hour, they were driving her crazy.

Most of the employees hadn't even met Roshdi Whitford. A few didn't know his first name. Some had no idea what the company's hierarchy was. Most simply knew that they were expected to do their job, which was as narrowly defined as a job could be, and then go home.

Half the employees she talked to weren't even worried that their jobs might be in jeopardy now that the boss was dead. No one had bothered to reassure them that the job would remain. They just simply had no idea who was in charge or why.

All they knew was that money appeared in their accounts every pay period, so long as they showed up to work and performed within certain parameters.

And all of that very sincere ignorance made Romey want to scream.

The junior detectives who were also conducting interviews were reporting the same problems. Not only were the employees isolated from one another, but the computer systems within the company itself were isolated.

It seemed that Whitford Security had two dozen different networks, and the single computer tech the department could spare for this part of the case couldn't figure them out.

Someone needed to talk with Whitford's computer security manager and he wasn't going to say a word to the police, even with a warrant.

So Romey approached this next interview with more than the usual amount of discouragement. She wanted to go home. She wanted to see her sons.

And she had a hunch she wouldn't get a chance to for hours, maybe days.

The door to the conference room opened and a very pretty twenty-something woman walked in. She had hair that was so gold that it was clearly fake, and her delicate features were flecked with gold glitter. She looked almost like an android, but the way that her hands were shaking told Romey the woman was all too human.

"Medora Lenox? I'm Detective Romey. Please sit down."

Romey indicated the chair next to hers, but like most of the other employees, Medora Lenox chose the seat farthest away. She folded her shaking hands together and set them on the fake wood tabletop.

"What is your job description, Medora?" Romey asked.

"I organize transmissions from security teams," Lenox said, speaking so softly that Romey had to strain to hear her.

Romey felt her heart leap. For the first time, she was speaking to someone who monitored more than one group of people.

"Do you organize the transmissions from more than one team at a time?"

"I'm sorry," Lenox said. "I don't understand."

Romey felt the hope she'd had a moment ago fade. "When the teams are out, how do you chose whose transmissions to organize?"

"I get assigned one team. I follow them through their assignment, until the security detail is over."

Her shaking voice made her hands start shaking again. She clenched them tighter, then slid them under the table.

"So if a security team has permanent residency at someone's business or house—"

"I don't work permanent teams," Lenox said. "That's a whole different department."

Of course it is, Romey thought. Then she sighed. "So, what team were you running today?"

"I'm working on team B-One."

"Which is?"

Lenox shrugged. "We only work by code."

"But if you're organizing the transmissions, you must know the name of the client."

"I know the name of the subjects," Lenox said. "The client is usually someone different."

Romey frowned. "What do you mean?"

"The client is the person who pays. The subject is the person guarded. They're not always the same."

For the first time, Romey spoke to someone who had more than a passing knowledge of the firm. "Why not?"

"Mostly it's parents, you know, hiring protection for their kids. But sometimes it's more than that. Sometimes we do government contracts for alien ambassadors—you know, the kind of thing that the city or the United Domes doesn't dare spend its money on for fear of having the security budget slashed."

Romey didn't know, but it was an interesting tidbit. She wondered how it fit into her investigation. "So, who was the subject today?"

Lenox's face had gone so pale that the glitter looked like color in an incomplete child's drawing.

"Ki Bowles," she whispered.

So that was why she was so nervous.

"Did you hear what happened on the grounds of the Hunting Club?"

"She's dead, I know. It's horrible."

Romey suppressed a sigh. Clearly Lenox wasn't much brighter than the rest of the staff. "I meant, did you get any transmissions from the grounds? Did you hear what happened to Bowles?"

"See, not hear," Lenox said. "Our transmissions are audio and visual."

Romey sent a message through her links immediately to Gumiela. *We need a special warrant for Whitford Security. It appears they have transmission records on every surveillance detail they've run.*

Romey signed off before she could get Gumiela's answer.

"All right," Romey said as she was finishing her message. "Did you see anything?"

"No," Lenox said. "The Hunting Club jams our signals. We've protested in the past. It's never done any good. They claim their security is good enough."

"It obviously wasn't."

"I know." Lenox sounded sad. She rubbed her thumbs together so hard that the skin around the knuckles turned red.

"Medora," Romey said. "Are you all right?"

Lenox stopped rubbing her thumbs and pulled her hands apart. She put them on the edge of the table as if she were bracing herself.

"Can I ask you a question?" Lenox's voice was soft, softer than it had been before.

Romey wasn't quite sure how it managed to carry the length of the table. "Go ahead."

"Has anyone found Gulliver?" Lenox swallowed hard. "I've been trying to reach him since this morning, and I'm not getting anything."

Romey frowned. The staff wasn't supposed to be able to communicate with the outside during lockdown.

"Not," Lenox said quickly, "that I could do anything since we found out about Mr. Whitford. But you know what I mean."

"No," Romey said. "Explain it to me."

"I mean, I tried from the time I came into work, and I couldn't get him. And I didn't get any transmissions from him. Then we heard about Mr. Whitford, and I tried again, and you know, Mr. Monteith was all panicked, and I'm just worried, that's all."

"Mr. Monteith?" Romey asked.

"He was heading the B-One detail. He was the one who let us know something was wrong, but he wouldn't say what. He had me look for Mr. Whitford, but he hadn't come into work today, so Mr. Monteith went to talk to him." Lenox threaded her hands together again. "I thought you knew that."

Romey didn't. Or maybe Nyquist had mentioned something like that. There were too many details, and until now she hadn't really thought of Bowles as her case, so she hadn't concentrated on them.

"I prefer you tell me," Romey said.

Lenox started rubbing her thumbs together. Her eyes filled with tears, but she didn't say anything.

Romey waited for a moment, but the day had already been too long for her. She didn't have her usual amount of patience.

"Was it unusual that you couldn't reach Gulliver?" she finally asked.

A single tear ran down Lenox's cheek, making the glitter sparkle, but not dislodging it. Romey stared at that path. The stupid woman had had the glitter embedded into her skin. It was some kind of enhancement that made her sparkle like that, not something she'd added later.

"Medora? Was it—"

"Yes." Lenox raised her chin slightly. "He would always contact me all day."

"I thought you just monitored transmissions."

"I did," Lenox said. "But Gulliver . . . me and Gulliver . . . we . . ."

This time Romey did wait. She knew better than to fill in what some subject was trying to say. Often the subject would parrot what the interviewer said, trying to please the interviewer.

"Gulliver," Lenox said, "he liked to talk to me."

Romey nodded, knowing that wasn't what Lenox initially planned to say. "When did he contact you last?"

"This morning." Lenox swallowed hard. "He—we— you're not going to tell, right?"

"Tell what?" Romey said.

"That he stays at my house. We could get fired."

Interesting, Romey thought. "You could get fired for what?"

"Fraternizing." The word seemed too big for Lenox. But she spoke it bitterly. "No one is supposed to socialize outside of work."

"And you two socialized?" Romey understood what Lenox meant, but she wanted Lenox to tell her.

Lenox's cheeks flushed a pale pink. It accented the gold beneath her skin.

"He's gonna marry me," she said proudly.

"Doesn't that violate company policy?" Romey asked.

"One of us will quit. We don't know who yet. When we have enough money. He gave me a ring, but I can't wear it at work because people will ask."

Romey nodded. "But they don't ask about the time you spend together?"

"They don't know." Lenox whispered this last. "He comes to my house after midnight, leaves before dawn."

"Do you go to his place?" Romey asked.

Lenox shook her head. "He shares with some friends. We can't let anyone know."

Something about this bothered Romey. It seemed too cautious even for employees who might lose their jobs if they "fraternized."

"Has anyone seen you together?" Romey asked.

Lenox kept shaking her head. "We don't dare risk it."

"The job is that important," Romey said.

"Until we save up enough money."

"Hmmm." Romey wasn't sure how to ask this next part. But she decided to give it a try. "Is your employer worried that you'd talk about work?"

"I don't know," Lenox said. "I don't see how it would matter."

This felt like something Lennox had said many times before, probably to Gulliver.

"Why wouldn't it matter?" Romey asked.

"In our case, anyway," Lenox said. "I mean, I monitor his transmissions. I know what's going on with his case."

"I see," Romey said.

And she did—a little. She asked a few more questions about transmission procedure, things that held no surprises at all. She didn't want Lenox to know that the questions she'd asked about Gulliver and the questions she was about to ask were connected.

"I assume," Romey said as she finished the basic transmission questions, "that each member of the team is privy to what the other members of the team are doing?"

"They have a plan," Lenox said. "But the transmissions are separate."

Romey nodded. Her heart was pounding. Finally something useful. "So if one team member is monitoring, say, the subject's home, and another is monitoring, say, the subject's office, the team members don't communicate about what they see?"

"Through me they do," Lenox said. "They tell me if something is suspicious and I relay it to the other."

"Why can't they do it directly?"

"I don't know," Lenox said. "Too much information, I guess."

"Too much information?" Romey asked.

"It's like the employee motto. It's posted all over our break rooms. Too much information is dangerous in the wrong hands."

"So information must be secured as well as the subject herself."

"Yeah," Lenox said. "Everything has channels."

"Do you think team members should talk to each other more?"

"Not me," Lenox said.

"But Gulliver?"

Lenox looked down. "He says it handicaps him, not knowing what the others are doing."

"Have you ever told him what they're doing?"

Lenox swallowed hard again. Those thumbs were rubbing each other raw.

"It's okay, Medora," Romey said. "I'm not going to get you in trouble with your employer. All I care about are the things that might pertain to the death of Mr. Whitford."

"How does this pertain?" Lenox asked softly.

"We think his death and Ki Bowles's death might be linked."

"Because Enzio died?"

Enzio Lamfier, the other bodyguard.

"Yes," Romey said.

"Gulliver was supposed to be with him," Lenox said. "That's why I asked if you'd heard from him."

Romey frowned just a little. "I do know that our people searched the entire Hunting Club grounds and didn't find anyone else who was hurt."

She almost said "dead," but knew better.

But Lenox didn't look relieved. Apparently she knew that much.

"So," Romey asked, "did you ever tell Gulliver what the others were doing?"

"On which case?" Lenox asked.

"On the Bowles case."

"He said she was difficult. He said she was hard to guard. She didn't listen to them. He had to know where the others were all the time or she might die." Lenox wiped at her face. "She died anyway, didn't she?"

Romey nodded. "I'm afraid so."

"He was right, then," Lenox said.

He might have been right or he might have been using Lenox to find out where the other bodyguards were at all times.

"It would seem so," Romey said.

"Promise me you'll tell me when you find him," Lenox said.

Such a small request from such a desperate woman.

"I promise," Romey said.

But she had a hunch she wouldn't find Gulliver—at least not easily. And maybe not even alive.

39

The computer tech stood three meters away from Van Alen's desk, shifting nervously from foot to foot. The tech was a heavyset woman whose expensive clothing didn't quite fit—either she ate more than her weight-loss enhancements could keep up with or she didn't have weight-loss enhancements.

She certainly never exercised. Even the skin on her face jiggled as she moved from side to side.

Van Alen had only seen aliens that had jiggling skin. She found herself staring at it, hoping that the woman—named Fifine ("Don't call me Fifi, please") Ito—wouldn't notice.

"I found an encroachment." Ito threaded her hands together. Her fingers were startlingly small given the size of the rest of her.

Van Alen placed her own hands on her desk and leaned forward. It was a position she used to intimidate. She hoped that intimidation might get this woman to speak quicker, since she'd already been in the office five minutes before she admitted to the "encroachment."

Van Alen had called her because the maintenance team had been stumped. The power had cut to Van Alen's building, but something had kept the computer systems' separate line up. The maintenance team thought it could be that the "something" was built into the separate line (they would have to check and that would take time) or because someone had deliberately maintained the power to the separate line.

They didn't know yet. They wouldn't know for hours.

So Van Alen figured a computer tech might know.

Well, she hadn't figured it exactly. That had been one of Flint's suggestions.

If the maintenance team has no idea what happened, call in computer experts. And have them look for these things . . .

"What do you mean, an encroachment?" Van Alen asked.

"Something—something rather sophisticated—used that momentary glitch to search our network." Ito licked her lips as if she were afraid of Van Alen's response.

"Search our systems?" Van Alen felt cold.

Ito nodded.

"Did it take anything off our systems?"

"Not that I can tell," Ito said. "It was looking for something very specific."

"What, exactly?" Van Alen asked.

"I don't know. It's like—a net came into the system and tried to catch something, then disappeared. I have evidence of the net, but not evidence of what it was trying to catch."

"Can you tell if it caught anything?" Van Alen stood up. Her back hurt when she leaned forward too long.

"I don't think so," Ito said. "The sophisticated something remained the same size going in as it did coming out. If you think of the net analogy again, a net full of, say, fish would make a bigger wave in the water than a net that didn't catch any."

Van Alen's understanding of water and fish and nets was almost as poor as her understanding of computer networks. But she did get water displacement images.

"Can you be sure nothing left the system?" Van Alen asked.

"I can't be sure. I can be reasonably certain. Honestly, though, ma'am, this thing was beyond my capacity. That's why I'm calling it sophisticated. We don't have anything in Armstrong that I know of that can run into a full computer network filled with so much data, pinpoint one area, and then remove it without leaving so much as a trace."

"But you just said there was a trace."

"Of the search. And only because I was looking for it in those two seconds. Whatever it was, it was looking for something very specific. When it didn't get that something, it vanished. Or . . ."

Ito's voice trailed off. She continued her back-and-forth shifting.

"Or?" Van Alen asked, not liking that she had to continually prompt this woman.

"It left something."

"As in a virus?"

"As in an alert or a message system, something that might contact whoever set the program up in the first place."

Van Alen frowned. She had heard of things like that. "Shouldn't you be able to find that?"

"Eventually," Ito said. "But we're working with a sophisticated program. For all I know, the power glitch and the resulting trail through our computer networks was a Trojan horse."

"Something snuck in here?" Van Alen at least understood that metaphor. She'd used it a few times herself in court cases.

"And it'll attack when it's ready. Or . . ."

This woman had irritating speech patterns. Van Alen wanted to shake her.

"Or?"

"It will send information out of the system when it finds the information. Not an attack so much as a prolonged search."

"In other words," Van Alen said, "you have no idea what happened."

Ito flushed. Her face turned so red it almost looked painful. "No. Something came into our systems during the glitch. I think the glitch was designed to mask that. While we were all dealing with a momentary power issue—which distracted us and shut down our external security—something got into our computer systems."

"Which should have shut down but didn't. Do you know why?"

"There's a backup power system on them," Ito said.

"I know that," Van Alen said. "But a backup system should be buildingwide, not just on the computer systems."

"Really?" Ito sounded breathless. "Because as far as I can tell, it's only on the computer networks."

"No," Van Alen said. "It's on everything. I had that system put in myself. We don't want to lose information . . ."

It was her turn to trail off. She had specifically wanted this building to remain active when there was a problem in the power supply.

"Ma'am?" Ito asked. "You want me to check to see when the backup equipment got changed?"

"I'll have maintenance do that," Van Alen said. "You find out if there's some kind of Trojan horse in my network. And even better, see if you can find what kind of information that damn search was looking for."

"Yes, ma'am. Can I bring in some help?"

"Inside help only," Van Alen said. "I don't want to have outsiders looking at my systems again today. I think we've had a big enough breach, don't you?"

Ito nodded probably because she had no other choice. Then she shifted from foot to foot again.

"Go," Van Alen said. "And report back as soon as you can."

"Yes, ma'am."

Van Alen sighed. She needed maintenance again. She wanted to know when the systems were tampered with.

Timing mattered, but not as much as the missing information.

Although she had a hunch she knew what the search was looking for.

Ki Bowles's files. Someone from the outside would think that Bowles had case files here. Instead, Bowles came every week for some new tidbit that Flint would send her out to investigate.

The files Flint kept here were not on the networked computers.

So the thing that had invaded Van Alen's systems had done so searching for something it couldn't find.

Something that didn't really exist.

Still, it made her nervous.

She felt vulnerable for the first time in years.

And she didn't like the feeling at all.

40

He noticed them out of the corner of his eye: a group of large men who seemed more like athletes than law students. Flint kept his head down but stopped looking at his screen. Instead, he watched them.

They carried handhelds and one even had a thick book with a green cover, something Flint had seen law students carry before. The men leaned toward one another and began to talk in an animated way. One of them studied the menu on the table, while another opened the book.

No one else seemed to notice them. The Peyti study group didn't even look up. Neither did the Sequev and human group.

Maybe they were used to seeing this group of large men gather in the library in the afternoon. Or maybe they had seen the men around campus.

It wouldn't be the first time that a group of humans— maybe from an area off the Moon—had come to the same university to study together.

For all Flint knew, they could be brothers.

Talia was still going through the information before her. She hadn't noticed the newcomers at all, which surprised

Flint. He would have thought that she would notice everything new, considering how on edge she was.

He turned his attention back to the screen before him. Ki Bowles had been an only child. Her parents had lavished her with affection, and given her the best education possible. She had gone to college on Earth, where she majored in, of all things, art history.

That surprised him, but it explained why she had once said in one of her news reports that Flint looked like a pre-Raphaelite angel—"fallen, of course," she had added with a laugh.

One of his links cheeped.

Talia looked up. She had heard it as well.

"What now?" she asked.

A message scrolled underneath his vision: *Possible client. Urgent.* And then his link cheeped again.

The link was one of the few contacts he had attached to the sign outside his office door.

He didn't need any clients. He probably wasn't going to take any for quite a while, maybe years.

But the cheeping continued.

"It's a possible client," he said. "I'm just going to wait until they go away."

"Just talk to them," Talia said. "That noise is annoying."

Flint smiled at her, then stood. He didn't want her to hear how harsh he could be. He walked back over to the pastry counter. The damn things looked no more appetizing than they had earlier.

His link cheeped again. He wished he hadn't set the stupid thing up to be audible, but he had. He'd figured he would need it, back when he thought he would need a lot of clients.

With a sigh, he answered the link—and found no one there. He frowned. He used the link to back-trace the communication, and got a visual in the bottom corner of his right eye. He saw the sign outside his office. The sign had a tiny black dot near the communications chip.

Someone had set up an automatic page.

He frowned. He didn't like that. Automatic pages often had tracking equipment built into them. Whoever had contacted him might have used it to determine where he was located.

He and Talia would have to find another place to do their research—and they'd have to do so quickly.

He disconnected the link, then started back to Talia's booth. As he did, the men got up from their table and casually kept pace with him.

Then two fell in behind him and one stopped in front of him. The other kept to his side.

Flint realized that the one beside him was jamming his links. He stopped walking. He didn't want to lead them to Talia.

"Miles Flint?" The man in front of him spoke softly. "You're to come with us."

"I don't do anything people tell me to do," Flint said. "Now let me pass."

One of the men behind him grabbed his arm. The grip was tight.

"I'm sorry, sir," said the first man. "We need you to come with us."

"I don't care what you need," Flint said, refusing to speak softly.

But none of the students looked up. No one did. No one seemed to notice his plight.

"Come with us," the first man said so softly that Flint had to strain to hear him, "or we'll take your daughter."

"And some of us," said the man holding Flint's arm, "are quite fond of young girls."

Flint felt his stomach turn. The man's grip had grown so tight that it cut off blood to his hand.

He needed to get them out of the cafeteria, away from Talia. Then he would take them on. If nothing else, a brawl would bring the campus police.

"All right," he said to the first man, "so long as your goon here lets go of my arm."

The first man nodded at the other one. The one behind Flint let go. Blood immediately began flowing again, sending a feeling of pins and needles into Flint's hand.

The men surrounded him and walked with him toward the door. He hoped Talia didn't see—or if she did, he hoped that she was sending for help through her links.

He needed to figure out how to get away from these men.

He had no weapons, nothing except his own strength and cunning.

His strength looked like no match for these guys.

He hoped his cunning would be.

41

Bowles's handhelds were still in her apartment. The techs hadn't finished with everything. Apparently Gumiela had instructed them to bag and tag anything that might be construed as evidence, so the techs were being extra cautious.

As he pulled up beside the building, Nyquist understood why. He hadn't seen so many reporters in one place, all of them pushing and shoving each other in an attempt to get some kind of story.

A few were reporting live from the scene. Others were trying to interview the poor street cops who had been assigned to guard the building itself.

The noise was incredible, and for a moment, Nyquist, who was still feeling wrung out from his memory attempt, didn't want to go inside.

But he had to. If Bowles had those files, it might explain why Wagner had gone after her.

So Nyquist squared his shoulders and walked onto the sidewalk. One reporter saw him, then looked away. Another frowned, and a third stopped interviewing a street cop and headed straight for Nyquist.

Which started the avalanche of people.

"Detective Nyquist?" said a man he didn't recognize. "Are you on this case?"

"What case?" Nyquist asked.

"Detective Nyquist?" one reporter asked another. "Wasn't he the guy who nearly died last year?"

"Detective Nyquist?" a third reporter shouted. "Who murdered Ki Bowles?"

He kept his head down. He'd shoved his way through crowds before. A few times, he'd shoved his way through crowds of reporters.

It hadn't made him nervous before, but it made him nervous now. He still wasn't over that attack—and remembering it just a few moments ago, no matter how much it had served this case—only seemed to make him even more uneasy.

He wanted to brush away anything that looked ropelike. He hated the touch of hair or fabric against his skin.

His heart was pounding and the distance to the door looked like kilometers.

"Detective Nyquist, why would anyone want Ki Bowles dead?"

"You tell me," he shouted back at them, knowing that sometimes statements like that brought actual results.

"Is it true that she was returning to InterDome?" someone asked.

"Do you think this was an in-house rivalry?" asked someone else.

"How could anyone get killed on the grounds of the Hunting Club?" asked a third. "I thought they had the best security in Armstrong."

He finally made it to the door. Someone inside opened it for him and he slid through the crack. Then the two of them leaned on it so that no reporter followed.

The street cop inside looked even more harried than the street cops outside.

"Sorry," she said. "I'm told it's only going to get worse."

"The story of the year," Nyquist said. "Nothing reporters like more than a story about a reporter."

He sounded more cynical than he felt. He was actually feeling sorry for Bowles. Especially if she had died for her profession. That showed more courage than he would have expected.

He adjusted his coat, made sure no one had stuck a tracking device or a microphone on him.

"Can you see if I'm chipped?" he asked the street cop.

The cop grinned. She held out a gloved hand. He recognized the glove. It was black with gold lining, designed to catch most noninternal chips and tracking devices.

She ran it across the air near him, but found nothing.

"Thanks," he said. He would still run the check himself when he got into the elevator. He hated it when some reporter got news that way. The courts always ruled such actions illegal, but that was long after the story aired and a case was ruined.

He stopped outside the elevator when Romey appeared in the lower corner of his left eye. He hated that, and wished he could shut off the feature, even though he knew better than to do so in the middle of an investigation.

"You secure?" she asked.

"God knows," he said. "I just ran a reporter gauntlet."

"Ooof." She rolled her eyes. He didn't recognize the backdrop behind her. Improbably, it was all white. "I'll try to phrase this as cautiously as I can, then."

"Okay." He decided not to step into the open elevator. He moved away from the doors and closer to the walls. "What do you have?"

"Did you tell me that a bodyguard is in custody?"

She meant a bodyguard of Ki Bowles, but she didn't say so.

"Yeah," Nyquist said. "Someone's doing preliminaries right now. I planned to talk to him when I got back to the station."

"Might be worth a conversation together," Romey said. "You want to meet me there?"

"Now?" he asked.

"Yeah," she said.

"I thought you had to do hundreds of interviews," he said.

"Whitford Security is the most annoying organization," she said. "They parcel out information so no employee knows more than one thing. It's like putting a puzzle together. I'd rather wait for the reports. Hell, I'd rather wait for a computer analysis of the reports."

"Well, I actually have something pressing," he said. "Why don't you interview him?"

"Because I know something you don't," Romey said, "but I'm pretty sure you know a lot of things that I don't. The interview will relate more to your side of this investigation than mine. I need you there."

"You think this is crucial?" Nyquist asked.

"If my hunch is right," Romey said, "I might know the name of our killer."

"You think there is only one?" Nyquist asked.

"Don't know that yet," Romey said. "But I suspect we're going to find out."

42

Something made Talia look up. She'd been lost in the data, finding the details of these court cases fascinating despite herself. She had no idea how someone could live happily from day to day when so many people hated her.

Maybe Ki Bowles hadn't lived happily.

Maybe she had just lived.

Talia was beginning to understand that. She sometimes found herself thinking that she didn't deserve to be happy—she couldn't be, not with her mom dead.

And then she'd feel guilty when she was.

It was bad, but not as bad as some of the stuff she'd been reading about Bowles.

Talia had just been looking at an interview with some guy who'd followed Bowles around Armstrong for nearly a year before the police managed to find him, when her heart started pounding hard.

She had grown nervous and she wasn't sure why.

She looked up and saw her father standing near the pastries, talking to four guys.

Why would her dad talk to four guys? And why now?

Talia almost sent for help along her emergency links, but

she could just imagine her dad telling her that she was over-reacting. *They're friends, Talia. Calm down.*

But she couldn't calm down. And there was something about her dad's expression that disturbed her.

She tried to send him a message along her links—*You okay?*—but the message bounced back to her almost instantly.

It should have gone through.

He didn't even look up at her.

Then some guy grabbed her dad's arm.

Talia swore.

Her dad kept talking to these men and then they started walking with him. One stopped in front of him. Her dad raised his voice a little, but Talia couldn't quite hear what he was saying.

The man still had his hand on her dad's arm.

She didn't need to hear. She wasn't going to let something happen to another parent. Not now.

She sent for help along all her emergency links. *Police! My father's being kidnapped! Help! Help!*

Then she activated her recording chip, lifting her hand so that she could catch the entire thing.

The man behind her dad let go of his arm, and her dad started walking with them toward the door. He didn't glance at Talia. Not once.

She cursed again.

He was doing this to protect her.

Help! We're at the cafeteria in the law library. Please help!

But no one moved. The students didn't seem to notice anything and no one answered on Talia's links. She got out of the booth.

In Valhalla Dome, where she had grown up, there were police on every corner. Sometimes even in official buildings, like this one.

Someone would have answered her by now. Someone might even have made it down here.

But Armstrong was a big city, and her dad once laughed when she asked why the police weren't everywhere.

There can't be that many police in a free society, Tal, he'd said. As if Valhalla Dome hadn't been free. As if Armstrong was somehow better.

He'd thought it was.

But she didn't. Not now.

She set her help message on automatic and then she got out of the booth. The men were marching her dad toward the door. One man had his hand near her dad, probably using a jammer for his links.

Didn't any of the students notice? Weren't their links momentarily checking in and out?

The guys surrounding her dad were big, but all she needed to do was distract them. Her dad was tough. If she distracted the guys, her dad could fight back.

And when he did, maybe the students would help, too.

This was her only chance.

She'd never gotten the opportunity to save her mom.

She could save her dad.

And she had to do it now.

43

Romey beat Nyquist to the precinct, which surprised her. Maybe he had stopped off at the Detective Division before coming to the interview area. She had thought he was closer to the City Complex than she was when she contacted him.

The interviews were still continuing at Whitford Security. She reviewed several of them, mostly by asking investigators what—if anything—they had learned that was of interest. Most claimed they hadn't learned anything.

But a few of the investigators had discovered some interesting tidbits. Such as the fact that that bunker beneath Roshdi Whitford's body wasn't for human protection, but protection of a high-end computer system, one that wasn't linked to anything else.

What if, the investigator postulated, someone discovered that the bunker existed, figured out how to break in, and got caught by Whitford? Maybe that was why he died.

It was a good theory, although it was as yet unprovable. The evidence hadn't yet shown whether Whitford was home when the break-in occurred or he had opened the door to someone he knew (who also knew how to turn off the alarm systems) or he had stumbled on some kind of major break-in in progress.

And as yet, Romey couldn't even tell if someone at Whitford Security had been notified that the boss's house was being broken into. Even that information was parceled out.

Still, she felt encouraged by something one of her other investigators had said: *You know, when we're done with all this talking, we'll know more about Whitford Security than anyone who works there.*

And they would. It was the downside to the parceling out information. If a determined someone put all of that information together, then that someone would know more than anyone who worked for the company—and might be unstoppable.

In fact, as Romey headed to the interview room to see Pelham Monteith, she turned that very idea over in her head. Maybe her team wasn't the first to come up with the idea that one person could know more than all of Whitford Security combined.

All it would take would be some careful conversations— a bit of information here and a bit of information there. In fact, it might be relatively simple.

A conversation could go like this: *I heard you're handling the Bowles case.*

Naw. I'm taking care of XYZ case. I have no idea who is handling other cases.

And so on and so forth.

She let out a small breath. If that someone worked for the company, then the other employees might be willing to divulge information. Just as Medora Lenox had to her friend Gulliver.

Maybe she hadn't been the only one to give him tidbits of information. She certainly wouldn't have known if he spent time with someone else.

He had only spent midnight to six with her.

The interview room where they had stashed Monteith was at the end of a long hallway. The room was one of the larger units, designed for long-term interrogations. It had the most equipment and the most environmental controls.

Romey could play all kinds of games if she wanted to, cutting down the oxygen, amping it up, making the room warmer or colder, depending on what she wanted to do.

But she wasn't going to play any of those games—not yet. Maybe not ever.

She knew that the street cops who had brought Monteith in had placed him here because the case was high profile. High-profile interviews often got stuck here because they could be easily monitored.

Romey peered inside the interview room before she went in. Two extremely junior detectives sat on either side of Monteith.

Monteith himself seemed calmer than she expected. He was also older. He sat between the two detectives, answering each question with a deliberation that was obvious even with the sound off.

He was balding. All of his enhancement money seemed to have gone to his muscles, which bulged out of his black suit. Or maybe he had somehow done that on his own.

Romey didn't want to think about it.

And she didn't want to start without Nyquist.

But she would if he didn't get here soon.

She had a feeling that interviewing this man was the key to the entire case.

44

Talia let out an ear-shattering scream. It took Flint a moment to realize that a word was buried in that sound.

"Noooooooooooooooooooooooo!"

She raced across the cafeteria and launched herself at the man behind Flint.

"God, Talia, no," Flint said. "Go away. Go away!"

But his words were doing no good. She landed on the man's back, her hands pulling his hair, her knees pressing into his kidneys. The man's face turned red.

Flint had no choice. He elbowed the man on the other side of him, then reached for the guy in front of him and slammed him into the Peyti's table. The guy to the right reached for Talia, but she had somehow gotten the guy she had attacked to turn and turn and turn.

As Flint punched the man on the Peyti's table, he realized that Talia was biting the other guy on the ear.

The man Flint had elbowed was standing up. Flint kicked him in the stomach, figuring a second hit would help.

That man had been the one with the jammer, and for a moment, Flint's links kicked back in. He sent a message along the emergency links; then he sent one—he hoped—to Nyquist:

Ki Bowles's killers have come for me—

The jammer went back on. The man who had done all the talking held it up like a prize.

The law students had backed away from the fight, but Flint knew they had to be sending for help as well.

Flint reached for the jammer, but the man pulled it out of his reach.

Then Talia screamed.

The man Flint had kicked in the stomach had pulled her off the first man's back. That man's ear was bleeding. It looked like Talia might have ripped part of it off.

Talia was spitting blood into the face of the man who held her. She wasn't screaming at all. She was shouting, and flailing at him, trying to get him to let go of her.

Flint went for the man holding her. Then the man with the bloody ear pulled her away and put a laser pistol to her head.

"We wanted you to cooperate, Mr. Flint," said the man with the jammer.

Flint did not turn around to look at him.

"We wanted this to be a nice, polite little conversation. We'll take you to our boss, and you'll talk, and then you can leave."

"I don't go with anyone unless I know who I'm going to talk to," Flint said.

The man with the jammer laughed. "Nice try. But I'm not going to tell these fine students where we're going."

He turned toward them, waving the jammer like a weapon.

"Mr. Flint and his daughter will be fine. You can tell the police that. And tell the police that the attack came from the girl. She's out of control. We're just going to get her some help."

"No!" Talia said, still kicking at the man holding her. "Dad, stop them. Stop them. Don't worry about me."

As if he could do that.

"Regretfully, we've been told that the loss of this girl here isn't all that important," said the man with the jammer. "I understand that there are replacements? She's not unique, am I right?"

Talia flushed and immediately stopped flailing.

"She is unique," Flint said.

The man with the jammer laughed. "Then you'll protect her. And the best way to do that is for both of you to come with us. Calmly."

Calmly. As if Flint could be calm. But he didn't see any choice. He had to trust that Nyquist got his message. He had to hope that he was right—that these thugs were from Wagner.

But he didn't really know.

"If someone comes," he said to the law students, "tell them—"

"You'll tell them that there was a fight and it got settled," the man with the jammer said. "Don't try anything else, Mr. Flint. I've heard you're pretty smart. But we have the weapons. And that lovely child whom you think is unique. So behave."

"Dad," Talia said, her voice filled with tears. But her eyes weren't. She was pretending to be limp so that he could try an attack. She was letting him know that she was ready.

He shook his head ever so slightly.

"We'll come with you," Flint said. He really didn't see any other choice.

<u>45</u>

Romey was already inside the interrogation room when Nyquist arrived. He switched off all but his emergency and police links as he approached the door, just like he did every time he conducted an interview of this magnitude.

But his personal links gave a cheep of protest. A message had come through.

For a moment, he debated checking it. Then he decided it could wait.

He stepped into the interrogation room. The room was normal temperature, which he hadn't suspected. All of the environmental controls were at normal levels. Usually interrogators tried to make the subject uncomfortable.

It seemed Romey was doing the opposite.

"Detective Nyquist," Romey said as Nyquist closed the door. "This is Pelham Monteith. He headed the security team for Ki Bowles."

Nyquist was about to say, *Well, that worked*, when something in Romey's face caught him.

"Mr. Monteith is about as upset as I've ever seen a man. He's never lost anyone he was guarding before." Romey was finessing the guy, and she clearly wanted him to do the same. "We've been talking about procedures from Whitford.

They're proprietary, but Mr. Monteith is willing to tell us what the systems are so long as we keep them confidential."

Monteith was nodding. The crown of the man's head was shiny with sweat. He almost seemed relieved that someone was treating him with respect.

Nyquist gave Romey a surprised look. He'd never seen this kind of interview work before, but he was willing to give it a chance.

"He was about to tell me about the poor guard who died trying to save Ms. Bowles," Romey said.

"Enzio Lamfier," Nyquist said, trying to make his voice as sympathetic as he could.

"Yeah," Monteith said. "I didn't know him well."

"Was he a new hire?" Romey asked.

"New to our team," Monteith said. "Illiyitch recommended him."

"Gulliver Illiyitch?" Romey asked.

Monteith nodded.

"And Mr. Illiyitch is missing now, right?"

"You didn't find him?" Color appeared in Monteith's cheeks. "I thought the police were going to look for him. He had to be in those woods."

"Near the Hunting Club?" Romey asked.

"Surrounding the Hunting Club." Nyquist finally understood why Romey wanted him here, and why she wanted him to go lightly. Monteith felt aggrieved—a professional who hadn't been treated like one—and he was more likely to share information with peers than he was with authority figures.

"Yes," Monteith said.

"I must have arrived on the scene after you left," Nyquist said. "I coordinated the search for Mr. Illiyitch."

"And you didn't find him?"

Nyquist shook his head. "We didn't find him. I wasn't even sure if the second person in that forest was another guard for a while. The Hunting Club didn't know, and we couldn't find any representatives from Whitford."

Monteith's mouth thinned. He might have heard that last comment as disapproval.

So before Monteith could say anything, Nyquist added, "I had a hunch that was standard procedure. Most security organizations run their own investigations when something goes wrong."

"Exactly," Monteith said, sounding relieved. He glanced at Romey as if looking for her approval. "I have strict instructions for what to do when there's a problem. I call off the team. Then I have to report to the team coordinator, and then we decide how to handle everything."

"So you called off the team," Romey said. "And spoke to the coordinator."

Monteith ran a hand over his skull. He glanced at his palm, seeming surprised that it was covered with sweat. "My coordinator on this one was Roshdi Whitford."

"That seems unusual," Romey said. Nyquist let her take the Whitford questions. He'd bring it back to Bowles in a minute.

"It is," Monteith said. "But Ms. Bowles was so high profile and her handlers were paying a lot, so Mr. Whitford wanted to oversee the case himself."

Romey looked at Nyquist to see if he wanted to pursue the handlers question. He didn't, not yet.

"You went to the office to find him," Romey said.

"No, I tried to contact him on his links, but they were off. I sent ahead to the office, but his assistant said he hadn't arrived yet and I should go to his house. So I did."

Monteith looked nervously from Romey to Nyquist, then back to Romey.

"You found the body," she said.

Monteith nodded. "I went in. It's protocol. Some of us have the house codes."

Nyquist raised his eyebrows but didn't say anything. That sounded like a major security breach to him, especially for someone as paranoid as Whitford had seemed.

"What happened when you went in?" Romey asked.

"I went to the main room. I could smell the blood before I saw it. I . . ." Monteith's voice faded. "We're not supposed to go to the police. Sometimes our clients are being protected from police forces from other countries. You understand."

Nyquist felt his own face flush. He did understand. Sometimes Whitford Security was protecting a Disappeared. Then the company couldn't go to the police.

But he didn't like it.

Romey saw that. She said, "We do understand. You had your orders. And in this case, they were to go to a lawyer?"

"No," Monteith said. "We went to the client if the client was different from the person being protected, which in this case it was. I had the name of the lawyer who hired us. Turns out she did so in the name of someone else."

"Who is?" Romey asked.

Monteith licked his lips. "I shouldn't say."

"Remember the promise I made," Romey said. "This is important."

Monteith sighed. "I probably don't have a job anymore, anyway," he said, and for the first time, Nyquist felt some sympathy for him. He probably didn't have a job. And after this, he probably wouldn't be able to get a job in security. Even if the police didn't say a word about the interview, the fact that he had lost a subject under his protection would probably count against him in any future job interview.

Monteith was looking at Romey.

"The man was named . . . Flint," he said.

"Miles Flint?" Nyquist asked, feeling stunned.

"Yeah, I think so. Weird blond guy."

"You met him," Romey said.

"He's the one who told me to come to you. Or he approved it. The lawyer had already called the police." Monteith didn't sound too happy about the arrangement.

"Do you know why Flint had hired you to take care of Bowles?" Nyquist asked.

"You mean besides to keep her alive?" Monteith's answer bordered on sarcasm.

"Yes," Romey said in that gentle tone. She gave Nyquist a warning glance. Apparently she had worked hard at softening Monteith and didn't want Nyquist to ruin it.

"No," Monteith said. "But we did know that once some stories ran, she would be an even bigger target. I tried to talk her out of the Hunting Club. It doesn't like outside security agencies. It thinks it's the best. But it really screwed us. We had a team inside, a team with her, and I was on the street. But someone still got her."

"And Mr. Lamfier," Nyquist said.

"And probably Mr. Illiyitch," Monteith said sadly. "He's probably somewhere nearby."

"We're searching the entire area near the Hunting Club now," Nyquist lied.

"Tell me abut Mr. Illiyitch," Romey said. "You said Lamfier was new to your team. Was Illiyitch?"

"Assigned that morning. But he'd been with the company for a while. Everyone liked him."

"Did you?" Nyquist asked.

Monteith looked away.

"It's all right, Mr. Monteith," Romey said.

Monteith nodded. He looked at Nyquist. "Illiyitch broke the rules sometimes. He gossiped."

"Talked to people he shouldn't have?" Romey asked.

"Not clients or anything. Just people in other parts of the company. We're not supposed to socialize, but he did. I think he was sleeping with some of the women."

"Not just one?" Romey sounded surprised.

Monteith shook his head. "I saw him with at least three. He—I don't know—I asked him to be put on a different team. But he'd been pushing for the assignment and he'd been moving up in the company, so I got overruled."

"By whom?" Nyquist asked.

"The memo came from Mr. Whitford. But it seemed odd to me. I tried to ask Mr. Whitford about it, but our appointment wasn't until tomorrow."

Nyquist's gaze met Romey's. She raised her eyebrows, giving him some kind of signal.

"I'm so sorry about this, Mr. Monteith," she said. "I'm getting an urgent message on my links. Detective Nyquist and I have to go look at some evidence, but we'll be back shortly. Can we bring you anything?"

Monteith shook his head. Then he sighed.

Nyquist stood, wanting out of the room. He opened the door, and Romey walked through it. Once it was closed, she said, "I interviewed a lot of people. All the information in Whitford Security is segregated. No one person can have more than one piece of information. But it seems that this Illiyitch was talking to everyone. He could be your killer."

"Our killer," Nyquist said. "Especially if Whitford decided to talk to him before Monteith did."

Romey nodded. "This would have taken a lot of planning."

"It seems more like opportunity. He got himself assigned to Bowles's detail and looked for the moment. Lamfier was new to the detail as well. If they were in it together, it would explain how Bowles died so quickly."

"Quickly? What do you mean?" Romey asked.

"It only takes a few seconds to walk through that forest around the Hunting Club. But if Lamfier grabbed Bowles and then Illiyitch shot her, she would have died in those few seconds and no one would have been there to help her."

"Then Illiyitch murdered Lamfier to keep him quiet."

"Or to avoid paying him," Nyquist said.

"It's all supposition right now," Romey said.

"But it's good supposition."

"Only this Illiyitch guy is missing."

Nyquist smiled. "But not for long."

"How do you plan to catch him? He had to know we'd be looking."

"But he probably hadn't counted on Bowles being news." Nyquist grinned. "Let's give his image to the press."

"That results in so many bad leads," Romey said.

"You have a better idea?" Nyquist asked.

She frowned for a moment. "Let's just call him a potential witness."

"Then the press might try to interview him first."

"And he's going to what? Admit he killed her?" Romey grinned back at him. "We'll hear about it no matter what."

"We'll have someone monitoring the news nets."

"And taking any tips." She put a hand on Nyquist's arm. "See? I told you this interview would be important."

He nodded. "It just might be the break we needed," he said.

46

Flint didn't want to be in Wagner's office, but he saw no other choice. Those thugs Wagner had sent still had a laser pistol to Talia's head, and they had a jammer.

Had Flint been alone, he could have knocked the pistol away and tossed himself out of the air car, using his emergency links on the way to the ground to let the authorities know where he was.

He would have risked injury to himself.

He couldn't risk any injury to Talia.

So he let these four guys drag him and Talia into Wagner's office. Fittingly, the office was in the middle of the building that housed WSX. Wagner tried to hide the office's location with fancy elevator tricks and some floating corridors, but Flint wasn't fooled.

He also knew that even if the thugs left, it would be nearly impossible to get out of WSX alive.

Of course, if Wagner had wanted Flint dead, he wouldn't have dragged him to the office. Especially in such a public way.

The office itself was wide and spacious, with a skylight that was open to the dome. Flint only looked at the skylight as a possible escape route.

But everything he could think of wouldn't work for Talia. She had given the thugs as good as she'd gotten—the one was limping because she had managed a well-placed kick, and the who held her was missing part of his ear and probably had a major infection growing in there—but she looked a bit worn herself, and Flint didn't want that.

He didn't want any of this.

So he told Talia to stop fighting and to come along. She had given him an anger-filled look, but she had stopped.

And then she seemed close to tears.

"You may go," the voice came from darkness near the back of the office.

Flint recognized the voice. It belonged to Justinian Wagner.

"I'd love to go," Flint said, "but it seems your goons are holding my daughter."

"You mean a clone of your daughter, don't you?" Wagner asked. "You can always replace her."

Flint clenched his fists so that he wouldn't lunge at the man.

"Besides, I wasn't talking to you, Flint. I was talking to my men. They can leave. Take the clone with you."

"She stays." Flint wasn't going to let her out of his sight.

Wagner stepped into the light pouring from the dome opening. He looked tired. Flint had never seen the man look tired before.

"We're going to be talking business," Wagner said. "No child needs to hear that."

"I'm not a child," Talia said.

"Technically," Wagner said, "you're barely a person."

Flint didn't like the fact that Wagner knew that Talia was a clone. "Leave her alone, Wagner. She's more human than you are."

Wagner stared at Flint for a moment, then inclined his head slightly to one side. "By your definition of human, that might actually be true," Wagner said. Then he waved a hand at the thugs. "Get out. Leave the clone, the child, whatever Flint here calls her."

"My daughter," Flint snapped.

"Well, technically, I suppose she is. If you claim all your random DNA," Wagner said.

One of the thugs shoved Flint forward. The one holding Talia didn't let go until he was almost through the door.

They left the room, closing the door behind them.

Talia wiped a hand over her face. The look she gave Flint was one part defiance and two parts terror.

"What do you want, Wagner?" Flint needed to know what this was about before he could figure out how to leave.

He also checked his links. Even though the portable jammer was gone, the links still weren't working.

"I want to know why you're trying to destroy me," Wagner said.

Flint smiled. "Destroy you? Don't you think that's a bit dramatic?"

Talia came up beside him and stuck her hand through his arm. She was shaking. He put it around her shoulder, pulling her close.

She continued to stand straight, though. She clearly wasn't going to let Wagner see how he had frightened her.

Wagner took a step toward them. "You sicced that reporter on me. You gave her protection and files. Then you arranged to have her killed so that everyone will blame me."

The man's clothing was in disarray. His hair was slightly messy.

Flint guessed that was what passed for distraught in Wagner's universe.

"You're telling me you didn't order her killed?" Flint asked.

"I've never ordered anyone killed in my life," Wagner snapped.

Flint made a sound of disgust. "Don't lie, Justinian."

"I'm not," Wagner said.

"Maybe you didn't order your parents' deaths," Flint

said, "but you sure as hell guaranteed it. I know you let the Bixian government know how to find your parents. And I also know you're smart enough to know that once the Bixian government could find them, the assassins would come to kill them."

Wagner's face had turned waxy. His eyes glittered.

"I never ordered anyone killed," he said. "Why should I? I own the largest law firm in the Earth Alliance. I can destroy my enemies with lawsuits and motions and court cases that would last decades."

Wagner's voice was shrill. Talia leaned closer to Flint. He tightened his grip on her.

"You didn't want anyone to know about the ESI lawsuits," Flint said. "You didn't want anyone to know that it was WSX's advice that got people killed, not negligence."

This time, Wagner made the sound of disgust. "That was my parents' problem," he said. "I can and did disavow any culpability there. I wasn't even a lawyer when all that happened. I was a boy."

"There are other things in the files," Flint said. "Things you did."

"Yes," Wagner said. "The files. I thought you returned those to me untouched, Miles."

"You can think whatever you want, Justinian. Amazing how trusting you are, for a lawyer."

Wagner's eyes narrowed. "I still don't see why you had to kill Bowles. I can prove I was here. I can prove that I hadn't hired anyone. Nothing will hold up in a court of law, not even if you made up evidence."

Flint was feeling uneasy, and it wasn't just because he was in Wagner's office. "You didn't have Ki Bowles killed?"

"I've been spending all day trying to hold on to clients. Why the hell would I hire a killer in the middle of all that? And how would I? I barely have time to talk to you."

Flint said, "Yet you managed to hire some goons to kidnap me and my daughter."

"Kidnap is a harsh word. Besides, it only applies to legal

humans. I'm sure you and I can come to some agreement where we concede that I brought you here for a meeting. I'm sure we can work that out."

Flint ignored the second part of that statement and focused on the first part. "Talia is legal. She's legally my child. You can check the records, Justinian. Any of those witness in the law school cafeteria will testify to the fact Talia left the cafeteria with a laser pistol to her head. You had no reason to meet with her."

Wagner waved a hand in dismissal. "If I'd summoned you, you wouldn't have come here."

"Probably not," Flint said. "But I might have met you in a neutral place."

"Without protection? Thinking I had killed Ki Bowles?"

"I can protect myself," Flint said.

"That's clear," Wagner said with great sarcasm.

Flint didn't answer that. He wasn't going to say that the only reason he'd come had been Talia. He didn't want to give Wagner that much ammunition, even if Wagner was smart enough to figure it out himself.

"Besides," Wagner said, "why would I kill you? I'd sue your ass for my files. The ones you have illegally. The ones that you turned over to a reporter for no real reason."

"Prove that I have the files," Flint said. "There were witnesses to the fact I returned them."

"Because," Wagner said, "there's no way Bowles could have known about ESI and Aleyd and Gramming. Not in the detail she was promising."

Talia had tensed. Flint wondered what she saw. He looked out of the corner of his eye but saw nothing.

"Promised," he said. "You never waited to see if she'd deliver. It's Ki Bowles we're talking about here. She could have had only innuendo."

"Possibly," Wagner said. "But not even innuendo could have dug up Gramming."

"Gramming," Talia said softly.

Flint turned toward her.

"Gramming is on my certificate, Dad." She was whispering. "It's all over my research."

"Research?" Wagner asked.

Talia flushed.

"What research?"

Flint narrowed his eyes. Wagner seemed flustered. Something about Gramming bothered him.

"Talia wanted her day of creation certificate," Flint said. "It took some work to get it."

"I'll bet," Wagner said, "considering creatures like you are owned by the corporations that created you."

"What?" Talia asked.

"Enough," Flint said.

"And the corporation that created you would be . . . what? Aleyd? Isn't that who your wife worked for, Flint?"

The attack surprised Flint. And Wagner's knowledge. The man had been keeping an eye on Flint, just like Flint had kept an eye on him.

"Talia is legally my child," Flint said. "She's not owned by anyone."

Although he couldn't say she never had been. If he hadn't taken her off Callisto, she would have become property of Aleyd Corporation.

"Why don't we call a truce, Flint?" Wagner said. "You stop trying to destroy me and I'll leave your so-called daughter alone."

"That's blackmail," Flint said.

Wagner waved that hand again. "Kidnapping, blackmail, murder. You seem to think I'm capable of all of it."

"Because you've done it all," Flint said. "To say that you represent the law is a joke, Justinian. You're a power-mad egomaniac who seems to believe he's above the law."

"Dad," Talia whispered warningly.

"You're in my office," Wagner said. "Do you realize how easy it would be to make you vanish? All I have to do is tell your friends that you've Disappeared with that daughter of yours. They'd think it was inevitable, given the kinds of trouble you've been in over the years."

"They wouldn't believe anything you say," Flint snapped.

"Sure they would," Wagner said. "You helped my brother Disappear. I know that. I'm sure your lawyer, Van Alen, does, too. She'd believe. If she believes, so would everyone else."

"Threatening me does you no good, Justinian," Flint said. "Ki Bowles was doing her own reports from materials she gathered."

Which was true enough. Just because he had jump-started her with tidbits of information from confidential files didn't make it any less true.

"When you killed her," Flint said, "you made sure that the source of that information went with her."

"*I didn't kill her!*" Wagner sprayed spit as he yelled. "I didn't order her killed and I didn't do it. You'd think I'd destroy my law firm like that? You did it."

"No, he didn't," Talia said. "My dad would never kill anyone."

Wagner stared at her. Then he looked at Flint.

"Is that true?" Wagner asked in a completely different tone.

Flint wasn't going to answer the implied second question. He had killed, more than once, but only when he had no other choice.

"I didn't kill Ki Bowles. And I certainly would never have killed anyone to frame you." He put all the hatred he felt toward Wagner in his voice.

"Interesting," Wagner said. He sank into a nearby chair as if all the fight had gone out of him. "If one of us didn't kill her, then who the hell did?"

47

Nyquist and Romey left the interrogation area. Romey wanted to ask Monteith more questions, but Nyquist felt that first, they needed to get officers tracking Illiyitch.

"I'll contact the team still at Whitford," Romey said. "I'm sure they have holoimages and descriptions. He had to have had a résumé or—"

A piercing shriek resounded in the corridor. Nyquist put a hand to his ear.

"You all right?" Romey asked.

He started to say, "Didn't you hear that?" but before he could, static filled his ears, followed by: "Ki Bowles's killers have come for me."

And then, silence.

Nyquist had a sudden headache. The sounds were so loud he'd actually thought they were inside the building, not coming from his links.

Normally links had filters to protect the receiver from things like that.

Only in cases of emergency did those filters sometimes malfunction.

"You didn't hear anything, did you?" he asked, knowing his own voice was too loud.

Romey shook her head.

His ears were ringing. He wasn't sure he knew where the message had come from.

He instructed his links to replay it.

"Ki Bowles's killers have come for me—"

The message was actually cut off. That was probably why it had so much sound with it. The sound amplified an emergency message, making it seem even more urgent.

He had his links trace the source of the message, and it only took a few seconds to get an answer back.

Miles Flint.

Nyquist swore.

Romey looked concerned. "What is it?"

"See if you can find out if there's some kind of emergency with Miles Flint." Nyquist went to the end of the corridor where the police networks had on-screen access.

He looked for any emergency call with Flint and found one he didn't expect.

Emergency call from the cafeteria in the law school at Dome University, Armstrong Branch from Talia Shindo (Flint). Call interrupted.

Nyquist played that back. Romey had joined him.

Police! My father's being kidnapped! Help! Help! Help! We're at the cafeteria in the law library. Please help!

"I got several reports of an incident in that cafeteria," Romey said. "It came through many emergency links, including those weird ones issued to resident aliens. A few said that some guys took a man and his daughter away at gunpoint, and that the guys called the man Flint."

"Crap," Nyquist said.

"He's the one who contacted you?" Romey asked.

"It was broken off. He said Ki Bowles's killers had come for him and Talia."

"But we don't know who Ki Bowles's killers are," Romey said.

"Yeah." Nyquist frowned. "But we have a suspect."

"Illiyitch?"

"Justinian Wagner." Nyquist waved a finger. "You make sure that the responding officers at the cafeteria know how important this is."

"What are you going to do?"

"I'm heading to Wagner, Stuart, and Xendor."

"You're not going alone," Romey said.

"You're staying here and coordinating the search for Illiyitch."

"I didn't mean me," she snapped. "Take a team."

He nodded as he hurried out of the interrogation area. "Don't worry," he said over his shoulder. "I will."

48

Popova sat cross-legged on one of plush chairs. She was going through one of the handhelds and comparing it to a clear net screen that was open on a table in front of her.

DeRicci had assigned Popova to search through the nut ball data—the saved information from the public nets—while DeRicci herself looked over the power glitch information.

She was stunned that no one had ever noticed these glitches before. They had occurred off and on throughout the last fifteen years.

The glitches might have occurred before that as well, but she was searching through that data. She only started with information from fifteen years ago, thinking that if fifteen-year-old information was stolen recently, maybe an attempt had been made earlier as well.

She found some longer glitches, ones that occurred intermittently throughout the system.

Initially, Armstrong's city engineers thought the glitches part of the aging environmental systems array, something that worried her almost more than the glitches did. Because, it seemed to her, the engineers were awfully calm about potential problems in the environmental systems, the only thing that kept Armstrong's residents alive in the harsh environment on the Moon.

But she had to force herself not to read the engineering reports. Instead, she had been looking at the number of power glitches since the dome's systems had been rebuilt after the bombing.

If she had had to guess, she would have wagered that the number of glitches went down after the rebuild—and initially they did.

But about a year after the rebuild, the glitches started again. Only this time, they'd gotten worse.

And they were concentrated on specific areas—sometimes down to specific buildings.

"Rudra," she said, "can our techs back-trace these glitches?"

"Hmmm?" Popova looked up. Her eyes were bleary from looking back and forth at two different-sized screens. "Um, I'm not sure. I would assume so."

"Find out," DeRicci said, and looked back at the data.

She heard rather than saw Popova get up from her chair. Then Popova walked over to DeRicci's desk.

"Before I forget," Popova said, "I found some of what's missing. It seems innocuous enough."

"Write it up," DeRicci said.

"I will," Popova said. "But it's weird."

DeRicci looked up. She really didn't want to lose her concentration. She had numbers floating around in her mind—the number of glitches, the address of the areas where the most glitches occurred, the different types of businesses located there.

But Popova seemed determined.

So DeRicci sighed. "Go ahead."

"It's mostly names. People's addresses and backgrounds vanished from the public networks."

"Everyone has the right to remove their name and address from the public boards," DeRicci said.

"Remove yes," Popova said. "But not obliterate all traces

of those names. And even stranger, before the traces were obliterated, every single one of those people came through the Port of Armstrong."

DeRicci leaned back in her chair. Her breath had caught. She had to remind herself to breathe.

"Every one of them?" she asked.

Popova nodded.

"Did they stay at the hotels that lost records?" DeRicci asked. "Did they bank at the banks?"

"All of the people were from off-Moon," Popova said.

"Still, some of our banks have branches off-Moon," De-Ricci said.

"I don't know the answer to that. I didn't have time to check. But I would wager they stayed at the hotels. Most of them used the port again about two weeks after they arrived."

"They came into Armstrong, then left two weeks later," DeRicci said.

Popova nodded.

"What can you find out about these people?"

"That's the strange thing," Popova said. "I can't find anything. What vanished is work records, birth and death records, records of marriages or divorces. Mundane stuff."

"Anything unusual in it?"

"No," Popova said. "They didn't even work for the same companies."

"Did they come to Armstrong at the same time?"

"The first group did. About five of them, during that initial missing period. But they didn't seem to hang out together, and they didn't seem to know one another."

"Did they frequent the same places?" DeRicci asked.

"I haven't had enough time to look." Popova tucked a long strand of hair behind her ear. Her hands were shaking.

She was clearly frustrated.

"We need more people working on this," DeRicci said.

"I don't know that, either," Popova said. "I mean, the data is years old. So why the hurry now?"

"The glitches have increased in the past week," DeRicci said.

"Meaning what?"

DeRicci shrugged, and then she closed her eyes as a realization hit her. She should have been examining the glitch information around the time of the dome explosion. They'd never caught the bomber.

Maybe these people whose information vanished were saboteurs or part of terror cells. Maybe the people who came in had some kind of horrible plan to harm—or even destroy—Armstrong.

"Sir?" Popova asked.

DeRicci opened her eyes. Her mouth was dry. She was making things up. She didn't have enough information yet.

But the information she did have was making her very, very nervous.

"See if these glitches can be back-traced," she said. "And if they can, make the traces a priority. I want to know who—if anyone—is causing this."

"Yes, sir," Popova said. "Should I bring in someone else to search the information?"

DeRicci thought for a moment. If this was some kind of well-coordinated outside attack, then each glitch had meaning. And people with no history of trouble were causing the problems.

People with no history of trouble. Like the people who got vetted before becoming government employees.

"Not yet," DeRicci said. "If we need more eyes on this, we'll get them."

"Yes, sir," Popova said.

Popova was almost to the door when DeRicci said, "Rudra?"

"Yes, sir?"

"What do you think is going on?"

Popova bit her lower lip. "I don't like to speculate, sir," she said after a moment.

"Do it anyway," DeRicci said.

"It could be anything," Popova said. "From some kind of plan or plans against Armstrong to the placing of illegals throughout the city. I mean, what better way to become a part of a community if all you have to do is wipe out any record of your past, and create some new identity?"

What better way indeed? DeRicci made herself breathe. Or, she suddenly realized, it could be a combination of both. People who shouldn't be in Armstrong establishing new identities—and then planning to do some harm.

"Thanks, Rudra," DeRicci said, effectively dismissing her.

DeRicci looked at the data in front of her. She hadn't yet compared the recent glitches to this week's crime reports.

But she had a hunch she'd find something—something she wouldn't like at all.

<u>49</u>

Nyquist had never bullied his way into a law office before. He'd gone into doctor's offices and high-end brokerage firms. He'd arrested people in schools and restaurants and museums.

But he'd never gone into a law office on official business. At least not on business that involved a possible crime still under way.

He had a team of ten officers behind him. He used his "official business" line with the expensive android that guarded the door. He overrode the circuitry with his police-issued chips when the android wouldn't let him pass.

He had all of the officers draw their weapons as he hurried through Wagner, Stuart, and Xendor's large lobby, demanding to know where Justinian Wagner was.

Assistant after assistant tried to stop him, and he wouldn't be stopped.

He remembered how to get to Wagner's office. He used his chip again to override the privacy controls in the need-lessly fancy elevator, and commanded it to hurry.

It moved faster than he wanted it to, and if he had anyone to confess to, he would have told that person that the speed of the elevator made him slightly queasy.

But it didn't get rid of the feeling of elation that had accompanied him from the moment he entered this place.

Even if his information—his guess—was wrong, he was enjoying this. He had a reason to be here.

He hadn't realized how much he hated Wagner, how much he blamed the bastard for every single painful day in that hospital, for each and every agonizing movement in physical therapy, for all those excruciating surgeries designed to rebuild him the way he had been before.

As if he could ever be the way he had been before.

The elevator stopped. He remembered the way that the doors opened onto the reception area, the way that Wagner's office seemed like its own fortress.

Well, Nyquist was storming that fortress now. Despite all the associates gathered in front of the doors, trying to protect their boss.

"Detective," one of the associates said, "I'm sure we can come to some kind of agreement—"

"And I'm sure we can't," Nyquist said. "Step aside, or I'll arrest you."

"You can't arrest everyone in the firm," said another associate, a thin young woman with glittery eyes.

He stopped for the first time since he started his charge into WSX. "Of course I can," he said. "We have a report here of a kidnapping in progress. I can do anything I want to do. Now get the hell out of my way."

They got. Leaving him and his team in front of that big black door.

Nyquist was about to open it when another associate stepped in front of him.

"At least let me tell him you're here," the associate said.

But Nyquist shoved him aside.

He'd tell Wagner himself why he was here.

And then he'd arrest the bastard, whether Flint was inside the room or not.

50

"Hear me out," Wagner said, his hand up, as if Flint could flee from the sound of the man's voice.

Flint had been listening to the man ever since they both realized that neither of them had killed Ki Bowles, and he didn't want to listen anymore.

He just couldn't think of an alternative. If he grabbed Talia's hand and burst out of the office, he'd get caught by those thugs again—and this time they might kill his daughter, especially after what Wagner had said about her.

Some people didn't consider clones human. Apparently Wagner was one of those.

"You're an investigator, right?" Wagner said. "I mean, you make your money finding people, but you've taken on stranger assignments, not quite specific ones. What if we team up? My resources, your skills, and we find who killed Bowles. Someone is trying to frame us both, and we shouldn't allow it."

Flint froze. Talia was staring at Wagner in disbelief. Flint wondered if he was, too.

"Team *up*?" Flint asked.

"We're both businessmen," Wagner said. "We have similar interests. I know you dislike me and I'm not real fond of you, but we could work something out—"

"You're serious," Flint said.

"Of course I am," Wagner said. "Occasionally a man must ally with someone he dislikes to get a job done. We need to know what's going on in the Bowles case. I think that by doing it together—"

"You actually think I'd work with you?" Flint asked.

"Of course," Wagner said. "You're a smart man. It's in both of our interests—"

"I don't work with murderers," Flint said.

"I told you," Wagner said. "I didn't kill Ki Bowles. Weren't you paying attention? I—"

"Or kidnappers," Talia said with so much anger that for a moment, Flint thought she was going to jump on Wagner like she'd jumped on that thug.

"Child," Wagner said, "your—father—and I are having a discussion. It doesn't concern you."

"It concerns her," Flint said. "Because if I were a man unethical enough to tie myself to you, then she would have to deal with that. And she knows better. *I* know better. I want you to pay for Paloma's murder. I'm not going to help you out of this mess."

"But I have nothing to do with it," Wagner said.

"Even if that's true," Flint said, "I don't care. You can't bring us in here at gunpoint and assume we'll help you."

"Surely—"

"Surely you're not that stupid," Flint said. "Surely you understand that I'll make sure someone pays for Paloma's murder."

"The Bixian assassins are dead. The Bixian government can't be charged."

"And neither can the man who tipped them off," Flint said. "But I stopped working for the police, remember?"

At that moment, the door to the office slammed open. Bartholomew Nyquist stood there, with a group of officers in uniform behind him.

Some associate—a man—waved his hands. "I tried to stop them, sir. They say there's a kidnapping in progress."

"There is," Flint said. "Wagner brought me and Talia here at gunpoint."

"I recorded it all," Talia said, holding up a fist. She pointed to a chip on her knuckle. "You want it?"

Nyquist's eyes were sparkling. But his expression was serious. "Are you injured?"

"No—" Talia started, but Flint put a hand on her arm.

"We'll have to have someone make sure," he said. "My daughter is probably badly bruised."

"It's not a kidnapping," Wagner said. "I invited Mr. Flint here to discuss business."

"He took us," Talia said. "I have proof."

"And witnesses," Flint said. "Ask anyone in the law school cafeteria."

"We already are." Nyquist walked deeper into the office. He looked jaunty. "Justinian Wagner, you are under arrest for the kidnapping of Miles Flint and Talia Shindo. Other charges, including attempted murder or murder by hire, might be added later. Have you anything to say?"

"I'm one of the most respected lawyers in Armstrong. You have no right—"

"You know the law, sir. Do you contend the charges or accept them?"

Wagner's lips thinned. He looked like he wanted to punch Nyquist. Instead he said tightly, "Contend."

"Excellent." Nyquist removed the lightlocks from his pocket. "Turn around."

"Surely that's not necessary."

"You're being charged with a felony, sir," Nyquist said. "It's necessary."

Then he grinned at Flint over Wagner's shoulder. Flint grinned back.

"Took you long enough," Flint said softly.

"Came as soon as I heard." Nyquist finished attaching the locks, then roughly turned Wagner around and shoved him forward. "Figured this was one arrest I didn't want to miss."

51

It had only been a half hour since the images of Gulliver Illiyitch were displayed all over Armstrong, but sighting reports had already overwhelmed the police station.

Romey had examined a dozen herself. The most credible
seemed to come from the area around the port, but she
couldn't get confirmation. And she didn't want to go in,
weapons drawn, without it.

"Savita." Gumiela had come out of her office. She stood
in the hallway just outside Romey's small cubicle.

Gumiela looked even more put together than usual. She
had probably refreshed her clothes several times during the
day and reapplied her hair gel, all because she had known
this was going to be a media kind of day.

Romey looked up from her desk. She was using the
scratched screen to make a map of the city, trying to trace a
trajectory of a possible Illiyitch path.

"You need to come see this." Gumiela moved away from
Romey's line of sight.

Romey suppressed a sigh and stood. Her sons would be
doing their homework or watching some vids. Maybe they'd
even left the house, knowing their mom wouldn't be back
until long after their bedtime.

She stepped into the hallway. Gumiela had turned on a wall screen.

There, in the middle of a throng of people, stood Gulliver Illiyitch.

He looked just like the identification photos that Whitford Security had. He hadn't even changed out of his black suit.

"Where's this?" Romey asked.

"The port, just like we thought. The media tracked him down. They're questioning him right now. I'm having Space Traffic Control pick him up. You want to go down there and cap off the arrest?"

Gumiela was actually being kind. She wanted to know whether Romey would like to make a high-profile arrest, the kind that would launch a career—turn Romey from a detective into an assistant chief or a media coordinator.

Into a junior Gumiela.

Romey made herself smile. "I think Space Traffic can handle it. I'll take care of him in interview."

Gumiela studied her for a moment, as if trying to figure her out. "You sure?"

"Yeah," Romey said.

"Are you worried that he's not your killer? Because I'm convinced he is. I've looked at the reports. No one else could have gotten close to Bowles. And certainly no one else could have taken out the other guard so easily."

Gumiela was being so nice that Romey wanted to ask why.

But she had a hunch she knew why. If this case got resolved today, then the department would get kudos, and the media would be grateful.

The longer this thing went on, the harder it would be for the department to take any credit—even if that credit was deserved.

"I agree," Romey said. "But I've looked at this guy's record. He's got a suspicious history, and it looks phony to me. I'm reasonably sure he's a hired killer. I'd rather get the person who paid for the murder than the murderer himself."

"Interesting," Gumiela said. "You know, sometimes we just have to be satisfied with the shooter."

"Yeah," Romey said, feeling almost like she was admitting defeat before she'd even started to fight. "I know."

52

After some argument, Flint got Nyquist to drop him and
Talia at Van Alen's. Nyquist wanted to take them first to a
hospital and then to the precinct. To make the charges
against Wagner even harsher, Nyquist wanted doctors to de-
clare Talia injured. Then he wanted to take a statement from
both of them.

"You got a statement," Flint said. "We made them at the
crime scene. And you have Talia's recordings. That should
be plenty."

Besides, he wanted to say, but didn't, charges against
Wagner wouldn't stick. Or if they did, they'd be reduced significantly. Wagner had too many judges in his pocket. He
had worked for half the city government and most of the
people who ran the United Domes of the Moon as well.

He would get out of this.

Although his law firm might not survive the negative
publicity.

But Flint had other things to do and he wasn't going to
tell Nyquist what they were. Flint wanted to check the name
of that corporation that had Wagner so upset—the one Talia
recognized.

And he wanted to make sure his daughter was protected.

But mostly, he wanted Van Alen to initiate a civil suit against Wagner. If the criminal case died—and it probably would—the civil suit would ensure that WSX and its shady senior partner would remain in the news, at least until Flint could decide what to do with the remaining files.

Van Alen's office was still in an uproar. People were examining networks, talking excitedly, and double-checking everything from their computer screens to their backups.

No one questioned Flint's entry, and no one asked how Talia was, even though she was leaning heavily on Flint. He knew she wasn't injured—he'd checked himself—but she was frightened deeper than she had been since Rhonda died.

In fact, the whole incident had probably brought Rhonda's death back. Flint was going to have to get Talia home soon.

But he knew this place, at least, would make her feel protected while he worked.

"Miles, thank God." Van Alen hurried toward him, wobbling on her heels. Her feet clearly hurt again. She only wobbled when she was tired.

She stopped just a few meters from him, frowning.

"What happened?" she asked.

He looked up at her. He didn't want to go through the whole story of the kidnapping and the arrest, but he didn't see a choice.

He told it as quickly as he could, as tersely as he could.

And to her credit, Van Alen didn't gloat that Wagner was arrested or even mention the shocking fact that Wagner probably wasn't involved in Bowles's death.

Instead, she walked over to Talia and put a hand on her shoulder.

"Come on," she said, glaring at Flint over Talia's shoulder, "let's take you to my office. It's quiet there. You can clean up, put on some comfortable clothes, and get something to eat."

"I don't have any clothes here," Talia said, and in that tone, Flint heard *I want to go home.*

But he also knew she didn't think of his apartment as

home. To her, the house she'd left on Callisto was the only home she'd ever had.

"I have some things that'll fit you," Van Alen said. "I also have a full bathroom so you can shower, and a lot of hot water, so you don't have to worry about it running out."

"Not to mention the fluffiest towels I've ever used," Flint said.

His daughter looked at him in shock and he realized she suddenly thought he was having an affair with Van Alen.

"Maxine let me hide out here back when Paloma died," Flint said. "I think I lived in her office for an entire day."

"More like two," Van Alen said. "Or three. I forget."

"I need to use your nonnetworked machines," Flint said.

"Before you do, I need you to back-trace that glitch," Van Alen said. "Particularly now that we know Wagner wasn't involved."

"I'll back-trace it," Flint said. "After I check the files."

"Dad, let's just go," Talia said.

He looked at her. He did need to take her home.

But he couldn't do that yet.

He'd actually believed Wagner. And if Wagner hadn't ordered Bowles's death, then someone else had.

And Flint was beginning to wonder if it wasn't one of the corporations that Wagner had mentioned.

Corporations could easily hire a killer and then deny it. Or slough it off on a lower-level employee.

"I'd love to go," he said to Talia. "But I can't. Not yet. We don't know everything that's going on."

"Mr. Wagner's been arrested," Talia said. "The news says they found Ki Bowles's killer. We can go."

"They found the killer?" Flint asked Van Alen. He hadn't been monitoring his links. He hated listening to news while trying to concentrate on other things.

"The shooter," Van Alen said. "They think someone hired him."

She gave Talia a pointed look.

Talia's eyes filled with tears. "I'm really tired."

"I know," Flint said. "Go with Maxine. I'll be working in the same office, which is right near the bathroom. We'll have food ready by the time you get out of the shower."

"I don't want to sleep here," Talia said.

Flint nodded. "I know."

But he didn't promise her that she would be able to go home. He couldn't, not yet.

He needed answers before he could do that.

And he needed them now.

53

Gulliver Illiyitch didn't look all that tough. He didn't look strong. He wasn't all that big.

And to top it off, he didn't even look all that bright.

Savita Romey found that comforting. She'd been afraid, deep down, that he would have the brains of a master criminal.

She watched two space traffic cops bring him into the precinct. She kept an eye on him as they booked him and took him to interrogation, but she didn't introduce herself.

Instead, she studied him.

He had an oily charm. He smiled a little too much. He also had the square jaw and broad forehead that some people thought composed classic handsomeness. His black hair was thick and glossy, and his clothes almost looked tailored, although they'd gotten quite messed up during the pursuit and arrest.

She'd watched the news reports.

Sightings had come into the police precinct and media outlets at the same time. While Gumiela had dispatched street cops to investigate sightings, the media sent junior reporters with cameras, hoping to find the man who'd killed one of their own.

And they had.

Romey would never know how many reporters went to dead ends, looking for the best scoop in years, but she suspected the number was probably in the hundreds.

And for once, she was glad of it.

She wanted this guy off the street.

For the first time, however, she wished she had a partner. A real one. She didn't want to go into interrogation alone. This case was too important. There were too many eyes on her, and one mistake could cost her career.

She didn't dare lose this job, not with the boys to support.

Not to mention the fact that she loved it.

Except when she was exhausted and overwhelmed, like now.

She hoped that booking would take longer than usual. Maybe by then, Nyquist would be done with Wagner.

Nyquist wouldn't be able to interview Wagner. That cagey lawyer would hire another cagey lawyer to protect him from everything. Wagner would never admit to hiring a man to murder Ki Bowles.

But maybe Illiyitch would admit to taking the money.

Or in exchange for some kind of reduced sentence, he'd talk about Wagner.

She could only hope.

Just like she could hope that she managed to make no mistakes in the interrogation.

Not one.

Especially one that would let Gulliver Illiyitch go free.

54

Flint settled at the nonnetworked computer closest to the wall. He turned it on, checked to make sure that no one else had used it since the last time he had, and then got to work.

Talia was still in the bathroom. Van Alen had ordered a feast, and then settled at her desk just behind Flint to draw up a civil complaint against Wagner.

She would file the motions and notify the media at the same time. Over Flint's objection, she also said she'd tell the reporters of her suspicion that Wagner had murdered Ki Bowles.

I don't think it's true, Flint had said.

Based on what? Van Alen had asked. *A feeling? Something the man said to you? Don't you know his office is designed to reflect his moods? Literally reflect them. He has some pheromones in there or something that make the people who visit him feel like he wants them to feel.*

I doubt that, Flint had said, *unless he wanted Talia to feel scared and me to feel pissed off.*

Van Alen had shaken her head at him. *Trust me. We're letting the press know he's behind the killings. If we're wrong, the fact that it was our suspicion will be forgotten in all the back-and-forthing the talking heads will do over the next*

*twenty-four hours. If we're right, we'll make it even more
difficult for Wagner to get away with the kidnapping.*

Flint was too tired to argue. And he rather liked her
analysis. So he let her do her job. It kept her from nagging
him about checking into that glitch.

He wanted to look through Paloma's files first.

Over the past few months, he'd set up a sophisticated
search engine that combined Paloma's files for names,
places, and crimes. Paloma had developed an unusual system for keeping track of the files, so a standard search
wouldn't work.

Most of the time he had been grateful for that, but once
he started feeding information to Ki Bowles, he found he
needed something more specific.

He didn't want to give her something he hadn't vetted yet.

Although it appeared that he had without realizing it.

Gramming Corporation was a wholly owned subsidiary
of Speidel Corporation, one of the many cloning firms that
had offices in Armstrong. Speidel worked mostly with the
Growing Pits and other food organizations, but Speidel also
did some corporate work for places like Aleyd.

And they had a small human cloning facility. They re-
stricted use to employees of Aleyd and the handful of other
people who could pay exorbitant prices for a clone. The corporation's bylaws also stated that clones could only be of
someone who had already died.

Some human communities didn't allow cloning of the
dead, but it was legal on the Moon. Which brought a lot of
people from outside Armstrong to the cloning firms. Speidel
tried to prevent being overrun by requests, so it charged the
highest prices in Armstrong.

Flint knew that Speidel had cloned Emmeline, even
though when they had initially done so, she hadn't been
dead. The corporation wouldn't release the files to him because the files didn't belong to him.

The files belonged either to Rhonda or to Aleyd Corporation.

Flint wouldn't have been surprised if Speidel's name had been on Talia's day of creation certificate, but it hadn't been.

Talia said the name on the certificate was Gramming's.

So he opened Gramming's files.

And wished he hadn't.

55

Van Alen's shower had a chair carved in the very center. Talia found the chair by pushing buttons. The chair rose from the tile floor and became the centerpiece of the shower itself.

The shower could be either a sonic shower like most in the dome or a water shower, the height of luxury. A sign appeared when Talia hit the water button, letting her know that the water she was using had been recycled and would be recycled again.

But that didn't make her feel any less decadent. Especially when she sat in that chair, water dripping around her like those pictures of rain forests she'd seen in school. She'd set the water as hot as she could stand it. It was working some of the soreness out of her shoulders and back, but it wasn't quite enough to make her feel better.

She wasn't sure anything could make her feel better.

What was wrong with her? The people around her, the people who cared for her, got attacked. Her dad could have died. Then she went to help him like she'd promised herself she would after her mother got kidnapped, and that man had put a gun against her neck.

The spot was still sore. So was her stomach. She had a

long bruise that ran from her hip to her rib cage where his arm had clutched her so tightly she was afraid she was going to vomit.

She hadn't, of course. But she'd been hoping she would. She would have gotten him with it, startling him, and helping herself and her dad escape.

All those fantasies, and they never came true. Not even the attack fantasy. Attacking the attacker didn't make things better, like she had always thought.

It had made things worse.

She wiped her wet hair off her face. Steam rose around her, coating the etched glass that protected the shower area from the rest of the bathroom.

This was nice. It was the kind of thing her dad could afford but wouldn't. He was weirdly stingy, wanting a kind of life that didn't rely on money.

Maybe that was why he worked so hard, even when he said he wouldn't.

Because he didn't want to think about the money he had.

She wasn't sure how she could deal with him working anymore, now that she knew the danger he was always talking about was real. And how focused he got. Just like Mom. Mom wasn't ever thinking about Talia.

Mom was thinking about the next experiment, the problems on the job, the way that the company wanted her to be.

And all she'd done was get mad at Talia.

At least, her dad had let Talia help.

Although that hadn't made her feel better, either. All that stuff she'd learned about Ki Bowles had been disturbing. Ki Bowles had a lot of people after her, so she needed orders of protection. And a lot of people hated her because she was so good at her job.

Talia didn't understand any of it.

She wasn't sure she wanted to.

Maybe that was why she'd been trying to leave. To visit those other girls, who were just exactly like her—exactly like her, down to the DNA structure—to see if they'd found a life that was better, one that didn't involve parents who worked too hard or people who hated them because of their jobs or, God forbid, kidnapping.

Talia ran a hand over her face, smoothing the water off it. Then she closed her eyes and tilted her head back.

At least here she felt better than she had all day.

Here she could pretend everything was all right, even when it wasn't.

She could pretend that she was cherished and loved and safe.

Just like the girls she called sisters.

56

Flint hunched over the nonnetworked computer in Van Alen's office, blocking her view of his work with his body. Not that she was trying to look at it. She was doing her own work, setting up his case, handling parts of the crisis that had descended on the office during the power glitch.

Talia was still in the bathroom. He was going to send Van Alen for her if she hadn't come out when the food arrived.

But he wanted to be calmer by then. Because he'd been reading Gramming's legal files, and they turned his stomach.

Gramming had originally been set up as a humanitarian corporation attached to Speidel Corporation. Cloning sometimes went wrong. Not the way it had in the spectacular early years, when a cloned child might have a finger growing out of its belly, but something a bit more subtle.

If an elderly couple wanted to clone their dead adult child, they'd often instruct the company to make several attempts. Gene manipulation, particularly certain kinds of enhancements, made the adult different than the baby had been.

Some parents wanted a child just like the one they'd

raised. Others wanted a child just like the adult the dead person had made himself into.

Often cloning companies like Speidel showed the parents the cloned child, only to have them reject that child as "not right." That child—a living, breathing human being—then became property of Speidel.

And Speidel wasn't set up to raise dozens (and in the early days hundreds) of children.

So it set up Gramming, where, for a small fee, families who wanted to could adopt the clones and raise them as their own.

Adoption had fallen out of favor in many parts of the sector. It was easier to have a child carried through a surrogate or grown in a vat from the parents' mixed sperm and egg than it used to be. But creating an original child from sperm and egg, however it was done, remained expensive.

And the people who couldn't afford to create their own children and who couldn't have them the natural way often adopted because adoption was so much cheaper.

The one thing Gramming did from the beginning was insist that Speidel hide the clone mark. Most clone marks were visible behind the neck. But Talia's, like that of every other clone made at Speidel, was behind the ear and under the skin.

Most adoptive parents would never know that the baby they'd raised from a few weeks of age was a clone. Gramming had done studies. People didn't want to raise clones. They wanted to raise "real children."

As Speidel cut the amount of human cloning work it did in favor of agricultural products, the money that went to Gramming faded as well.

That loss of revenue threatened Gramming since, despite the intent of the corporation's founders, it had become a tidy for-profit business.

So the new CEO—Ohari Kinoy—had spoken to his lawyers about that. His lawyer.

Justinian Wagner.

Who suggested that certain clones might have more value than others. Say, clones of a highly regarded scientist who married one of the most gifted computer programmers in the city. Clones whose original had a tested intelligence that was higher than her parents' combined.

Flint went cold as he stared at that. Because Justinian Wagner—years younger, but just as cold—had been talking about five clones of Emmeline, clones that Rhonda had made to protect herself, not their living, breathing daughter.

He made himself continue. Wagner had made the same argument about babies whose parents had award-winning beauty or some highly desirable talent, things that got passed through the genes.

As close to designer babies as a company could get.

The clones were created for other reasons that, like Rhonda's, often weren't specified in the files.

And the clones that weren't wanted—the "defective" ones, the ones that didn't quite look like Uncle John or Aunt Susan—were property of Speidel or Aleyd or whatever corporation had paid for the cloning.

So, Wagner had suggested, on special children, bump the fee. Deal with the parents yourself so that no one else would know.

And Kinoy had done that.

For almost twenty years.

He'd sold babies and made a hefty profit for Gramming. Some of that profit went to WSX in the form of consulting fees—probably keeping-quiet fees—and some of it went directly into Kinoy's pocket, before it ever saw Gramming's books.

Gramming itself, the five regular employees and the six part-timers, only saw the standard fee. They handled the records exactly as they would handle them for a straight adoption.

The only difference was that the boss handled the case and kept the most damning records on file with his law firm. WSX.

And Paloma had meticulously copied those files along with all the others.

Flint rubbed a hand over his forehead. He could comfort himself with the knowledge that the families were vetted, like the other adoptive families. Gramming employees found no history of child abuse or alcoholism anywhere in the family's past, made sure the financial records were in order, demanded a written commitment to education, and a determination to raise the child within the best guidelines of the family's community.

The rules had come from Gramming's early days. Then it had had a political mission. It had wanted clones to become the best human beings in the universe. The corporation wanted to prove that clones were as good as and sometimes better than their originals.

The initial founder of Gramming had wanted to help clones obtain their legal rights all over the Earth Alliance.

Then he'd retired and someone else had taken over and the mission got lost.

Then Kinoy became CEO.

And sold babies.

"You all right?" Van Alen asked. She was standing beside her desk.

"I don't know," Flint said.

"Were you injured earlier?"

He shook his head. "Just some information I found."

Van Alen knew better than to ask him what that information was. "Well, they tell me that the food is here. Can they bring it up?"

"Of course." He darkened the screen, but not before checking his own logs.

He hadn't given any of this to Ki Bowles. He'd given her some material on ESI and some on Aleyd, but nothing on Speidel and Gramming.

He moved to one of the other nonnetworked computers, where he kept Ki Bowles's interview lists and her own research material—things he had insisted on having from the beginning of her work, so that he could monitor her.

He found three former legal assistants to Justinian Wagner. They had told Bowles that if she wanted a scandal that would break WSX open, she should investigate Gramming.

And that was all she had.

She'd used it as a threat in her first piece without knowing what she was digging into.

Kinoy had made millions selling babies. Clones. If Bowles had completed her investigation and reported it, the news would have destroyed families.

Families that had paid too much for their children, but families that had, so far as Flint could tell from the small sample Talia had found, kept up their bargain with Gramming. They'd educated their children, raised them to be solid citizens, and given them the best advantages within the Earth Alliance.

"How bad is it?" Van Alen asked as she raised the etched-glass door.

"Bad," Flint said.

And he wasn't sure exactly what he could do.

57

Nyquist stopped outside the interrogation room and watched Romey work. The elation he'd felt with Wagner's arrest still hovered at the edges of his emotions. He needed to calm down.

He had to remind himself that things could go very wrong with the Wagner case.

If Wagner were anyone else, the interrogation room that Nyquist would be about to enter would have Wagner in it. And Nyquist would be able to get him to answer each and every question he asked.

Instead, Wagner had one of the best criminal defense attorneys in the Earth Alliance on his way here from Cairo on Earth, and a surrogate who just happened to be the best criminal defense attorney in Armstrong standing in until the other attorney got here.

Nyquist would probably lose his prize.

But he'd make sure the press knew each and every detail of his case. He'd already leaked the arrest and the reasons for it, along with parts of Talia's recording.

That kid was brilliant. She'd gotten everything, from the men encircling her father to the ride to WSX and the "talk" with Wagner himself.

If WSX survived that little recording, then there was such a thing as miracles.

Or maybe, to put it more accurately, if Wagner survived it. The law firm might have a life of its own, but it wouldn't be as powerful as it had been, and it certainly wouldn't have that man at its head. Not with all he'd admitted to in the privacy of his own office.

And Nyquist had to admit he found some satisfaction in that. Even if Wagner hadn't killed Ki Bowles—and Nyquist wasn't yet convinced of that—the poetic justice was still nice.

Wagner, in trying to get rid of a media gadfly, was going to be brought down.

By the media.

And one kid he'd called barely human. Talia was certainly a lot more human than Wagner could ever be.

And smarter, too.

Nyquist would have to think of a way to let her know what she'd done was great. She'd been too shaken in the car for him to really talk with her—not about what happened, she'd been clear about that—but about how she felt about it.

Not that it was his concern.

But he'd gotten to know her a little in the months that she'd lived here, and while he'd always liked her, he never really realized what a thinker she was.

Which shouldn't have surprised him, given that she was Miles Flint's daughter.

Whom Wagner had called a clone.

Nyquist hadn't released that part of the recording to the media. He'd keep that as quiet as he could. He'd been surprised by it, but it made more sense than Flint's story—that Rhonda had had a second child and kept that child hidden from him.

Still, not everyone would be understanding if the word got out.

And not everyone would treat Talia with the kindness that she deserved.

Nyquist turned up the sound from the interview room. Romey had been going through Illiyitch's fake history with him, the stuff the man had put on his résumé. The résumé hadn't been that deep. If Whitford Security had done the kind of background check that the police department did, they would have found that Illiyitch was using one of his many false names.

They would also have found a half dozen arrest warrants from all over the Earth Alliance, many for murder, and a few for murder for hire.

Romey hadn't had that information when she started the interrogation. She'd asked a junior detective to do the research and he'd handed it to Nyquist as Nyquist finished with Wagner.

Now all Nyquist had to do was bring it inside.

He wondered how many other cops had tried to interview this bastard, how many cops had failed to get information from him, how many times charges had been pressed only to be dismissed later on.

He didn't have the time to look all that up.

He just had to assume that the other cops all over the sector had failed with this guy.

So he wouldn't.

Nyquist pushed the door open. Romey was leaning over the table, her hands splayed, Illiyitch cuffed to the chair near her. The fact that he didn't complain about his treatment proved that he had been arrested a number of times before.

Nyquist plugged the chip that the junior detective gave him into the table screen. Images of Illiyitch appeared all over it—some with blond hair, some with brown, some with dark skin, some with light.

"Murder for hire, Gulliver?" Nyquist said. "That's quite a gig you've gotten for yourself. How do your subjects contact you? Through a friend? Some sort of advertising? Or do you go to them and ask them if they want anyone killed?"

Illiyitch swallowed so hard his Adam's apple bobbed. "I

work for a security company. They wouldn't hire me if I had the kind of background you say."

"I'll wager if we look at your Whitford Security records, we'll find them to be incomplete. And I'll wager that someone—maybe you—hacked into their systems and made sure your résumé was at the top of some stack, already marked as one that was approved by whatever system they used."

Nyquist sat down across from Illiyitch.

"Was that what was in that underground room at Whitford's house? His secure files? Or did you destroy the protection down there so that someone could access the information he stored there?"

Illiyitch frowned at Nyquist. Romey raised her eyebrows.

"You want to tell me about that?" Nyquist asked. "Or should we just put the case together on our own?"

"Someone's setting me up," Illiyitch said without enough fear to be convincing.

Romey's eyes twinkled as she looked at Nyquist, but to her credit, she didn't smile. Instead, she tapped one of the images.

"Murder for hire. Amazing," she said. "Who hired you this time?"

"I want a lawyer," Illiyitch said.

Romey raised her eyebrows as she looked at Nyquist. "We must have hit a nerve. He hasn't asked for help until now."

"Send for someone," Nyquist said. "But make sure it's someone good. Maybe your friends from WSX."

"Where?"

"They've already got a criminal defense attorney working with your buddy Wagner," Nyquist said.

"Who?" Illiyitch looked confused, and this time, his acting job had improved. He didn't seem to know who Nyquist was talking about.

"Tell us who to send for, and we'll do so," Romey said.

"I got a guy in Gagarin Dome," Illiyitch said. "He handled my dad's estate. Maybe—"

"Stop playing," Nyquist said. "You'll need a good attorney, since we have a record of the murders you committed."

"A record?" Illiyitch asked, further giving himself away.

Romey gave Nyquist a harsh glance. She had no idea what he was talking about because he was lying, and he hadn't told her what he was going to do. He hoped she'd play along.

And he hoped that the coroner had interpreted the evidence on the bodies correctly.

"You know," Nyquist said, "you made one serious mistake. You shouldn't have had your buddy—Lamfier, was that his name?—hold Bowles steady. You should have just shot him, then let her run. That's how most people would have done it. They'd shoot the bodyguard first, then go after the potential victim."

Romey sank into a chair beside Nyquist. Because she didn't know where this was going, she focused on Illiyitch.

Nyquist appreciated that.

"You could've gotten her before she made it out of the Hunting Club's protected grounds. You're a good shot. She would have been terrified. It would have been over in a matter of seconds. And . . ."

Nyquist paused for effect. Illiyitch was watching him, a pulse throbbing in his neck. The man looked scared for the first time since Nyquist arrived.

"And," Nyquist said again, "we wouldn't have gotten a record of the kill. Your jammer took out all of the Hunting Club's cameras. That was good work. But you didn't take out Bowles's personal cameras. She had four on various parts of her body. You know, killing a reporter isn't easy. And she was looking at you the entire time."

Color rose in Illiyitch's cheeks. Nyquist almost breathed a sigh of relief.

The man had believed him.

One more thing to thank Talia Shindo for. The girl had given Nyquist this idea.

Even if it was a lie.

"If you give us the person who hired you," Romey said, "we can make sure your charges are reduced. We'll also make sure you go to a minimum-security facility, rather than maximum. We won't tell the judge about any of the other warrants, and we won't let the other jurisdictions know we have you."

Illiyitch was watching both of them. The pulse visibly beating in his neck was going faster.

"That's a hell of a deal," Nyquist said. "You'll probably get twenty years instead of consecutive life terms."

"And you'll be in a facility that allows visitors, has great workout areas, and net capabilities. It'll be easy, at least compared to some of the prisons I've seen." Romey smiled at him.

He looked at her, then at Nyquist.

"The deal is good for the next fifteen minutes," Nyquist said. "The longer you wait, the more we take off the table. Starting with the other warrants."

Illiyitch bit his lower lip. "I want a lawyer," he said again.

"Who do we contact?" Romey asked.

"I want one before you take stuff off the table," Illiyitch said.

"Fine," Romey said. "We'll video-conference you. Who do we contact?"

"What if . . ." Illiyitch was looking at Nyquist now. "What if I don't have a name?"

"We'll find you a lawyer, then. Or let WSX do it."

"No, no," Illiyitch said. "Of the person who hired me. What if all I have is some contact information?"

His voice shook enough for that to be true.

"Why wouldn't you have a name?" Romey asked.

"I never ask," Illiyitch said, admitting to all the murder-for-hire cases. "I don't dare. It's better to get the assignment and the money in my account and move on. Safer, too."

"If you don't have a name, there's no deal," Nyquist said.

"I have contact information," Illiyitch said.

"If it leads to a person, then maybe we can do something," Nyquist said. "But contact information isn't the same as a name and a witness. You wouldn't be a good witness to contact information. It could be anyone using someone else's passwords and accounts."

Illiyitch swore. "I want to deal."

"Then give us a name," Nyquist said.

"I don't have one," Illiyitch said. "Just the contact information."

Nyquist shook his head and stood. He headed out of the room. As he pulled the door open, he heard Romey say, "Give me the name of your lawyer. We'll get him down here."

Illiyitch answered, but Nyquist didn't hear the name. He didn't care. He let the door close behind him. He leaned against the wall until Romey came out.

"I believe him," she said.

Nyquist sighed. "I'm hoping it's a tactic. Maybe we'll get a name after the lawyer comes."

"You don't believe that, though, do you?"

"No names would make more sense on a murder-for-hire agreement," Nyquist said.

"I know. Do you think the contact information will lead us to anyone?" Romey asked.

Nyquist shook his head. "I was hoping we could wrap this up today, but we're not going to. We might never get the person who hired Illiyitch."

"So what do you want to do? Rescind the deal?"

"Yeah," Nyquist said. "We gave it a time limit. We'll just act on that. Besides, it was contingent on a name."

"At least we can give the press Illiyitch."

"Without telling them it's murder for hire?"

Romey shrugged. "Let them think the case is closed. It's easier for us. We'll spin some story about him being a dis-gruntled Whitford employee, and Bowles got caught in the cross fire."

"Won't that hurt at trial?"

"You think there's going to be a trial?" Romey asked.

Nyquist closed his eyes. Of course there wouldn't be a trial. Illiyitch would make a deal—not as good a deal as Nyquist offered him, but one all the same—and they'd get the useless contact information.

Then they'd keep the file open for decades. Periodically, someone would poke at it and see if they could find anything.

"You can't give up," Romey said.

Nyquist opened his eyes. "I'm not giving up," he said. "I have to remind myself I am having a good day. I arrested Justinian Wagner on kidnapping charges, charges that could stick with some effort on the part of the prosecutors and with the right judge. I've resolved two cases in less than twelve hours, and all that in my first week back. I'm even going to make friends with the press. That's a good day."

"That's a stellar day." Romey smiled at him. "You're damn good. I don't say that lightly. Any time you want an affair . . ."

He smiled back. "I'll call you."

58

"You know," Van Alen said, "sometimes taking your mind off things helps your subconscious come up with a solution."

Flint knew that. He also knew he wouldn't be able to stop thinking about Gramming while he ate rich food and talked with his daughter.

His cloned daughter.

Whom he hadn't paid for.

So he knocked on the bathroom door, told her in a loud voice that the food was here, then went to Van Alen's networked computer.

"What are you doing?" she asked.

"What you wanted me to," he said. "I'm going to look into your power glitch."

And think about something else for a little while.

He settled into the chair behind Van Alen's desk and leaned forward, touching the screen to scroll back through the last few hours.

In a wave of steam and perfume, Talia came out of the bathroom. Flint looked up. She was wearing a long dress, belted at the waist. Grown-up clothing. Her hair was pulled back and her face, freshly scrubbed, looked vibrant.

His heart stopped for just a moment. She looked like an adult.

And he found that he didn't want that yet. He didn't want her to grow up any faster.

She had already aged years today. He'd seen that in her eyes.

He had promised her she'd be safe in Armstrong and then the day's events had replayed the horror she'd experienced the day her mother had been kidnapped.

"I'm not that hungry," Talia said.

Van Alen was helping an assistant put food on the conference table near the window.

"None of us are," Van Alen said. "But food is a great comforter. Let's soothe our bodies and maybe we'll feel better. Right, Miles?"

He didn't want to go over there. He didn't want to have a discussion.

"Just bring me something," he said.

"I can help you," Talia said, looking at the activated screen, which now showed mostly code.

"Everything on that computer is confidential," Van Alen said.

So long as no one broke into the network. And someone had. But Flint was wise enough not to correct her.

"So? My dad doesn't work for you," Talia said.

"We trade services. He can keep secrets."

"So can I." Talia sounded sullen but she walked to the table, anyway. She grabbed an apple, sat down, and surveyed the feast before her.

Van Alen filled a plate for Flint, mostly finger food. She'd seen him do this before.

He decided to ignore both of them. Instead he focused on the screen.

Van Alen's maintenance people had managed to trace some of the information. They'd plugged the leak and done everything that Flint had told them to do.

But they hadn't been able to see where the problem had come from.

It didn't take him long to find it.

Whoever had invaded Van Alen's systems had done so rather crudely. They'd used the power glitch to invade, but had isolated the glitch so that it distracted the people in the office while leaving the network up.

That had shown some planning and a knowledge of Van Alen's systems.

Then a search program, not nearly as refined as the one he'd designed to go through Paloma's files, had slid into Van Alen's systems. The maintenance team had managed to disable the search program, so that it didn't send messages back to its host.

But Flint didn't care about that. He wanted to see what the search parameters were.

Most of them were simple: anything with Bowles's identification on it, anything to do with WSX, and anything to do with Justinian Wagner.

But there were two other things that caught Flint's attention. The word *Gramming* and the word *clone*.

His hands were shaking now. He worked faster. He decided to enable part of the host program, to see where the information would go.

The trace was simple because he knew what he was looking for.

It went back to a computer system that had an anonymous identification code. But all computers also had manufacturers codes unless they were rebuilds like Flint's. He looked at the manufacturer's code, then traced it to the buyer.

Gramming Corporation.

"Son of a bitch," he said.

His daughter and Van Alen both looked at him.

"I think I know who killed Ki Bowles," he said. "And why."

"Excellent," Van Alen said. "Let's get the police on it and finish our meal."

Flint shook his head. He needed to think about this. Particularly the families, like the ones raising the other clones, the missing copies of Emmeline.

Yes, they had paid for those girls, but they were also raising them in an existing family, and had done so for years. He'd seen how shattered Talia had been to discover, not just how her mother betrayed her, but also how empty she felt when she realized she was a manufactured person rather than one born the natural way.

She was still coping with it.

"It's not quite that simple," he said to Van Alen.

He knew he would have to explain it.

Then he would need some kind of solution.

He disabled the tracking system, then shut it down, and turned off Van Alen's computer. He picked up his plate and went back to the table.

"Let me explain my dilemma," he said to Van Alen and his daughter. "Maybe you guys can help me figure out exactly what to do."

59

When her dad finished talking, Talia got up from the table. Van Alen had been wrong. Food didn't soothe. Talia's stomach was queasy from everything she'd eaten.

Or maybe it was what her dad had said—how the other girls would learn that their family wasn't their real family and they weren't real people.

Just like she had.

Only maybe their families—or the people they thought were their families—wouldn't be as accepting of clones as her dad was.

She remembered how it felt: She hadn't felt real after learning that she was a copy of someone else. Sometimes she still didn't feel real. Sometimes she felt like a pale imitation of that baby she'd seen in her dad's arms, the one he still mourned, the one he'd named his ship after.

And he was trying.

Imagine if the other parents didn't.

"It seems straightforward to me," Van Alen said. "If what you found is accurate, then someone at Gramming— probably the CEO—has ordered the death of at least one person. The security guard with Ki Bowles was probably collateral damage."

"He would still be responsible for the guard's death," Talia's dad said.

"Yes," Van Alen said. "And if he knows that we know his secret, then we might be in danger as well. You have to turn him in."

"And destroy countless lives." Talia's dad pushed his plate away.

"You said not everybody that went through the adoption process at Gramming was bought," Talia said. "Just a few, right? The rest paid normal fees, right?"

"That's right," her dad said.

"What if we don't turn Gramming in for murder?" Talia said. "What if you turn them in for something else, like—what's it called when you steal money from your own company?"

"Embezzlement," Van Alen said. "The punishment isn't nearly severe enough."

"And there's not enough here without revealing the sales," her dad said. Then he frowned. "But you might be on to something, Talia. There are several crimes here. Including tampering with the power systems in the dome."

"Which is considered an act of terrorism," Van Alen said. She was smiling.

Talia came back to the table. She wasn't exactly sure why that had cheered them both up.

"I'll let Noelle know," her dad said.

"Why?" Talia asked. "What does that mean?"

Van Alen picked up her glass. It was full of wine that Talia's dad wouldn't let her have.

"Ever since the dome bombing," Van Alen said, "acts of terrorism have special status in the United Domes. All of the domes have passed laws saying that anyone tampering with dome systems—life-enhancing systems, like the power grid—are attempting mass murder. They've beefed up not just the punishments, but the liberties the law can take in arrests."

"They can seize everything in a home or an office if

someone in those places has committed an act of terrorism," Talia's dad said.

He sounded pleased.

Van Alen's smile faded. "You know, I've been protesting these new laws for years. I think they're harmful."

"But they exist," Talia's dad said. "So we're going to use them. I'll contact Noelle."

Talia still wasn't sure she followed everything. "What will she do?"

"She'll make an arrest in the name of the United Domes," Talia's dad said. "She'll make sure no one ever comes after us."

"And maybe," Van Alen said, "no one will ever know why the CEO of Gramming invaded the public power grid."

Talia's dad nodded. "No one will even care."

"I will," Talia said. "The records will be open to anyone. Do you know how many families will be destroyed?"

"Yeah." Her dad looked serious. "Which is why I'm going to ask to go along on any arrest. I'll make sure the information disappears, Talia. No one will know."

"Except us," Van Alen said.

60

DeRicci stared at the information in front of her. It made no sense—and she'd already interrogated her techs about it.

The glitches could all be traced back to an adoption agency. One computer inside that agency caused all the problems.

And the techs told her they believed the problems were deliberate.

She cupped her cheeks with her hands and rested her elbows on her desk. Sometimes she felt buried in too much information.

She'd found—on her own—that some of the glitches were tied to crime reports. One happened near the time that Roshdi Whitford was murdered. Another near a break-in at a bank, although all that was stolen were transaction records. Not account numbers, not identifying information, not even passwords.

Just a few transaction records.

The bank's backups didn't have them, but one of the officers claimed that judging by the size of the whole in the transaction record, the information removed was probably for a sizable deposit or withdrawal.

Or both.

Normally, DeRicci would think that someone was covering his tracks, but so far, it made no sense.

Maybe the trail to the adoption agency was a false one.

Or maybe one of the employees had another agenda, one that had nothing to do with children.

Her links beeped at her. She had an incoming visual contact.

It was from Miles Flint.

He rarely used visuals. That, more than the urgent tag he'd put on the contact, made her answer.

He appeared as a holoimage on her desk. She didn't know he had that capability. In fact, she didn't know that her desk could show holoimages.

Then she realized he wasn't using his usual system. He was coming through someone else's security filter, and instead of creating a two-dimensional visual image of his face in front of her vision, it created a holoimage.

"Where are you?" she asked.

"My lawyer's," he said, apparently not minding that she hadn't said hello.

DeRicci nodded.

"We had a power glitch here," he said. "I traced it to the source. It came from Gramming Corporation."

"We've had a number of those glitches," DeRicci said, "and we know that Gramming is causing them. Do you know why?"

Flint's mouth narrowed. DeRicci knew that expression. Her old partner wasn't going to tell her everything.

She hated it when he did that.

"Let's just say that Gramming is trolling for information it shouldn't have."

"In a lawyer's office?" DeRicci asked.

"And other places," Flint said. "It's also deleting records."

DeRicci frowned. "Do you know why?"

"It's a security breach," Flint said, not answering her at all. "A serious one. Gramming has gotten into the public database and now it's working on some private ones. The company is misusing minute power failures to interrupt and destroy information in various locations. It seems to me that such behavior should worry the Security Chief for the United Domes of the Moon. Imagine if this gets bigger. Imagine if they want to shut down the environmental systems domewide."

"Imagine if you just answered my question instead of giving me information I already know," DeRicci said. "Do you know why?"

"Shouldn't you stop them and ask them yourself?" Flint asked.

DeRicci grinned at him. "You want me to go into Gramming and seize their equipment."

"Seems to me the situation warrants it. And the police can't do it. Only the Moon's security chief has the authority for such a large seizure."

"And you want to come with me, right?" DeRicci asked.

Flint smiled back at her and nodded. "You know me well, Noelle."

"I know you well enough to know you have your own agenda here. You'll compromise my raid."

"I will not," he said.

She tilted her head, unsure how he would see her. "You realize you're transmitting a holoimage."

"Yeah. It's one of the security protocols that I haven't shut off yet. When this system feels threatened, it goes to more complex matrices." He paused, then gave her his most charming look. "Take me along. I promise I won't compromise anything."

"A civilian on a government raid will compromise this," DeRicci said. "Especially when said civilian just completed an adoption of his own."

"I didn't work through Gramming," Flint said.

"Yes, but Ki Bowles mentioned them in that brand-new report of hers." DeRicci was finally glad she'd watched it more than once. "Is that what got her killed?"

"Probably," Flint said with reluctance.

"Have you told Bartholomew yet?" DeRicci asked.

"No," Flint said.

"You probably should."

"You're not going to take him on the raid, either, are you?" Flint asked.

"Nope," DeRicci said. "Although I will share information with him. Which is more than you're probably going to do."

Flint's entire body looked deflated. Or maybe that was just the smallness of his image, standing there on her desk.

"You're going to need me on this, Noelle."

"I already have enough to arrest everyone at Gramming and seize their assets," DeRicci said. "I don't need you at all. But I appreciate the heads-up."

"Noelle—"

"Tell me one thing, Miles. How come you're just letting me know about this now?"

"Because I just found it," he said.

"I wish I could believe that," DeRicci said, and signed off. Flint was planning something. He wanted access, and he wanted her to give it to him.

So she had to act quickly.

61

Flint felt rather than saw DeRicci sever the connection. One moment they were talking, the next he felt like he was on his own.

He put a hand to his forehead and closed his eyes.

"What's wrong?" Talia asked.

He didn't have a lot of time. If he'd gone with DeRicci he could have taken some of the records on his own. But he couldn't do that now.

"Dad?" Talia asked.

Flint opened his eyes. Both Van Alen and Talia were watching him from the table.

"Maxine, contact Nyquist. Let him know that Gramming is connected to Ki Bowles's death. Tell him that DeRicci is going to run a raid on that organization and he needs a court order to get some of the records."

"All right," Van Alen said. "But what about this discussion of revealing to children that they're clones, maybe destroying families?"

"I'm going to have to wipe the records," Flint said. He didn't want to, but he would have to. It was the only way to protect the children.

"Then there'll be no case," Van Alen said. "At least not

for the murder, and maybe not even for the United Domes. They'll be accused of harassment."

"Gramming did use power glitches to steal information."

"Or maybe its system malfunctioned and sent out some virus that did that. Without motive, a case could fall apart. You can't touch those records."

"He can't just leave them," Talia said, her voice rising. "The news stories alone will break up families. And maybe parents will get arrested for buying children."

"Probably not," Van Alen said. "I'm sorry to say that clones are viewed differently."

"And that's the problem," Talia said. "Dad, you can't let those records get out."

Flint stared at Talia for a moment, then at Van Alen. They both had valid points, and while he contemplated them, he was losing time.

Families were fragile, but families broke up naturally when the children grew up. The child left home and the family re-formed into something different.

Gramming had been doing this for twenty years. Which meant that the older children had reached eighteen, which was the age of majority in the Earth Alliance.

He could use the files from eighteen to twenty years ago. Those clones would legally be adults.

And he could use the pending files as well, the children that weren't yet sold. That would be more than enough to convict anyone of baby selling—or whatever DeRicci wanted to do. It would give her motive if nothing else.

If he deleted the information properly, it would look like Gramming itself was trying to cover its own tracks.

He didn't have a lot of time. And he couldn't follow the back trace all by himself, not and complete this before DeRicci arrived. All of the material had to be gone before she seized the computer systems.

"Talia," Flint said. "Get a networked notebook in here, and sit down beside me. I'm going to need your help."

62

Nyquist was having a very strange day. First he arrested one of the most powerful attorneys in the Earth Alliance on charges that just might stick, and then he got a message from another attorney, not quite as powerful, that told him the people who killed Ki Bowles had been hired by Gramming Corporation.

Oh, and that he was not to contact the second attorney with questions. She wouldn't answer them. But she recommended that he petition a court for a warrant to look at the material Noelle DeRicci was about to seize from Gramming in a raid she was conducting now.

He sat at his desk, feeling a bit stunned. Gramming had been in Bowles's report. He remembered the name. He also remembered that she had mentioned it in passing.

Which meant that Gramming was tied to WSX, and Flint had implied—in that one strange communiqué before he got kidnapped—that WSX's files were tied to Bowles.

So there was a link; Nyquist just didn't know what it was.

And he probably wouldn't know, not without files that DeRicci was somehow going to get.

He shook his head. After DeRicci's coldness to his request to shut off the Hunting Club's security system earlier, he wasn't going to contact her about this.

Instead, he was going to take Maxine Van Alen's advice and request a warrant for the information. It wouldn't be hard to get: He had an ongoing investigation and a tip from an informant. Plus a mention of the company by the victim.

If it all worked, he would finally get his answers.

63

Gramming Corporation was at the outskirts of Armstrong, in an older section of the dome. The dome here wasn't as old as it was near Flint's building, but it was old enough to have a yellowish tinge to its plastic and chips in its exterior that looked dangerous enough to warrant replacement.

DeRicci had already studied the maps. Gramming's building was small. The corporation itself had eleven employees, and they filled the single-story rectangular building almost to capacity.

The building had six windows, four doors—two industrial strength—and no basement level.

DeRicci brought a team of twenty, all in survival gear, all with laser pistols and laser rifles and an emergency knife. They wore masks, just in case someone used a gas in part of an attack, and they moved with quiet deliberation.

She'd made the security vehicles park nearly a block away. She monitored Gramming's communications before she approached, and jammed them after the vehicles were in position.

By now, the company's employees had to know something was up, but they wouldn't know what.

She doubted that people who worked in an adoption

agency—no matter what illegal activities some of them were participating in—would expect a full-fledged security raid.

When she told the governor-general she was planning this, she had said she would just supervise. But they both knew better.

DeRicci did send the first team in, so that they could surround the exits, but she was going to break into the building herself.

She hadn't done something like this since she had been a detective, and she missed it.

She slipped the environmental mask over her face, let it distort her vision for a moment, and then took her position at the front of the phalanx.

Her team spread beside and behind her in an open triangle. They moved slowly, taking each step as if they expected an attack.

Someone announced to the building that they were being raided and that they'd better open the doors, or the doors would be opened for them. The voice, distorted by the mask and the amplifier, was one DeRicci didn't recognize.

She held her laser rifle tightly, crouching just a little, as the double doors up front swung open.

The woman who stood behind them was slight and gray haired. She wore a dress that didn't quite fit properly and she was in her stocking feet.

She raised her hands and yelled, "You have the wrong building. We're an adoption agency."

"Gramming?" DeRicci shouted. Her voice didn't sound like her own, either.

"Yes."

"We have the right building." DeRicci turned to the man beside her. "Secure that woman. The rest of us are going in."

The woman screamed as the security officer grabbed her and moved her out of the way. The rest of the team poured through the door, laser rifles out, ready to shoot if necessary.

Other employees, standing near the door, fell to their

knees, covering their heads. A few screamed. Others started to cry.

DeRicci's sense of enjoyment was fading. She didn't want to terrorize do-gooders.

She could feel the energy leave the bust. So she went through the central door first.

Now she saw some desks and a few more employees. They hid behind the chairs or the desks and peered around them, shivering in terror.

Only one door remained closed.

It had a sign in the center: PRESIDENT AND CHIEF: OHARI KINOY.

The sign itself seemed a bit pretentious for the business, and that sinking feeling that DeRicci had faded. This was right. She knew it.

She kicked the door open. It slammed backward with a bang.

A small redheaded man sat behind a very big desk. He had a laser pistol pointed at his own head.

Behind him, a computer screen rose, ostentatiously deleting information.

"Stay back," he said.

DeRicci pulled up her mask. "You're going to kill yourself? Are you kidding?"

"I mean it," he said. "Stay back."

She let her own rifle down. "You realize this is a security raid. You've been messing with the power grid. That's illegal."

And then she recited the code. "But it's certainly not something to kill yourself over."

He was shaking. His eyes were full of tears.

"Oh, for God's sake," she said, and dropped her own rifle. She motioned at everyone else to come in the door. "Seize the computers and stop them from deleting information."

"I'm going to shoot myself," the man said.

"Go ahead," DeRicci snapped. "But realize if you do,

you'll guarantee that your employees and your family will pay for your mistakes."

His chin wobbled and then the tears that had threatened became reality. He set the pistol down, and DeRicci grabbed it.

She had been playing a hunch, but it was a hunch based on countless arrests as a police officer. People who threatened suicide when they were about to be arrested were more afraid of the social consequences of that arrest than they were of going to prison.

He'd done something besides tamper with the information grids all over the dome. He'd done something that people would condemn him for, and he had probably done it for money.

She couldn't wait to see those files.

She cuffed his hands behind his back and tossed him to another security officer.

"Get rid of this idiot," she said.

Then she turned to the computer screen before her. Even she could tell that the deletions had been extensive. All she could hope was that their techs could reconstruct the deleted information.

She doubted that any of the employees outside knew what this idiot had done, or they would have been trying to cover up as well.

Her heart was pounding, but she felt better than she had in days.

She had an investigation to complete.

She had a bad guy in custody.

She had stopped a threat to the dome.

For once, she used every skill she had. And she'd stopped a problem before it threatened Armstrong or the United Domes.

Just as she'd been hired to do.

64

The screens in front of Flint went dark.

"Dad!" Talia said. "I just lost everything."

Flint's connection with Gramming disappeared. DeRicci must have gotten inside the building and found a way to shut down the deletions.

He hoped her techs weren't good enough to trace this back to him.

"Dad!" Talia said again.

"It's okay," he said. "I expected it. Don't do anything."

Van Alen was still at the table. She watched with concern on her face.

Flint went through the back trace and deleted any evidence of the work he did to get to Gramming's files. He did not delete the back trace, however. That would be suspicious. DeRicci knew he had figured out that Gramming had attacked Van Alen's office. DeRicci would expect the back trace.

After a few minutes, he was through. He stood up. His back cracked.

"Well?" Van Alen asked. "Did you get the files?"

"I didn't capture them," Flint said. "I had Talia run a standard deletion program for the moneyed accounts that Kinoy kept in his personal files. Then I got rid of all the names that he mentioned in the years we agreed on."

"If it's standard, Dad," Talia said, "they can reconstruct it."

"No," he said. "That's why I had you do it. I followed you in and cleaned up the remnants of the information. They won't be able to find the information. They'll just find that it existed once and got deleted."

"I hope you left enough to convict the bastard," Van Alen said. "Selling children."

"I did," Flint said. "The old accounts and the pending ones are still there."

He wiped a hand over his face. He hadn't worked that hard on a computer program in years.

"What about the kids?" Talia asked softly. "Are they going to be okay?"

He looked at his daughter. He could see more than concern on her face. She was afraid.

"No one'll find them," he said.

"I know," she said. "Is that going to be okay? I mean, did we make a mistake? Their parents paid for them."

Second thoughts were common after an operation of this size. He'd tell her that later, though.

"It's the best we could come up with on short notice," he said. "That's all we can do."

Van Alen was nodding. Talia sighed. Early lessons in adulthood. Flint hadn't expected to do that.

"What about—you know—the others?" Talia asked. "You saved that stuff, right?"

She was asking about the girls she called her sisters. The other clones of Emmeline.

"No," he said. "I didn't save anything."

Except their names. Kahlila El Alamen and Gita Havos. He had their names and their family's names and where they were right now. And that information was in his memory, not in a network somewhere.

He would never forget any of that.

He doubted Talia would, either.

"What now?" Van Alen asked. "Do we find a new reporter?"

Flint shook his head. He was a little stunned that Van Alen could be so callous. Ki Bowles hadn't even been dead for twelve hours. "I think Nyquist has a good case against Justinian Wagner, thanks to Talia, and I have a hunch all of this will be in the news—the phony adoptions and the embezzlement and the ties to Wagner. WSX as we know it is gone."

"Law firms don't disappear," Van Alen said.

"But they don't recover from bad publicity, either. WSX won't be the powerhouse that it once was," Flint said. "So we don't need another reporter. I wouldn't risk someone else's life like that."

Including his own. And Talia's.

She was watching him. "What are we going to do, Dad?"

He walked over to her, took the notepad off her lap, and then helped her up. He put his arm around her shoulder and pulled her close.

"We shut down my office," he said. "And we find you a good school."

"Dad," she said in a voice only a teenager could manage. "I mean you. What are you doing?"

"Nothing," he said. "I'm not taking new clients. I can't handle the old ones right now. It's too much of a risk."

Talia backed away from him and rolled her eyes. "Dad, you have to work. Besides, I can help now. You said I was good."

"You are," he said. And it frightened him. She was this good at thirteen. If he kept his office open, her whole life could be about illegal computer activity and the occasional encounter with someone dangerous. He didn't want that for her.

He didn't want it for either of them.

"Tell you what," he said. "When you finish school, we'll

talk about opening the office again. If you're interested then."

Talia frowned at him. "That's five years from now."

"Eight," he said. "College."

"What if I don't want to go to college?" she asked.

He shrugged. "We'll talk about it."

She frowned at him. "You should work. You like being a Retrieval Artist."

He did. But he hadn't done much of it in recent years. And it was better if he started anew. His office was too tainted with Paloma's methods, Paloma's systems.

He needed to clear his head.

He needed to see what other choices he had.

"I'll be fine," he said.

"Dad," Talia said.

"You're not going to settle it now," Van Alen said. "This whole case was a mistake. We have funerals to attend and lawsuits to file. We have some reassessing to do. All of us."

She looked pointedly at Flint.

He nodded. He found himself wondering whether Ki Bowles had anyone in Armstrong who was a close enough friend to plan a funeral for her.

He doubted it. He hadn't found any connection like that in all the research he'd done today.

Which meant he and Van Alen would have to do it. Two people who had worked with Bowles, and hadn't really liked her.

Hadn't liked her at all.

And if he had continued on the same path, working alone, alienating his friends, he would have ended up just like Bowles.

Instead, he had Talia. And Van Alen. And DeRicci. Not to mention Nyquist, who was probably wondering how Flint had found this stuff—and how to make Flint admit what he knew in a court of law.

Too many connections, Paloma would have said.

But Paloma had been murdered by her own son. Her

other son had claimed she hadn't spent any time with them. She'd abandoned them.

She hadn't loved them enough.

Flint wouldn't make that mistake with Talia. She hadn't had a father for the first thirteen years of her life.

She would have one now.

"Dad," Talia said, "if you're not working, we have time to find a better apartment."

He looked at her.

"One with, you know, a shower like the one in here."

He raised his eyebrows. He didn't remember the shower here, although he remembered how luxurious the bathroom was.

"Are you gonna run away again?" he asked.

She shook her head. "I didn't know the problems I'd cause for the other families."

"What about me?" he asked.

She frowned.

"What about the problems you would have caused for me?"

"I wouldn't cause problems for you," she said. "You could go back to your old life instead of give it up for me."

His breath caught. Was that what she thought? That he regretted finding her? "What if I want to give up my old life?"

She stared at him. "You don't."

"If you'd asked me all those years ago, when Emmeline died and your mom left, if I wanted to be a successful businessman or if I wanted my family back, I would have asked for my family, every single time."

"But Mom's dead, and I'm not Emmeline."

"I know," he said. "But you're my daughter. And you have no idea how lucky that makes me."

Talia was frowning. Flint clapped his daughter on her back.

"Come on," he said. "Let's go to that apartment you don't like and forget about all this."

Talia looked at Van Alen, then at the notebook Flint had placed on the chair.

"I'm not going to forget," Talia said.

"I know," Flint said softly.

He wouldn't forget, either. Not now.

Not ever.

Classic Science Fiction & Fantasy
from
ROC

2001: A SPACE ODYSSEY by Arthur C. Clarke
Based on the screenplay written with Stanley Kubrick, this
novel represents a milestone in the genre.
"The greatest science fiction novel of all time." —*Time*

ROBOT VISIONS by Isaac Asimov
Here are 36 magnificent stories and essays about Asimov's
most beloved creations—Robots. This collection includes
some of his best known and best loved robot stories.

THE FOREST HOUSE by Marion Zimmer Bradley
The stunning prequel to *The Mists of Avalon*, this is
the story of Druidic priestesses who guard their ancient
rites from the encroaching might of Imperial Rome.

BORED OF THE RINGS by The Harvard Lampoon
This hilarious spoof lambastes all the favorite
characters from Tolkien's fantasy trilogy. An instant
cult classic, this is a must read for anyone who has ever
wished to wander the green hills of the shire—and after
almost sixty years in print, it has become a classic itself.

S527

THE ULTIMATE IN
SCIENCE FICTION AND FANTASY!

From magical tales of distant worlds to stories of technological advances beyond the grasp of man, Penguin has everything you need to stretch your imagination to its limits.

penguin.com

ACE
Get the latest information on favorites like William Gibson, T.A. Barron, Brian Jacques, Ursula K. Le Guin, Sharon Shinn, and Charlaine Harris, as well as updates on the best new authors.

ROC
Escape with Harry Turtledove, Anne Bishop, S.M. Stirling, Simon R. Green, Chris Bunch, Jim Butcher, E.E. Knight, and many others—plus news on the latest and hottest in science fiction and fantasy.

DAW
Mercedes Lackey, Kristen Britain, Tanya Huff, Tad Williams, C.J. Cherryh, and many more—DAW has something to satisfy the cravings of any science fiction and fantasy lover.
Also visit dawbooks.com.

Get the best of science fiction and fantasy at your fingertips!